SHELTER IN PLACE

Also by Nora Roberts

Series

Irish Born Trilogy
BORN IN FIRE
BORN IN ICE
BORN IN SHAME

Dream Trilogy
DARING TO DREAM
HOLDING THE DREAM
FINDING THE DREAM

Chesapeake Bay Saga
SEA SWEPT
RISING TIDES
INNER HARBOR
CHESAPEAKE BLUE

Gallaghers of Ardmore Trilogy
JEWELS OF THE SUN
TEARS OF THE MOON
HEART OF THE SEA

Three Sisters Island Trilogy
DANCE UPON THE AIR
HEAVEN AND EARTH
FACE THE FIRE

Key Trilogy
KEY OF LIGHT
KEY OF KNOWLEDGE
KEY OF VALOR

In the Garden Trilogy
BLUE DAHLIA
BLACK ROSE
RED LILY

Circle Trilogy
MORRIGAN'S CROSS
DANCE OF THE GODS
VALLEY OF SILENCE

Sign of Seven Trilogy
BLOOD BROTHERS
THE HOLLOW
THE PAGAN STONE

Bride Quartet
VISION IN WHITE
BED OF ROSES
SAVOR THE MOMENT
HAPPY EVER AFTER

The Inn BoonsBoro Trilogy
THE NEXT ALWAYS
THE LAST BOYFRIEND
THE PERFECT HOPE

The Cousins O'Dwyer Trilogy
DARK WITCH
SHADOW SPELL
BLOOD MAGICK

The Guardians Trilogy
STARS OF FORTUNE
BAY OF SIGHS
ISLAND OF GLASS

Chronicles of the One
YEAR ONE
OF BLOOD AND BONE

eBooks by Nora Roberts

Nora Roberts & J. D. Robb

REMEMBER WHEN

J. D. Robb

Anthologies

FROM THE HEART

A LITTLE MAGIC

A LITTLE FATE

MOON SHADOWS
(with Jill Gregory, Ruth Ryan Langan, and Marianne Willman)

The Once Upon Series
(with Jill Gregory, Ruth Ryan Langan, and Marianne Willman)

ONCE UPON A CASTLE   ONCE UPON A ROSE

ONCE UPON A STAR   ONCE UPON A KISS

ONCE UPON A DREAM   ONCE UPON A MIDNIGHT

SILENT NIGHT
(with Susan Plunkett, Dee Holmes, and Claire Cross)

OUT OF THIS WORLD
(with Laurell K. Hamilton, Susan Krinard, and Maggie Shayne)

BUMP IN THE NIGHT
(with Mary Blayney, Ruth Ryan Langan, and Mary Kay McComas)

DEAD OF NIGHT
(with Mary Blayney, Ruth Ryan Langan, and Mary Kay McComas)

THREE IN DEATH

SUITE 606
(with Mary Blayney, Ruth Ryan Langan, and Mary Kay McComas)

IN DEATH

THE LOST
(with Patricia Gaffney, Ruth Ryan Langan, and Mary Kay McComas)

THE OTHER SIDE
(with Mary Blayney, Patricia Gaffney, Ruth Ryan Langan, and Mary Kay McComas)

TIME OF DEATH

THE UNQUIET
(with Mary Blayney, Patricia Gaffney, Ruth Ryan Langan, and Mary Kay McComas)

MIRROR, MIRROR
(with Mary Blayney, Elaine Fox, Mary Kay McComas, and R. C. Ryan)

DOWN THE RABBIT HOLE
(with Mary Blayney, Elaine Fox, Mary Kay McComas, and R. C. Ryan)

Also Available . . .

THE OFFICIAL NORA ROBERTS COMPANION
(edited by Denise Little and Laura Hayden)

SHELTER IN PLACE

NORA ROBERTS

ST. MARTIN'S GRIFFIN ≋ NEW YORK

The official Nora Roberts seal guarantees that this is a new work.

SHELTER IN PLACE. Copyright © 2018 by Nora Roberts. All rights reserved. Printed in the United States of America. For information, address St. Martin's Press, 175 Fifth Avenue, New York, N.Y. 10010.

www.stmartins.com

Excerpt from *Under Currents* copyright © 2019 by Nora Roberts

Designed by James Sinclair

The Library of Congress has cataloged the hardcover edition as follows:

Names: Roberts, Nora, author.
Title: Shelter in place / Nora Roberts.
Description: First edition. | New York : St. Martin's Press, 2018.
Identifiers: LCCN 2017060315 | ISBN 9781250161598 (hardcover) | ISBN 9781250193988
    (international, sold outside the U.S., subject to rights availability) | ISBN 9781250161611 (ebook)
Subjects: | GSAFD: Romantic suspense.
Classification: LCC PS3568.O243 S54 2018 | DDC 813/.54—dc23
LC record available at https://lccn.loc.gov/2017060315

ISBN 978-1-250-16160-4 (trade paperback)

Our books may be purchased in bulk for promotional, educational, or business use. Please contact your local bookseller or the Macmillan Corporate and Premium Sales Department at 1-800-221-7945, extension 5442, or by email at MacmillanSpecialMarkets@macmillan.com.

First St. Martin's Griffin Edition: May 2019

10 9 8 7 6 5 4 3 2 1

In memory of my grandmother
with the bright red hair

PART ONE

Innocence Lost

No acquisitions of guilt can compensate the loss of that solid inward comfort of mind, which is the sure companion of innocence and virtue; nor can in the least balance the evil of that horror and anxiety which, in their room, guilt introduces into our bosoms.

—Henry Fielding

CHAPTER ONE

On Friday, July 22, 2005, Simone Knox ordered a large Fanta—orange—to go with her popcorn and Swedish Fish. The choice, her standard night-at-the-movies fare, changed her life, and very likely saved it. Still, she'd never drink Fanta again.

But at that moment she only wanted to settle down in the theater with her two best friends forEVER and lose herself in the dark.

Because her life—currently and absolutely for the rest of the summer, and maybe for all time—sucked beyond infinity.

The boy she loved, the boy she'd dated *exclusively* for seven months, two weeks, and four days, the boy she'd imagined cruising through her upcoming senior year with—hand in hand, heart to heart—had dumped her.

In a text.

done wasting time cuz i got 2 b with somebody ready to b all the way with me and thats not u so we r done c u

Certain he couldn't have meant it, she'd tried to call him—but he didn't answer. She'd texted three times, humiliating herself.

Then she'd gone to his MySpace page. *Humiliation* was too weak a word for what she suffered.

Traded in the old DEFECTIVE model for a hot new one.
Simone out!
Tiffany in!
Shook off a LOSER and I'll be rolling through the summer and into senior year with the hottest girl in the class of 2006.

His post—with pictures—had already generated comments. She might've been smart enough to know he'd ordered his friends to say mean, ugly things about her, but that didn't lessen the sting or the embarrassment.

She grieved for days. She wallowed in the comfort and righteous anger of her two closest friends. She raged at her younger sister's taunts, dragged herself to her summer job and the weekly tennis lessons at the club that her mother insisted on.

A text from her grandmother made her sniffle. CiCi might be meditating with the Dalai Lama in Tibet, rocking it out with the Stones in London, or painting in her studio on Tranquility Island, but she had a way of finding out anything and everything.

It hurts now, and the pain's real, so hugs, my treasure. But give it a few weeks, and you'll realize he's just another asshole. Kick butt and namaste.

Simone didn't think Trent was an asshole (though both Tish and Mi agreed with CiCi). Maybe he'd tossed her aside—and in a really mean way—just because she wouldn't do it with him. She just wasn't ready to do it. Besides, Tish had done it with her ex-boyfriend after the junior prom—and twice more—and he'd dumped her anyway.

The worst was, she still loved Trent and, in her desperate sixteen-year-old heart, knew she'd never love anyone else, ever again. Even though she'd torn out the pages of her journal where she'd written her future names—Mrs. Trent Woolworth, Simone Knox-Woolworth, S. K. Woolworth—ripped them to shreds, then burned them, along with every photo she had of him, in the patio firepit during a girl-power ceremony with her friends, she still loved him.

But, as Mi pointed out, she had to live, even though part of her just wanted to die, so she let her friends drag her to the movies.

Anyway, she was tired of sulking in her room, and she really didn't want to slump around the mall with her mother and little sister, so the movies won. Mi won, too, as it was her turn to pick, so Simone was stuck with some science-fiction deal called *The Island* Mi was crazy to see.

Tish didn't mind the pick. As a future actress, she felt that experiencing movies and plays was both a duty and pre-career training. Plus Ewan McGregor ranked in Tish's top five movie boyfriends.

"Let's get seats. I want good ones." Mi, small, compact, with dark, dramatic eyes and a thick wedge of black hair, gathered her popcorn—no fake butter—her drink, and the peanut M&M's she favored.

Mi had turned seventeen in May, dated sporadically, as she currently preferred science to boys, and skimmed just above the nerd line only because of her prowess as a gymnast and solid slot on the cheerleading squad.

A squad unfortunately captained by one Tiffany Bryce, boyfriend stealer and slut.

"I need the ladies'." Tish—double-fake-butter popcorn, a Coke, and Junior Mints—pushed her snacks at her friends. "I'll find you."

"Don't fool around with your face and hair," Mi warned her. "Nobody can see them anyway, once the movie starts."

And she was already perfect, Simone thought as she juggled Tish's popcorn on the way to one of the three theaters in the DownEast Mall Cineplex.

Tish had long, smooth, silky chestnut-brown hair—with professional golden highlights because *her* mother wasn't stuck in nineteen-fifty-whatever. Her face—Simone loved studying faces—a classic oval, added flirty charm with dimples; and the dimples flirted often, as Tish always found something to smile about. Simone figured she'd smile a lot, too, if she'd turned out tall and curvy, with bright blue eyes and dimples.

On top of *everything*, Tish's parents totally supported her ambition to pursue acting. She'd hit the jackpot in Simone's mind. Looks, personality, brains, *and* parents who actually had a clue.

But Simone loved Tish anyway.

The three of them already had plans—secret ones for now because Simone's parents completely did not have a clue—to spend the summer after graduation in New York.

Maybe they'd even move there—it had to be more exciting than Rockpoint, Maine.

Simone figured a sand dune in the Sahara had to be more exciting than Rockpoint, Maine.

But New York? Bright lights, hordes of people.

Freedom!

Mi could study to be a doctor at Columbia, Tish could study acting and go on auditions. And she . . . could study something.

Something that wasn't law, as her own clueless parents wanted. Not surprising, and *so* lame and clichéd because her father was a big-shot lawyer.

Ward Knox would be disappointed, but that's how it had to be.

Maybe she'd study art and become a famous artist like CiCi. *That* would freak her parents out awesomely. And, like CiCi, she'd take and discard lovers at her whim. (When she was ready to do it).

That would show Trent Woolworth.

"Come out," Mi ordered, giving her an elbow bump.

"What? I'm right here."

"No, you're in the Simone Brood Zone. Come out, join the world."

Maybe she liked it in the SBZ, but . . . "I have to open the door with the power of my mind because my hands are full. Okay, done. I'm back."

"The mind of Simone Knox is an awesome thing to behold."

"I must use it for good, and not use it to melt Tiffany into a puddle of slut goo."

"You don't have to anyway. Her brain's already a puddle of slut goo."

Friends, Simone thought, always knew the right thing to say. She would rejoin the world with Mi—and Tish, whenever Tish stopped playing with her already-perfect face and hair and came out—and leave the SBZ behind.

A Friday night opening meant she walked into a theater already half-full. Mi grabbed three seats dead center, took the third one in from the aisle so Simone—still heart tender—could take the one between her and Tish, whose longer legs earned the aisle seat.

Mi shifted in her seat. She'd already calculated they had six minutes until the lights dimmed.

"You've got to go to Allie's party tomorrow night."

The SBZ beckoned. "I'm not ready for a party, and you know Trent's going to be there with that slut-goo-brain Tiffany."

"That's the *point*, Sim. If you don't go, everybody's going to think you're, like, hiding out, that you're not over him."

"I am, and I'm not."

"The *point*," Mi insisted. "You don't give him the satisfaction. You go with us—Tish is going with Scott, but he's cool—and you wear something amazing, let Tish do your makeup because she's got the skills. And you act like: Who, what, him? You know, you're so over that. You make a statement."

Simone felt the SBZ pulling her. "I don't think I can face it. Tish is the actress, not me."

"You played Rizzo in *Grease* for the spring musical. Tish was awesome as Sandy, but you were an equally awesome Rizzo."

"Because I've had dance lessons and can sing a little."

"You sing great—and you did great. Be Rizzo at Allie's party, you know, all confident and sexy and up yours."

"I don't know, Mi." But she could, sort of, imagine it. And how Trent, seeing her all confident and sexy and up yours, would want her again.

Then Tish rushed in, dropped down, gripped Simone's hand. "You're not going to freak."

"Why would I . . . Oh no. Please!"

"The slut's putting on fresh lip gloss, and the creep's hanging outside the ladies' like a good dog."

"Crap." Mi curled her fingers around Simone's arm. "Maybe they're going to one of the other movies."

"No, they're coming here, because that's what my life is."

Mi tightened her grip. "Don't even think about leaving. He'd see you and you'd look and feel like a loser. You're not a loser. This is your dress rehearsal for Allie's party."

"She's going?" Tish's dimples flashed and flickered. "You talked her into it?"

"We're working on it. Just sit." Mi angled herself just enough. "You're right, they're coming in. Just stay," she hissed as Simone's arm trembled under her hand. "You don't even notice them. We're right here."

"Right here, now and forever," Tish echoed, giving Simone's hand a squeeze. "We're a . . . a wall of disdain. Got it?"

They walked by, the blonde with the tumble of curls and snugly cropped jeans, and the golden boy—tall, so handsome, quarterback of the championship Wildcats.

Trent gave Simone the slow smile that had once melted her heart, and deliberately ran a hand down Tiffany's back, letting it slide to her butt and linger there.

Tiffany turned her head as Trent whispered in her ear and looked over her shoulder. Smirked with her perfect, freshly glossed lips.

Brokenhearted, her life a Trent-less void, Simone still had too much of her grandmother in her to take that kind of insult.

She smirked right back and shot up her middle finger.

Mi let out a snorting giggle. "Way to go, Rizzo."

Though Simone's broken heart thudded, she made herself watch as Trent and Tiffany sat three rows ahead, and immediately began to make out.

"All men want sex," Tish said wisely. "I mean, why wouldn't they? But when that's all they want, they're not worth it."

"We're better than she is." Mi passed Tish her Junior Mints and Coke. "Because that's all she's got."

"You're right." Maybe her eyes stung a little, but there was a burning inside her heart, and the burn felt like healing. She handed Tish her popcorn. "I'm going to Allie's party."

Tish let out a laugh—deliberately mocking and loud. Enough to make Tiffany jerk. Tish shot Simone a grin. "We'll rule that party."

Simone clamped her popcorn between her thighs so she could link hands with her friends. "I love you guys."

By the time the previews ended Simone had stopped watching the silhouettes three rows down. Mostly. She'd expected to brood through the movie—actually planned on it—but found herself caught up. Ewan McGregor *was* dreamy, and she liked how strong and brave Scarlett Johansson came across.

But fifteen minutes in, she realized she should've gone to the bathroom with Tish—though that would've been a disaster with lip-gloss Tiffany in there—or she should've taken it a lot easier on the Fanta.

Twenty minutes in, she gave up. "I've gotta pee," she whispered.

"Come on!" Mi whispered back.

"I'll be fast."

"You want me to go with you?"

She shook her head at Tish, gave her what was left of the popcorn and Fanta to hold.

She shuffled by, strode quickly up the aisle. After making the turn to the right, she hurried to the ladies', shoved the door open.

Empty, no waiting. Relieved, she grabbed a stall, and contemplated as she emptied her bladder.

She'd handled the situation. Maybe CiCi had been right. Maybe she was close to realizing Trent was an asshole.

But he was so, so cute, and he had that smile, and—

"Doesn't matter," she muttered. "Assholes can be cute."

Still, she thought about it as she washed her hands, as she studied herself in the mirror over the sink.

She didn't have Tiffany's long blond curls or bold blue eyes or killer bod. She was, as far as she could tell, just average.

Average brown hair her mother wouldn't let her have highlighted. Just wait until she hit eighteen and could do whatever she wanted with her *own* hair. She wished she hadn't worn it in a ponytail tonight, because it suddenly made her feel juvenile. Maybe she'd cut it. Spike and punk it up. Maybe.

Her mouth was too wide, even if Tish said it was sexy, like Julia Roberts.

Brown eyes, but not deep and dramatic like Mi's. Just brown, like her stupid hair. Of course Tish, being Tish, said they were amber.

But that was just a fancy word for brown.

That didn't matter, either. Maybe she was average, but she wasn't fake. Like Tiffany, whose hair was brown, too, under the bleach.

"I'm not a fake," she said to the mirror. "And Trent Woolworth's an asshole. Tiffany Bryce is a slut-bitch. They can both go to hell."

With a decisive nod, she held her head high and walked out of the bathroom.

She thought the loud pops—firecrackers?—and the screams were from the movie. Cursing herself for stalling and missing an important scene, she quickened her pace.

As she neared the theater door, it burst open. The man, eyes wild, took one stumbling step before he fell forward.

Blood—was that blood? His hands clawed at the green carpet—the carpet where red spread—then stilled.

Flashes, she saw flashes through the door that was wedged open a few inches by the man's legs. Blasts and blasts, screams. And people, shadows and silhouettes, falling, running, falling.

And the figure, dark in the dark, walking methodically up the rows.

She watched, frozen, as that figure turned and shot a woman in the back who was running.

She couldn't breathe. If she'd been capable of drawing a breath, it would've expelled in a scream.

Part of her brain rejected what she'd seen. It couldn't be real. It had to be like the movie. Just pretend. But instinct kicked in, had her running back to the bathroom, crouching behind the door.

Her hands didn't want to work, fumbled on her purse, fumbled on her phone.

Her father had insisted on nine-one-one as her first memory code on the phone.

Her vision wavered, and her breath came now, came in ragged pants.

"Nine-one-one. What is your emergency?"

"He's killing them. He's killing them. Help! My friends. Oh God, oh God. He's shooting people."

Reed Quartermaine hated working weekends. He wasn't crazy about working in the mall, either, but he wanted to go back to college in the fall. And college included this little detail they called tuition. Add in books, housing, food, and you had to work weekends at the mall.

His parents covered most of the freight, but they couldn't manage it all. Not with his sister heading off in another year, and his brother already three years in at American University in D.C.

He sure as hell didn't want to wait tables for the rest of his life, so college. And maybe before he donned another cap and gown he would figure out just what the hell he did want to do for the rest of his life.

But summers, he waited tables, and tried to look on the bright side. The restaurant's mall location worked okay, and the tips didn't suck. Maybe waiting tables at Mangia five nights a week with a double shift on Saturdays killed his social life, but he ate well.

Bowls of pasta, loaded pizzas, hunks of Mangia's renowned tiramisu hadn't put much meat on his long, bony frame, but it wasn't for lack of trying.

His father once had hope his middle child would follow in his football-star cleat-prints, as his oldest son had—resoundingly. But Reed's complete lack of skill on the field and skinny frame dashed those hopes. Still, standing on a yard of leg by the time he'd hit sixteen, with a willingness to run all damn day, had made him a minor sort of star on varsity track, so that balanced it out some.

Then his sister took the heat off with her fierce talent on the soccer field.

He served a table of four their starters—*insalata mista* for the mother, gnocchi for the dad, mozzarella sticks for the boy, and fried ravioli for the girl.

He flirted harmlessly with the girl, who gave him long, shy smiles. Harmless because he figured she was maybe fourteen and off the radar for a college man heading into his sophomore year.

Reed knew how to flirt harmlessly with young girls, older women, and pretty much all in between. Tips mattered, and he'd honed the charm for customers after four summers of waiting tables.

He covered his section—families, some old couples, a scatter of date-night thirty-whatevers. Probably dinner and a movie, which made him think he'd see if Chaz—assistant manager at GameStop—wanted to catch the late showing of *The Island* after their shifts.

He ran credit cards—chatting up table three had bagged him a solid twenty percent—turned tables, swung in and out of the insane kitchen, and finally hit break time.

"Dory, taking my ten."

The head waitress gave his section a quick scan, gave him the nod.

He stepped out of the double glass doors and into the Friday night mayhem. He had considered texting Chaz and taking his ten in the kitchen, but he wanted out. Plus he knew Angie worked the Fun In The Sun kiosk on Friday nights, and he could take four or five of his ten for some not-so-harmless flirting.

She had an off-and-on boyfriend, but the last word he heard said off. He could try his luck there and maybe score a date with somebody whose miserable schedule matched his own.

He moved fast on long legs through shoppers, through cliques of teenage girls and the teenage boys who scouted them, around moms pushing strollers or herding toddlers, through the incessant brain-numbing music he no longer heard.

He had a mop of black hair—his mother's Italian half. Dory didn't bug him about getting a trim, and his dad had finally given up. His eyes, deep set, pale green against olive-toned skin, brightened when he saw Angie at the kiosk. He slowed his pace, slipped his hands into his trouser pockets—casual—and sauntered over.

"Hey. How's it going?"

She flashed him a smile, rolled her pretty brown eyes. "Busy. Everybody's going to the beach but me."

"And me." He leaned on the counter with its display of sunglasses, hoping he looked smooth in his uniform of white shirt, black vest and pants. "I'm thinking of catching *The Island*, it's got a ten-forty-five last show. It's almost like a trip to the beach, am I right? Want in?"

"Oh . . . I don't know." She fussed with her hair, a beachy blond that went with the golden tan he suspected she got from the self-tanner in another display. "I do kind of want to see it."

Hope sprang, and Chaz was bumped off his list.

"Gotta make some fun, right?"

"Yeah, but . . . I sort of told Misty we'd hang after closing."

Chaz jumped back on the list. "That's cool. I was heading down to see if Chaz wanted to catch it. We could all go."

"Maybe." She flashed that smile again. "Yeah, maybe. I'll ask her."

"Great. I'm heading down to see Chaz." He shifted to give more room to the woman waiting patiently while her kid—another who hit about fourteen—tried on half a zillion pairs of sunglasses. "You can text me either way."

"If I could have two pairs," the girl began, checking herself out in a pair with metallic blue lenses, "I'd have a spare."

"One, Natalie. This *is* your spare."

"I'll text you," Angie murmured, then shifted to work mode. "Those look awesome on you."

"Really?"

"Totally," Reed heard Angie say as he headed off. He quickened his pace—he had to make up time.

GameStop buzzed with its usual crowd of geeks and nerds and, for the younger geeks and nerds, the glazed-eyed parents trying to move them along.

Monitors previewed a variety of games—the PG variety on the wall screens. The less friendly ones were on individual laptops—for use with over-eighteen ID or with parental supervision.

He spotted Chaz—king of the nerds—explaining some game to a confused-looking woman.

"If he's into military-style game play, strategy and arc building, he'd go for it." Chaz shoved his coke-bottle glasses up on his nose. "It's only been out a couple weeks."

"It seems so . . . violent. Is it appropriate?"

"Sixteenth birthday, you said." He gave Reed a quick nod. "And he's into the Splinter Cell series. If he's good with those, he'd be good with this."

She sighed. "I guess boys are always going to play war. I'll take it, thanks."

"They'll ring you up at the register. Thanks for shopping at GameStop. Can't hang, man," he told Reed as the customer walked away. "Slammed."

"Thirty seconds. Late show, *The Island*."

"I'm all about it. Clones, baby."

"Solid. I've got Angie on the hook for it, but she wants to bring Misty on."

"Oh, well, I—"

"Don't let me down, man. It's the closest I've got to a date out of her."

"Yeah, but Misty's a little scary. And . . . Do I have to pay for her?"

"It's not a date. I'm working on turning it into a date. For me, not for you. You're my wingman, and Misty's Angie's. Clones," he reminded Chaz.

"Okay. I guess. Jeez. I wasn't figuring on—"

"Great," Reed said before Chaz changed his mind. "Gotta book. Meet you there."

He rushed out. It was happening! Group nondate could clear the way for a one-on-one let's-hang-out and that opened the door to the possibility of a little touch.

He could use a little touch. But right now he had three minutes to make it back to Mangia or Dory would scorch his ass.

He started to lope when he heard what sounded like firecrackers or a series of backfires. It made him think of GameStop's shooting games. More puzzled than alarmed, he glanced back.

Then the screaming started. And the thunder.

Not from behind, he realized, from up ahead. The thunder was dozens of people running. He jumped out of the way as a woman careened toward him racing behind a stroller where the kid inside wailed.

Was that blood on her face?

"What—"

She kept running, her mouth wide in a silent scream.

An avalanche rolled behind her. People stampeding, stomping on discarded shopping bags, tripping over them, and as some fell, over each other.

A man skidded over the floor, his glasses bouncing off to be crushed under someone's foot. Reed grabbed his arm.

"What's happening?"

"He's got a gun. He shot—he shot—"

The man shoved to his feet, ran on in a limping sprint. A couple of teenage girls ran weeping and screaming into a store at his left.

And he realized the noise—*gunfire*—came not only from in front of him, but also from behind him. He thought of Chaz, a thirty-second sprint behind him, and his restaurant family, double that ahead.

"Hide, man," he muttered to Chaz. "Find somewhere to hide."

And he ran toward the restaurant.

The cracking, popping sounds went on and on, seeming to come from everywhere now. Glass shattered and crashed, a woman with a bloodied leg huddled under a bench and moaned. He heard more screams—and, worse, the way they cut off, like a sliced tape.

Then he saw the little boy in red shorts and an Elmo T-shirt staggering like a drunk past Abercrombie & Fitch.

The display window exploded. People scattered, dived for cover, and the kid fell down, crying for his mother.

Across the mall, he saw a gunman—boy?—laughing as he fired, fired, fired. On the ground, a man's body jerked as the bullets tore into him.

Reed scooped up the kid in the Elmo T-shirt on the run, hooking him under one arm like the football he'd never been able to handle.

The gunfire—and he would never, never forget the sound of it—came closer. Front and back. Everywhere.

He'd never make it to Mangia, not with the kid. He veered off, running on instinct, did a kind of sliding dive into the kiosk.

Angie, the girl he'd flirted with five minutes before, a lifetime before, lay sprawled in a pool of blood. Her pretty brown eyes stared at him while the kid hooked under his arm wailed.

"Oh God, oh Jesus. Oh Jesus, oh God."

The shooting wouldn't stop, wouldn't stop.

"Okay, okay, you're okay. What's your name? I'm Reed, what's your name?"

"Brady. I want Mommy!"

"Okay, Brady, we're going to find her in just a minute, but now we have to be really quiet. Brady! How old are you?"

"This many." He held up four fingers as fat tears splashed on his cheeks.

"That's a big guy, right? We have to be quiet. There are bad guys. You know about bad guys?"

With tears and snot running down his face, eyes huge with shock, Brady nodded.

"We're going to be quiet so the bad guys don't find us. And I'm going to call for the good guys. For the police." He did his best to block the boy's view of Angie, did his best to block his own mind from the idea of her, of her and death.

He yanked open one of the sliding doors for storage, shoved out stock. "Climb in there, okay? Like Hide and Seek. I'm right here, but you get in there while I call the good guys."

He nudged the kid in, got out his phone, and that's when he saw how badly his hands shook.

"Nine-one-one, what is your emergency?"

"DownEast Mall," he began.

"Police are responding. Are you in the mall?"

"Yeah. I've got a kid with me. I put him in the stock cabinet in the Fun In The Sun kiosk. Angie—the girl who worked it. She's dead. She's dead. God. There are at least two of them shooting people."

"Can you tell me your name?"

"Reed Quartermaine."

"Okay, Reed, do you feel you're safe where you are?"

"Are you fucking kidding me?"

"Sorry. You're in a kiosk so you have some cover. I'm going to advise you to stay where you are, to shelter in place. You have a child with you?"

"He said his name's Brady, and he's four. He got separated from his mother. I don't know if she's . . ." He looked around, saw Brady had curled up, eyes glazed over, as he sucked his thumb. "He's probably, you know, in shock or whatever."

"Try to stay calm, Reed, and quiet. The police are on scene."

"They're still shooting. They just keep shooting. Laughing. I heard him laughing."

"Who was laughing, Reed?"

"He was shooting, the glass exploded, the guy on the ground, he kept shooting him and laughing. Jesus God."

He heard shouting—not the screams, but like war cries. Something tribal and triumphant. And more shots, then . . .

"It stopped. The shooting stopped."

"Stay where you are, Reed. Help is coming to you. Stay where you are."

He looked down at the boy again. The glassy eyes met his. He said, "Mommy."

"We're going to find her in a minute. The good guys are coming. They're coming."

That was the worst part, he'd think later. The waiting . . . with the smell of gunfire burning the air, the calls for help, the moans and sobbing. And seeing the blood on his own shoes of the girl he would never take to the movies.

CHAPTER TWO

At seven-twenty-five on July 22, Officer Essie McVee finished the on-site report on a fender bender in the parking lot of the DownEast Mall.

No injuries, minimal damage, but the driver of the Lexus got pretty aggressive with the trio of college girls in the Mustang convertible.

Though the Mustang was clearly at fault—the weeping twenty-year-old driver admitted it—by backing out of the space without checking, the hotshot and his mortified date in the Lexus had—also clearly—had more than a few drinks.

Essie let her partner handle the Lexus, knowing Barry would pull out the old women-drivers bullshit. She'd ignore that, also knowing Barry would cite the guy on an OUI.

She calmed the girls, took statements and information, wrote the ticket. Lexus didn't take kindly to the OUI—or to the cab Barry ordered—but Barry handled it in his "Aw, shucks" way.

When the radio squawked, she tuned her ear to it. Four years on the job didn't stop her heart from banging.

She jerked around to Barry, saw by his face his ear had been tuned in as well. She turned her head to her mic.

"Unit four-five is on scene. We're right outside the theater."

Barry popped the trunk, tossed her a vest.

Mouth dry as dust, Essie strapped it on, checked her sidearm—she'd never fired it off the range.

"Backup's coming, three minutes out. SWAT's mobilizing. Jesus, Barry."

"Can't wait."

She knew the drill, she'd had the training—though she'd never really expected to use it. *Active shooter* meant every second counted.

Essie raced with Barry toward the wide glass doors.

She knew the mall and wondered what twist of fate had put her and her partner seconds outside the theater entrance.

She didn't wonder if she would get home to feed her aging cat or to finish the book she'd started. She couldn't.

Locate, detain, distract, neutralize.

She put the scene inside her head before they hit the doors.

Theater lobby opening to the main mall, turn right to ticket booth, move to concessions, left to corridor to the three theaters. Nine-one-one stated shooter in One—the biggest of the three.

She scanned through the glass, went through, tacked left as Barry tacked right. She heard the piped music from the mall, the rumble of shoppers.

The two guys at concessions gawked at the pair of cops, weapons drawn. Both shot their hands up. The jumbo soda in the hand of the one on the left hit the counter, smashed and splashed.

"Anybody else here?" Barry demanded.

"J-j-just Julie, in the lockers."

"Get her, get outside. Now! Go, go!"

One of them leaped toward a door behind the counter. The other stood, hands up, still stammering, "What? What? What?"

"Move!"

He moved.

Essie turned left, cleared the corner, saw the body, facedown outside the doors of One, and the blood trail behind it.

"We got a body," she told dispatch, and kept moving. Slow, careful. Past the laughter in the theater on her right, and toward the sounds pushing against the door of One.

Shots, screams.

She exchanged a look with Barry, stepped over the body. At his nod, she thought: Here we go.

When they dragged open the theater doors, the sounds of violence and fear flooded out, and the muted light from the corridor slid into the dark.

She saw the shooter—male, Kevlar vest, helmet, night-vision goggles, an assault rifle in one hand, a handgun in the other.

In the instant it took her to register, he shot a male—who was fleeing for the side exit—in the back.

Then he swung the rifle toward the theater doors, and opened fire.

Essie dived for cover behind the wall behind the last row, saw Barry take a hit in the vest that flung him back and down.

Not center mass, she told herself as adrenaline pumped through her, not center mass because, like Barry, the shooter wore a vest. She sucked in three quick breaths, rolled, and to her shock saw he was charging up the sloping aisle toward her.

She fired low—hips, crotch, legs, ankles—and just kept firing even when he went down.

She had to shove aside the instinct to go to her partner, pushed herself to the shooter.

"Shooter down." Keeping her weapon trained on him, she pulled the pistol out of his hand, slapped her foot on the rifle he'd dropped. "Officer down. My partner took a hit. We need medical. God, multiple gunshot victims. We need help here. We need help."

"Reports of another active shooter, possibly two or more in the mall area. You confirm one shooter down?"

"He's down." She scanned his lower body, the mass of blood. "He's not getting up." Even as she said it, the shooter's harsh, rapid breaths went out.

He had a pimple on his chin. She stared at it until she could lift her head, until she could look at what he'd done.

Bodies, splayed in the aisle, slumped in the seats, crumpled in the narrow spaces between rows where they'd fallen or tried to hide.

She'd never forget it.

When a quad team burst through the theater doors, she held up a hand. "Officer McVee. Shooter's neutralized. My partner."

As she spoke, Barry coughed, moaned. She started to straighten from her crouch, swayed as her head swam.

"You hit, McVee?"

"No. No, just . . . No." Bearing down, she went to Barry.

"Next time I bitch about how hot and heavy these vests are, slug me." He hissed in a breath. "Hurts like a motherfucker."

She swallowed bile, took Barry's hand. "Would've hurt more without it."

"You got him, Essie. You got the bastard."

"Yeah." She had to swallow again, hard, but she nodded. "I think he's a kid. Barry, he's not alone."

More cops poured in, and medical first responders. While other police units rushed into the mall hunting for the other shooter or shooters, Essie worked with Barry to clear the theater's bathrooms, storage area, lockers.

"You need medical," she told him as they approached the ladies' room.

"I'll get it later. Nine-one-one caller." He nodded toward the bathroom door.

Essie shoved it open, swept with her weapon, and caught a glimpse of her own face in the mirrors over the sink. Sickly pale, but better than the gray tone under Barry's deep brown skin.

"This is the police," Essie called out. "Simone Knox? This is the police."

Silence echoed back.

"Maybe she got out."

The stall doors stood open, but one hardly more than a crack. "Simone," Essie repeated as she walked over. "I'm Officer McVee with the Rockpoint police. You're safe now."

She eased the door open, saw the girl crouched on the toilet seat, her hands pressed to her ears.

"Simone." Hunkering down, Essie laid a hand on Simone's knee. "You're all right now."

"They're screaming. He's killing them. Tish, Mi, my mom, my sister."

"Help's here now. We'll find them for you. Let's get you out of here, okay? You were really smart. You saved lives tonight, Simone, by calling for help."

Simone looked up then, huge brown eyes drenched with tears and shock. "My phone died. I forgot to charge it, and it died. So I hid in here."

"That's good, that's fine. Come on with me now. I'm Officer McVee. This is Officer Simpson."

"The man, the man ran out, and fell. The blood. I saw—I saw—Tish and Mi are in the movie. My mom and sister are shopping."

"We're going to find them for you." She put an arm around Simone, helped her down, helped her out. "You're going to go with Officer Simpson. And I'm going to go find your mom and your sister and your friends."

"Essie."

"You're hurt, Barry. Take the kid. Get her checked out."

She led the girl down the corridor, past the theaters. The situation report on her radio claimed two more shooters were down. She hoped that was all of them, but she needed to be sure.

But when Barry took over, steering Simone toward the glass doors and the flashing lights of cop cars and ambulances, Simone stopped, looked directly into Essie's eyes.

"Tulip and Natalie Knox. Mi-Hi Jung and Tish Olsen. You have to find them. Please. Please find them."

"Got it. On it."

Essie headed the opposite way. She didn't hear gunfire anymore and some-body, thank Christ, had shut off the music. Her radio crackled about areas cleared, calls for medical assistance.

She stopped, stared at the mall she'd shopped in, wandered in, grabbed her first meal in for as long as she could remember.

It would take time, she thought, almost numb, to clear the dead, to treat and transport the wounded, to take statements from those who'd escaped injury—physical injury, she corrected. She doubted anyone who lived through this night would come through unscathed.

Paramedics poured in now, but there were so many beyond their help.

A woman with blood running down her arm cradled a man—beyond help—in her lap. A male in a Red Sox jersey lay facedown. She could see gray matter in his head wound. A female, early twenties, sat weeping in front of Starbucks, her apron spattered with blood.

She saw a little pink sneaker, and though she prayed the girl who'd lost it found safety, it wrenched her heart.

She saw a man—early twenties/late teens—stagger out of GameStop. His thick glasses sat askew over eyes as dazed as a dreamer's.

"Is it over?" he asked her. "Is it over?"

"Are you injured?"

"No. I banged my elbow. I . . ." Those dazed eyes skimmed over her, then over the bleeding, the dead. "Oh jeez, oh jeez. In the—in the back room. I got people in the back room. Like they said to do if . . . They're in the back room."

"Just hold on a minute." She turned away to use her radio, to ask if she could lead a group out, and to what checkpoint.

"What's your name?" she asked him.

"I'm Chaz Bergman. I'm, like, the manager on duty tonight."

"Okay, Chaz, you did good. Let's get your people out now. There are officers outside who'll take your statements, but let's get everybody outside."

"I've got a friend. Reed, Reed Quartermaine. He works at Mangia—the restaurant. Can you find him?"

"I'll find him." Essie added him to her list.

"Is it over?" Chaz asked again.

"Yes," she told him, knowing it for a lie.

For everyone touched by the violence that day, it would never be over.

Reed had Brady on his hip when he spotted some of the Mangia crew. Some sat on a curb, holding each other. Rosie, still in her cook's apron, covered her face with her hands.

Eat that pasta, she always said to him. *Fatten you up, skinny boy.*

"You're okay, you're okay." Reed closed his eyes as he started to crouch down to her. She leaped up, wrapped her arms around him.

"You're not hurt." Rosie cupped Reed's face.

He shook his head. "Is everybody okay?"

Rosie let out a sound, like something tearing.

"He came in and . . ." Rosie broke off as she registered the boy Reed held. "We'll talk about it later. Who is this handsome fellow?"

"This is Brady." Not everyone was okay, Reed thought. "We, ah, hung out together. I need to help him find his mom."

And call his own, Reed thought. He'd texted her from inside, told her he was okay, not to worry. But he needed to call home.

"The good guys came. Reed said."

"Yes, they did." Rosie worked up a smile with tears flowing over it.

"I want Mommy."

"I'm going to ask one of the cops to help."

Reed straightened again, walked toward a cop—a girl cop, because he thought Brady might go with a woman. "Officer? Can you help me? This is Brady, and he can't find his mom."

"Hey, Brady. What's your mom's name?"

"Mommy."

"What's your daddy call her?"

"Honey."

Essie smiled. "I bet she has another name."

"Lisa Honey."

"Okay, and what's your whole name?"

"I'm Brady Michael Foster. I'm four years old. My daddy is a fireman and I have a dog named Mac."

"A fireman, and what's his whole name?"

"He's Michael Honey."

"Okay. Hold on a minute."

Firefighters were among the first responders, so Essie tracked one down. "I need a Michael Foster. I've got his son."

"Foster's one of mine. You've got Brady? Is he hurt?"

"No."

"His mother's en route to the hospital. Two shots in the back, fuck me. Foster's looking for the boy now. He didn't know they were here until our paramedics found Lisa." He rubbed his hands over his face. "Can't say if she'll make it. Here he comes."

Essie saw the man rushing through the shell-shocked crowd. Compact build, brown, close-cropped hair. His body jerked, sagged, then shifted direction as he ran toward his son.

In Reed's arms, Brady let out a squeal. "Daddy!"

Michael grabbed his son from Reed, folded him in, ran kisses over his head, his face. "Brady, thank God, thank God. Are you hurt? Did anybody hurt you?"

"Mommy fell down, and I couldn't find her. Reed found me and he said we had to be real quiet and wait for the good guys. I was real quiet like he said, even when he put me in the cupboard."

Michael's eyes swirled with tears when they met Reed's. "You're Reed?"

"Yes, sir."

Michael shot out a hand, gripped Reed's. "I'm never going to be able to thank you. I've got things to say to you, but—" He broke off as his mind cleared enough to notice the blood on Reed's pants and shoes. "You're hurt."

"No. I don't think . . . It's not mine. It's not . . ." Words dried up.

"Okay. Okay, Reed. Listen, I've got to get Brady out of here. Do you need help?"

"I have to find Chaz. I don't know if he's okay. I have to find him."

"Hold on."

Michael shifted Brady on his hip, pulled out his radio.

"I want Mommy."

"Okay, pal, but we're going to help Reed out."

While Michael talked into the radio, Reed looked around. So many lights, everything bright and blurring. So much noise. Talking, shouting, crying. He saw a man, moaning, bleeding, on a stretcher being loaded into an ambulance.

A woman wearing one shoe and with a slow trickle of blood sliding down the side of her face limped in circles, calling for Judy, until somebody in a uniform led her away.

A girl with a long brown ponytail sat on a curb talking to a police officer. She just kept shaking her head, and her eyes—like a tiger color—glinted in the whirling, swirling lights.

He saw television vans and more bright lights behind the yellow police tape. People were crowded behind the tape, some of them calling out names.

It struck him, suddenly and hard: Some of the names they called would never answer again.

He started to shake from the inside out. Gut, bowels, heart. His ears started to buzz, his vision blurred.

"Hey, Reed, how about you sit down a minute? I'm going to find out about your friend."

"No, I need to—" He saw Chaz, coming out with a group of people, with cops moving them along. "Jesus. Jesus. Chaz!"

He shouted it, like one of the people behind the police tape, and sprinted.

On the curb, Simone waited to feel her legs again. To feel everything again. Her body had gone numb, like someone had given her a full-body shot of novocaine.

"Your mom and sister are okay."

She heard Officer McVee's words, tried to feel them. "Where are they? Where are they?"

"They're going to bring them out soon. Your mom has some minor injuries. Minor, Simone. She's fine. They got inside one of the shops, got to safety. Your mom got some cuts from flying glass, and hit her head. But she's fine, okay?"

All Simone could do was shake her head. "Mom hit her head."

"But she's going to be fine. They got to safety, and they're coming out soon."

"Mi, Tish."

She knew, she knew by the way Officer McVee put an arm around her shoulders. She couldn't feel it, not really, just the weight.

The weight.

"Mi's on her way to the hospital. They're going to take good care of her, do everything they can."

"Mi. He shot her?" Her voice spiked, stabbing her own ears. "He shot her?"

"She's going to the hospital, and they're waiting to take care of her."

"I had to pee. I wasn't there. I had to pee. Tish was there. Where's Tish?"

"We have to wait until everyone's out, and everyone's accounted for."

Simone kept shaking her head. "No, no, no. They were sitting together. I had to pee. He shot Mi. He shot her. Tish. Sitting together."

She looked at Essie, and knew. And knowing caused her to feel again. To feel everything.

Reed caught Chaz in a bear hug, felt at least some of the world was right again. They stood gripping each other in front of the girl with the long brown ponytail and tiger eyes.

When she let out a wordless, keening wail, Reed dropped his head onto Chaz's shoulder.

Inside the wail, he knew, was a name that would never answer again.

They couldn't make her go home. Everything was jumbled and tangled together, but she knew she sat in a hospital waiting room on a hard plastic chair. She had a Coke in her hands.

Her sister and their father sat with her. Natalie curled against Dad, but Simone didn't want to be held or touched.

She didn't know how long they'd waited. A long time? Five minutes?

Other people waited, too.

She heard numbers, different numbers.

Three shooters. Eighty-six injured. Sometimes the number of injured went up, sometimes down.

Thirty-six dead. Fifty-eight.

Numbers changing, always changing.

Tish was dead. That wouldn't change.

They had to wait in the hard chairs while somebody picked glass out of her mother's head, and treated the cuts on her face.

She had an image of that face in her head, all those little nicks, and the face pale, pale, pale under the makeup. Her mother's blond hair—always perfect—bloody and tangled.

They'd brought her out on one of those rolling stretcher things with Natalie clinging to her hand and crying.

Natalie didn't get hurt because Mom had shoved her into the shop, and Mom had fallen. Natalie pulled and dragged her inside, and behind a display counter of summer tanks and tees.

Natalie was brave. Simone would tell her she was brave when she could speak again.

But now they had to get the glass out of her mother's head, and examine her because she'd hit her head, too, and it had knocked her out for a couple minutes.

Concussion.

She knew Natalie wanted to go home because Dad kept telling her that Mom was going to be fine, and she'd be coming out soon, and they'd go home.

But Simone wouldn't go, and they couldn't make her.

Tish was dead, Mi was in surgery, and they couldn't make her.

She kept the Coke can in both hands so her father wouldn't take her hand again. She didn't want anyone to hold her hand or cuddle her. Not yet. Maybe not ever.

She just needed to wait on the hard plastic chair.

The doctor came out first, and her father surged to his feet.

Dad is so tall, Simone thought vaguely, so tall and handsome. He still wore his business suit and tie because he'd just come home from a business dinner, turned on the news.

Then he'd rushed straight out to drive to the mall.

The doctor gave her father some instructions. Minor concussion, some stitches.

When her mother came out, Simone got shakily to her feet. Until that moment she hadn't understood she'd been afraid her mother really wasn't okay.

Her mother would be like Mi, or worse, like Tish.

But her mother came into the waiting room. She had those weird bandages in a couple places on her face, but she didn't look pale, pale, pale the way she had. The way Simone imagined dead people looked.

Natalie leaped up, flung her arms around their mother.

"There's my brave girl," Tulip murmured. "My brave girls," she said, reaching out for Simone.

And finally Simone wanted to be touched, wanted to hold and to be held. She wrapped her arms around her mother with Natalie between.

"I'm okay, a bump on the head. Let's take our girls home, Ward."

Simone heard the tears in her mother's voice, clung tighter for one more moment. And closed her eyes when her father wrapped his arms around the three of them.

"I'll go get the car."

Simone pulled back. "I'm not going. I'm not going home now."

"Sweetheart—"

But Simone shook her head fiercely, moved another step away from her mother's tired face with its nicks and bandages. "I'm not going. Mi— They're operating on Mi. I'm not going."

"Sweetheart," Tulip tried again, "there's nothing you can do here, and—"

"I can *be* here."

"Nat, do you remember where we parked the car?"

"Yeah, Dad, but—"

"Take your mom out." He passed Natalie the key. "You two go out to the car, and give me and Simone a minute."

"Ward, the girls need to be home. They need to be away from here."

"Go on out to the car," he repeated, even as Simone sat again, her arms folded in a picture of defiant misery. He pressed his lips to his wife's cheek, murmured something, then sat beside Simone.

"I know you're scared. We all are."

"You weren't there."

"I know that, too." She heard the misery in his voice now, but shook it off. Pushed it away. "Simone, I'm sick and sorry about Tish. I'm sick and sorry about Mi. I promise you we'll check on Mi from home, and I'll bring you to see her tomorrow. But your mother needs to go home, so does Natalie."

"Take them home."

"I can't leave you here."

"I have to stay. I left them. I left them."

He pulled her to him. She resisted, tried to yank free, but he was stronger and held her until she broke.

"I'm sick and sorry about Tish and Mi," he repeated. "And I'll be grateful for the rest of my life you weren't in the theater. I need to take care of your mom and your sister now. I need to take care of you."

"I can't leave Mi. I can't, I can't. Please don't try to make me."

He might have, and Simone worried he would have, but as she pulled back from him, CiCi rushed in.

Long, flying red hair, a half-dozen strings of beads and crystals around her neck, a swirling blue skirt and Doc Martens sandals.

She scooped Simone up, enfolded her in yoga-fit arms and a cloud of peachy perfume with just the faintest hint of marijuana.

"Thank God! Oh, baby! Oh thank every god and goddess. Tulip?" she demanded of Ward. "Natalie?"

"They just went out to the car. Tulip got a couple of bumps and scrapes, that's all. Nat's fine."

"CiCi will stay with me." Simone turned her lips to her grandmother's ear. "Please, please."

"Sure I will. Are you hurt? Are you—"

"He killed Tish. Mi—they're operating."

"Oh no." CiCi rocked her, swayed her, wept with her. "Those sweet girls, those sweet young girls."

"Dad has to take Mom and Natalie home. I have to wait here. I have to wait for Mi. Please."

"Of course you do. I've got her, Ward. I'll stay with her. I'll bring her home when Mi's out of surgery. I've got her."

Simone heard the snap of steel in CiCi's words and knew her father had been about to object.

"All right. Simone." He cupped her face, kissed her forehead. "You call if you need me. We'll pray for Mi."

She watched him go, slipped her hand into CiCi's. "I don't know where she is. Can you find out?"

CiCi Lennon had a way of getting people to tell her what she wanted to know, of doing what she thought they should do. It didn't take long for her to lead Simone up to another waiting room.

This one had chairs with pads, sofas and benches, even vending machines.

She saw Mi's parents, her older sister, her younger brother, her grandparents. Mi's father saw her first. He looked a thousand years older than he had when they'd picked up Mi for the movies.

He'd been working in his front garden, she remembered, and had waved them off.

He rose, walked over with tears swirling in his eyes to hug her.

"I'm so glad you weren't hurt." His English was perfect and precise, and he smelled of freshly cut grass.

"I left them. I had to use the bathroom, and I left them. Then—"

"Ah. I'm glad for it. Ms. Lennon, it's kind of you to come."

"CiCi," she corrected. "We're all family now. We'd like to wait with you, send all our healing thoughts and lights to Mi."

His chin wobbled as he fought to compose himself.

"Simone, my treasure, why don't you go sit with Mi's mom?" She put an arm around Mr. Jung's shoulders. "Let's take a little walk."

Simone went over to sit by Mrs. Jung. And when Mrs. Jung gripped her hand, Simone held tight.

She knew CiCi believed in vibes and light and burning sage and meditation. And all sorts of things that made her daughter roll her eyes.

Simone also knew that if anyone could make Mi be okay through sheer force of will, it was CiCi.

So she clung to that just like she clung to Mi's mother's hand.

CHAPTER THREE

When CiCi came back, Simone got up so Mr. Jung could sit next to his wife. Before she took another seat, Mi's sister, Nari, took her arm.

"Help me get tea."

Simone went with her across the big room to a counter with pots of hot water, coffee, tea bags, and disposable cups.

Nari, slim, studious, in her second year at MIT, efficiently set up a cardboard tray. "They won't tell you." She spoke quietly, giving Simone a long look—dark eyes through the lenses of dark-framed glasses. "It's bad. Mi was shot three times."

Simone opened her mouth, but no words came out. There were no words.

"I heard one of the police talking to a nurse after they took her to surgery. She lost so much blood. She's so tiny, and she lost a lot of blood. Will you go with me to give blood for her? It might not go to her, but—"

"Yes. What do we do? Where do we go?"

Because she was a minor, Simone needed CiCi. They took turns because so many people were doing just as they were.

Simone looked away before the needle went in because needles made her feel a little sick. She drank the little cup of orange juice after, as instructed.

On the way back, she told CiCi she needed to use the bathroom.

"I'll go with you."

"No, that's okay. I'll be right there."

She wanted to go alone, mostly because she needed to throw up the orange juice.

But when she went inside she saw a woman standing at one of the sinks, crying.

Tiffany's mother. Mrs. Bryce had been her seventh-grade language arts teacher. That same year—and everyone knew—Mr. Bryce had divorced her to marry the woman (*lots* younger) he'd had an affair with because the woman was pregnant.

Simone realized she hadn't thought of Tiffany or Trent—the boy she'd thought she loved.

"Mrs. Bryce."

Still sobbing, the woman turned.

"I'm sorry. I'm Simone Knox. You taught me in middle school. I know Tiffany. I saw her tonight before . . . Before."

"You were there?"

"With Mi-Hi Jung and Tish Olsen. In the movies. They're operating on Mi. She got shot. She got shot. He killed Tish."

"Oh God." They stood, tears streaming. "Tish? Tish Olsen? Oh God, oh God." When she threw her arms around Simone, Simone clung to her.

"Tiffany's in surgery. She . . . they can't tell me."

"Trent? She was with Trent."

Mrs. Bryce stepped back, pressed the heels of her hands to her eyes, shook her head. "I'll pray for Mi." She turned back to the sink, ran water, splashed and splashed it on her face. "You'll pray for Tiffany."

"I will," she promised, and meant it.

She didn't need to throw up anymore. She already felt empty.

In the waiting room she fell asleep with her head in CiCi's lap. When she woke she stayed curled there, her mind so foggy it seemed a thin layer of smoke blurred the room.

Through it she saw a man with gray hair and blue scrubs talking to Mrs. Bryce. And Mr. Bryce, she realized, and the woman he'd gotten pregnant and married.

Mrs. Bryce was crying again, but not the way she had in the bathroom. She had her hands clutched together in her lap, her lips pressed tight, but she kept nodding. And even through the layer of haze, Simone saw gratitude.

Tiffany hadn't died, not like Tish. Not like Trent.

Mi wouldn't die, either. She couldn't.

They waited. She drifted off again, but lightly now, so she felt CiCi shift.

This doctor was a woman with ink-black hair pulled back from her face. She had an accent—Indian, maybe. Simone heard it, but it faded off as the words registered through the fog as she pushed herself up.

Mi had come through surgery.

Bullet wound in the right arm. No muscle damage.

Bullet nicked the right kidney. Repaired, no permanent damage likely.

Chest wound. Lungs full of blood. Draining, repairing, transfusions. The next twenty-four hours critical. Mi—young and strong.

"Once she's out of Recovery and in ICU, you can see her. Briefly, only two at a time. She's sedated," the doctor continued. "She should sleep for several hours. You should try to get some rest."

Mrs. Jung cried, but like Mrs. Bryce had.

"Thank you. Thank you. We'll wait, and go see her." Mr. Jung put an arm around his wife.

"I'll have you taken up to ICU. But only family," she added, with a glance at Simone and CiCi.

"This girl is family," Mr. Jung said.

Relenting, the doctor looked back at Simone. "I'll need your name for the approved visitors list."

"Simone Knox."

"'Simone Knox'? The first nine-one-one caller?"

"I don't know. I called them."

"Simone, you should know: By calling them so quickly, you gave Mi a fighting chance. I'll put your name on the list."

After Simone had gone home to her bed, to dark, fractured dreams, Michael Foster sat by his wife's hospital bed while she slept.

She'd wake, ask about Brady again. Her short-term memory was disrupted, but would come back, they told him. For now, he needed to reassure her anytime she surfaced that their son hadn't been harmed.

Reed Quartermaine. They owed Reed Quartermaine for that.

She'd wake, he thought. She'd live.

And, due to a bullet in the spine, she'd never walk again.

One bullet struck her just below the shoulder blade, but the other hit her lower spinal cord.

He tried to believe they'd been lucky, because he'd have to believe it to convince her. If the bullet had hit higher, she could've lost feeling in her trunk, in her arms. She might have needed a breathing tube, might not have been able to turn her neck.

But they'd been lucky. She'd been spared the trauma of losing control of her bladder and bowels. With time and therapy, she'd be able to operate a motorized wheelchair, even drive.

But his beautiful wife, his wife who loved to dance, wouldn't walk again.

She'd never run on the beach again with Brady, go hiking, jog up and down the stairs in the house they'd scrimped and saved for.

All because three sick, selfish bastards had gone on some senseless murder spree.

He didn't even know which one of the three had hurt his wife, the mother of his child, the love of his goddamn life.

It didn't matter which, he thought. They'd all done it.

John Jefferson Hobart, aka JJ, age seventeen.

Kent Francis Whitehall, age sixteen.

Devon Lawrence Paulson, age sixteen.

Teenagers. Sociopaths, psychopaths. He didn't care what label the shrinks slapped on them.

He knew the death count, at least as of four a.m. when he'd last checked. Eighty-nine. And his Lisa was one of the two hundred and forty-two injured.

Because three twisted boys, armed to the fucking teeth, had walked into the mall on a Friday night with a mission to kill and maim.

Mission accomplished.

He didn't count them among the dead—they didn't deserve to be counted. But he could be grateful to the cop who'd taken out Hobart, and grateful the other two had killed themselves—or each other.

That detail remained unclear as of four a.m.

He could be grateful there would be no trial. Grateful he, a man who'd dedicated himself to saving lives, wouldn't spend sleepless nights imagining killing them himself.

Lisa stirred so he shifted closer. When her eyes opened, he brought her hand to his lips.

"Brady?"

"He's fine, baby. He's with your mom and dad. He's fine."

"I had his hand. I started to grab him up and run, but then . . ."

"He's fine, Lisa honey, he's fine."

"So tired."

When she drifted off, he went back to watching her sleep.

Reed woke at dawn with his head banging, his eyes burning, his throat desert dry. The world's worst hangover without a single drop of alcohol.

He showered—his third since coming home to his exhausted, grateful parents and his clinging, weeping sister. He just couldn't get over the way Angie's blood had soaked through his pants and onto his skin.

He knocked back some Advil, guzzled water straight from the faucet.

Then he booted up his computer. He didn't have any problem finding stories on the shooting.

He studied the three names listed, then the photographs. He thought maybe he recognized Whitehall, but couldn't figure from where.

He knew he recognized Paulson. He'd seen him riddle a man's body with bullets and laugh.

One of the two had killed Angie, as the reports said the third, Hobart, never got out of the theater.

One of them had killed Justin, a busboy at Mangia, his first summer job. And Lucy, a waitress who'd planned to retire at the end of the year and hop into their RV to tour the country with her husband.

Customers, too. He didn't know how many.

Dory was in the hospital. So were Bobby and Jack and Mary.

Rosie told him the boy with the guns had walked through the glass doors, sprayed the main dining room with bullets, then walked out again. Ten seconds, twenty. No more.

He read eyewitness reports, stopped and read the one on GameStop twice.

We heard the shooting, but didn't really know what it was. The shop's noisy. Then somebody came running in yelling somebody was shooting people. He was bleeding, but didn't even seem to know he'd been shot.

That's when the store manager—I don't know his name—started telling everybody to get into this back room. Some people started to run out, but the shooting got closer. You could hear it, and the manager kept telling people to get in the back. It was really tight in there, the store was crowded. I was never so scared in my life as being crammed in that room. People were crying and praying, and he said we had to be quiet.

Then we heard it, the shooting, really loud. Right out in the store. Glass breaking. I thought we were all going to die, but then it stopped. Or I guess it moved away. He wanted us to stay in there until the police came, but somebody panicked, I guess, and pushed out of the door. Some people ran out. Then police came and took us outside. That boy saved our lives, the young manager with the thick glasses. I'm convinced he saved our lives.

"Way to go, Chaz," Reed murmured.

In the little kitchen of her little apartment, Essie brewed a full pot of coffee. She'd have plenty of time to drink it as she'd been taken off the roll.

Her CO assured her she'd be back on—and likely get a medal—but the process had to play out. She'd not only fired her weapon, she'd killed.

She believed her CO and knew she'd done her job, but figured she'd stay half on edge until being cleared for duty. She hadn't realized just how much she needed to be a cop until there'd been the tiniest doubt that she could be dismissed.

While the old cat slept on a cushion, Essie made herself a bagel and took her last banana. Since the size and layout of the apartment allowed her to see the screen from her kitchen/dining/worktable, she sat there and switched on the TV.

She knew the press had her name, and an earlier glimpse out the window proved they'd tracked her down. She wouldn't go out of the apartment and into the volley of questions and cameras. Someone had leaked her land-line number, so she'd unplugged it. The constant ringing bugged the shit out of her.

So far her cell phone remained secure. If her partner or her CO wanted to reach her, they would. Plus she still had e-mail.

She opened her laptop as she ate and watched the early news shows for any information she didn't already have.

Using the laptop, she made a list of names she had in her head.

Simone Knox, her mother, her sister. Reed Quartermaine. Chaz Bergman. Michael, Lisa, and Brady Foster. Mi-Hi Jung.

She'd follow up with all of them, even if it had to be on her own time.

She noted down the names of the shooters. She intended to dig out everything she could on them, on their families, their teachers, their friends, employers, if any. She wanted to know them.

She typed out the numbers—current—of dead, of wounded. Added names when she had them. She'd get the rest.

She'd been doing her job, she thought as she watched, as she ate, as she worked. But that didn't mean it wasn't personal.

CiCi Lennon lived life by her own rules. Two of the top rules—Try Not to Hurt Anybody, and Have the Balls to Say What You Think—often clashed, but the results blended with her Be An Asshole When Necessary rule, so it worked for her.

She'd been raised by sober Methodist, traditional Republican parents in Rockpoint, an upper-class suburban haven of Portland, Maine. Her father, a financial executive, and her mother, a housewife (self-proclaimed and proudly), had belonged to the country club, attended church every Sunday, and hosted dinner parties. Her father had bought a new Cadillac every three years, played golf on Saturday mornings and tennis (doubles with his wife) on Sunday afternoons, and collected stamps.

Her mother had had her hair done on Mondays, played bridge on Wednesdays, and belonged to the garden club. Deborah (never Deb or Debbie) Lennon had kept her pin money inside a white glove in her top dresser drawer, had never in her life written a check or otherwise paid a bill, and greeted her husband with freshened makeup after his day of work. She had mixed his evening drink—a dry gin martini, one olive, except during the summer season, when he switched to gin and tonic with a twist of lime—so he could unwind until dinner.

The Lennons had employed a daily housekeeper, a weekly groundskeeper, and—in the season—a pool boy. They had owned a vacation home in Kennebunkport and were considered, by themselves and others, pillars of the community.

Naturally, CiCi rebelled against everything they were and stood for.

What was a child of the sixties to do but appall her conservative parents with her passionate embrace of the counterculture? She denounced the patriarchal structure of the church—and their lifestyle—railed against the government, actively protested the war in Vietnam, and literally burned her bra.

At seventeen, CiCi packed a bag and hitchhiked to Washington to march. From there, along with sex, drugs, and rock and roll, she traveled. She spent springtime in New Orleans sharing a ramshackle house with a group of artists and musicians. She painted for tourists—she'd been born with the talent.

She rode to Woodstock in a van she helped paint into psychedelic wonder. Sometime during the rain-soaked bliss of that weekend in August, she conceived a child.

When she realized she was pregnant, she cut out the drugs and alcohol, adjusted her vegetarian diet (as she would do countless times for countless reasons over the decades), and joined a commune in California.

She painted, learned to weave, planted and harvested vegetables, tried and failed at a lesbian relationship—but she tried.

She gave birth to her daughter on a cot in a dilapidated farmhouse on a pretty spring afternoon as Janis Joplin rocked it out on the record player and tulips swayed in the breeze outside the open window.

When Tulip Joplin Lennon was six months old, CiCi, missing the green of the East Coast, caught a ride with a group of musicians. Along the way she hooked up briefly with another musician/songwriter who, stoned, offered her three thousand to paint him.

She did, with him wearing only his Fender Stratocaster and a pair of shit-kicker boots.

CiCi moved on, the subject of her painting got a record deal and used her painting for the album cover. As luck would have it, he had a major Top 40 hit with the single, "Farewell, CiCi," and the album went gold.

Two years later, while CiCi and Tulip lived in a group house in Nantucket, the songwriter OD'd. The painting went on the auction block, sold for three million dollars.

And CiCi's career as an artist truly launched.

Seven years after she'd hitchhiked to D.C., CiCi's father contracted pancreatic cancer. Though she'd sent postcards and mailed photos of their granddaughter, called them two or three times a year, communications had remained scattered and tense.

But her mother breaking down over the phone had CiCi following another of her rules: Help When You Can.

She packed up her daughter, her art supplies, and her bike in a thirdhand beater of a station wagon and went home.

She learned a few things. She learned her parents loved each other, deeply. And that deep love didn't mean her mother could handle the dirty work. She learned the house where she grew up would never be her home again, but she could live there as long as she served a purpose.

She learned her father wanted to die at home and because she loved him—surprise—she would damn well make sure he got his wish. While she drew the line at her mother's *strong* suggestion of private school, she enrolled Tulip in the local public elementary. While she drove her father to chemo, to his doctor's appointments, cleaned up puke, her mother happily tended to Tulip.

CiCi hired a male nurse whose compassion, kindness, and love of rock made them lifelong friends.

For twenty-one months she helped nurse her dying father and ran the household accounts, while her mother clung to denial and spoiled Tulip.

Her father died at home with the wife who loved him curled beside him in their bed, and his daughter holding his hand.

Over the next few months she accepted that her mother would never become independent, would never learn how to balance a checkbook or fix her own leaky faucet.

And accepted she would go raving mad if she stayed in suburbia in a not-so-mini mansion with a woman who could barely figure out how to change a light bulb.

As her father had left her mother more than financially secure, CiCi hired a business manager, an on-call handyman, and an eager young housekeeper, as the other had retired, who would also stand as a companion.

When she learned, during those twenty-one months, her father had changed his will and left her a million dollars—after taxes—her first reaction was rage. She didn't need or want his conservative right-wing establishment money. She could—and was—supporting herself and her daughter through her art.

The rage faded when she took Tulip for a ferry ride to Tranquility Island and saw the house. She loved the ramble of it, the wide terraces—on the first and second levels. The views of the water, its narrow little strip of beach, that curve of rocky coastline.

She could paint forever.

The FOR SALE sign was just that to CiCi. A sign.

Only a forty-minute ferry ride from Portland—far enough (thank God!)

from her mother, but close enough to assuage any guilt. A village with a cheerful artists community an easy bike ride away.

She bought it—after a hard-eyed negotiation—for cash, and began the next chapter of her life.

Now she was back in upper-class suburbia—briefly, she hoped—in the home of a daughter who'd always been more like her grandmother than the mother who'd tried to give her a sense of adventure, independence, and freedom.

Because Help When You Can was still a rule. And she loved her grand-children beyond measure.

She made breakfast for her daughter and Ward in their sleekly modern kitchen. She'd unplugged the phones, closed the curtains and drapes as re-porters gathered outside.

She'd listened to the news on the guest-room TV, and heard the replay of Simone's nine-one-one call. It had chilled her to the bone. Someone had leaked not only the call but Simone's name.

She sat with Ward and Tulip in the breakfast nook of the kitchen, made her pitch.

"Let me take Simone to the island, at least until school starts."

"She needs to be home," Tulip began.

"The press isn't going to leave her alone. She was the first call for help, she's a beautiful sixteen-year-old girl. One of her friends died, and the other is in the hospital. Mi made it through the night," CiCi added. "She's still critical, but she made it."

Ward let out a shaky breath. "They wouldn't give me any information on her when I called."

CiCi looked at him. He was a good man, she thought. A good man, good husband, good father. At the moment, he looked exhausted.

"Hwan had them put my name and Simone's on the family list." Because he was a good man, CiCi reached out, laid her hand over his. "You should call him."

"I will. Yes, I'll call him."

Now CiCi laid a hand over her daughter's. "Tulip, I know you need your girls, and they need you right now. I'll stay as long as I can help. Simone won't leave until she's sure you're all right, and Mi's all right. And I imagine the police are going to need to talk to her."

"We'll have to make a statement to the press," Ward added. "You're right. They won't leave her alone."

"You're right, too. But after all that, let me take her, give her a few weeks of peace and quiet. Even with the crazy of summer people on the island I can give her that—and Mi when she's well enough. No one will bother her, or them, I'll see to that. And Simone's going to need someone to talk to about everything, besides us. I have a friend. He spends part of the summer on the island. He's a therapist with offices in Portland. You can check out his credentials, Ward. You can meet him, talk to him."

"I'd have to do all of that."

"I know, but you'll learn he's very good. She'll need to talk to someone. So will you and Natalie, baby."

"I don't want to talk to anyone, see anyone right now. I just want to be home, with my family."

CiCi started to speak, but Ward shook his head in warning.

"Okay, think about this instead. After you've had that, a few weeks on the island might help Simone get away from all of it. Natalie, too, if she wants to come, but I know she's had her heart set on that equestrian camp, and that's coming up in a couple weeks. She likes spending time on the island, but Simone loves it."

"We'll talk about it," Ward said. "We're grateful, CiCi, for—"

"None of that. Family does what family needs. And right now, I think this family needs more coffee."

As she stood, Simone came in.

Dark circles under her dazed, heavy eyes stood out stark against her pallor.

"Mi woke up. The nurse said the doctor was in with her, and her dad said—he said she asked for me. I have to go see Mi."

"Sure you do, but you need to have some breakfast. You don't want Mi to see you looking so pale. That won't help her feel better, will it, Tulip?"

"Come, sit down, sweetie," her mother urged.

"I'm not hungry."

"Just a little bit. CiCi's going to fix you just a little bit."

She sat, looked at her mother's face. The bandages, the bruises. "Are you feeling better?"

"Yes." But her eyes welled.

"Don't cry, Mom. Please."

"I didn't know where you were. I hit my head, and poor Nat . . . It was only for a minute," she said, "but I was confused and scared. I could hear the shooting, the screaming, and I didn't know if you were all right, if you were safe. I know Mi needs to see you, but I need you for just a little while first."

"I didn't know if you and Nat . . . I didn't know." She sat next to her mother, pressed her face to Tulip's shoulder. "When I woke up, I thought it was a bad dream. But it wasn't."

"We're okay now."

"Tish isn't."

Tulip stroked, rocked. "I'm going to call her aunt. I'd call her mother, but— I think I'll call her aunt. I'll ask if there's anything we can do."

"Trent's dead, too."

"Oh, Simone."

"I saw on the news . . . I looked before I came down, and I saw the names, the pictures of who did this. They went to my school. I know them. I went to school with them. I had classes with one of them, and they killed Tish and Trent."

"Don't think about it right now."

Denial, CiCi thought, like her grandmother. Close your eyes to the bad shit until you couldn't.

CiCi watched Simone get up and go sit on the other bench to face her parents.

"They said my name in the news report. I looked outside, and there are people, reporters."

"You don't need to worry about that," Ward told her. "I'll take care of it."

"It's my name, Dad. And my voice—they played my call to the police. They had my yearbook picture. I don't want to talk to them, not now. I need to see Mi."

"Your dad'll talk to them," CiCi said briskly as she brought over a single scrambled egg, two strips of bacon, a piece of toast with butter. "And your mom's going to help you with some makeup. My Tule always had a hand with makeup. We're going to put your hair up under a ball cap, you're going to put your Wayfarers on, and you and I are going out the back while your dad has them busy out front. We're going to cut across the backyards to where I parked the car in the Jeffersons' driveway. I called them last night to clear that. Then all we have to do is call the hospital and have them get us in a side entrance."

"That's a damn good plan," Ward murmured.

"When you have to make some quick exits from hotels, motels, wherever, you learn the ropes. We'll get you to Mi." CiCi smoothed a hand over the tangle of Simone's hair. "Just eat a little first."

CHAPTER FOUR

It worked, exactly the way CiCi said it would. Though it seemed to Simone like some weird dream, like the ones she'd have when she wasn't exactly awake or exactly asleep. Everything felt vivid and blurred at the same time, with sounds coming down some echoing tunnel.

But when CiCi guided her into ICU, Simone's heart started beating so loud and fast inside what felt like squeezing hands. The sensation shot her straight back to the bathroom stall where she'd crouched with her dead phone and terror.

"CiCi."

"Breathe. In through your nose, like your belly's a balloon you're inflating, then out through your nose, like it's deflating. In and out," she crooned, an arm around Simone's waist. "That's right. You're all right. Mi's going to be all right, so you'll breathe for her. Look, there's Nari."

Nari, face pale with fatigue, eyes bruised from it, rose and walked to them. "Our parents are in with Mi. The doctor said they'll put her in a step-down room soon, maybe today, because her condition's improved."

"She's better?" Simone's throat filled. "She's really better?"

"She's better, I promise. She looks . . ." Nari pressed her lips together when they trembled. "She looks very frail, but she's better. We had to tell her about Tish. She needs to see you, Simone, very much."

"Nari, sweetie, have you been here all night?" CiCi asked her.

"My grandparents took my brother home. I stayed with my parents. We just couldn't leave her."

"I'm going to get you some coffee. Or tea? A soda?"

"I'd be grateful for coffee."

"Simone, sit with Nari. And, Nari, when your mom and dad come out, the three of you should go home and get some sleep. Simone and I'll stay. We're going to start taking shifts so someone's always here. Go on and sit."

"I don't know if they'll leave," Nari said after CiCi had gone to find coffee.

"CiCi will convince them. She's good at that." To be brave for Mi meant starting now, Simone thought, leading Nari back to the chairs. "We'll take turns so Mi isn't ever alone."

"She remembers. Some anyway, she remembers. The police talked to her this morning. The doctor only let them talk to her for a few minutes. Have you talked to the police?"

"Not today. Not yet today."

CiCi came back with a Coke for Simone, coffee for Nari. "A lot of cream, a little sugar, right?"

"Yes." Nari managed a smile. "You remembered."

"Got it locked in." CiCi tapped a finger on her temple, sat. "I was a roadie on and off for a few years. You learn to lock in how people like their coffee, their liquor, their sex."

"CiCi."

"Facts of life, my girls. Are you seeing anyone, Nari?"

Simone didn't know how her grandmother did it, but even then could see why she did. She took Nari out of the terrifying moment and into the normal; in three minutes she learned more than Simone suspected Mi or their parents knew of the boy Nari had started dating. An Irish Catholic boy from Boston who was, even now, driving up to be with her.

When Mi's parents came out, CiCi rose, went over to quickly embrace each of them. During their murmured conversation, Simone saw Mrs. Jung look back toward the doors with tears in her eyes, but CiCi kept talking in that low, soothing way.

Like a dream, Simone thought again, when, within minutes, the Jungs agreed to go home for a little while.

When it was done, CiCi sat again, patted Simone's knee. "They don't think they'll sleep, but they will. The body and the spirit need recharging, and the spirit will guide the body."

"I didn't know Nari had a real boyfriend."

"I don't think she did, either, until he said he was dropping everything and coming to be with her. Now. I want you to think strong, positive thoughts."

With a finger tapping in the air, CiCi gave Simone a knowing look out of eyes Simone thought of as golden, and were, in fact, the same shade as her own.

"And don't think I can't see the smirk you're giving me inside your head. Think them anyway. You're going to cry together, but that's a healing thing whether it feels like it now or not. You're going to listen to her, to whatever she needs to say. And you're going to tell her the truth about whatever she asks you because if you break trust with each other now, you may not get it back."

"I don't want to say anything that makes it worse."

"It's already worse, and you're going through it together. You need truth between you. There's her nurse now. Go see your sister, baby. Strong and brave."

She didn't feel strong and brave, not with the buzzing in her head and that squeezing inside her chest. She nodded at the nurse, but didn't really comprehend what she said.

It all got worse when she saw Mi through the glass.

Mi looked so small, so sick. *Frail*, Nari had said, but to Simone's eyes Mi looked broken. Something fragile already dropped and shattered.

Mi's exhausted eyes met hers, and tears spilled.

She didn't remember going in. Couldn't remember if the nurse had told her not to touch Mi. But she had to, had to.

She pressed her cheek to Mi's, gripped hands that felt as thin as bird wings.

"I thought— I was afraid they lied." Mi's voice, thin as her hands, choked with sobs. "I was afraid you were dead, too, and they weren't telling me. I was afraid . . ."

"I'm not. I'm here. I didn't get hurt. I wasn't there. I left—"

Simone heard herself—and heard CiCi: Listen to her.

"Is Tish really dead?"

Her cheek still pressed to Mi's, Simone nodded.

They cried together, with Mi's frail body shaking under hers.

Simone shifted so she could sit on the side of the bed, hold Mi's hand.

"He came in. I didn't see him at first. Then we heard the shooting and the screaming, but it happened so fast, and we didn't know what was happening. Tish said, 'What's happening?' and then . . ."

Mi closed her eyes. "Can I have some water?"

Simone got the cup with the bendy straw, held it for Mi.

"He shot her. Simone, he shot her, and I felt this—like, this awful pain, and Tish fell on me, just sort of tipped over on me, and I felt more pain, and she was, I don't know, jerking. Simone, he kept shooting her, and she was kind of over me, so she died. I didn't. She saved me. I told the police. I couldn't move. I couldn't help her. And I was awake, but it didn't seem real. He just kept shooting and shooting, then it all stopped. The shooting. But people were screaming and crying. I couldn't scream, and I couldn't move. I thought I was dead, and then I . . . I just went away, I guess. I don't remember until I woke up here."

Her fingers squeezed, light as wings, on Simone's. "Am I going to die?"

Tell her the truth.

"You were really hurt, and we were so scared. It took hours before the doctor came out, but she said you did really well. And today they said they're going to take you out of ICU because you're not critical anymore. CiCi's here with me, and she talked your parents into going home for a little while to sleep. They'd never go home if you were going to die."

Mi closed her eyes again. "Tish did. Why?"

"I don't know. I can't— I still think it's not real."

"You went to the bathroom. What happened?"

"I was coming back, and I thought the noise was from the movie. But someone—a man—tried to run out, and he fell. I saw the blood all over him. I looked in, just for a second, and I saw— I saw somebody shooting, and I heard everything. I ran back to the bathroom and called nine-one-one. They said for me to stay where I was, to hide and wait, and while I was talking my phone died."

Mi smiled a little. "You forgot to charge it again."

"I never will again, ever. The police came. A policewoman, I gave her your names, and my mom's and Natalie's."

"They were in the mall. I forgot."

"There were three of them, Mi. That's what the news said. Two in the mall, one in the theater."

"Your mom and Natalie? No, Simone, no."

"They're okay. Mom got a concussion and some cuts from flying glass. Nat dragged her behind a counter. She's okay. They're okay." She hesitated a moment, then pushed on. "Three of them, killing people. Killing Tish. And we knew them."

" 'We knew them'?" Mi repeated slowly.

"They're dead. I'm glad they're dead. JJ Hobart."

"Oh my God."

"Kent Whitehall and Devon Paulson were in the mall. JJ was in the theater."

"He killed Tish. I saw them in school almost every day. They killed Tish."

"And Trent. He's dead. Tiffany's hurt bad. I saw her mom last night. Tiffany's. JJ shot her. She might have brain damage and her face . . . I only heard a little. I don't know how bad she is."

"I knew JJ especially was mean, stupid mean sometimes, but . . ." Mi's bruised eyes spilled over with tears again. "I'm the one who picked that movie. I wanted to see that movie especially, and now Tish is dead."

"It's not your fault. It's not my fault I went to the bathroom and wasn't there. But it feels like it. It really feels like it. But it's their fault, Mi. I hate them. I'll hate them forever."

"I'm so tired," Mi murmured as her eyes closed. "Don't go."

"I'll be right outside," Simone said after the nurse came to the door and signaled her time was up. "I won't go."

Once or twice in the past Reed had had very interesting dreams about getting Angie naked. Now, after recurring nightmares of hiding beside her dead body, he sat in the back row of the Methodist church for her funeral.

He'd nearly talked himself out of coming. They hadn't really been friends. He hadn't really known her. Like, he hadn't known her parents were divorced or that she'd played the flute or had a brother in the Marine Corps.

Maybe he'd have learned those things if they'd gone to the movies or grabbed a pizza or taken a walk on the beach. But they hadn't.

Now he felt lost and guilty and stupid, sitting there while people who had known her, loved her, cried.

But he'd had to come. He'd probably been the last person—who was not a customer—to have an actual conversation with her. He'd spent those terrifying minutes hiding a little boy in her kiosk with her body right . . . there.

He'd had her blood on his shoes, his pants.

So he sat through the prayers, the weeping, the heartbreaking eulogies in a suit too tight in the shoulders. His mother had told him when he'd come home for the summer to get a new suit, and he'd ignored the idea as a waste of money.

As usual, his mother was right.

Thinking about his suit made him feel disrespectful. So he thought about the three faces he'd seen again and again on the news.

Younger than he was, all of them, and one of them had killed Angie.

Not Hobart, he remembered. He'd been in the theater, and the cop—Officer McVee—killed him. The reports said Hobart had worked in the theater. They said he'd been the ringleader.

But either Whitehall or Paulson had killed Angie.

They looked normal in the pictures on TV and in the papers, on the Internet.

But they hadn't been normal.

The one he'd seen—still saw in nightmares—all geared up in Kevlar, laughing as he shot a man in the head, hadn't been normal.

He knew more about them now, the three who'd killed a girl he'd liked during their eight-minute slaughter. Hobart had lived with his father after an ugly divorce. His younger sister lived with the mother. The father, an avid gun collector, taught his children to hunt, to shoot.

Whitehall had lived with his mother, stepfather, half brother, and stepsister. His father, currently unemployed, had a couple of arrests: drunk and disorderly, driving under the influence. Whitehall—the neighbors said—kept to himself and had some drug issues.

Paulson appeared to be a model student. Good grades, no trouble, solid home life, only child. He'd been a Boy Scout—and had a sports shooting merit badge. He'd been a junior member of the USA Shooting organization, with an eye toward the Olympics.

His father had competed for the USA in Sydney in 2000, and Athens in 2004.

People who knew Paulson said they'd noticed a change (hindsight) maybe six months ago when he'd seemed to become more closed in.

That would be about the time the girl he liked decided she liked someone else better, and he'd hooked up with Hobart.

About the time the three who'd become mass murderers began to feed each other's internal rage.

They'd documented it, so the reports claimed, on computer files the authorities were still studying. Reed, in turn, studied the reports, dug into speculation on the Internet, watched news broadcasts, talked endlessly with Chaz and others.

As much as he wanted to *know*, just know why, he expected it would take forever for it all to come out. If then.

As he saw it, from the pieces he put together from the reports, the gossip, the conversations, Hobart hated everybody. His mother, his teachers, his coworkers. He hated blacks and Jews and gays, but mostly just hated. And he liked to kill things.

Whitehall hated his life, wanted to *be* somebody, and believed everything and everyone worked against him. He'd gotten a summer job—at the mall— and had been fired within two weeks. For showing up high, a former co-worker claimed, when he showed up at all.

Paulson hated his luck. He'd concluded he'd done everything right all his life, but still lost his girl, and wasn't quite as good as his father at anything. He'd decided it was time to be bad.

They'd targeted the mall for impact, and Hobart took the theater because he wanted to destroy the place that expected him to work for a living.

Rumors claimed they'd done three dry runs, timing them, refining them. They'd planned to regroup at Abercrombie & Fitch, barricade themselves inside, taking hostages as bargaining chips, and taking out as many cops as possible.

Whitehall and Paulson nearly made it, but they'd taken an oath. If one of them fell, they all fell.

When Hobart didn't show, and with the cops closing in, Whitehall and Paulson—according to witnesses—bumped fists, shouted, *"Fuck yeah!"* and turned their weapons on each other.

Maybe some of it was true. Maybe even most. But Reed expected more and more would come out. They'd do a book, probably a freaking TV movie.

He wished to hell they wouldn't.

He came back to the moment when people started to stand, and felt a wave of shame that he'd been inside his own head instead of paying attention.

He got to his feet, waiting while the pallbearers carried Angie out. He couldn't imagine her inside that box, didn't want to imagine her there. Her family filed out, grouped tight together as if holding each other up.

He saw a couple people he knew now—Angie's friend Misty, some others who worked at the mall. It shouldn't have surprised him to see Rosie. He'd sat with her the day before at Justin the busboy's funeral.

He knew Rosie had spent the last few days at funerals or in hospital rooms.

He hung back, let her go on her way. Probably to another memorial, or to visit one of the injured, maybe to take food to someone who'd suffered a loss or was recovering at home.

That was Rosie.

The opposite of the three who'd killed.

When he stepped out of the church, he walked into a perfect summer afternoon. The sun shined out of a blue, blue sky dotted with soft white clouds. Grass grew summer green. A squirrel darted up a tree.

It didn't seem real.

He saw reporters across the street, shooting video or taking photographs. He wanted to despise them for it, but wasn't he clinging to every word they reported, every photo they published?

Still, he angled away from them, started for the car he'd parked nearly two blocks away. When he heard his name called, he hunched his shoulders rather than turn. But a hand dropped lightly on his arm.

"Reed. It's Officer McVee."

He gave her a blank look. Her hair fell down her back in a bouncy honey-blond ponytail. She wore a plain white T-shirt and khakis. She looked younger.

"Sorry, I didn't recognize you. No uniform. Were you at the funeral?"

"No. I waited out here. I called your house. Your mom told me where you were."

"I gave my statement and all. A couple times."

"I'm off duty. I'm just, well, trying to do my own personal follow-up with anybody I connected with that night. For myself. Are you going to the cemetery?"

"No, I don't feel right about it. Her family and all that. I didn't know Angie all that well. I just . . . I was trying to get her to go out with me. We were maybe going to that same movie, the last show, and . . . Jesus."

He fumbled on sunglasses with shaking hands.

"You want to go over to the park? Sit and look at the water for a while? It always helps me level out."

"I don't know. Maybe. Yeah, I guess."

"How about you ride with me, and I'll bring you back for your car after?"

"Okay, sure."

When he thought of it later, he wondered why he'd gone with her. He didn't know her. She'd been a blurred face and a uniform inside the madness and shock.

But she'd been there. She'd been in it, like he had.

When he got in her car, he had a moment to think it was older and crappier than his—if a lot cleaner. Then he remembered.

"You shot Hobart."

"Yes."

"Man, they didn't fire you or anything for it, did they?"

"No. I'm cleared. Back on the job tomorrow. How are your parents dealing?"

"They're pretty messed up, but they're handling it."

"And the people at the restaurant?"

"I think it's harder. We were there, and we saw . . . You can't stop seeing it. But we're doing okay. Like Rosie—head cook? She's doing a lot of stuff. The funerals, hospital visits, taking food to people. It helps, I think. I don't know."

"What's helping you, Reed?"

"I don't know."

He felt the air on his face, through the open window—breeze off the water. That was real. Cars zipped by, a woman pushed a kid in a stroller down the sidewalk. All real.

Life just kept going. And he was in it. Lucky to be in it.

"I talk to Chaz a lot. My friend at GameStop."

"I remember. He saved lives. So did you."

"The kid? Brady? His dad called me. He wants to bring Brady to see me maybe next week. He said his wife's getting better."

Essie said nothing for a moment, but, like CiCi, she believed in truth and trust.

"She's going to make it, but she's paralyzed. She won't walk again. He probably didn't want to lay that on you, but you'd find out."

"Goddamn it. Goddamn it."

He put his head back on the seat until he could breathe clear again. "I try to listen to music, or shoot hoops in the backyard, but I can't stop reading about it, or listening to the news. I can't stop."

"You were part of it."

"My parents want me to see somebody. You know, a shrink or something."

"It's a good idea. I have to see one. Department rules, and for a reason."

He opened his eyes again, frowned at her. "You have to talk to a shrink?"

"Already have. I'm cleared—it was a good shoot—for desk duty. And I'm talking to the department shrink. I'll be back on full active in a while. I don't mind working through it. I killed somebody."

She parked, turned off the engine. "I did it to save lives, including my own and my partner's. But I killed a seventeen-year-old boy. If I could just shrug that off without a single regret, I shouldn't be a cop."

She got out of the car, waited for him.

They walked for a while, past a playground, along a promenade, then sat on a bench where gulls swooped and cried, and the bay rolled blue as the sky.

Boats glided on the bay, and Reed heard kids laughing. A woman with a killer body inside spandex shorts and a tank jogged by. A couple who looked a thousand years old to his eyes strolled, holding hands.

"Is it true, what the papers and TV are saying, that he—that Hobart—was the main guy?"

"I'm going to say it's likely he was the strongest-willed, pushed for the plan. But the three of them? It seems to me they were like pieces of a sick, sad puzzle that fit together, and at the worst time. A few months sooner, a few months later, Paulson probably wouldn't have fit."

Reed knew what the papers and TV said about Paulson, what neighbors and teachers said. How shocked they were, how he'd never been violent. Always bright and helpful.

Fucking Boy Scout.

They were putting Angie in the ground now. They'd put a kid on his first summer job in the ground yesterday. How many others?

"I don't think you can kill like that, just kill people the way they did, if it's not in you. I mean, maybe—probably—everybody's capable of killing, but like you did. To save lives, to protect people. In self-defense or like a soldier, that's different. But what they did, for that something else has to be inside."

"You're not wrong. I think with Paulson's background, his family, they'd have gotten him help. But he linked with the others at a dark time, and those pieces came together."

He listened to the soft lap of the water, the call of birds, somebody's radio. Realized the world seemed more real as he sat there, talking to her.

He felt himself slide more inside it as he sat with her.

"What was it like? When you shot him?"

"I'd never fired my weapon off the range before last Friday night. I was scared shitless," she told him, "but that mostly came before and after. In the moment? I guess it came down to training and instinct. He shot my partner. I could see people, dead and dying. He shot at me, and I just did what I'd trained to do. Take out the threat. Then I had to do what came next. My partner—down, but not seriously injured. There was the kid in the bathroom. The first nine-one-one caller."

"That's, ah . . . Simone Knox."

"Right. You know her?"

"No, I just . . . can't stop reading and watching. I remember her name."

"She's in your club. She saved lives. She kept her head, hid, contacted the police. Barry and I—my partner—were right outside in the parking lot."

"I read that, too. You were right there."

"It's playing out that Simone's call came in about a minute, maybe two, after Hobart pushed in the exit door he'd left unlocked. She lost a friend that night, and another's still in the hospital, recovering. She's coping, but it's rough."

"You talked to her, too."

"To her, to her friend Mi, to Brady and his dad." With a sigh, Essie lifted her face to the sun. "It helps me, and I like to think maybe it helps them."

"Why'd you become a cop?"

"Seemed like a good idea at the time." She smiled, then sighed again as she looked out over the water. "I like order. I believe in law, but it's the combination that works for me. It's a good fit for me. Rules and procedure, and trying to help people. I never saw myself in a situation like Friday, but now I know I can get through it. I can do the job."

"How do you get to be a cop?"

She turned her head, gave him a raised eyebrow. "Interested?"

"Maybe. No. Yeah," he realized. "I am. I never thought much about what I was going to do. Just get a job eventually. I like college. My grades are okay, but I just like being there, so I haven't been thinking too hard about what happens when I'm out. I told Brady we were waiting for the good guys, because we were. So yeah, I'd like to know how to become a cop."

By the time she took him to his car, Reed had, for the first time, a life plan. It had forged itself out of death, but it was his life he could see rising from it.

Seleena McMullen had ambitions and a smoking habit. Her ambition to rise to fame as an Internet blogger put her outside the church during the funeral. As a reporter for *Hot Scoops*, with its somewhat questionable reputation, she didn't get much respect from the print and on-air reporters gathered outside.

It didn't bother her. One day, she'd be bigger than any of them.

She'd developed both the attitude and the ambition during high school and college. There'd been no question in her mind that she was smarter than any of her peers—so she didn't have a problem letting them know it.

If that meant she had no real friends, so what? She had clients. She credited Jimmy Rodgers in eighth grade for helping her forge a clear path. By pretending to like her, telling her she was pretty—all so she'd gullibly do his homework while he laughed behind her back—he'd provided her with the impetus to start her own business.

Sure, she'd do homework assignments, for a fee.

By the time she'd graduated high school she'd had a considerable nest egg, and had grown it throughout college.

Fresh out of college, her journalism degree hot in her hand, she'd snagged a job on the *Portland Press*. It hadn't lasted long. She had considered her editor and her coworkers idiots, and didn't trouble with tact.

Still, she'd seen the Internet as the future, and at twenty-four hitched her wagon to *Hot Scoops*. She worked primarily out of her own apartment, and since she saw her current position as no more than a stepping-stone toward her own site, her own successful blog, she tolerated editorial interference and crap assignments.

Then the DownEast Mall Massacre fell into her lap.

She'd actually walked into the mall, on a quest for new running shoes, seconds before the first shots were fired. She'd seen one of the shooters—identified as Devon Lawrence Paulson—cutting his bloody swath, and had hunkered behind a mall map as she'd pulled out her camera, her recorder.

She had scooped every paper, network, site, and reporter.

As follow-ups she'd dogged victims, family members, hospital staff. She'd bribed an orderly and gained access long enough to get a few pictures of patients, even slipped into one of the rooms after one had been transferred down from ICU.

The recorder in her pocket had caught some of the conversation between Mi-Hi Jung and—bonus—Simone Knox for her to flesh out another story.

By her calculation, she only needed a few more to take that leap off her current stepping-stone. She'd already had offers.

And now her smoking habit tossed another into her lap.

She'd stepped away from the other reporters to have a smoke, moving a half block down to lean on a tree, smoke, and think. She could head to the cemetery when the church portion ended, but how many clicks would yet more pictures of people in black generate?

Maybe someone would faint—like the dead kid's mother had the day before. But, well, been there, done that.

Time for more dish on the shooters, she decided, and had nearly started for her car when she spotted the cop.

Officer McVee, she thought, edging around the tree. She'd tried to pigeonhole McVee a couple of times—the young female officer who'd shot and killed John Jefferson Hobart equaled pure clickbait. McVee wasn't the cooperative sort, but right now said cop was hanging back, avoiding the gaggle of reporters and cameras.

Waiting.

Interesting, Seleena thought, settling down to wait herself.

The casket came out, so she took a couple shots with her long lens, just in case nothing better came along. She watched McVee moving up, and spotted one more prize.

Reed Quartermaine—teenage protector of the firefighter's kid, the kid whose mother took one in the spine.

Seleena took a couple shots of them talking, then walking together, then getting in the cop's car. And while everyone else headed to the cemetery, she ran to her own car.

She nearly lost them twice, but considered that more good luck. If she looked like a tail, the cop might spot her.

Running potential copy in her head, she parked a good distance away, watched from the car until her quarry settled on a bench.

Pleased with the investment she'd made in the lens, she wandered as close as she dared. She was just one more person casually taking photos of the bay, of the boats.

Maybe she couldn't get close enough to hear the conversation—the cop wouldn't talk to her—but she had her lead as she framed her shots.

On another painful day in Rockpoint, death unites heroes of the DownEast Mall Massacre.

Oh yeah, that leap was coming soon.

CHAPTER FIVE

— Three years later —

Simone rolled up to sit and nudged the man who shared her bed. "You gotta go."

He grunted.

She knew his name, even knew why she'd decided to have sex with him. He looked clean, in good shape, and had wanted just what she had.

Plus he had an interesting face, sort of chipped and chiseled and sharp. In her head she'd seen him as a modern-day Billy the Kid. The hard-boned western outlaw.

It had taken her awhile to embrace the idea that one-night-stands had particular and peculiar advantages over the drama and hassle of relationships—or the pretext of them.

It wasn't taking quite as long for her to realize they also carried a whole lot of boredom in their wake.

The guy, Ansel, dressed in the dim glow of light through the window. She hadn't pulled the shades—why bother?

She liked looking out at New York, and didn't mind if some of New York liked looking back at her.

He said, "I had a good time."

She said, "Me, too," and meant it enough that it didn't qualify as a lie.

"I'll call you."

"Great." Maybe he would, maybe he wouldn't. It didn't matter much either way.

Since she didn't bother to get up, he made his own way out. When she heard the door shut, she grabbed a sleepshirt, quick-walked out to lock the apartment door.

She wanted a shower and turned into the bathroom she shared with Mi in their tiny apartment. The fact that it boasted two bedrooms and was reasonably close to the campus offset the fourth-floor walk-up, the unreliable hot water, and the sting of the monthly rent.

But they were together, in New York. Sometimes they forgot to look for the ghost of the friend who wasn't there.

Simone showered off the sex, stuck her head under the stingy spray of lukewarm water. She'd cut her hair into a short wedge and had recently dyed it the purple of a ripe eggplant.

It made her feel different. It seemed she searched forever for something that made her feel different from the girl from Rockpoint, Maine. Something that would make her look in the mirror one day and think: Oh, *there* you are!

She liked New York, liked the crowds, the rush, the noise, the color. And God yes, the freedom from parental criticism, questions, and expectations.

But she knew she'd come to fulfill Tish's dream.

She liked Columbia, had worked her ass off to get in, but knew she'd done that to be a part of Mi's dream.

She couldn't find her own, and wasn't sure she had one.

But being there on borrowed dreams was better than being home where everything reminded her. Where her mother would look at her choice of hair color with puzzled disapproval or her father, with that worried look in his eyes, would casually ask how she was doing.

She was fine. How many times did she have to say it? It was Mi who still suffered from anxiety attacks and nightmares. Though they came less frequently now.

She'd done everything possible to bury that night along with her friend. Since Mi's release from the hospital, Simone read nothing that connected to that night, watched no reports on it. Every anniversary, she watched and read no news at all, in case she tripped over some mention.

She went home only on winter break and for a week in the summer—and the summer week she spent on the island with CiCi. When she wasn't in class, she worked. When she wasn't in class or working, she played—hard.

Out of the shower, she wrapped herself in a bath sheet—Egyptian cotton, courtesy of her mother—then swiped off the skinny mirror over the teacup sink.

No, she thought, not yet. She saw a girl with tired eyes and wet hair, and nothing more.

She hung the towel, dragged the sleepshirt back on. When she stepped out of the bathroom, she saw Mi in their sorry excuse of a kitchen, putting a kettle on their two-burner stove.

"Can't sleep?"

"Restless. I heard the door."

Mi had let her hair grow into a straight rain of black. When she turned, Simone saw another pair of tired eyes.

"I'm sorry."

"Doesn't matter. Do I know him?"

"I don't think so. Doesn't matter, either." Moving into the kitchen, Simone got out two cups. "The music was good, and he wasn't a bad dancer. I wish you'd come with me."

"I needed to study."

"You're acing everything—again."

"Because I study."

Simone waited while Mi fiddled with the tea. "Something's up, I can see it."

"I've been accepted for a summer research program."

"That's great—like last summer? Dr. Jung, biomedical engineer."

"That's the dream. Not exactly like last summer. The program's in London."

"Holy shit, Mi!" Grabbing her friend, Simone danced her around the room. "London! You're going to London."

"It's not until the end of June, and . . . my family's asked me to come home first. To spend the time after the semester ends and before I leave for London at home. I need to give them that."

"Okay." Maybe her heart dropped a little, but Simone nodded.

"Come home with me. Come home, Simone."

"I've got a job—"

"You hate that job," Mi interrupted. "If you want to waitress at some dump of a coffeehouse, you can do it anywhere. You're not happy here. You're doing okay at Columbia, but it doesn't make you happy. You have sex with guys that don't make you happy."

"Rockpoint's not going to make me happy."

Trim, tiny, with that gymnast's grace, Mi went back to finish making the tea.

"You need to find what does. You're here because of me and Tish, and I'm not going to be here all summer. You should find what makes you happy. Your art— Don't do that!" she snapped when Simone rolled her eyes. "You've got talent."

"CiCi has talent. I'm just playing around."

"So stop playing around!" Mi snapped again. "Stop playing around, stop screwing around, stop fucking around!"

"Wow." Simone picked up the tea she no longer wanted, leaned back on a fridge manufactured in the last century. "I like playing around, screwing around, and fucking around. I'm not going to spend my life studying, researching, holed up in a lab because I don't want to *have* a life. Jesus, when's the last time you had sex?"

"You have enough for both of us."

"Maybe if you got laid, you wouldn't be such a bitch. You won't go to parties, won't go to clubs, you haven't had a date in months. It's school, labs, or this shithole apartment. Happy, my ass."

As her eyes fired, Mi curled one hand into a fist. "I'm going to make something of myself. I didn't die, and I'm going to make something out of my life. I am happy. Sometimes it's almost happy, and sometimes I hit it. But I know I'm working toward something, and I'm watching my best friend pushing back at everything."

"I go to classes, I go to work, I go to clubs. How's that pushing back at anything, much less everything?"

"You go to classes, but you don't care enough about any of them to do more than get by. You go to work at a job that means less than nothing to you, instead of looking for something that would." It poured out now, a flood over a broken dam. "You go to clubs because you can't stand being alone, being quiet for more than an hour. And you hook up with guys you have no intention of seeing again *because* you have no intention of seeing them again. Not letting yourself be close or involved with anything or anyone is the freaking definition of pushing everything away."

Simone smirked, adding nasty to it. "I was damn close to the guy who just left."

"What's his name?"

Austin, Angel, Adam . . . shit, shit, shit. "Ansel," she remembered.

"You had to dig for it. You brought some guy home, had sex with him, and have to dig for his name in less than an hour."

"So what? So the fuck what? If I'm such a ho, why do you care what I do, what I feel?"

"Because, goddamn it, you're *my* ho."

Simone opened her mouth to rage, and laughter gurgled out. As Mi—face bright pink with temper, tears of fury sparking in her eyes—stared at her, the gurgle built into a roll.

Even as Mi let out an insulted huff, Simone toasted with her tea. "This calls for a T-shirt. *Mi-Hi's Ho.*" She tapped her free hand on her chest.

While she knuckled temper tears out of her eyes, the absurdity pushed a watery laugh out of Mi. "You'd wear it proud, too."

"Why wouldn't I?"

"Oh hell, Sim." Mi set her tea aside, scrubbed her hands over her face. "I love you."

"I know. I know."

"You're wasting yourself, taking classes you can basically sleep through."

"I'm never going to be a biomedical freaking engineer, Mi. Most of us are still figuring stuff out."

"The only courses you've shown any real interest in are art related. So focus there, and figure it out. You're wasting yourself on a job you don't like, don't need, where you're so stupidly overqualified you should be running the shop."

"I don't want to run the shop. A lot of people don't like their jobs. And I need it because I'm going to at least pay for some of my own expenses."

"Then find a job you like. You're wasting yourself on sex with men you don't care about."

Now Simone had her own tears to knuckle away. "I don't want to care about anybody right now. I don't know if I ever will. I can care about you, about my family, and that's all I've got."

"I think it's sad I value you more than you value yourself, so it's a good thing I'm around to bitch and nag at you."

"You're really good at it."

"I'm president of the Bitch and Nag Club. You barely qualify as an honorary member. Take the summer, Sim. We can hang out at the beach until I leave for London. You can spend time with CiCi, even let her take you around Europe like she wanted to after graduation. We can sublet the apartment. Don't stay here alone."

"I'll think about it."

"That's what you say when you want me to shut up."

"Maybe. Look, I'm tired, and I've got to be at the shop at eight to do the job I don't like. I want to get some sleep."

Mi nodded, dumped the tea neither of them had finished in the sink.

Simone knew the quality of that silence, and it read anxiety.

"Sleepover time?" she suggested.

Mi's shoulders dropped in relief. "That'd be good."

"We'll use your virginal bed for obvious reasons." She slung an arm around

Mi as they walked to Mi's bedroom. "I got Aaron's number. Maybe he has a friend."

"You said he name was Ansel."

"Damn it."

They crawled into Mi's bed, snuggled together for comfort.

"I miss her," Mi murmured.

"I know. Me, too."

"I think I'd feel different about New York, just being here, if she were. If Tish were here, we'd be different."

Everything would be, Simone thought.

She dreamed of it, of sitting with Mi, watching Tish, alive and vital, onstage. In the spotlight. Just owning it.

She dreamed of Mi working in her lab, so crisp and brilliant in her white coat.

And when the dreams turned inward, she saw herself sitting on a raft on a still and silent sea. Drifting nowhere.

She woke to the reality of serving the college crowd fancy, overpriced coffee most paid for with credit cards given to them by their parents—and they still couldn't be bothered to tack on a decent tip.

When she found herself, for the second time that week, scrubbing out the toilet in the unisex bathroom, she took yet another good look at herself in the mirror.

She knew the fuckhead of a manager dumped the bathroom duty on her twice as often as anyone else because she wouldn't have sex with him. (Married, at least forty, ponytail, so yuck.)

"So screw it," she told herself.

She walked out of air that smelled like bleach and fake lemons, into the constant hum of espresso machines and conversations pontificating about politics or whining about relationships.

She pulled off the stupid red apron she had to pay to have laundered, got her purse out of the skinny locker—the rent of which also came out of her sorry excuse for a paycheck.

Manager Fuckhead sneered at her. "It's not time for your break."

"You're wrong about that. It's past time for my break. I quit."

She strolled out into the world of noise and color, and realized she felt something she'd missed for entirely too long.

She felt happy.

Six months after graduating from the Academy, Reed rode patrol with Bull Stockwell. Officer Tidas Stockwell had earned the name "Bull" not only from his physicality, but from his personality. A fifteen-year vet, Bull was foulmouthed, hard-assed, and claimed to have a nose that could detect bullshit from two miles off.

He had several red flags that caused him to charge, including: anything he considered anti-American (a sliding scale), assholes (a wide range of qualifications), and motherfuckers. His top candidates for motherfuckers were anyone who harmed children, beat women, or abused animals.

He hadn't voted for Obama—he'd never voted for a Democrat in his life, and saw no reason to deviate. But the man was president of the United States and, as such, had his respect and loyalty.

He didn't have a bigoted bone in his body. He knew assholes and motherfuckers came in every color and creed. He might not understand the whole gay thing, but didn't actually give a shit one way or the other. He figured if you wanted to get off with somebody built the same as you, that was your business.

He had two divorces under his Sam Browne belt—from the first, a ten-year-old daughter he unabashedly worshipped—and he owned a one-eyed, one-legged cat he'd rescued after a drug bust.

Most days he berated Reed verbally for being too stupid, too slow, a college boy, and a dumbass rookie. And in the six months since he'd been on the job, Reed had learned more about the down-and-dirty and nitty-gritty of cop work than he had in all his college courses or in his months at the Academy.

He'd sure as hell learned, when answering a domestic disturbance call, to put himself between Bull and the offending party (male) before that red flag had his partner pawing the ground and snorting.

So when they rolled up to a potential double D in a townhome they'd visited for the same reason four times before, Reed prepared to do just that.

"She's got an RO on him now, so his ass is mine."

Reed recalled the *she* in question—one LaDonna Gray—had taken her husband—one Vic Gray—back after a black eye and split lip, and again after a broken arm and clear-cut marital rape.

But the third incident—knocking her unconscious, and knocking out two teeth—two months after she'd given birth to their son had been the restraining order charm.

"He better not have touched that baby." Bull hitched up his pants as they started for the door down a frost-heavy walkway slushy with snow.

A woman ran out of the connecting unit. "He's killing her! I swear this time he's killing her."

Reed heard it now—the screams, the shouts, the wails from the baby.

He had time to think: Oh, shit.

He saw, too, the front door had already been broken in.

He went through the doorway with his partner, noted the signs of violence on the main level, with the overturned table, broken lamp.

Upstairs the baby screamed as if someone had shoved an ice pick through his ear, but the shouts, curses, sobs, thuds came from the rear of the house.

Reed moved faster than Bull—younger, longer legs—and had time to see Vic Gray bolt out the back door. The woman lay moaning, sobbing, bleeding on the kitchen floor.

"I've got him." Reed sprinted out the back. As he ran, he called it in.

"Officer Quartermaine in pursuit of suspect in assault. Suspect is Victor Gray, Caucasian male, age twenty-eight, heading south on Prospect on foot. Suspect is five feet ten inches, a hundred and eighty pounds. He's wearing a black parka, red watch cap, jeans. Turning east on Mercer."

Gray cut across a yard, carving a path through the eight inches of snow from the fall the night before, scaled a fence. Reed thought how much faster he'd be if he had his Nikes instead of the uniform shoes.

His breath in visible clouds, Reed went over the fence, dropped into snow.

Heard screams, kicked up his speed. He hadn't lettered in track in high school for nothing.

He spotted a woman sprawled in the snow in her yard beside a half-built snowman. With her nose dripping blood, she clutched a wailing toddler.

"He tried to grab my baby!"

Reed kept going, saw Gray cut east again, reported it as he gained on him. He went over another fence, saw Gray veer toward the open door of another townhome where music and a woman's laugh pumped out.

Reed heard the woman say, "I don't need to see how well you shoveled the patio. Close the door. It's cold!"

His only thought: He's not getting in there and hurting somebody else. Reed may not have been his father's football star, but he knew how to tackle.

He leaped, left the ground, and took Gray out at the knees on the narrow patio outside the open door.

When Gray's face scraped along the stone, he screamed.

"Hey, hey, what the fuck!" A man stepped out, wineglass in one hand, iPhone in the other. "Jesus Christ, he's bleeding all over the place. I'm recording this. I'm recording this. This is police brutality."

"You go ahead and record it." Out of breath, with his own bones rattled from the hit, Reed pulled out his cuffs. "Go ahead and record the asshole who beat his wife to a pulp a few blocks over, assaulted a second woman, and tried to kidnap her child as a hostage. The guy who was heading straight into your house.

"I've got him," Reed reported into his radio. "Suspect's contained, may require medical attention. What's the address here?"

"I don't have to tell you dick."

"Shut up, Jerry." The woman who'd been laughing shoved the man with the phone aside. "It's 5237 Gilroy Place, Officer."

"In the rear of 5237 Gilroy Place. Thank you, ma'am. Victor Gray, you're under arrest for assault, two counts, for battery." He snapped the cuffs on Gray's wrists. "For attempted child abduction, resisting arrest, and violating the terms of a restraining order."

"That man has rights."

Reed looked up. "Are you a lawyer, sir?"

"No, but I know—"

"Then why don't you stop interfering with police business?"

"You're on private property."

"My property," the woman said, "so shut the hell up, Jerry. You're bleeding some, too, Officer."

He tasted it in his mouth, felt it on the stinging heels of his hands. "I'm okay, ma'am. Victor Gray, you have the right to remain silent."

As he recited the Miranda warning, Jerry smirked. "Took you long enough."

"Not a lawyer?" Reed pulled Gray to his feet. "Just a dick in general."

"I'm filing a complaint!"

"That's it. Out. Get out of my house, Jerry."

Reed heard the sirens as the woman handed the dick his ass. Since she appeared to have that situation under control, he stiff-walked Gray around to the front of the house.

"I'm gonna sue your fucking ass," Gray mumbled.

"Yeah, you do that, Vic."

LaDonna Gray suffered three broken ribs, a broken wrist, a broken nose, two black eyes, a shattered cheekbone, and internal injuries. Her son wasn't harmed.

Sheridan Bobbett, who'd been in her yard playing with her two-year-old, sustained minor injuries, and the minor child had some bruises on his arms and shoulders. According to her statement, Gray had rushed into her yard, knocked her down. She'd fought him when he attempted to yank her son out of her arms, then he had run away when a police officer had come over the fence in pursuit.

Eloise Matherson, resident of 5237 Gilroy Place, served as an eyewitness of the takedown and arrest, stating she'd seen through her open door the man identified as Victor Gray running toward her house, saw the officer tackle him just a foot away from her door, and restrain him when Gray attempted to resist. She expressed her gratitude for the officer stopping a violent man from entering her home.

And gave Reed her number on the sly.

Bull dumped the paperwork on Reed—that's how it went for rookies. And Reed overheard him talking to the hospital, checking on LaDonna Gray's condition.

By the time Reed had filed the paperwork, Jerry the Dick's phone video hit the local newscasts.

Reed took the ribbing—that's how it went for cops—winced a little at the cold fury on his face, and figured he'd take some heat from his CO over the *dick* remark.

"You hit the Internet already, Quartermaine."

One of the other uniforms tapped a computer screen. "McMullen's blog."

"Crap."

"Aw, she calls you young and studly, and . . ."

"What?"

"She brings up the DownEast Mall. Don't sweat it, rook. Nobody reads her bullshit."

Everybody read it, Reed thought. Including cops. Just like plenty had read the book she'd published the year before. *Massacre DownEast.* With her buzz, the likelihood of the damn phone video going viral—and national—catapulted to the top of the heap.

He knew the word had already started burning when Essie—now Detective McVee with the Portland PD—stepped in, signaled to him.

She walked him into the currently empty roll-call room.

"You okay?"

"Yeah, sure."

"Something left a mark." She tapped a finger to his bruised jaw.

"Hit the back of his head on the takedown. It's okay."

"Get some ice on it. The media's going to play with this a little. Young hero of DownEast Mall becomes hero cop—with a bite. And like that."

He shoved at his hair—cop short, as his sergeant insisted he keep his loosely curling mop trim. "Shit, Essie."

"You'll deal. Your sergeant's going to give you a little flick over the 'dick' remark. But he, and every cop in Portland and its 'burbs, is going to give you a nice golf clap over it. Don't worry about it, and don't worry about McMullen or the rest of the media. Keep your head down and do the job."

"Well, I was," he pointed out.

"That's right. And what the dick's video showed was a cop doing his job, maintaining his composure and control—with the exception of a muttered word. A word the video also shows was well earned by said dick. You did it right, Reed, and I wanted you to hear that from me, since I feel I had something to do with getting you in that uniform."

"You had a lot to do with it. I felt . . . I had to get him. When I saw that woman bleeding on the floor, I had to get him. It wasn't like a flashback sort of thing. I didn't flash back to that night or anything like that, but it was sort of like when I knew I had to get that kid."

"Instincts, Reed. You've got them." With approval, she gave him a fake punch on his bruised jaw. "Keep using them, and learn from Bull. He's a solid son of a bitch despite his bullshit."

"He rides my ass—that's not a complaint. Especially. He was gentle as a priest with LaDonna Gray. I guess that's something I'm learning from him— how to handle victims so they don't feel so victimized."

"That's a good one. How about you come to dinner next week?"

"I could eat. Are you still seeing that professor?"

"Some cop you are." She held up her left hand, wiggled her fingers to show off the ring.

"Holy shit, Essie." He started to reach out, stopped himself. "I can't hug a detective in the precinct. It'll wait. He's a lucky guy."

"Damn right. If you need to talk, you know who to call. I'll text you about dinner."

He went straight to the locker room to change out of uniform. He'd been off shift since before he'd filed the paperwork. He found Bull hanging up his own uniform jacket.

"You finished getting kissed from the Detective Bureau?"

"Can't kiss her. She just got engaged."

"Huh. Cops oughta know better than to get married." He pulled on a plain white T-shirt. "Did you call that civilian witness a dick when you fucking knew he was recording you?"

"It's on the recording, so I'd be stupid to deny saying it."

"Well." Studying himself in his locker mirror, Bull scraped a hand over his crew cut. "Looks like I'm going to buy you a beer." He shut his locker. "You might make a half-decent cop after all."

CHAPTER SIX

Patricia Jane Hobart devoured McMullen's blog along with a bowl of veggie sticks with gobs of hummus.

She'd been a tubby child, routinely indulged by her mother with cookies, snack cakes, and her favorite M&M's. Her interests—computers, reading, watching TV, and the occasional video game—merged well with her appetites. She'd often consumed an entire bag of Oreos (she preferred Double Stuf, chilled in the fridge) washed down with a liter of Coke while immersed in a spy novel, a murder mystery, the occasional romance, or testing her hacking skills.

While her father (redneck loser) and mother (hapless idiot) battled their marriage to dust, she enjoyed playing one against the other and reaping the rewards of more chaos—and more cookies.

By the age of twelve she carried one hundred and sixty pounds on a height of five feet two inches.

She played her teachers and neighbors as slyly as her parents, wearing the mask of a stoic child bullied by her peers. She was, in fact, bullied, but she invited it, embraced it, and used it to her advantage.

While the adults stroked and cosseted her, she plotted and executed vengeance with the stealth and focus a CIA operative would admire.

The boy who dubbed her Patty the Porker took a flying header off his Schwinn when the chain she'd compromised snapped.

She considered his fractured jaw, broken teeth, hospital stay, and the thousands for dental work his parents had to shell out almost enough payback.

The ringleader of the girls who'd stolen her underpants while she was in the shower after gym and then creatively tacked them to a drawing of an elephant before posting them on the bulletin board nearly died when the peanuts Patricia crushed to powder and slipped into her thermos of hot cocoa sent her into anaphylactic shock.

By the time she hit her teens, Patricia was a virtuoso of vengeance.

Occasionally she enlisted the aid of her brother, the only person in the world she loved almost as much as herself. Her schemes engaged him—she plotted several for him as well—enough to keep their bond strong after the divorce.

She hated that JJ lived with their worthless father, hated that he actually preferred it. She understood why. He could run wild with no repercussions, sneaking beer and weed while she remained stuck with their whiny martyr of a mother.

But JJ depended on her. He wasn't particularly bright, so he needed her help with schoolwork. He had impulse-control problems, and needed her to remind him that payback worked best when carefully crafted.

She enjoyed nothing more than carefully crafting payback.

At seventeen, her brother too often showed the world the angry, violent, bitter beast. On the other hand, Patricia's quiet, studious, kid-with-a-weight-problem façade hid a cunning, brutal psychopath.

Perfectly aware that teenage boys—and she considered all men on that level—would stick their dicks in anything, she had sex with both Whitehall and Paulson. She calculated it as a way to control them—useful tools—and to make them believe they controlled her.

JJ knew better, but blood was thicker.

She devised the plan. A mass shooting that would shake the core not just of the community she despised, but the city—the entire country. She worked on it for months, selecting and rejecting locations, refined and refined the timing, the weaponry.

She told no one, not even JJ, until she'd settled on the mall. The mall, where giggling teenage girls who treated her like dirt ran in packs. Where perfect parents with their perfect kids had pizza and went to the movies. Where old people who should just die already walked in their ugly tracksuits or rode around on scooters.

She considered the mall a perfect location for payback on everyone and everything she despised.

Even after she told JJ, she swore him to secrecy. He could tell no one, could write down nothing they discussed. When the time was right, when she had everything in place, all contingencies nailed down, they could bring in his two friends.

She walked miles in the mall—joining those revolting old people for their preopening exercise, and letting them make her a pet.

She took photographs, made maps, studied mall security. Took off a little weight as cover, and directed JJ to get a part-time job at the mall.

He chose the theater, so she worked that sector in for him.

By her calculations, Operation Born To Kill would go green mid-December, giving her time to work out kinks, and capitalizing on the holiday crowds for the most impact.

They would take out hundreds.

But then JJ, literally, jumped the gun. And hadn't even told her.

After all the work she'd done, he'd let his impulses rule him. She found out about the shooting from a bulletin when the local news broke in during a rerun of *Friends*.

She'd had to scramble to destroy her notes, her maps, her photos, every scrap of six-months' work. She hid her laptop in a neighbor's broken down garden shed. She'd bought the laptop—used exclusively for the mall project—for cash when visiting her grandparents in their big-ass, fancy house in Rockpoint.

The cops would come, she knew. They'd question her, her mother, they'd search the ratty, wrong-side-of-the-tracks rental from top to bottom. They'd talk to neighbors, teachers, other students.

Because JJ would get caught. Even if he had followed her plan as she'd laid it out so far, he'd get caught. He'd never implicate her, but his two ass-hole friends would.

But the cops would have nothing but that, the word of two assholes against a fifteen-year-old girl, a distinguished honor-roll student without a single mark on her record.

While she paced, waiting for the next bulletin, she worked out what she'd say, how she'd react, every word, every expression, her body language.

Shock and deep, genuine grief dropped her to the floor when the grim-eyed reporter announced the shooters—believed to number three—were dead.

Not JJ. Not the only person in the world who knew her and gave two shits about her. Not her brother.

That grief rose up in a single wail. Then she shoved it back. She'd save it for the police. Save it for her idiot mother when the cops pulled her out of her second job—cleaning the offices of a bunch of lying lawyers.

She'd save it for the cameras.

And when they came, when they notified her and questioned her—with her trembling mother beside her—when they searched the house from top to bottom, talked to the neighbors, they'd see a fifteen-year-old girl in shock. A girl who clung to her mother and sobbed. A girl as innocent as her brother was guilty.

As expected, her mother fell apart, her father raged and picked up a bottle he'd never come out of. She bore up, asked one of the lawyers from the of-fices where her mother cleaned to help write a statement expressing their shock and horror and grief, a statement, she insisted tearfully, that apolo-gized to everyone.

And because her parents couldn't handle it, she read the statement herself through choked sobs.

They had to move. She secreted the laptop in a box of stuffed animals. They couldn't move far—her mother needed her jobs, and her employers kept her on. She finished her high school years with a tutor—her wealthy paternal grandparents paid.

She kept her head down and gathered her vengeance to her, preparing to serve it ice cold.

At eighteen, she carried a sharply honed 112 on a five-foot-four-inch frame. Her family attributed her initial weight loss to stress and grief, but Patricia worked to turn herself into a whippy weapon.

She had people to kill, and compiled dossiers on all of them.

Time, she calculated, remained on her side, and she had college to finish. With her stellar grades and smarts she had numerous choices, and settled on Columbia, as two of her targets—and the one her primary—chose it.

How better to keep tabs on the person she held most responsible—even more than the cop who'd put the bullets in him—for her brother's death?

Without Simone Knox, the cops didn't get there so quickly, didn't enter the movie theater, didn't kill her brother. He'd have walked out the way he'd walked in, but for Simone Knox.

She could've killed Knox and finished JJ's job on her little Asian friend a thousand times already. But the dish was not cold enough.

And they would be far from the first to pay.

On the food chain of her revenge, she'd placed her parents first. But now, reading McMullen's blog in the studio apartment her grandparents paid for—she just couldn't live with people!—she reconsidered.

Not the cop, and not the boy hero who'd become one. They ranked too high to be shifted that far down. But maybe, just maybe, she could pick one of the lessers, run a kind of test.

She munched her hummus and veggie sticks in an apartment across the street from her prime target and began the selection process.

On July 22, 2005, Roberta Flisk was thirty-six. She'd gone to the mall with her sister and her young niece to have the ten-year-old Caitlyn's ears pierced.

They'd planned to conclude the rite of passage with ice cream sundaes. But as Caitlyn with her tiny gold studs, Shelby carrying the bag of overpriced daily cleaner, and Roberta strolled out of the earring boutique, everything changed.

Roberta stopped at a kiosk to buy her little boy some beach toys for his long weekend away with his grandparents. She and her husband had planned their own long weekend on Mount Desert Island in hopes of reviving their troubled marriage.

Later, she'd tell police, her family, reporters, how she'd seen the boy identified as Kent Francis Whitehall come into the mall as she, her sister, and her niece walked toward the same doors.

She'd thought he was wearing a costume for some event. Until he'd lifted the rifle. Her sister was the first victim of the attack.

As she'd fallen, Caitlyn screamed, dropping to the ground with her mother. Roberta threw herself over her niece and sister. Whitehall shot her twice—left shoulder, left leg—before he'd moved on to other targets.

With her sister dead, her niece traumatized, her own injuries requiring two surgeries and months of therapy—physical and emotional—Roberta hadn't been shy about talking to the press.

She became a passionate, vocal advocate for gun regulation. She helped launch For Shelby, an activist organization dedicated to Safe, Sane Solutions.

Their website and Facebook page ran totals daily of the number of gun deaths in the country—murder, suicide, accidental.

Her marriage died, another victim of DownEast.

She gave speeches, organized rallies and marches, appeared on television—always wearing the heart locket that held a photo of her sister.

In tragedy she became a warrior, a name, and a face, a well-known voice not only locally but nationally.

For that reason, she fit Patricia's needs perfectly.

Patricia took a full month to study, to stalk, to take notes and photos, to plan. Back in Rockpoint for most of the summer, ostensibly to spend time with her grandparents, she made meticulous records of Roberta's habits, routines.

In the end, she found it ridiculously easy.

Early one morning, before daybreak, she slipped out of her grandparents' house, jogged a half mile to the home of one of her grandmother's friends. After slipping on a short blond wig and latex gloves, she removed the spare key to the car from the magnetic box under the wheel well. She drove, carefully at the speed limit, to Roberta's quiet neighborhood, parked, took the gun and the silencer—taken from her father during one of his drunken stupors—out of her backpack.

At sunrise, like clockwork, Roberta came out of her back door. On a normal day she would have cut across her own backyard, through a neighbor's gate, and met up with the first of her two morning jogging companions.

But on this morning, Patricia waited.

She stepped out from behind a sturdy red maple.

As Roberta, adjusting her earbuds, glanced over in surprise, Patricia took her down with two quick shots to the chest. The silencer kept the sound to a harmless *pop*. The third shot—a kill shot to the head—popped louder, but it had to be done.

She took the sign she'd made out of the backpack, tossed it on Roberta's body.

HERE'S YOUR SECOND AMENDMENT, BITCH!

She policed her brass, secured them with the gun and silencer in the backpack. Light streaked in reds and pinks across the eastern sky as she drove back to the neighbor's, replaced the key.

With the wig and gloves in her backpack, she took out earbuds, put them in, and began to jog.

She felt . . . nothing special, she realized. She'd expected to feel some elation or amazement. Something. But she felt no more than she did when she completed a necessary task well.

A little satisfaction.

She jogged, as she'd made a habit to do since observing Roberta's morning routines, toward a bakery a full mile away.

She listened for the news reports—and the speculation that Roberta's visible and vocal advocacy had made her the target for some gun-rights nut.

Time to wait again, she decided. To wait and plot and study. But the test? She'd aced it. Killing was easy if you just made a plan and stuck to it.

She went into the bakery, got a big welcoming smile from the woman—Carole—who opened it every morning. "Hey there, Patricia. Right on time."

"Gorgeous day!" Beaming back, Patricia jogged lightly in place. "How about three of those apple muffins today, Carole."

"You got it. It's real sweet of you to get your grandparents a treat every morning."

"Best grandparents ever. I don't know what I'd do without them." Patricia dug the money out of the side pocket of her backpack, and angling it away, unzipped the main pack to tuck the bag of muffins in with the wig and the gun.

She got home and stowed the wig, the gloves, the gun, and the silencer. After a quick shower, she took the muffins to the kitchen and put them in a little bowl on the counter.

She'd just started the coffee when her grandmother shuffled in.

"You've been out running already!" she said, as she said every fricking day.

"Up with the sun, and what a gorgeous morning. Apple muffins today, Grammy."

"You just spoil us, sweetie pie. Just spoil us to death."

Patricia just smiled. She'd spoil them all right, and when they finally died, she'd get everything.

She could do a lot with everything.

That evening Essie and her fiancé hosted a summer barbecue in the little backyard of the house she'd talked herself into buying when she made detective.

It squeezed her budget, but by God, it made her happy to have her pretty three-bedroom house with its small, cheerful yard.

And since Hank had moved in, the budget could breathe just a little easier—and everything was happier.

Right now she had a house and a yard full of cops and teachers—with some family and neighbors tossed in. And it worked pretty damn well.

Hank, adorable to her eye with his trim goatee, scholarly glasses, and WILL COOK FOR SEX bib apron, manned the grill. He'd also made the potato salad, the deviled eggs, and other sides. She'd peeled and chopped, even stirred, but Hank's apron spoke truth—and he'd proven himself a damn good cook.

She poured herself a margarita—those she could make—and watched the man she loved joke with her former partner.

She and Barry hadn't parted ways, not personally, when she'd traded her uniform for a gold shield. It made her feel settled to see how well the cop she liked and respected blended with her man.

Maybe it surprised her that they blended, even that she blended with Professor Coleson, the Shakespearean scholar with his classy horn-rimmed glasses.

She certainly hadn't been looking for love, and had only gone on the blind date (her first and last) because a friend had nagged the resistance out of her.

She'd fallen into smitten over drinks, into sincere like during the main course, and into lust over dessert.

And into bed after the thin excuse of a nightcap—a word she'd never used before in her life.

When he'd cooked her breakfast in the morning, she'd made it all the way to love.

She walked to the grill, and her whole body smiled when he bent down to give her a casual kiss.

"Need any help here?"

"Soon as I flip these burgers onto the platter, you can take them and the dogs over to the table."

"Can do. Did you get your incinerated dog yet, Barry?"

"Got two. Place looks damn good, Essie. The trouble is, Ginny's looking around and starting to complain we don't have flower beds as nice."

"She needs a Terri." Essie gestured toward an energetic blonde running herd on a pair of toddler twins. "Our next-door neighbor's a genius with plants. She's teaching us."

"She's prevented several flora murders this summer," Hank added. "Essie's thumb's turning green. Mine's still questionable. Here you go, beautiful." He flipped burgers onto the platter, added the hot dogs.

"I've got it, and that ought to hold the horde awhile. You should take a break, get some food, Hank."

"Good idea. How about we get a cold adult beverage first, Barry?"

"I'm all in."

She wound her way toward the table—lost a few burgers and dogs on the way as people snagged them right off the moving platter.

She set it down, picked up the nearly empty bowl of potato salad. She took it and an empty plate that had held sliced tomatoes (Terri's garden) into the kitchen for refills.

She found Reed leaning on her counter, drinking a beer, and in what appeared to be a serious discussion with her current partner's ten-year-old son.

"No way, just no way, man," Reed said. "I'm going with you on crossing the streams on this, but there's no way Batman takes down Iron Man. Iron Man's got the suit."

Quentin—moonfaced, freckled, and bespectacled—begged to differ. "Batman's got the suit, too."

"He can't suit up and fly, bro."

Essie listened to the debate while she reloaded the bowl and plate.

"I'm going to write the story," Quentin claimed. "And you'll see. The Dark Knight rules."

"You write it, and I'll be the judge."

Obviously delighted, Quentin ran back outside.

"You're good with him," Essie observed.

"Easy to be. The kid's just great. Even if he's wrong about Tony Stark."

"Who's Tony Stark?"

"I don't think I can even talk to you right now." With a shake of his head, Reed downed some beer. Still, he reached for the bowl to carry it, and right then the phone in Essie's pocket signaled.

She pulled it out, frowned, then sighed. "Shit."

"You're not on the roll."

"Not that. I've got an alert set up that notifies me if anybody from the mall shooting comes over the wire. And we've got one."

"Who? What?"

"It's Roberta Flisk. Found dead in her backyard early this morning. Shot three times. She was—"

"I remember." Reed kept his own files. He'd pored over every report and news article, read every book on that night, and still did. "Her sister was listed as the first victim outside the theater. She took a couple hits herself. Major player now for gun regulation."

"Details leaked claim a sign was left with her body. 'Here's your Second Amendment, Bitch!' Fuck."

"Who found her?"

"A couple of friends. It's saying they jogged together every morning, sunrise."

"Every morning?"

Cop eyes met cop eyes as Essie glanced up, nodded. "Yeah, routine. Somebody knew her routine. Either knew her or watched her. More than some sick fuck with a Second Amendment fetish."

"Divorced, right? Did she ever remarry? Boyfriend? Ex?" Reed asked her.

"Bucking to make detective?"

"Just follows you've got to look there first."

"Yeah, it does." No longer a rookie, she thought, and Reed had the makings of a smart, solid investigator. "Not my case."

"But you're going to look," he countered. "She was there. We were there. You've got to look."

"Right again, but not now. Not today." She handed him the bowl, picked up the plate. "I'll reach out tomorrow to whoever caught it."

"Can you keep me in the loop?"

She nodded, looking out the back screen door. "It's never going to be really finished. It's the kind of thing you never just close and box away. But you can't live with it every day, either."

"The media will cycle it again. It's how it goes."

"Keep your head down, do the job."

"But you'll keep me in the loop?" he insisted.

"Yeah, yeah, now put it aside for today. Let's get you another beer."

Over the next few days, Reed spent any time he could carve out compiling information on the Flisk investigation. Good as her word, Essie kept him in the loop, even nudged the lead investigators to clear him to visit the murder scene.

He studied the yard—established trees and plantings offered plenty of cover for lying in wait.

The victim comes out her back door, he thought, as multiple statements confirmed that routine.

He walked it off himself, moving from the back door, crossing the patio, stopping at the bloodstained grass.

Take her out deeper in the yard, he concluded. Less chance for her to run back into the house, more difficult for anyone in the neighboring houses to witness the killing, and the view from the street was cut off.

Smart.

Three hits, two center mass, then the head shot.

Now he walked off the angle designated by the medical examiner and investigative team. Plenty of cover, he noted, off to the right while the target moved toward the gate in the fence.

Had the killer said anything? It seemed to Reed that if someone decided to murder a woman over her stand on gun regulations, he'd want to let her know why.

But all he heard, as he imagined it, was silence.

Had she flashed back, he wondered, to that moment in the mall, the moment she saw Whitehall raise the AR-15?

He sometimes caught himself wondering if fate was waiting to send a bullet into him that had missed that night. One caught in the air, like a video recording on pause, that would rip into him when fate hit the play button.

Had she?

Since he'd already concluded he could do nothing to change whatever button fate opted to push, he worked to live, and to make a difference, to try to at least. He thought Roberta Flisk had done the same.

He put the picture of her in his head. Black cap with its logo of a handgun in a circle with a slash through it over short, medium blond hair, earbuds in place. A dark blue support tank and dark blue running shorts on an athletic frame—scars on her leg a constant reminder of a nightmare—her house key tucked into the inner pocket at the waistband. Pink-and-white Nikes and white socks.

In his mind, she stopped her forward motion just for an instant.

Shock, awareness, resignation? That he'd never know.

Two soft *pops*, he thought, as ballistics verified a .32, silenced. Both struck center mass. Victim falls, he thought, once again crossing to the stains baked onto the grass by the summer sun.

Third *pop*—louder as the silencer weakened—angled from above to the back of the head.

Then the flourish of the sign, the message.

It struck him as wrong, just off. The killing had all the elements of a cold, even professional, hit; but the sign showed heat—angry and careless.

The killer had taken the time and caution to police the brass, to leave no trace but the bullets in the body, then adds a hand-printed sign announcing himself as a pissed-off defender of the Second Amendment?

It rubbed wrong because the killer hadn't been pissed-off, the murder didn't feel personal.

They'd cleared the ex-husband, Reed considered as he walked the scene one more time. He and the victim maintained a cordial relationship. He didn't own a gun, and, in fact, gave an annual donation to her organization in their son's name.

At the time of her murder, he'd been helping make breakfast—plenty of witnesses—for a couple dozen Boy Scouts, including his son, at a campground on Mount Desert Island.

She hadn't had a boyfriend, dated rarely and casually, no problems with neighbors, volunteers, or the staff of her organization.

Some death threats, sure, from the very type who'd have written that message. But it just didn't fit.

Or fit too well.

He walked back to his car, recalling that two people had crossed from their own yards to ask him what he was doing there when he'd parked. He'd had to show his police ID.

While statements from neighbors claimed they'd either still been in bed or been just getting up at the time of the murder, it seemed to him that the killer, in order to stalk the prey, had to have blended easily into the quiet, upper-middle-class neighborhood.

He got into his car, wrote careful notes on his observation and theories. Maybe his leading theory was just a rookie mistake, but he outlined it anyway.

The killer had patience and control, could blend in the victim's neighborhood, had killed with efficiency and precision. And the message?

A countermeasure.

Of course, none of his notes, theories, and speculation helped Roberta Flisk or her now motherless son one damn bit. But he'd transcribe all of it, file it.

And he wouldn't forget it.

When Simone heard about Roberta Flisk, and the violent death of a DownEast Mall survivor, she switched off the television.

She made it a point to forget.

She'd given Mi what she'd wanted: She sublet the apartment, went home.

And after one short week of sharing the house with her parents and sister, she'd fled to the island.

She loved her parents, truly. And if her sister's perfection—like mother, like daughter in this case—bugged the crap out of her, she loved Natalie, too.

She just couldn't live with them.

CiCi gave her space, literally, in the doll-like guest house over the glass-walled art studio. And she gave her space emotionally as well.

If she wanted to sleep half the day, CiCi didn't ask if she felt well. If she wanted to walk on the beach half the night, CiCi didn't wait up with a worried look on her face.

She didn't get a furrowed brow over quitting her job, a long sigh over the color of her hair.

She ran as many of CiCi's errands as she could, prepared some of the meals—though her cooking was nothing to brag about. She agreed to pose whenever asked.

As a result, after two weeks, Simone had to give Mi a virtual thanks. She felt more relaxed and easy than she had for months. Enough that she started to paint a little.

She set down her brush when CiCi came out on the patio with a tray holding a pitcher of sangria, glasses, a bowl of salsa and chips.

"If you don't want a break, I'm taking this to my studio and drinking the whole pitcher."

"Can't have that." Simone stepped back to study the seascape she'd worked on for the last three hours.

"It's good," CiCi told her.

"It's not."

"It certainly is."

Since CiCi, floppy-brimmed hat over her black-and-white-streaked braid (her newest look), poured the sangria, Simone dropped down in one of the patio chairs.

CiCi's latest tattoo wrapped Celtic symbols around her left wrist like a bracelet.

"That's my grandmother talking, not the artist."

"It's both." She tapped her glass to Simone's, sat, stretched out her legs, crossed her Birkenstock-clad feet at the ankles. "It is good—you've got a sense of movement and mood."

"The light isn't right, and screwing with it's made it less right. I love your seascapes. Your portraits are just incredible, every time, and you don't do seascapes often. But when you do, they're moody and magic."

"First, you're not me, and you should celebrate your youness. Second, I do sea- and landscapes, still lifes when I need calm, or my own mood strikes. Mostly I'd rather just sit here and look at the water. Portraits? People are endlessly fascinating, as is painting them. Painting, period, is my passion.

"It's not yours."

"Clearly."

"You're nineteen. Plenty of time to find your passion."

"I tried sex."

After a throaty laugh, CiCi toasted and drank. "Me, too. It's a damn happy hobby."

Amused, Simone scooped up some salsa. "I'm taking a break there."

"Me, too. You're an artist—and don't contradict your grandmother. You're an artist, with talent and with vision. Painting's a good discipline for you, but it's not your passion, and it's not going to be your primary medium. Experiment."

"With what? Dad's still trying to nudge me into prelaw, and Mom thinks I should find a nice, reliable boyfriend."

"They're traditionalists, baby. They can't help themselves. I'm not, but I can't help it, either. So I'm going to say you'd be stupid to do either of those. Experiment," she repeated, "with everything. For art, I'm going to give you what nobody wants: advice. You remember the August you spent here after the horrible?"

Simone looked out at the strip of beach, the rocks that edged it, the water beyond that never ended.

"I think it saved my sanity, so, yeah, I remember."

"You and Mi spent a lot of time on the beach the week she was here. You built sandcastles. Mi's were precise and pretty and traditional—very like her. And yours were fascinating and imaginative and fanciful."

Simone took another drink. "So I should build sandcastles?"

"Create. Try clay for a start, see where it takes you. You took the basics last year."

"How do you know?"

CiCi only smiled, sipped. "I know a lot of things. And knowing we were going to have this conversation, I ordered some supplies. They're in my studio. We can share it, we'll work out a rotation. Try it. If it's not clay, it'll be something else. Take the summer to start, see if you find out what your passion is."

CHAPTER SEVEN

After checking Roberta Flisk off her list, Patricia decided she'd had enough of college. Besides boring her brainless, actually attending class and doing the work restricted her time and cut into her focus now that she'd experienced her first kill.

She moved back to Rockpoint and, with a little finagling, in with her grandparents. It thrilled them to have their sweet, considerate, helpful granddaughter under their roof.

She made sure of it because there was no way she'd move back to some crappy rental with her useless whinefest of a mother.

To satisfy her grandparents' questions about her education, her future, Patricia took some online and community-college courses. They also served as a cover for her research on creating fake identification and credit cards.

She had plans.

She also had the run of her own wing in the dignified old mansion, a BMW Roadster, and already enough skills to skim from their accounts.

With the extra funds, she began to stockpile weapons, and to compile a healthy supply of cash.

She laughed at their jokes, ran errands, drove her grandmother to salon appointments, and made herself indispensable. The vague talk of looking for a job, investing in a career, faded like mist.

They never noticed.

At the same time, she bought and delivered groceries to her mother, made her duty visits, arranged for snow removal from the walk and driveway of the miserable rental.

And kept her head down.

She kept it down for the two years she waited to kill her mother. She considered it a reward for her patience, and her hard work playing the devoted daughter and granddaughter.

Everyone knew Marcia Hobart was a weak and troubled woman. A woman who had never sloughed off the guilt for her son's actions, or the grief of his death.

Even when she'd turned to God, she'd chosen His most vengeful and punishing form. Her penance—as a Daughter of Eve—demanded a lifetime of suffering and regret.

The only light in her personal darkness came from her daughter (Patricia made sure of it). Surely if she'd given birth to a child of kindness and compassion, a child with a bright mind and a quiet demeanor, that made up, in part, for birthing a monster.

And still, she loved the monster.

Patricia used that love as a stealth weapon in the five years since the DownEast Mall.

She saw to it that articles on the shootings, ugly letters reviling Marcia as responsible, and death threats ended up in her mother's hand. Some she mailed, others she taped to the front door or shoved under it. The night before she'd left for Columbia, she'd thrown a rock wrapped with a particularly vicious note through the living room window, then rushed inside to huddle screaming behind the sofa.

An anonymous tip had McMullen dogging Marcia—at home, at work. Marcia lost her second job. Though the lawyers would have kept her on, she moved farther away—another miserable rental—isolating herself.

She took pills to sleep, more pills to hold off the constant and increasing anxiety. Patricia planted the seeds with her grandparents of her own worries. Her mother sometimes mixed up the pills, or took a double dose because she'd forgotten she'd taken the first.

They, who'd cut Marcia off for divorcing their asshole of a son, showered Patricia with sympathy.

She planted nanny cams in her mother's house so she could watch her. She knew just when to call from the drop phone she'd bought, how to wake her groggy mother up out of a Xanax-assisted sleep and whisper her brother's name.

On visits she'd add an extra pill or two, grinding them into the soup the dutiful daughter prepared, then play old videos from when JJ was a baby.

She tearfully reported to her grandparents about finding her mother in a stupor on the couch with the videos playing. While still in college, she'd asked her instructors and professors—she'd majored in psychology—for advice. She arranged an accidental overdose, placed a frantic nine-one-one call, and held her mother's limp hand in the ambulance.

She left the trail of a worried, loving daughter with a mother lost in pills and guilt. Even as she attended support groups for children of addicts, she found fresh ways to gaslight her mother.

On the night before her brother's birthday, she slipped into the house, baked his favorite chocolate cake. Deliberately, she left ingredients scattered on the counter, the mixing bowl and pan in the sink, setting the stage.

Then she blew out the oven's pilot light.

After waking her drug-addled mother, she led her into a kitchen smelling of chocolate and baking.

"It's dark." Marcia shuffled and swayed. "What time is it?"

"It's time for cake! You baked such a nice one."

"I did? I don't remember."

"JJ's favorite chocolate cake. He wants you to light the candles, Mom."

Marcia's eyes darted around the room. "Is he here?"

"He's coming. Turn on the TV. There's the remote."

Obediently, Marcia picked up the remote, and with Patricia guiding her fingers, hit play. On the TV, a grinning, gap-toothed JJ giggled as his mother lit his birthday candles.

"Light the candles, Mom. For JJ."

"He was my sweet little boy." Tears, sentiment, and guilt filled Marcia's eyes. She took the long butane lighter, lit the candles. "He didn't mean to be bad. He's sorry. Look, look, he's so happy. Why did he stop being happy?"

"You need to take your pills. JJ wants you to take your pills. They're right there. You need to take your pills."

"I took them. Didn't I take them? I'm so tired. Where's JJ? It's dark outside. Little boys shouldn't be out in the dark."

"He's coming. You need to take your pills for JJ's birthday. I think you should take one for each candle."

"Six candles, six pills. My baby boy is six." Eyes damp as they stared at the TV screen, Marcia took six pills, one by one, with the wine Patricia had set beside them.

"That's good, very good. JJ needs more light. He needs more light to find his way home. I think he's lost!"

"No. No. Where's my little boy? JJ!"

"You have to light the curtains. If you squirt some of the lighter fluid on them, they make such a bright light. He'll see it, and he'll come home."

Marcia picked up the can of fluid. For a moment Patricia wondered if she saw a kind of awareness in her mother's eyes. Maybe a kind of relief. Marcia doused the curtains with the fluid, set them to flame.

"See how bright! You need to turn on the oven, Mom."

"I baked the cake?"

"Just like always." Taking Marcia's arm, Patricia led her to the oven. "Turn on the oven." And guided her mother's hand to the knob.

"I'm so sleepy. I need to sleep."

"Just turn on the oven, then you can take a nap."

"Then JJ will come?"

"Oh, you'll see JJ soon. Turn on the oven, that's right. Why don't you just lie down over here on the couch?"

As her mother collapsed on the couch, Patricia used a second lighter—one she would take with her—to light the already soaked living room curtains.

As she edged toward the door, she watched her mother's slack face. "Sing 'Happy Birthday' to JJ, Mom."

Her voice slurred, her eyes closed, Marcia tried to sing.

By the time the gas fumes did their work, when they met flame and combusted, Patricia was in her bed in her grandparents' house.

She slept like a baby.

The phone on Reed's nightstand signaled an alert. He rolled over, scooped it up, squinted at it.

"Ah, hell."

"Cop stuff?" Eloise Matherson stirred beside him.

"Yeah." Not directly, he thought, but since he'd followed Essie's tack with alerts on incidents connected to the DownEast Mall, not one he wanted to ignore, either.

"Sorry."

"How it goes." She stirred again. "Want me to take off?"

"No, go back to sleep. I'll text you later." He gave her butt an easy pat as he got out of bed.

Their friends with—occasional—benefits status suited them both. Nothing serious, as the friends aspect of the equation remained the priority.

He grabbed some clothes in the dark and, taking a quick shower, thought about Marcia Hobart.

He had a file on her, and he'd refresh himself there, but he remembered she'd been divorced when her son had opened fire in the DownEast Mall Cineplex. Hobart had lived with his father, and his younger sister with the mother.

Domestic worker, he recalled as he pulled on jeans. Moved twice—that he knew of—since the shooting.

His alert reported firefighters battling a five-alarm blaze at her current residence—one that threatened neighboring properties. They'd recovered a single body inside the Hobart residence.

He snapped on his off-duty weapon, grabbed his keys and a bottle of Mountain Dew from the refrigerator. Chugging some, he jogged down the two flights of steps from his apartment to the weedy gravel lot and his car.

The car, the same Dodge Neon his parents had given him when he'd graduated high school, was pretty much a piece of crap. Just the way his apartment building was pretty much a dump.

He'd opted to make do and follow Essie's lead, saving whatever he could toward a down payment to buy a house.

And as it turned out, his dump of an apartment put him five minutes from Marcia Hobart's address.

In under two he heard sirens.

When he spotted patrol cars, he pulled over to park. He recognized one of the uniforms working the barricades, aimed for him.

"Hey, Bushner."

"Quartermaine. In the neighborhood?"

"Not far. What do you know?"

"My ass from a hole in the ground."

"Good you confirmed that. What else?"

"Heard the nine-one-ones reported an explosion and the fire. House down there is toast with a crispy critter inside. Smoke eaters are still knocking it down. The house on the east side took a hit, but everybody got out."

"Mind if I walk down?"

"No skin off mine."

He could see the firefighters in turnout gear silhouetted against the snaps and pulse of fire. Spumes of water arced through the haze of smoke and raining ash. Civilians stood back, clutching children or each other. Some wept.

He heard the bark of orders, the crackle of radios.

And saw Bushner had it right. The house where the beleaguered Marcia Hobart lived was toast. He watched it fold in on itself, shooting flames and firefly sparks into the smoke-choked dark. More hoses attacked the flames crawling up the west wall of the house on the east side, still more soaked down the walls of the house on the west to stop the spread.

The patch of lawn in front of all three houses, the narrow strips between, were a blackened morass of soaked ash and mud.

He scanned the crowd, considered the young couple with the infant in the woman's arms and a yellow Lab at their feet. Tears streamed down the woman's face as they stared at the east-side house.

Reed moved toward them.

"Is that your place?"

The man, late twenties by Reed's gauge, with a sleep-tousled mop of blond hair, nodded as he put an arm around the woman. "It's burning. Our house is on fire."

"They're putting it out. And you got out. You and your family got out."

"We just moved in two weeks ago. We haven't even finished unpacking."

Reed watched the water drowning the flames. "You're going to have some damage, but nothing you can't fix."

The woman sucked in a sob, turned her face into her husband's shoulder. "It's our fixer-upper, Rob. We bought a fixer-upper."

"It'll be all right, Chloe. We're going to make it all right."

"Would you mind telling me what happened? What you know. Sorry." Reed pulled out his ID. "Not just nosy."

Chloe swiped at tears. "God. God. Custer, our dog, started barking and woke the baby. I was so mad because we'd barely gotten her down. She's not sleeping through the night, and I'd just fed her at around two. It was just after three when Custer started barking, and the baby started crying."

"I got up. My turn," Rob said. "I got up, and I yelled at the dog. I yelled at him." Rob bent down now to stroke the Lab, who leaned on him. "But he wouldn't quit. I glanced out the window. It just didn't register at first—the light—then I looked, and I saw the house next door. I saw the fire. I could see the fire through the windows of the house next door."

"Rob yelled at me to get up, get the baby. I grabbed Audra, and Rob grabbed the phone to call nine-one-one while we were running out of the bedroom."

"Something exploded." Fire reflected in Rob's eyes before he pressed his fingers to them. "It was just this *boom*. Our bedroom windows shattered."

"The glass. If Custer hadn't— The glass flew. Audra had been in her bassinet on the window side of our bed. If Custer hadn't barked, woken us up, the glass . . ."

"That's a good dog."

"We ran out," Chloe continued. "We didn't even stop to get anything, just ran out while Rob called nine-one-one."

"You did just right. You got your family out. That's what matters. Fire's out," he told them.

"Oh God. It didn't burn down. Rob, it didn't burn down."

"You'll fix it, and I'm betting you'll make something special out of it. Look, if you need anything—supplies, clothes, hands to help put things back together?" He pulled a card out of his pocket. "My mother's always organizing something, so she knows a lot of people. I can hook you up."

"Thank you." Chloe knuckled another tear away while Rob slipped the card in his pocket. "Do you know when they'll let us go back in? Go in and see?"

"That'll be up to the fire department, and they'll want to make sure it's safe. Let me see if I can find out anything, maybe get somebody to talk to you."

He moved off to one of the pumpers, spotted a sweat-and-soot-soaked Michael Foster.

"Michael."

"Reed. What are you doing out here?"

"JJ Hobart's mom—that used to be her house."

Michael's eyes sharpened in his soot-covered face. "You're sure about that?"

"That's my information."

"Son of a bitch." Michael sucked in air. "Son of a fucking bitch." And released it in a hiss. "Hobart," he murmured, "again."

"I know, man. Look, have you got a minute?"

"Not now, but I will have in a few."

"I'll hang until you do. Meanwhile, that couple over there with the dog and the baby? That's their house you guys just saved. Is there somebody who can talk to them?"

"Yeah, I'll send somebody over. Hobart's mother? Did she live alone?"

"As far as I know."

"Then there's not much left of her."

Reed figured there wasn't any harm in talking to some of the people still gathered outside, on the street, on their own lawns, on their porches.

The main impression he formed said Marcia Hobart hadn't just kept to herself, she'd isolated herself. His secondary impression was the neighbors hadn't known her relationship with the organizer of the DownEast Mall massacre.

"You, there!"

He turned, saw the old woman in a creaky rocker on a creaky porch. "Yes, ma'am."

"You a reporter or some such?"

"No, ma'am, I'm a police officer."

"You don't look much like a police. You come on up here."

She had a face like a raisin, golden brown and wrinkled beneath a snow-ball of hair. Glasses rested on the tip of her nose as she eyed him up and down.

"Good-looking boy, I'll give you that. What kind of police are you?"

"Officer Reed Quartermaine, ma'am."

"That's not what I asked."

"I'm trying to be good police."

"Well, some are, some aren't. Maybe you will be. Sit down here, 'cause I'm getting a crick in my neck looking up at you."

He sat in the equally creaky chair beside hers.

"You being the police, you'd know who the woman was who died in that house tonight." She pushed the glasses back up her nose to peer through them at the smoldering rubble across the street. "Maybe you're not stupid police as you know to keep your mouth shut waiting to see if I know what I know. That poor woman had a son go bad on her, and he killed people. DownEast Mall."

"Can I ask how you know that?"

"I pay attention, that's how. I got clippings from back when it happened, and some have her picture. She didn't age well since, but I saw who she was."

"Did you talk to her, or anybody else about that?"

"Why would I?" With a sad shake of her head, she looked back at Reed. "She was just trying to live her life, to get by. I had a son go bad on me. He didn't kill anybody, as far as I know, but he went bad all the same. I've got another son and a girl who make me proud every day. I did my best by all of them, but I had a son go bad. She was a sad, troubled woman."

"Were you friendly with her?"

"She wasn't friendly with anybody. She just holed up in there, went off to work, came back, and shut herself in."

"Any visitors?" Reed prodded.

"The only person I ever saw go inside would be her daughter. She'd come by now and again, stay awhile. She'd bring groceries every couple weeks. Saw her bring flowers this past Mother's Day. Did her duty."

Patricia Hobart, Reed remembered. JJ's younger sister. "Did you ever talk to the daughter?"

"Ayuh, a time or two. Polite, but closemouthed all the same. She asked me if there might be a young boy willing to cut the grass, shovel snow, and that sort of thing, so I told her to ask about Jenny Molar, two doors down there. She's a good girl, helps me out when I need it—and more reliable than most boys. Jenny, she told me the daughter paid her what she asked, and told her not to bother her mother. How she wasn't real well, and shy with it. So the daughter did her duty by her mother, no more, no less."

He caught the tone. "No more?"

"That's how I see it, but I have high standards." She smiled, then looked back across the street. "Shame about the house. It wasn't much, but it could've been better. The man who owns it isn't worth a half bucket of spit, so he didn't mind having it rented out to somebody who wouldn't dog him about repairs. I guess he'll collect his insurance and sell off the plot."

While Reed considered that, she gave him another long study. "My grandson's a police. Officer Curtis A. Sloop."

"Seriously? Come on. I know Sloopy."

She tipped down her glasses again. "Is that so?"

"Yes, ma'am. We went to the Academy together, and were rooks the same year. He's good police."

"He's trying to be. If you talk to him before I do, you tell him you met his granny." She offered a hand, small and delicate as a doll's. "Mrs. Leticia Johnson."

"I sure will, and I'm pleased to meet you, Mrs. Johnson."

"You go be good police, young, good-looking Reed Quartermaine. And maybe you'll come by and see me sometime."

"Yes, ma'am."

He left her rocking, hunted up Michael. Found him talking with Essie.

"Your case?" he asked her.

"It is now." With her hands on her hips, she studied the wreck and rubble. "The arson investigator's already in there, so we'll see. Official ID of the body's going to take awhile."

"I hear the landlord isn't big on repair and maintenance."

Essie slanted him a look. "Is that what you hear?"

"Mrs. Leticia Johnson—her grandson's on the job. I know him, he's solid. She's sitting on the porch across the street. You'll want to talk to her. Chloe and Rob, from the house next door, were awakened by their dog barking about three a.m. Rob got up, as the barking woke up the baby in the baby thing beside the bed. He saw the fire, got his wife up, grabbed the phone to call it in while they headed out. The explosion came next, shattered their bedroom windows."

Essie's eyebrows lifted. "You've been busy, Officer."

"Well, I was here anyway. She lived alone, didn't socialize, didn't have visitors except for the daughter. The daughter came by occasionally, brought groceries every couple weeks, hired a local kid to cut the grass, shovel snow in the winter."

"You bucking for a gold shield, Officer Quartermaine?"

He smiled. "Next year." He turned to Michael. "Do you think arson?"

"I can't say. I can say it looks like two points of origin—kitchen and living room, and my best guess would be curtains. It wasn't a gas leak, most likely gas from the stove. Actually, the explosion was fairly contained, and that'll help the investigators determine cause."

"My partner's talking to the neighbors. I think I'll walk over and have a chat with Mrs. Johnson. Officer Quartermaine?"

"Detective McVee."

"I'm requesting you be assigned to this investigative unit."

"Hot damn."

"Start by canvassing the block. Write up your notes."

She walked across the street, leaving him grinning.

Simone broke under relentless, benign family pressure. While her father conceded his dream of his oldest following in his lawyer footsteps wasn't to be, the change of tack worked.

She would focus her studies on business management. She'd had her scattershot period, her parents told her, and now she had to buckle down. A degree in business management would keep her focused, open doors, forge a future.

She tried. She pushed herself so hard in the next semester even the responsible Mi urged her to ease off, take some breaks.

She ended the year with grades that made her parents beam, and spent the summer working as an assistant to the assistant of the manager of the accounting branch of her father's firm.

By the end of June, she was back in therapy.

In August, plagued with headaches, ten pounds underweight, with a wardrobe of suits she hated, she thought of the girl she'd been, the one who'd called for help, then hidden in a bathroom stall.

The one who'd feared she'd die before she'd lived.

And realized there were other ways to die.

She chose to live.

On the night before she left for New York, she sat down with her parents and Natalie.

"I can't believe both our girls are heading off to college," Tulip began. "What are we going to do, Ward, with our empty nest? Natalie off to Harvard, and Simone off to Columbia."

"I'm not going back to Columbia."

"We're just so . . . What?"

Simone kept her hands gripped together in her lap. They wanted to shake. "I'm going back to New York, but I'm not going back to college."

"Of course you are. You had a brilliant third year."

"I hated every minute of it. I hated working in the law firm this summer. I can't keep doing what I hate, what I'm not."

"This is the first I'm hearing about it." Ward shoved up, stalked across the room to mix himself a drink. "Your evaluations were glowing. Just as Natalie's were in her internship. We don't quit in this family, Simone, or take our advantages for granted. You disappoint me."

It stung. Of course it stung, as he'd meant it to. But she'd prepared herself for that.

"I know I do, and I know I might always disappoint you. But I gave you a year of my life. I did everything you wanted me to do, and I can't do it anymore."

"Why do you have to spoil everything?"

She spun around to face Natalie to take some of the burning sting out on her sister. "What am I spoiling for you? You're doing what you want, what you're good at. Go do it, be good at it. Be the perfect white sheep to my black."

"Your sister's mature enough to understand she needs a foundation, she needs goals, and she has parents who've given her a foundation, and support her goals."

"They match yours," Simone told her mother. "Mine don't."

"Since when have you had goals?" Natalie muttered.

"I'm working on it. I'm going back to New York. I'm going to take some art classes—"

"Oh, for God's sake." Tulip threw up her hands. "I knew this was CiCi's doing."

"I haven't even talked to her about it. While I've been trying to please you, I disappointed her. But here's the thing. She's never thrown it in my face, not once. That's the difference. She's never tried to shove me into a box where I don't fit because it was what she wanted. I'm going to take art classes, I'm going to find out if I'm any good. I'm going to find out if I can be better than good."

"And just how do you plan to support yourself?" Ward demanded. "You can't throw your education away and expect us to pay for it."

"I don't. I'll get a job."

"At some dump of a coffee shop?" Natalie tossed out.

"If necessary."

"It's obvious you haven't thought this through."

"Mom, I haven't thought of anything else for weeks. Look at me. Please, really look at me. I can't sleep. I can't eat. I've got a closet full of clothes you picked out and bought. My social life this summer's revolved around the appropriate son of a friend you handpicked for me. The clothes don't fit, and the son of a friend bores me to death. But I wore them, and I dated him, and I lay awake at night with my head pounding. I've been seeing Dr. Mattis since June, three times a week, and paying for it out of my savings so you wouldn't know."

"You'll take a semester off," Tulip decided, her eyes going shiny with tears. "You'll rest, and we'll take a trip. We'll—"

"Tulip." Ward spoke gently now, coming back to sit without his drink. "Simone, why didn't you tell us you starting seeing Dr. Mattis again?"

"Because I knew part of the reason I needed to go back to him was you, and it's not your fault. It's just reality. It's me not being what you hope for. It's me closing myself into that bathroom stall in my head, and being afraid to open the door. I have to open the door. I'm sorry," she said as she rose, "but you have to let me. I'm of age, and I've made my choice. I'm leaving tonight."

"We're going to talk this through," Tulip insisted.

"There's nothing more to say, so I'm leaving tonight. My bags are in my car," she added, but didn't tell them she intended to go to the island first. She needed that bridge before she stepped into the unknown. "Natalie's leaving tomorrow, and you should have tonight with her. I love you, but I can't be here."

She walked out quickly, and Natalie ran after her.

"How could you treat them that way?" Furious, she grabbed Simone's arm. "You're ungrateful and mean. Why can't you just be normal?"

"You sucked up all the normal left around here. Enjoy it."

She wrenched her arm away, got in her car as Natalie shouted at her. "Self-ish, stupid, crazy."

As she drove, she thought of the day she'd walked out of her old coffee shop job. She couldn't say she felt happy this time, but she could say she felt free.

For a year she waited tables to pay her share of the rent. She wasn't so proud and independent that she refused checks from CiCi to help defray other expenses, including her classes, her supplies. But she helped herself there, too, by modeling for students.

As she did two nights a week—three, if she got lucky—Simone stepped onto the platform in front of a class, shed her robe, and posed as instructed. Tonight, right arm bent at the elbow, palm open and up, left hand resting just above and between her breasts.

It didn't embarrass her to pose naked any more than it embarrassed her to sketch or to sculpt a naked model. And the modeling fees helped pay for the instruction, the sketchbooks, the clay, the firing, the tools.

She'd learned she was good, and believed she could be better than good.

While Patricia baked her dead brother a birthday cake to commemorate the anniversary of her mother's death, Simone let herself back into her apartment after a long day, poured herself a glass of wine, and was happy.

CHAPTER EIGHT

In April of 2013, Essie gave birth to a healthy baby boy she and the besotted father named Dylan. As her partner retired that same month, she requested Detective Reed Quartermaine as her new partner when she returned from maternity leave.

Though she happily took that leave, she kept her finger in the pie with regular news, gossip, and reports from her future partner.

Her life, Essie thought as she crept out of the bedroom where her husband and baby slept, had taken so many unexpected turns.

She'd never expected to become a detective second grade, much less part of the Major Crimes squad. She'd never expected to have a man as sweet, funny, smart, and sexy as Hank in her life. She sure as hell hadn't expected the dizzying wave of love she felt whenever she looked at or even thought about her son.

Her life had taken a turn one night in July, and out of tragedy, the path from it had been, well, pretty damn great.

She poured herself a glass of herbal tea over ice, grabbed one of the magazines off the stack, walked out to sit on the front porch and watch her little world go by.

She'd probably fall asleep—and she should be upstairs doing just that. *Sleep when the baby sleeps* had been her mother's advice. But she wanted the spring air and a little time to bask.

Maybe they'd take the baby out for a stroll later. And maybe the fresh air would help three-week-old Dylan sleep longer than his record of two hours and thirty-seven minutes.

It could happen.

Maybe she and Hank could snuggle up together, watch a movie—and, if she pumped first, drink a little wine.

Maybe . . .

She dozed off in her Adirondack chair.

Came awake with a start, reaching for the weapon she wasn't wearing.

"Sorry! Sorry." Reed held his hands up. One of them held a bouquet of pink-and-white-striped tulips. "I didn't mean to wake you up. I was just going to leave these."

"What time is it?"

"About five-thirty."

"Okay, okay." She sighed. "I just dropped off for a few minutes. You brought me tulips."

"I have it on good authority—my sister—that people tend to forget the sleep-deprived mom after the first couple weeks. Why aren't you sleeping inside the house?"

"I wasn't going to sleep yet. Sit down. My boys are snoozing upstairs. I could use the company to keep me from drooling on the porch. Wait, go on in and get a drink first. There's this tea, there's beer."

"I could use a beer."

At home at her place, he went in, got a cold bottle, popped it. He came back, sat down with her. "How ya doing?"

"Honestly, I never thought anybody could be so damn happy. And the hits keep coming. Hank told me today he's decided to take a year's sabbatical.

He's going to be a stay-at-home dad. I don't have to think about leaving Dylan with a nanny or at a daycare."

When her eyes teared up, she slapped her own cheeks. "God, God, hormones. Will they ever go back to normal? Talk cop to me. That'll work."

"We closed the Bower case."

"You got her."

"Yeah, the greedy, scheming widow's booked. Her boyfriend flipped. He gets the deal, she gets murder one."

He filled her in on a couple of open cases, made her laugh over some office gossip.

"I looked at a couple more houses over the weekend."

"Reed, you've been looking at houses for nearly a year now."

"Yeah, but none looks back and says: Here I am."

"Maybe you're too fussy, and you're going to end up living your life in that shitcan of an apartment."

"An apartment's just a place to sleep. A house has to be right."

She couldn't disagree, and yet. "That place I waddled into with you a couple months ago was great."

"It was close. No direct hit. I'll know it when I see it."

"Maybe it's Portland."

"Portland's okay. I'm close to family, I'll be working with you. That makes up for the shitcan until I get the direct hit."

"I'd say that's the same attitude that keeps you from having a serious relationship, but I was the same way there until Hank."

"No direct hit," he agreed. "I got an invitation to Eloise's wedding. June."

"She's really doing it."

"Looks that way. Eloise is taking the plunge, and I think it's working for her."

"There's something else." She poked his arm. "I can see it."

He studied his beer a moment, shook back the mop of hair he no longer had to shear short. "You didn't get the alert?"

"Shit. I don't even know where my phone is right now. Who?"

"Marshall Finestein. He's the one who took one in the hip, managed to crawl off."

"And served as an eyewit, with considerable detail, on Paulson. He consulted on a documentary. He pops up on TV at every anniversary."

"He won't make the next one. Hit-and-run. He jogged every morning, started it after he got back on his feet after the incident. The car didn't even slow down, knocked him out of his Adidas, and kept on going."

"Any witnesses?"

"Quiet stretch of road, early morning. But a Toyota Land Cruiser with front-edge damage and blood, fiber, skin, turned up abandoned a half mile from the scene. The owners—parents of two, a CPA and a pediatrician—reported it stolen about the time it was mowing Finestein down. We'll take a harder look, but they're clean, Essie."

"Somebody knew Finestein's routine and his route, stole the car to take him out."

"That's six deaths with the victims connected to the DownEast Mall. Three murders with this one, two suicides, and Marcia Hobart's one accidental. There's a pattern, Essie."

"One of the suicides was in Delaware, the other in Boston, one of the murders—deemed gang related—was in Baltimore." She held up a hand before he objected. "I'm not saying you're wrong, Reed. But it's still a stretch. A connection pattern, yeah, but statistically you're going to have deaths, especially that include suicide and accidental, in any large group. There's no pattern to the method. A silenced handgun, a knifing, a hit-and-run."

"Overkill's a pattern," he insisted. "Three bullets in Roberta Flisk. Thirteen stab wounds in Martin Bowlinger, ramming a big-ass SUV at high speed into Finestein. Bowlinger, in his first month as mall security, panics and runs when the shooting started. He can't live with it, moves away, starts using. He's zoned when he's stabbed, dead after a couple of holes go into him, but the killer keeps slicing. Overkill.

"And the suicides," he continued, warming up. "What if they weren't? Add Hobart's mother's accidental, which still doesn't sit all the way right for me, and you've got too damn many."

"The pattern breaks down with Hobart's mother. She wasn't a victim. She wasn't a survivor."

"She was a victim," he insisted, his green eyes going hard. "Maybe she wasn't a terrific mother, maybe she was weak, but she was a victim. Her son made her a victim."

"Motive?"

"Sometimes crazy's motive enough. I know it's a stretch, but it just keeps circling back."

Though the ice had melted, diluting it, Essie drank more tea. "And that might be the real reason you're still in that shitcan. You can't keep circling back, Reed. Keeping track, that's one thing. I'm never going to not keep track. But you have to move on, too."

"I wouldn't be a cop if it wasn't for that night, if it wasn't for you. And the cop's saying it feels like a pattern, all the way through it. I want to look closer at the suicides and the accidental. On my own time," he said quickly. "But I want you to know I'm going to look closer."

"Okay, all right. If you find anything, I'll be the first one to help you push."

"Good enough."

They both heard the first fussy cries through the upstairs window. "That's my cue," Essie said. "do you want to come in, stay for dinner?"

"Not tonight, thanks. Next time I'll bring dinner."

"I'll take it." She picked up the tulips. "Thanks for the flowers, partner."

"You bet. Have fun, Mom."

"I could sleep standing up." She paused at the door. "My boobs are a milk factory and I haven't had sex for a month. And you know what? It's fun. Come back, bring pizza."

"You got it."

He walked to his car, decided he'd go back to his shitcan, toss a frozen pizza in the oven, and dig a little into a couple of suicides.

Simone hauled suitcases and boxes down four flights of steps to Mi's Prius. Fork in the road, she told herself, determinedly cheerful. This was just a fork in the road, and a big, bright opening for Mi with the move to Boston, the position at Mass General.

Mi deserved it, had worked for it, would be great at it.

"How are you going to get all this stuff in there? You should've shipped all these books."

"Everything'll fit." Mi tapped a finger to her temple. "I've got it all worked out. It's like Tetris."

"I never understood that game, but once a geek . . ."

Realizing her skill had been in the hauling, Simone stood back, watched Mi—her long, sleek ponytail through the back loop of a Boston Red Sox hat (a gift)—calculate, arrange, shift.

She wore cropped jeans, pink sneakers, and a Columbia T-shirt. Small hands, Simone thought, boxing away every detail. Short nails, never painted. The little Vietnamese symbol tattooed under her right thumb that meant *hope*.

Lovely long, dark eyes, soft jawline, slim bladed nose.

An oversize watch on a slender left wrist, tiny gold studs in small, close-to-the-head earlobes.

And, of course, the brain, as within minutes Mi had everything loaded. "There! See?"

"Yeah. How could I have doubted. Except there's one more." Simone held out the box she'd kept behind her back. "You can find room, and open it when you get there."

"I'll find room, but I'm opening it now."

Mi tugged off the raffia tie, took off the lid, peeled back the cotton batting. "Oh. Oh, Sim."

The sculpture, no bigger than Mi's hand, formed three faces. Mi and Simone, with Tish centered between them.

"I was just going to do you and me, but . . . she wanted to be there. It's how I think she'd look. If."

"It's beautiful." Tears rose up, thickened the words. "We're beautiful. She's with us."

"She'd have been so proud of you, Almost Dr. Jung."

"Still have a ways to go for that. She'd've been proud of you, too. Look how talented you are." Gently Mi traced the features of her friends. "She'd have been a star," Mi murmured.

"Damn straight."

"It's the first thing I'll put out in my new apartment." Carefully Mi replaced the cotton, the lid. "Oh God, Sim. I'm going to miss you."

"We'll text and call and e-mail and FaceTime. We'll visit."

"Who am I going to talk to when I can't sleep?"

"Me. You'll call me." Wrapping Mi in a hard hug, Simone rocked them both. "You're allowed to make friends. You go ahead and do that. But you're never allowed to make another best-best friend."

"You, either."

"Not a chance. You have to go, you have to go." Still she clung. "Text me when you get there."

"I love you."

"I love you." Simone made herself pull back. "Go. Kick ass, Mi-Hi. Kick ass, cure the common cold, and be happy."

"Kick ass, Simone. Kick ass, make great art, and be happy."

Mi got behind the wheel, put sunglasses over streaming eyes, and with one last wave, took her own fork in the road.

Simone went back in, up the flights, and into the apartment to face living alone for the first time in her life.

She could afford it—and didn't want a roommate. She had a job, her modeling fees, and had even sold a few pieces here and there through a local gallery.

Plus her trust fund had kicked in, so she could—when stretched—dip into that.

Mi's bedroom would become her studio, her workshop.

Though she cried more than a little while she did it, she moved supplies from her bedroom, from the section of the living room she'd claimed. She dragged shelves, her bench and stool.

Now, she thought as she set up, she'd be able to get in and out of bed without climbing over and around art supplies.

The light in Mi's room—correction, her studio—would do very well. She could bring up models instead of paying or bartering for space in someone else's studio.

As she arranged and rearranged things, she made plans. Without Mi's companionship, she wouldn't be so tempted to just hang out, wouldn't have those long conversations or impulse evenings out. She'd use that time to work.

Not that she didn't have other friends, she assured herself. Not best-best friends, of course, and maybe she didn't make friends easily, but she had people she could go out with or hang out with.

She didn't have to be alone; she was choosing to be alone.

After two hours alone in the apartment, she grabbed her purse and went out.

Three hours later, she came back with her hair cut on an angle along her jaw, a long sweep of bangs, in a shade the salon called Icy Indigo.

She took a selfie and texted it to Mi, who'd already arrived in Boston.

Then she looked around, sighed. She took one of the sketches she'd pinned to her board, sat down, and began to do more precise measurements of a nude caught in a crouch, long hair spilling, spiraling, the fingertips of one hand pressed to the ground, the other hand with its palm up, slightly extended.

What's she doing? Simone wondered. What's she looking at? Where is she?

As she worked her measurements, she played with stories, considering, rejecting. Hitting.

"She's taken the leap," Simone murmured. "Not of faith, of courage. She jumped with nothing but herself, that's courage. I see you."

With no classes, no tables to serve for the evening, she got her wire for the armature, laid it on her template.

Too quiet, she decided, and switched on music.

Not rock, she realized, not classical.

Tribal. Her woman would seek a tribe.

Then she would lead it.

With the image clear in her mind, the framework ready, Simone chose her clay, her tools, and began to free the woman who would lead a tribe.

The feet, long, narrow; the ankles strong, slender; calf muscles defined.

She built, carved away, brushed, sprayed the clay with water, smoothed the knees.

As the figure emerged, she worked her way up the body until she realized the light had changed.

Evening was sliding in.

She covered the figure, made herself get off the stool, walk, stretch. A little wine, she decided, then ordered in Chinese because if she went back to work, she'd forget to eat.

Forget to eat, hydrate, move, the work often showed the neglect.

She spent her first night alone drinking wine, rotating it with water, eating noodles and stir-fried pork, and bringing her vision to life.

For three weeks she followed the same routine. Work—the sort that brought a paycheck with it—class, work—the sort that fed her soul.

After a fifteen-hour day, much of it on her feet, she came home to the creeping silence of her apartment.

She missed Mi like a limb, she couldn't deny it, but that wasn't the core of the problem. She sat, studying the sculpture she'd begun that first night.

It was good—really good. One of the best pieces she'd done, but she couldn't make herself take it to the gallery.

"Because I need it," she said aloud. "She's telling me something, and has been all along. I'm talking to myself." She sighed, tipped her head back. "So what? So what? I have something to say, too. It's time to take a leap. I've done what I came to New York to do. It's time to move on."

She closed her eyes. "No more waiting tables, no more modeling for a fee or for supplies or for class time. I'm an artist, goddamn it."

She had another two months on the lease. She'd either tough it out, or eat the cost.

Eat it, she decided.

She pulled out her phone, saw the time, and calculated the odds CiCi was still up.

She waited, and when her grandmother's voice came on clear and alert, smiled. "Having a party?"

"No, and I know it's late."

"Never too."

"Exactly. So, I think it's time I had a taste of Europe. Do you know anybody, say, in Florence, with a flat to rent?"

"Baby doll, I know everybody everywhere. How about we take a trip, and I introduce you?"

The smile turned into a laugh. "How about I pack?"

During the eighteen months Simone spent in Florence, she learned the language, grew tomatoes and geraniums on the tiny balcony of her flat overlooking Piazza San Marco, and took an Italian lover named Dante.

Dante, absurdly handsome, played the cello and liked making Simone pasta. As he traveled with the symphony, their relationship didn't crowd her, and left her all the time she needed to devote to her work.

The fact that he had other women on his travels didn't concern her. For her, Dante was part of a lovely interlude of sun, sex, and sculpting. She'd given herself this time and place, saturating herself with all it offered.

She studied, spent time with artists, with masters, with artisans and technicians. And sweated on the pouring floor of a foundry to learn more about casting in bronze.

As she learned, experimented, discovered, she built enough confidence to wheedle her way into a show at a trendy art gallery, then spent four months completing more pieces for what she called *Gods and Goddesses*.

Simone invited her family out of duty. They declined, but sent two dozen red roses to the gallery with a card wishing her luck.

Helping load in her art and debating with the gallery manager on placement ate up any time for nerves. She'd already told herself, countless times, if the show failed it meant she wasn't good enough.

Yet.

It didn't mean she'd go home a failure. Her parents might—correction, *would*, she thought as she debated, again, between a severe and serious black dress and a bold, sexy red one—think her a failure. But she would never meet their standards anyway. They had Natalie for that. She'd forever be their college dropout daughter who threw away all the advantages they'd offered her.

Her mother would vote for the black, Simone thought. Be sedate, be sophisticated.

She went for the red and worked it with killer-heel gold sandals that would make her feet weep. But they'd show off the toes painted the same pomegranate as her base hair color.

She'd added streaks and sweeps of turquoise, plum, flame to that base to set off her haircut of varying angles.

To add more bohemian, she added cascading gold disks to her ears and an army of bangles on her arm.

Trying too hard? Maybe the black after all.

Before she could snatch it out of the wardrobe, her buzzer sounded. Another delivery from Dante, she decided as she clipped from the bedroom through her parlor already fragrant with the white roses he'd sent the night before, the red lilies that morning, the orchids in the early afternoon, and the pink tulips after that.

She opened the door, squealed, and threw her arms around her grandmother.

"CiCi! CiCi! You're here!"

"Where else would I be?"

"You came. You came all this way."

"Wild horses, *cara*. Wild, wild horses."

"Oh, come in, sit down. Did you just get here? Let me get your bag."

"I came straight here, but don't worry, I'm staying with Francesca and Isabel."

"No, no, they can't have you! You have to stay here. Please."

CiCi shook back the hair that fell past her shoulder blades—now in burnished copper. "I'd love a threesome with that luscious Italian pastry of yours, but it's too awkward when one of the three's my grandbaby."

"Dante's in Vienna. The schedule just didn't click. But he's everywhere." She opened her arms to the roomful of flowers.

"The man's a romantic. Then if it's just you and me, I'm happy to stay.

I'll let Francesca and Isabel know. They're coming tonight, and I'm going to take us all out to celebrate after. God." Beaming, CiCi let herself soak in her greatest treasure. "Just look at you! Your hair's a work of art. And that dress!"

"I was just thinking I should change. I have a black dress that might—"

"Clichéd, expected. Don't be."

"Really? Are you sure?"

"You look bold and confident and ready, but do yourself a favor and take the shoes off until we leave. How long do we have?"

"We've got over an hour."

"Good. Time enough for you to get me a glass of wine before I make myself beautiful."

"You're the most beautiful woman in the world. I can't tell you what it means to me that you'd come for this, for me."

"No tears." CiCi tapped a finger to Simone's nose. "Your eyes look fantastic. In fact, I'm going to have you do my makeup. After wine."

After stepping out of her shoes, Simone padded over to the kitchen, chose a local red, tossed together a quick plate of cheese and bread and olives.

"I know it's not an important show," she began.

"Stop that right now—no negative vibes allowed. They're all important, and this one is especially. It's yours. It's your first European show." Opening the balcony doors, CiCi took one of the metal chairs, then the wine Simone set on the table beside her. "Salute, my treasure."

Simone clinked glasses with CiCi. "I'm grateful for the chance. I just don't want to overdo my expectations."

"Well, I can see I'm sure as hell needed here to keep you from dimming your own star. It's going to shine tonight—trust me there. You know I'm a little bit psychic. And you're going to let it shine or I'll have to kick your ass."

"I'm so glad you're here. How long can you stay?"

"I'm taking a couple of weeks to catch up with you, some friends, do some painting. It's a beautiful city," CiCi murmured, looking out at the piazza, the red-tile roofs and sun-washed stucco. "Is it your place, Simone?"

"I love it. I love the light and the people, the art. The air breathes art here.

I love the color and the history, the food, the wine. I think being here didn't just open something in me, but fed it. And who feeds body and soul better than the Italians?"

"And still?"

"And still. While it's a place I'll need to come back to, it's not mine. If you can stay three weeks, I'll fly back with you. I'm ready."

"Then I'll stay."

At the opening, Simone played her part, making conversation in Italian and English, answering questions about particular pieces. People wandered in, milled around—she knew many came for the little cups of wine.

But they came.

She greeted Francesca and Isabel when they arrived, exchanged warm hugs and kisses with the longtime couple who'd taken her under their wings when she'd arrived in Florence.

The gallery manager—a woman of fifty who made severe and sober black look spectacular—slipped up and murmured in Simone's ear.

"We have just sold your *Awakened*."

Simone opened her mouth, but nothing came out. The piece, one of the few she'd chosen to do in bronze, had involved weeks of planning and countless second guesses about the pose, the medium—and then the price the gallery set.

And now the figure of a woman half rising from a bed of flowers, one arm stretched up as if to take the sun, the hint of a smile Simone had agonized over getting exactly right, belonged to someone.

"Who— Oh God, don't tell me my grandmother bought her."

"She did not. Come and meet who did."

Her ears buzzed when she walked through the serpentine layout of the gallery to meet the businessman and his stylish wife who'd given Simone her first major sale.

Then the buzzing gave way to cheering inside as she shook hands, chatted.

She had to tell CiCi.

She worked her way through, finally found CiCi standing by a piece she'd titled *Emergence.* While she considered the bronze her most complicated and difficult piece in the show, this was her personal favorite.

Because it held her heart.

The female head and shoulders rose out of a pool, the head tipped back, the hair flowing down sleek and wet, the eyes closed, the face rapturous.

She'd done it in pale blues.

"CiCi, I . . . What's wrong?" Seeing tears in her grandmother's eyes, she rushed forward. "You're not feeling well? Do you need air? Do you need some water?"

"No. No." CiCi gripped her hand. "Step outside with me a minute, before I embarrass myself."

"Okay. Here." She slipped an arm around CiCi's waist, guided her out. "It's hot and crowded. I'm going to find you a chair."

"I'm fine. I'm fine. Jesus, don't treat me like an old lady. I just need a second."

Outside, the air smelled of flowers and food. People sat on the patio of the restaurant across the street, enjoying dinner, conversation. A woman walked by—long legs in a short skirt—with a dog on a leash.

"I knew you were talented. I knew it would be clay. I'm a little bit psychic, as you know." CiCi took the wine Simone had forgotten she held, sipped. "I could see your work moving when I visited last fall. And you've sent me pictures, videos. But they don't show it, my baby. They don't show it like this. Like seeing it. The textures, the details, the *feeling.* There's so much brilliance here, I can't begin. And you've barely started."

CiCi patted away tears. "I'm telling you this, artist to artist, so don't give me any crap when I say that your *Emergence* has to be mine. I'm buying it not because you're my granddaughter. I'm buying it because it made me weep, it touched my soul."

"It's . . . It's Tish."

"Yes, I know. And she, and you, touched my soul."

"Then it's a gift."

"No. It will *not* be a gift. You can give me something else, but not that. Now go in there and tell them it's sold before somebody buys it out from under me. I need to drink this wine and pull myself together. Hurry up!"

"I'll be right back."

When she came back, she found CiCi leaning against the wall, smiling. "I've still got it. The most charming man—not much older than you—stopped and offered to buy me a real glass of wine. We should go back in before I create a sexual disturbance."

"Now I need a minute. CiCi." She groped for her grandmother's hand. "CiCi, I've sold four pieces—five," she corrected. "Five with yours. Anna-Tereza is thrilled. I swear, I almost took a page out of your book, almost lit candles and tried to do a spell so I could sell one and not humiliate myself."

"No witchcraft for your own gain." Sipping with one hand, CiCi squeezed Simone's with the other. "It's tacky."

"Right. Dante's going to be pretty pleased, as he was the model for two of the sales."

"And the night's not over. When this part is, we're going to have ourselves one hell of a celebration. And look who's going to be raising glasses with us."

"Who—" Simone looked in the direction CiCi pointed.

She saw the woman running, short, black bob bouncing. Sneakers, a backpack.

"Mi. Oh God, Mi!"

Despite the heels, Simone sprinted to meet her.

"My flight from London was delayed. I didn't have time to change. I'm a mess. I'm here. I'm not too late."

The breathless volley of words came with hugs.

"But you had that conference. You're speaking. You—"

"I've only got tonight. I have to fly back first thing in the morning. Jeez, you look fabulous. I'm not worthy."

"Dr. Jung. My Dr. Jung." She pulled her over to CiCi, embraced them both. "This is the best night of my life."

CHAPTER NINE

In the eighteen months and three weeks Simone spent in Florence, Patricia Hobart killed three people.

Killing Hilda Barclay, who'd cradled her dying husband of forty-seven years in her arms during the attack, meant traveling to Tampa, where Hilda had moved to be closer to her daughter. But Patricia considered the time and expense worth it.

She thoroughly resented the press Hilda generated, especially after Hilda created a scholarship for underprivileged youths in her husband's name.

Underprivileged, my ass, Patricia thought. Freeloaders and assholes coddled by whiny liberal do-gooders.

Plus her target gave her ten days away from the nasty Maine winter—and her will-they-ever-just-die grandparents.

She did her research, of course, before she kissed her annoyingly long-lived grandparents goodbye, and headed off on what everyone agreed was a well-deserved vacation.

Maybe they'd both die in their sleep before she got back, and the equally detestable cat her grandmother spoiled like a baby would eat their eyeballs.

A girl had to have her dreams.

She loved Florida, and that surprised her. She loved the sun and the palm trees, the blue of the sky and the water. As she studied the view from her hotel suite—why not splurge?—and took pictures to send home, she imagined living there.

She might consider it, if it wasn't for all the old people.

And Jews.

She'd consider it anyway.

In any case, she found it ridiculously simple to stalk Hilda and case the two-bedroom bungalow she lived in—on the same block as her daughter's family.

Within three days, she concluded she had Hilda's daily routine down pat. The old bat lived a simple life. She liked to garden, had several bird feeders she kept stocked, and rode a three-wheeled bike around the neighborhood like some wrinkled toddler.

On the fourth day, with ideas of tragic gardening or biking accidents in the hopper, Patricia cruised by as Hilda filled a bird feeder built to replicate a restaurant—complete with flower-boxed windows and a sign proclaiming FOOD FOR FEATHERS.

She pulled over, patted her short black wig, adjusted her amber-lensed sunglasses, then got out of the car.

"Excuse me? Ma'am?"

Hilda, spry and wiry in her floppy-brimmed hat, turned. "Can I help you?"

"I hope this isn't too odd, but can you tell me where you got that adorable birdhouse? My mother would just love it."

"Oh." With a laugh, Hilda gestured Patricia closer. "Is she a bird lover?"

"Big-time. Gosh, it's even cuter up close. Is it one of a kind?"

"It's local work, but the shop that carries them has others like it. The Bird House."

She proceeded to give Patricia detailed directions, which Patricia dutifully tapped into her phone. "This is great."

"I think I saw you drive by yesterday."

Patricia's smile froze for a bare instant. "You probably did. My parents are just getting settled into a house a few blocks away. I'm running errands for them. They just couldn't take the winters in Saint Paul anymore."

"I hear that. I escaped the winters in Maine."

"Then you'd know," Patricia said with a laugh. "If I can find something like this, it would be a great housewarming gift for Mom."

"My favorite is in the back, so I can see it from the kitchen window. It's an English cottage."

"You're kidding me!" Inspired, Patricia lifted her hands. "My mother was raised in an English cottage in the Lake District. She moved to the States as a young teenager. An English cottage bird feeder—she'd just love that."

"They can nest in it, too. Come on back, I'll show you."

"Oh, you're so kind. If it's not too much trouble?"

"Happy to." As they walked, Hilda waved to a man who came out of the house next door. "Hi there, Pete."

"Morning, Hilda. I'm heading out on a grocery run. You need anything?"

"I'm good, thanks. Your parents will love it here," she added as they rounded the side of the house.

"I hope so. I'm going to miss them like crazy, but I hope so."

Can't kill her now, Patricia thought. Car's out front, stupid neighbor. "Oh, what a beautiful lanai. I bet you can swim year-round."

"And do," Hilda confirmed. "Every morning before breakfast."

Patricia smiled. "That's why you're in such wonderful shape."

She oohed and aahed over the ridiculous bird feeder, complimented the garden, the lanai plants and pots, and thanked the soon-to-be dead woman profusely.

She didn't follow the directions to the Bird House, but hit a Walmart for a toaster and an extension cord.

Promptly at seven-fifteen the next morning, Hilda walked out of the house, onto the lanai, shed a blue terry-cloth robe, and slipped into the pool in her simple chocolate-brown tank suit.

While she did her smooth, easy laps, Patricia stepped onto the lanai through its unlocked screen door, plugged the extension cord into the wall socket on the back of the house, and tossed the toaster into the pool.

She watched Hilda's body flop as the water flashed. Watched it float, face-down, as she unplugged the cord, used the pool net to scoop out the toaster.

They'd figure it out—probably—but why give them any help? She stuck the murder weapons into her backpack and, dressed in her running capris, a tank, and a ball cap, jogged three blocks to her rental car.

She tossed the toaster in a Dumpster behind a restaurant, dumped the extension cord a couple miles away in the parking lot of a strip mall.

That done, she stuffed her auburn wig back in her pack, went back to her hotel to enjoy a hearty room-service breakfast of a spinach omelette, turkey bacon, berries, and fresh orange juice.

She wondered who'd find Hilda floating. Her daughter? One of the grand-kids? Good neighbor Pete?

Maybe she'd keep an eye on the local papers.

But for the moment, she decided—without irony—to spend the rest of the day by the hotel pool.

Her grandparents failed to accommodate her by dying in their sleep. She settled for indulging herself with dreams of various methods of killing them. Actually killing them had to wait, but her father obliged her by getting ham-mered before getting behind the wheel of his Ford pickup.

He took a mother of two and her teenage son with him when he crossed the center line and plowed into their compact, but those were the breaks to Patricia's mind.

Now she could cross another off her list.

She'd crossed Frederick Mosebly off the list on a balmy summer night—pre-Hilda—with an explosive device she'd stuck under the driver's seat of his unlocked car.

That check mark especially pleased her as Mosebly had some minor local success with a self-published book he'd written about the DownEast Mall. And more, it was the first time she'd built a bomb.

She thought she had a knack for it.

She checked off her third for the year—had to spread them out awhile longer—by bumping into him in a crowded bar and jabbing him with a syringe of botulinum toxin. It seemed poetic as Dr. David Wu—who'd been having predinner drinks with his wife and another couple at the upscale restaurant and had been credited with having saved lives on that fateful night—was a cosmetic surgeon.

Patricia figured since he made a living (a rich one) injecting people with Botox, he could die being injected with the same basic substance.

She disposed of the syringe on the way home, and slipped quietly into the house.

For a moment, a sweet, sweet moment, she thought her prayers had been answered.

Her grandmother lay on the floor of the foyer. Moaning, so . . . still breathing, but that could be remedied.

On another moan, her grandmother turned her head. "Patti, Patti. (God, she *hated* that nickname.) Thank God. I—I fell. I hit my head. I think, oh, oh, I think I broke my hip."

Could be finished, Patricia thought. She just had to put a hand over the old bitch's mouth, pinch her nose closed, and—

"Agnes! I can't find the remote! Where did you . . ."

Her grandfather shuffled out of the first-floor master suite, brow furrowed in annoyance over his bifocals.

He saw his wife, let out a cry, and Patricia acted fast.

"Oh my God, Gram!" She lunged forward, dropped to her knees, gripped her grandmother's hand.

"I fell. I fell."

"It's all right. It's going to be all right." She yanked her phone out of her purse, hit nine-one-one. "I need an ambulance!" She rattled off the address, careful to put a good shake into her voice. "My grandmother fell. Hurry, please hurry. Grandpa, get Gram a blanket. She's shivering. Get the throw off the sofa. I think she's in shock. Hold on, Gram. I'm right here."

So the night wouldn't be a lucky twofer, Patricia thought as she gently, so gently, stroked her grandmother's cheek. But a broken hip (hopefully!) and an eighty-three-year-old woman had lots of potential.

Patricia hid her bitter disappointment when Agnes recovered. And she earned the admiration of the medical staff, the aides, and the neighbors with every performance of devoted caregiving.

She used the time to persuade her grandparents to not only give her power of attorney—the lawyers agreed—but to put her name on every account—checking, investments, the main residence, and the vacation home/investment property they owned on Cape May.

As she'd inherit her grandmother's jewelry anyway, she took some pieces now and again and converted them into cash on drives to Augusta or Bangor—and once on a weekend holiday (at the urging of the doctors)—to Bar Harbor.

She converted some of the cash into good fake identification, and used that to open a small bank account—and to rent a safe-deposit box in a bank in Rochester, New Hampshire.

Between the jewelry, the regular skimming, the sale of the vacation home her grandparents were too stupid to know they signed off on, she had more than three million dollars in the box, along with four fake IDs, including passports and credit cards.

She kept a cool hundred thousand in cash with other essentials in a run-for-the-hills bag in the top of her closet, and had started a second bag.

As neither of her grandparents used the steps any longer, she had the entire second floor to herself. She installed police locks on her master suite, and the guest suite she used as a workshop.

If the weekly housekeeper found it odd the second floor was off-limits, she said nothing. She was paid well, and it meant less work.

As the next anniversary of the DownEast Mall approached, Patricia made plans. Lots of plans.

And crossed a couple more off the list.

Seleena McMullen rode the approach to July 22 on her blog and on her talk show. It gave her a chance to hype the updated edition of her book.

She didn't quibble over the fact that the tragedy had made her career. As a matter of routine, every time a lunatic shot up a public place, she served as a talking head on cable TV.

She did the circuit every couple of years and raked in decent speaking fees. She'd copped a gig as executive producer on a well-received documentary about the shooting and, when things were really cooking, snagged a small guest shot on *Law & Order: SVU.*

It ebbed and flowed, she could admit that; every anniversary she pumped it up, and she'd be front and center.

She had staff, an agent, a hot boyfriend—after a brief marriage and a messy divorce. Still, the divorce and the hot boyfriend had bumped up the ratings and clicks.

They'd go through the roof with the lineup she had for the anniversary week.

She had the cop who'd taken out Hobart. Admittedly, Seleena had to pressure the mayor to pressure the cop's captain to pressure the cop, but she had her. She couldn't get the once teenage hero, now the cop's partner, and that stuck in her throat.

Portland PD had given her a choice, one or the other, not both. She'd gone with the female cop, the first on scene, and let the other go.

She had a woman who'd been in the theater and nearly died—and lived with facial scarring and brain trauma. She'd booked the geek who'd saved a store full of people by barricading them in a back room, some other victims, an EMT, one of the ER doctors from that night.

But the shining jewel? The sister of the shooter, the baby sister of the ringleader.

She had Patricia Jane Hobart.

Even with that, and that was huge as Hobart's sister had never, to date, given a formal interview, Seleena stalked around her office fuming.

She wanted the damn hat trick. The cop, Hobart's sister, *and* Simone Knox—the nine-one-one caller who'd first alerted the police so McVee took Hobart out.

The bitch wouldn't even take her calls. Had actually had some asshole lawyer send her a cease and desist when she'd tracked Simone down at an art gallery in New York.

A public event, Seleena thought now. And she'd had a perfect—First fucking Amendment right—to stick a mic in her face.

She didn't appreciate being kicked out of the gallery for doing her *job*.

She'd written a blistering editorial on the treatment she'd received, and on the bitch herself. And would have printed it, too, if her ex—before he found out about the boyfriend and became her ex—hadn't convinced her it would make her look like the bitch.

She hated knowing he'd had that right.

Well, she could play that nine-one-one call, and would. She could toss Simone Knox's name around and maybe insinuate that, as a somewhat celebrated artist, Miss Knox no longer wanted an association with the tragedy of DownEast Mall.

"Work on that," she murmured. "Work on how to say it. Throwing shade at her, but keeping the high road, the sympathy road."

She wrenched open her door, shouted: "Marlie! Where the hell is my macchiato?"

"Luca should be back with it any minute."

"For Christ's sake. Find out where Simone Knox is, and where she's going to be next week."

"Oh, Ms. McMullen, the lawyer—"

Seleena whirled around, making the mousy Marlie jump back a step. "Did I ask you what the fuck? Just find out. I want to know where she is when I interview Patricia Hobart and the cop who killed her brother. And I want then and now pictures of her. Move your ass, Marlie."

Seleena slapped the door closed.

"We'll see who wins this round," she muttered.

Simone won. She spent the weeks surrounding the anniversary traveling in Arizona, New Mexico, Nevada. She did sketches, took photos of the desert, the canyons, the people, imagined translating those colors, textures, shapes, those faces and forms, into art with clay.

She basked in the solitude, reveled in exploring a land as different to her eye from the east coast of Maine as Mars was from Venus. With no one to answer to but her own whims, she stopped when and where she liked, stayed as long as it suited her.

When she finally headed east, she detoured north through Wyoming, into Montana, where she bought more sketchbooks, and gave in to an impulse for cowboy boots.

By the time she crossed the Maine border, the calendar had flipped to August, and despite the constant use of sunblock and a hat, she was tanned, her hair sunstreaked.

And her mood high and happy.

She wanted to get to work, to sort through the hundreds of sketches and photos, the ideas and visions. She wanted to feel clay under her hands.

She considered texting CiCi, then decided to surprise her instead. After a stop for a bottle of champagne—hell, make it two—she planned to drive straight to the ferry.

But a twinge of guilt had her changing directions. She'd just stop off at her parents' house. A quick courtesy call.

Maybe her relationship with her parents, and her sister, remained strained, but she couldn't claim to be blameless. Since the day she'd walked out of her childhood home to pursue her own dreams, she mostly kept out of their way.

It saved arguing.

But avoidance meant traditions like Christmases, birthdays, weddings, funerals became stilted demilitarized zones—or battlefields.

Why not make an effort? she told herself. Stop by on a pretty Saturday afternoon, touch base, maybe have a drink, admire the garden, pull out a few anecdotes from her travels.

How sad and pitiful was it that she needed to outline an agenda to visit her own parents?

So she wouldn't. She would handle it just as she had her travels. She'd play it by ear.

Somebody's having a big summer party, she thought, noting the cars parked along the street. When she saw a line of them in her parents' long U of a driveway, more jockeyed into the service area, she realized she'd been about to crash a party.

Not the best time for a drop-in, she decided, but hesitated just long enough for one of the valets to block her quick exit. As she waited for the road to clear, to make her escape, Natalie and a couple of women in equally elegant garden-party dresses crossed the lush green of the front lawn.

Appalled that her first instinct was to duck down, she forced a smile on her face when Natalie spotted her.

Her sister didn't smile, but tipped her glamour-girl sunglasses down to peer over them. And that, for Simone, was that.

Deliberately, she pushed open the car door and climbed out in her traveling outfit of Army-green cargo shorts, red cowboy boots, a wide-brimmed straw hat, and a novelty tank that read: RED, WINE AND BLUE.

"Hey, Nat."

Natalie said something to her companions that had one of the women patting her arm before they wandered off—not without long, backward glances that clearly transmitted disapproval.

Natalie crossed to the sidewalk.

She looks like Mom, Simone thought, a perfect example of the polished female.

"Simone. We weren't expecting you."

"Obviously. I just got back. I thought I'd stop in to say hi."

"It's not the best time."

Simone didn't miss the tone—one used for an acquaintance you had to tolerate occasionally.

"Also obviously. You can tell them I'm back, and I'll be at CiCi's. I'll give them a call."

"That would be novel."

"Last I checked, phones work two ways. Anyway, you look great."

"Thanks. I'll let Mom and Dad know you—"

"Natalie!"

The man who crossed the lawn in the palest of pale gray loafers to match his crisp linen slacks boasted the charm of dimples in a Hollywood handsome face. His elegance—the white shirt topped with a navy blazer, the sundashed gold of wavy hair—matched Natalie's perfectly.

Though she knew him a little, it took Simone a minute to come up with his name. Harry (Harrison) Brookefield, one of the young guns in her father's law firm.

And, according to CiCi, Natalie's parentally approved boyfriend.

"There you are. I was just— Simone?" Dimples flashing, he held out a hand to shake hers. "I didn't know you were here. This is great. How long have you been back?"

"About five minutes."

"Then I bet you could use a drink." He'd slipped an arm around Natalie's waist as he spoke—and, to Simone's mind, hadn't yet clued in on her stiffness. Then he reached out again for Simone's hand.

"Oh, thanks, but I'm not dressed for a party. I'm just going to go—"

"Don't be silly." Harry took a good grip on her hand. "Keys in the car?"

"Yes, but—"

"Great." He signaled to the valet. "Family vehicle."

"Really, Harry, Simone's got to be tired after the drive."

"All the more reason she needs that drink." Like a carpenter's plane wrapped in velvet, he smoothed right over the rough bark. "Now you've got your whole family here to celebrate, sweets."

The man had a grip and a will like iron, Simone thought, but the main reason she allowed him to pull her along—however petty—was Natalie's blatant discomfort.

"What are we celebrating?"

"You didn't tell her? Good Lord, Natalie." Harry looked at Simone, added a wink. "She said yes."

Simone felt her brain empty out for three solid seconds. "You're engaged. To be married?"

"Which makes me the luckiest man in the world."

She heard music now, and voices, as they started up the walk that would wind through the side garden to the backyard.

"Congratulations."

How had it happened? she wondered. How had it happened that the sister who'd once slipped into her bed to whisper secrets hadn't shared such vital, life-changing news? Such happy news that rated a party with elegant dresses and white tablecloths decked with white flowers, with uniformed servers carrying trays of drinks and pretty finger foods.

"This is wonderful. Exciting."

You're still so young, and so . . . pampered, Simone thought. Are you sure? Would you tell me?

Harry stopped a server, took three flutes of champagne. "To the wonderful and exciting," he said after he passed them around.

"Absolutely. So have you set a date?"

"October—a year from this October," Natalie said.

"I couldn't talk her into the spring. I'll wait. If you'll excuse me a minute, I want to find my mother. She'd love to meet you, Simone. She's especially admired the statue of Natalie, holding the scales of justice, you made her when she graduated law school. I'll be right back."

"You're engaged. God, Nat, engaged! He's gorgeous, and he seems like a terrific guy. I—"

"If you'd bothered to get to know him over the last two years, you'd know he *is* terrific."

"I'm happy for you," Simone said carefully. "He's obviously crazy about you, and I'm happy for you. If I'd known about the party, I'd've come home sooner, and I'd have dressed appropriately. I'm going to leave, slip out before I embarrass you."

"Simone!" CiCi's cheerful shout cut through the music and conversations.

"Too late," Natalie stated as their grandmother rushed across the patio, gypsy skirts flying.

"There's my traveling girl!" She caught Simone in a fierce hug. "Look at you, all toned and tanned. Isn't this a kick in the ass?" She caught Natalie into the hug. "Our baby girl's hooked herself a fiancé. And he is *yum-mee*."

She let out one of her big, beautiful laughs, squeezed them both. "Let's drink ourselves a shit ton of champagne."

"Mother."

"Uh-oh." Snickering, CiCi drew back. "Busted." She shifted, hooked arms around her granddaughters' waists, and grinned at her daughter. "Look who's here, Tule."

"So I see. Simone." Lovely in silk shantung the color of crushed rose petals, Tulip leaned in to kiss Simone's cheek. "We didn't know you were back."

"I just got back."

"That explains it." With her company smile seamless, her eyes sparking annoyance, Tulip turned to Natalie. "Sweetheart, why don't you take your sister upstairs so she can freshen up? I'm sure you have something you can lend her to wear."

"Don't be such a buzzkill, Tulip."

Tulip simply turned those sparking eyes on her mother. "This is Natalie's day. I won't have it spoiled."

"I won't spoil it. I won't stay." Simone handed her flute to Natalie. "Tell Harry I wasn't feeling well."

"I'll come with you," CiCi began.

"No. It's Natalie's day, and you should be here. I'll see you later."

"That was a dick move, Tulip," CiCi said when Simone walked away. "And from the look on your face, Nat? Apple, tree. I'm ashamed of both of you."

Simone had to hunt down the valet who'd parked her car, then wait while he retrieved her keys.

While she waited, her father strode briskly down the walkway.

Oh well, she thought, what was one more elbow in the gut?

Instead, he put his arms around her, drew her close. "Welcome home."

The snipes and jabs hadn't filled her throat with tears, but his gesture did.

"Thanks."

"I only just heard you'd gotten back, then that you'd left. You need to come back out, honey. It's a big day for Natalie."

"That's why I'm leaving. She doesn't want me here."

"That's nonsense."

"She made it clear. My unexpected arrival, in attire inappropriate for the occasion, embarrassed your wife and daughter."

"You could have come home a bit earlier, worn the appropriate."

"I would have if I'd known."

"Natalie contacted you two weeks ago," he began, then saw her face. Sighed. "I see. I'm sorry. I'm sorry, she indicated she had, otherwise, I'd have contacted you myself. Come back with me. I'll have a word with her."

"No, don't, please. She doesn't want me here, and I don't want to be here." Sorrow clouded Ward's eyes. "It hurts me to hear you say that."

"I'm sorry. I wanted to come by, see you and Mom, to try to . . . turn some of it around. Some of it. I had a good summer. Productive, satisfying, illuminating. I wanted to tell you about it. And maybe you'd see I did the right thing, for me. Maybe you'd see that."

"I have seen it," he said quietly. "I've seen I was wrong. I clung to wanting to be right, and lost you. And losing you, it was easier to blame you than myself. Now my younger daughter's going to be married. She'll be a wife, and not just my little girl. It struck me that, with you, I wanted to be right more than I wanted you to be happy. It shames me to look that square in the face, but I have. I hope you'll forgive me."

"Daddy." She went into his arms, wept a little. "It's my fault, too. It was easier to pull back, to stay away."

"Let's agree. I accept I'm not always right, and you don't pull away from me." She nodded, rested her cheek on his chest. "It's a good homecoming after all."

"Come on back to the party. Be my date."

"I can't. Honestly, Nat bugs the crap out of me, but I don't want to spoil her party. Maybe you could come out to the island sometime, and I'll tell you about the trip, and show you some things I'm working on."

"All right." He kissed her forehead. "I'm glad you're back."

"So am I."

Glad to be back, she thought, especially when she stood at the rail of the ferry and watched the island come closer.

CHAPTER TEN

CiCi's house offered views of the bay, the ocean beyond, and the tumbled coastline of Tranquility Island, including the jut of rocky land on the far eastern point where the lighthouse perched.

When CiCi first settled on the island, the lighthouse had been a stark, uninspired white.

She'd fixed that.

Lobbying with the artists community, she'd convinced the island council, as well as the business and property owners, to kick things up. There had been doubters, of course, at the idea of a group of artists on ladders and scaffolds painting the slender lighthouse with sea flowers, shells, mermaids, sea fans, and coral.

But she'd been right.

Since its completion—and even during the work—tourists came to snap pictures, and other artists featured the now unique lighthouse in their seascapes. It was a rare visitor who left the island without one or more of the Light of Tranquility souvenirs sold in any number of village and beachside shops.

Every few years, the community refreshed the paint—and often added another flourish or two.

CiCi enjoyed looking down the coast, admiring that spear of color and creativity.

Her home stood west of the light, on a rise above another jut of the uneven coast. Big windows, stone terraces, graced its two stories—plus the converted attic with its little balcony, which made three. A generous patio skirted the water side, her favorite side, where in season she had dramatic pots of flowers and herbs soaking in the sun along with oversize chairs with brightly colored cushions and some painted tables.

More flowers and comfortable seating ranged along the wide terrace on the second floor. It also held a hot tub, which she used year-round, under a pergola where she often lounged—happily naked—with a glass of wine while watching the water and the boats that plied it.

She could enter her studio with its bay-facing wall of glass—designed and added after she'd bought the house—from the great room or the patio. She loved painting there when the water gleamed blue as a jewel, or when it went icy gray and thrashing in the grip of a winter storm.

She'd converted the attic—or Jasper Mink (who'd warmed her bed a time or two between his marriages) and his crew had converted it when Simone had gone to Italy.

It offered lovely light, plenty of space, and now had a charming little powder room.

As she liked to say, CiCi was a little bit psychic. She'd imagined Simone working in that space, staying in the rambling house until she found her place.

CiCi, a little bit psychic, had no doubt where that place was, but the girl had to find it for herself.

Meanwhile, whenever Simone came back to Maine, she always came back to CiCi.

Despite two artistic temperaments, they lived together easily. Each had their own work and their own habits, and they might go for days barely seeing each other. Or they might spend hours sitting together on the patio, biking into the village, walking the narrow strip of sand by the water, or just sitting on the coastline rocks in comfortable silence.

After Simone returned from the west, they spent hours with CiCi looking through Simone's photos and sketches. CiCi borrowed a couple of the photos—a street fair in Santa Fe, a stark shot of buttes in Canyon de Chelly—to use in her own work.

When Ward came to visit, CiCi slipped away to light candles and incense and meditate, pleased father and daughter were making an effort to reconcile.

For ten days, while the summer people thronged the island, they lived happily enough in their own world, with their art, the water, and cocktails at sunset.

Then the storm came.

Natalie whirled into the house like a force of nature. CiCi, still on her first cup of coffee (she still preferred seeing a sunrise as the last thing before bed instead of the first out of it), blinked owlishly.

"Hi, honey. What flew up your ass?"

"Where is she?"

"I'd offer you coffee, but you seem pretty hyped already. Why don't you sit down, catch your breath, my cutie?"

"I don't want to sit down. *Simone!* Goddamn it!" She shouted, raging as she stormed through the house, swirling negative energy CiCi already accepted she'd have to white sage away. "Is she upstairs?"

"I wouldn't know," CiCi said coolly. "I just got up. And while I'm all for self-expression, you're going to want to watch your tone with me."

"I'm sick of it, sick of all of it. She can do whatever she wants, whenever she wants, and you're just fine with it. I work my butt off, I graduate in the top five percent of my class—top *five*—and the two of you can hardly be bothered to show up."

Sincerely stunned, CiCi lowered her coffee mug. "Have you lost your mind? We were both there, with fucking bells on, young lady. And I can't believe you just pissed me into saying 'young lady.' I sounded like my *mother*! Simone worked weeks on your gift, and—"

"Simone, Simone, Si-fucking-mone."

"Now you're the X-rated Jan Brady. Get a grip, Natalie."

"What's going on?" Simone came in, in a fast trot. "I could hear you yelling all the way up in my studio."

"Your studio. Yours, your, you!" Natalie whirled, shoved Simone three steps back.

"Hold it!" Stepping forward, CiCi snapped out the order. "There will be no physical violence in my house. Shouting, foul language, fine, but no physical violence. Don't cross my lines."

"What the hell, Natalie?" Shifting, Simone laid a hand on CiCi's shoulder.

"Look at you! Always the two of you." Face bright pink with fury, blue eyes molten with it, Natalie jabbed out with a finger from each hand. "I'm sick of that, too. It's not right, it's not fair that you love her more than me."

"First, there's no 'fair' about love. And second, I love you just as much, even when you're being a crazy person. In fact, I might love you more when you're being a crazy person. It's an interesting change of pace."

"Just stop it." Tears spurted, hot with rage. "It's always been her. She's always been your favorite."

"If you're going to accuse me of things, be specific, because I can't remember ever slighting you."

"You didn't convert an attic for me."

Close to fed up, CiCi gulped down coffee. It didn't help. "Did you want me to?"

"That's not the point!"

"It is the goddamn point. I didn't take Simone to D.C. after her high school graduation and arrange for tours of Congress because she didn't want me to. You did, so I did. Get over yourself."

"I can't even come out here anymore because she lives here."

"That's on you, and it sure looks like you're here now. And one more thing before I trade this coffee in for the Bloody Mary I now crave, Simone can and will live here as long as she wants. It's not up to you who lives in my fucking house. If you wanted to move in, you'd be welcome, but it's not what you want."

CiCi went to the refrigerator. "Anybody else want a Bloody Mary?"

"As a matter of fact," Simone began.

"There it is." Natalie sneered. "Just like Mom says. Two peas in a snarky pod."

"So what?" Simone threw up her hands. "So we have things in common. You and Mom have things in common. So what?"

"You have no respect for my mother."

"*Our* mother, Nat the Brat, and I certainly do."

"Bull. You barely spend any time with her. You didn't even bother to spend any with her on Mother's Day."

"I was in New Mexico, for God's sake, Nat. I called her, I sent flowers."

Natalie's eyes, the same searing blue as their mother's, burned. "Do you think that means anything? Clicking on some flowers on the Internet?"

Simone angled her head. "You should tell Mom and Dad that, since that's what they've done for every one of my openings."

"That's different, and don't try to shift the blame. You don't care about her, or any of us, whatever you've convinced Dad to think. They've been arguing because of you. Because of you, Harry and I had a terrible fight on the night of our engagement party."

"Jesus Christ. Don't spare the vodka," Simone told CiCi.

"Believe me."

"The two of you," Natalie spat out. "All smug out here in your alternate reality. Well, I live in the *real* world. A world you barged into, uninvited, looking like something that just stumbled off the trail. But you managed to play up to Harry and Dad, didn't you, playing the victim."

"I didn't play up to anyone, or play anything. Maybe if you hadn't lied to both of them about contacting me, you wouldn't have had a problem."

"I didn't want you there!"

It ripped, ripped a jagged hole in Simone even though she already knew. "Clearly. But you weren't honest about it, and that's not on me."

"You're selfish, hateful, and don't care about anyone but yourself."

"I might be selfish by your gauge, but I don't have a lot of hate. And if I didn't care about anyone, I wouldn't have stopped off at Mom's and Dad's and ended up embarrassing both of us. You, on the other hand, you nasty little bitch, are a liar and a coward, and in your real world you don't take responsibility for being either. Fuck that, Natalie, and you along with it. I'm not going to be your punching bag or Mom's."

Though her heart thudded, and her hands wanted to shake, Simone picked up the drink CiCi had set on the counter, lifted it in a nasty toasting gesture. "Enjoy your version of reality, Nat. I'll stick with mine."

Tears, fired by rage, fumed in Natalie's eyes. "You disgust me. Do you know that?"

"I'm fairly astute, so yeah, I picked up on that."

"Okay, girls." CiCi stepped in. "That's enough now."

"You always take her side, don't you?"

Her own heart aching, CiCi forced herself to speak calm and clear. "I've been working hard over here not to take any side, but you're pushing it, Natalie. Now, you've blown off considerable steam, so—"

"I don't mean anything to either of you. You've turned her against me, too," she shouted at Simone. "I hate you. You're welcome to each other."

She turned to storm out, and blind and bitter, shoved the statue of *Emergence* from the stand CiCi had had made for it. Even as Simone cried out in grief, it fell, smashed to the floor. The lovely, serene face, that birth of joy, the face of a lost friend, broke into four pieces.

"Oh God, oh God." The sound, the sight of the destruction slapped Natalie's rage into horrified shock. "I'm sorry. Oh, Simone, I'm so sorry. I didn't mean—"

"You get out." Simone could barely whisper the words over the wound so deep it screamed inside her. She managed to put the drink in her hand down before she heaved it, because she knew if she struck out, she might never stop.

"Simone, CiCi, I'm so, so sorry. I can't—"

As Natalie stepped forward, hand out, Simone's head snapped up.

"Don't come near me. Don't. Get out. Get out!" With rage and grief choking her, Simone rushed out the back doors before she used fists instead of words.

Sobbing, Natalie covered her face with her hands. "I'm sorry. I'm sorry. CiCi, I didn't mean to."

"You did mean to. You meant to hurt her, and me. Sorry's not going to be enough this time."

When Natalie collapsed into her arms, CiCi patted her back for a moment, but then turned and steered her toward the front door. "You need to go, and you need to figure out why you'd do what you've done, why you said what you said, feel what you feel. And you have to figure out how to make amends."

"I'm sorry. Please."

"I'm sure you're sorry, but you destroyed a piece of your sister with a temper tantrum. You broke her heart, and mine."

"Don't hate me." As CiCi opened the door, Natalie clung to her. "She hates me. Don't hate me."

"I don't hate you, and neither does she. I hate the words I heard coming out of your mouth. I hate what you did because you wanted to hurt us both. And I hate having to say to my own grandchild—and I love you, Natalie—but you can't come back here until you face what you did, until you find a way to make those amends."

"She does hate me. She—"

"You stop." Snapping it out, CiCi pushed Natalie away. "You stop and look inside yourself instead of trying to put things inside someone you refuse to even try to understand. I love you, Natalie, but at this moment, I sure as hell don't like you. Go home."

It shattered another piece of her heart, but CiCi shut the door of her home in her granddaughter's face.

And leaning back against the door, staring at the beauty, the grace, the joy so recklessly destroyed, she let her own tears come.

Accepting them, she went to her other grandchild.

Simone sat on the patio stones, knees hugged tight to her chest, her face pressed against her knees as she sobbed. CiCi lowered to the patio floor, enfolded her, rocking until they'd both cried themselves out.

"How could she do that? How could she hate me that much?"

"She doesn't hate you. She's jealous and angry and, God, disdainful. She's her mother's daughter there. But I know, I do, Tulip would never have wanted this. You don't fit the mold, my darling girl, so they see that as an insult. We embarrass them, and that embarrassment makes them feel small, so they retreat into that disdain."

With her arm around Simone, Simone's head on her shoulder, CiCi looked out to the water, the deep blues and hints of green, the frisk of its slap against rock.

"I could take some of the blame, but what's the point?" CiCi considered. "I did the best I could. Tulip was a happy kid, and then my mother . . . Well, she's not to blame, either. We're who we are, and who we choose to be."

Gently, CiCi stroked Simone's hair. "She's devastated, baby. She's so sorry."

"Don't, don't, don't take up for her."

"Oh, I'm not. She struck out at me, too, and she had no right. It's long past time for her to deal with her inner toddler, to stop blaming you, me, or whatever the hell for her own issues. If she accepts what she did, does whatever she can to make up for it, it could be a turning point for her."

"I don't care."

"I know. I don't blame you. Families fuck up. Hell, families are fucked-up half the time. But fucked-up or not, she's always going to be your sister, always going to be my granddaughter. Forgiveness won't come easy for either of us, and it shouldn't. She'll have to earn it."

"I don't know if I can fix it. It's Tish, and I don't know if I can fix it. I don't know if I have it in me to try. And if I do, if I can, it wouldn't be the same."

"You'll fix it." CiCi turned to kiss the top of Simone's head. "You have it in you. No, it won't be the same. It will say something else, something more. Here's what we're going to do. We're going to go in, pick up the pieces, assess the damage. We'll take it up to your studio, and when you're ready, you'll start work on repairing it. In the meantime, we're going to white sage the house and banish all that negative energy."

"Okay, but can we just sit here a little longer?"

"Let's do that."

Harry came home from a round of golf feeling pumped. He'd knocked a couple strokes off his previous personal best to start what he had decided would be an excellent day.

He had an hour before he was due to pick up Natalie for lunch with friends, then he intended to surprise his bride-to-be with an early evening showing at a house he thought might suit them both.

A house, *their* house, equaled the next stage. Something they'd find and buy and outfit and *finally* live in together.

The lady wanted a fall wedding, he'd wait. She wanted a big, formal wedding, he got on board the train. But he wanted that next stage.

He let himself into his apartment, set his golf clubs by the door. Then he spotted Natalie curled on his living room sofa. His already bright mood went brighter still.

"Hey, sweets. I didn't—" Then he saw the tears, the ravaged face as her arms reached for him. "What's wrong? What happened?"

As he gathered her up, she broke into fresh sobs.

"Oh Jesus, is it your parents? Your grandmother?"

She shook her head fiercely. "Oh, Harry. I did something terrible."

"That's hard to believe. Shh, don't cry." He dug out a handkerchief—his mother had trained him to carry one at all times—dabbed at her face. "Did you rob a bank? Kick a puppy?"

"I went to see Simone."

"Okay. I'm guessing that didn't go well."

"She hates me, Harry. CiCi hates me, too."

"They don't."

"You don't *know*. You don't understand. Simone's always been CiCi's favorite. She dotes on her—peas in a pod, just like Mom says—and I get whatever's left."

"If that's true, there must be a lot left because every time I've seen you with your grandmother I've seen how much she loves you, how proud she is of you. I don't see any hate."

"They do hate me. If they didn't before, they do now after what happened."

"What happened?"

"I didn't mean to do it." Gripping his shirt, she burrowed against him. "I was just so mad, and Simone was saying awful, awful things to me. And CiCi's making them goddamn Bloody Marys, and I could just *feel* her laughing at me. I just lost my temper."

"God, Natalie, you didn't hit your sister, did you?"

"No! I just . . . I just lost my temper, and I pushed it over, and it broke. I didn't mean to do it, and I was so sorry, but they wouldn't listen."

"Pushed what?"

"The statue. The bust of the woman." Sick all over again, Natalie pressed the heels of her hands to her eyes. "Simone's statue from that damn show in Florence. CiCi bought it, was always showing it off. I just shoved it, and it fell, and it broke. And after, like a second after, it was like someone else had done it. I was so shocked and sorry, and I tried to tell them. They wouldn't listen."

"The woman coming out of the pool?" He'd seen it, admired it. "The one in CiCi's great room?"

"Yes, yes, yes. I just lost my temper. They—they ganged up on me, and I lost my temper, and then they wouldn't let me apologize."

He pushed off the sofa to walk to the window. He could see the piece in his head, remembered that when he'd admired it how CiCi had told him about the show, about how she'd felt when she'd seen it.

"Natalie, you knew what that piece meant to your grandmother, and to your sister."

"It was just there, and I didn't mean it."

He came back, sat again, took her hand. "Natalie, I know you, and I know you're not telling me the whole story."

"You're taking her side." She tried to pull her hand free, but he held tight.

"I'm listening to your side, but don't shade the truth."

"I didn't come here to fight with you. I didn't come here to fight with you over Simone. Again."

"We didn't fight over Simone. We fought because you hadn't told me the truth. You'd told me your sister couldn't make it home for the party. That she was too busy. You let me think you'd told her and she'd said she couldn't come."

"She was out west somewhere, so I assumed—"

"We're lawyers," he interrupted. "We both know how to use half-truths and semantics. Don't use them on me. What happened today?"

Genuinely terrified, she gripped his shirt again. "Don't turn on me, Harry. I couldn't stand it if you turned on me."

Now he cupped her face with his hands. "That's never going to happen. But we're going to be straight with each other. Honest with each other."

"My parents . . . My mother's upset because my father's gone over to the island twice since the party."

"Your mother's upset because your father's spent some time with your sister?"

"You don't understand! You don't understand. Simone's just full of disdain where my mother's concerned, and she's ungrateful. After all they did for her, she dropped out of college, ran off to Europe."

He'd heard all this before, and tried to be patient. "Which sounds like it was the right decision for her. And if there's an issue, it's between your mother and your sister. It's not your issue, Natalie."

"I love my mother."

"Of course you do. So do I." He smiled, kissed her lightly. "Peas in a pod. Did you go to see her to talk or to fight?"

"I'm a lawyer," she tossed back. "I went to talk, and then she . . ."

His gaze held hers, patiently. Love for him tangled up with guilt. "That's not true. It was when I left home, but by the time I got to the island, to CiCi's, I was furious. I started it. I started it. Oh God, Harry, I'm a terrible person."

"Don't say that about the woman I love." He gathered her up for a minute, loving her as much for her flaws as for her perfection. Just loving her. "Sit for a minute, sweets. I'm going to cancel our lunch plans." And the showing, he thought.

"I forgot. I forgot all about it."

"We'll reschedule. Then I'm going to pour us both some wine, and you're going to talk this through with me. We'll figure it out, sweets."

"I love you, Harry. I really love you." She clung to him, a port in a storm. "You're the best thing that ever happened to me."

"Right back at you."

"I want it to be all her fault. I want to stay mad at her. It's easier."

"I'm looking at your beautiful face, and those tears. So I don't think it's easier."

CiCi set up her easel on the patio. Summer would fade before she knew it, so she counted every day of it as precious. She wouldn't paint the view, but would continue to work on the study from one of Simone's photos.

The woman in the red hat—the wide, flat brim over a face lined with time and sun—perusing a bin of tomatoes at a street fair, with the wizened old man in the stall smiling at her.

In her version the tomatoes became magic eggs, bold as jewels, and the bird perched on the striped awning a winged dragon.

She'd played with the tones, the feel, the message for a week. Just as Simone had spent the week in focused, meticulous repair of the bust.

CiCi wished them both blessings on their work, lit a candle for each of them, and began to mix paints.

She called out a "Come in!" at the ring of her doorbell. She rarely locked the door—and this was one good reason. Whoever came calling could just come in rather than making her stop and go answer.

"I'm out here."

"CiCi."

Unsure whether to be relieved or wary at the sound of Natalie's voice, CiCi set aside her paints, turned.

The girl looked penitent, she decided. And full of nerves with her hand gripping the boy CiCi thought of as Handsome Harry.

"Since you've always been a rule-follower, I'm going to believe you've decided to take responsibility, and figured out how to make amends."

"I'm taking responsibility. I'm going to try to make amends. I don't know if I can, but I want to try. I'm so ashamed, CiCi, for what I said that day, for what I did. There are a lot of things I need to say to Simone, and I hope she'll listen. But I need to tell you I knew how much that piece meant to you. I knew it represented a bond between you and Simone. I broke it because I don't share that bond. And that's unforgivable."

"I decide what I can forgive."

"I think making amends to you starts with trying to make them to Simone. To try to do that, I have to say things to her."

"Then you should do that. She's up in her studio."

With a nod, Natalie released Harry's hand. "You've never been anything but wonderful to me, and I'm ashamed of what I said to you. You've never once let me down, ever, even when I deserved it."

"Long walk for her," CiCi murmured when Natalie went inside.

"Yeah, it is. We interrupted your work. I can wait out—"

"Don't be silly. I can't work wondering if I'll hear screaming, shouting, and cursing. Let's have a beer."

"I could use one."

CiCi stepped up to the doorway, reached up to pat his cheek. "You're good for her, Harry. I wasn't sure of it, but you're good for her."

"I love her."

"Love's the glue. Use it right, it can fix most anything."

Simone used glue, metal pins, sandpaper, paints. After a week of intense work, she began to believe she could bring Tish back. She could bring the life back into the face.

She heard the footsteps as she pushed back to study the morning's progress.

"Come see. I think . . . I think maybe."

Then she looked up, saw Natalie. Slowly, she got to her feet. "You're not welcome here."

"I know. I'm asking for five minutes. Please. There's nothing . . . Oh God! You fixed it."

"Don't you dare."

Natalie stopped her rush forward to the worktable, gripped her hands behind her back. "There's nothing you can say to me I don't deserve. Being sorry, ashamed, disgusted with myself isn't enough. Knowing you've fixed what I tried to ruin doesn't let me off the hook."

"She isn't fixed."

"But it—she . . . She's so beautiful, Simone. I resented that, resented what you can create out of freaking mud. I'm ashamed of that, I can't even explain how ashamed. I didn't tell you about the engagement, the party, because I didn't want you to come. I told myself you wouldn't anyway. It wouldn't matter to you. I was only going to have you in the wedding party because people would think poorly of me otherwise. I let myself think and feel terrible things about you."

"Why?"

"You left me. It felt like you left me. After the mall—" She broke off when Simone's face went blank, when she turned away. "Like that. You wouldn't talk about it with me."

"I talked about it in therapy. I talked about it to the police. Over and over."

"You wouldn't talk to *me*, and I needed my big sister. I was so scared. I'd wake up screaming, but you—"

"I had nightmares, Nat. Cold sweats, gasping for air. No screams, so Mom didn't rush in, but I had nightmares."

Staring, Natalie brushed tears from her cheek. "You never said."

"I didn't want to talk about it then. I don't want to talk about it now. I put it away."

"You put me away."

"Oh, bullshit." Simone whirled back. "Bullshit."

"It's not. It doesn't feel like bullshit, Simone, not to me. Before, you included me. It was you and Mi and Tish, but you included me. They were my friends, too. After, you shut me out. It was just you and Mi."

"Jesus Christ! Tish died. Mi was in the hospital for weeks."

"I know, I know. I was fourteen, Sim. Please, God. Have some pity. I thought she was dead. When I dragged Mom behind that counter, I thought she was dead. I thought you were dead. Then you weren't, and I kept dreaming you were. Everybody but me. Tish was my friend, too. And Mi. And all I saw was me being replaced as a sister. I know how stupid and selfish that sounds. The two of you came here when Mi got out of the hospital. To CiCi. And all I could think was Why did they leave me behind?"

"She needed me, and I needed—"

Natalie hadn't been hurt, Simone thought. But of course, she had. Of course she had.

"I didn't think," Simone managed. "I didn't think of it as leaving you out or behind. I just needed to get away from it. The reporters, the police, the talk, the looks. I was sixteen, Natalie. And broken inside."

"It was always Mi after that. You had each other. I was broken, too."

"I'm sorry." Simone dropped back on her stool, rubbed her hands over her face. "I'm sorry. I didn't see it. Maybe I didn't want to see it. You had Mom and Dad, CiCi, friends of your own. You got so involved in school, in projects."

"It helped me stop thinking. It helped stop the nightmares. But I wanted you, Simone. I was too mad to tell you. Not mad," she corrected. "More sorry for myself. Then you went to New York, to college. With Mi. You started dying your hair weird colors, wearing clothes Mom just hated. So I hated them, too. I wanted my sister back, but I wanted you back the way I wanted you. You weren't the way I wanted you, or I thought you should be. Then you sort of were, and . . . I didn't like you."

Finally, Natalie sat, let out a breath that ended with a baffled laugh. "I just realized that. I didn't like the Simone who wore business suits and dated that—what was his name?"

"Gerald Worth, the freaking Fourth."

"Oh yeah." Natalie sniffled. "He was kind of a jerk, but he didn't mean to be. I didn't like you that way, or the other way because you weren't the big sister I had before the world changed for us. Then you dropped out of college and went back to New York, then you went off to Italy, and I didn't know who the hell you were. You hardly came home."

"The welcome wasn't exactly warm there."

"You don't put much effort into it, either."

"Maybe not," Simone replied. "Maybe not."

"Everything I said last week, I felt. I believed. I was wrong, but I felt it, sincerely. I was wrong to expect you to, I don't know, freeze in place from before, when we all changed that night. I was so, so wrong to say those things to CiCi, who's the most loving and amazing person in the world, and I'll never stop being ashamed of that."

"She wouldn't want you to be ashamed forever."

"I know. Another reason for the shame. I'm here because of Harry, because he makes me a better person." Those blue eyes teared up again. "He makes me want to be a better person. You've been selfish, Simone. So have I. But this is who you are, and who I am. I'm going to try to be a better person—the one Harry sees when he looks at me. I'm going to try to be a better sister. It's the only way I know how to make amends for what I did."

"I don't know if we'd be any different from who we are, but I'm sorry. I am sorry I wasn't there for you, that I didn't see I wasn't there. We can try starting from here, with who we are now."

"Yeah. Yes." Tears swirling, Natalie got to her feet, stepped forward.

Her gaze fell on the bust, and she saw what she hadn't before.

"It's Tish."

"Yes."

Her hand flew up to her mouth, clamped there. More tears now, spilling over her fingers. "Oh God, oh my God. It's Tish. I never really looked—I didn't want to." Shuddering, Natalie lowered her hand, and as Simone rose, she saw deep grief. "It's Tish. You made something beautiful, and I . . . You had to feel as if she died again. Oh, Simone."

"Yes, I did." But she came around the worktable, felt herself able and more willing to pull Natalie to her. "I did. But I can bring her back. I can bring her back," she said, with her eyes on the clay. "This time, this way."

PART TWO

Passion of Purpose

Wealth lost, something lost,
Honor lost, something lost:
Courage lost, all lost.

—Johann Wolfgang von Goethe

CHAPTER ELEVEN

Reed sat with Chaz Bergman on the rocks watching the moonbeam light over the bay. They each had a bottle of Summer Pale Ale, a technical violation. But at two in the morning on the lonely stretch of coastline, Reed figured nobody cared.

Though Chaz had moved to Seattle for a job right out of college, they hadn't lost touch, and kept up sporadically through texts and e-mails.

Face-to-face time tended to be limited to Chaz's return for Christmas and the occasional long summer weekend.

"Sorry I couldn't make it earlier," Reed said as they settled in.

"Cop shit?"

"Yeah."

"You get the bad guy?"

With a nod, Reed took his first long drink. "Book 'em, Danno."

"Detective Quartermaine. It still slays me."

"Supreme IT Nerd Chaz Bergman. Doesn't surprise me a bit." Reed took another pull from the bottle, let the long day go. "I didn't expect to see you again this summer. You were just here in July."

"Yeah." Chaz took a slower, smaller sip, nudged his glasses up on his nose.

He'd kept his husky build, but put on some muscle. He had a lot more hair now, enough that he tied it back in a stub of a tail. He'd added a weird little soul patch that didn't disguise the geek.

Chaz looked out at the water, shrugged. "My mom really wanted me to fly in for that McMullen deal. I guess part of me wanted to. Not to talk about it so much, but to see some of the people who were in the store that night."

"That kid," Reed remembered. "He was, like, twelve, and now he's working on being a doctor."

"Yeah, and the pregnant woman. She's got those twins."

"You saved them, bro." Reed tapped his bottle to Chaz's.

"I guess. Speaking of, how's Brady Foster?"

"He's great. Batted three-forty on his high school team last year. They had another kid, you know, Lisa and Michael."

"Yeah, that's right. You told me."

"A girl. She's five. Camille. She's crazy smart, looks like her mom. I tell you, Chaz, Lisa's amazing. She lives with that night every day, but she doesn't let it, you know, define her. It sure as hell doesn't stop her. I guess I look at that family, and what that night cost them, and how they didn't just survive it, they didn't even just overcome it, they, well, they shine, you know? Like that damn moon up there."

"I never asked you, but do you ever go back there? To the mall?"

"Yeah." He'd drawn maps, marked points of attack, victims, movements, numbers. He had it all in his files. "It's changed a lot."

"I can't go in there. I don't even like driving by. I never told you, but I took the job in Seattle because it was the farthest away I could get and stay in the country. Well, the mainland—and I didn't get offers from Alaska or Hawaii. It's a great job, a good company," Chaz added. "But it was the distance."

"Nothing wrong with that," Reed said after a moment.

"I don't think about it for weeks, months. But I come back here and it hits me all over again. Weird . . . because I was in a locked, crowded room for the worst of it, not in the thick like you. Jesus, we were just kids, Reed."

Chaz took a longer drink. "Or I'll hear about another mass shooting, and it all flashes back."

"I hear that."

"I go to Seattle, and you go to the front line."

"You took a job, man. You built a career."

"Yeah, about that. The reason I'm back? I'm taking a transfer to New York. Taking a little downtime first, heading down to check out some apartments the company's got lined up." Chaz shrugged. "They want me to head up the cybersecurity division there."

"Head it? Holy shit, Chaz." Reed gave him a congratulatory elbow in the ribs. "You're a fucking honcho nerd."

It made him smile, but Chaz shook his head, shoved his glasses back up on his nose. "I almost turned it down. New York's a lot closer than Seattle, but I can't let that damn night, that damn mall—what did you call it?— define my damn life. So I'm moving to New York in November."

"Congratulations, man, all around."

"How do you do it? I mean, the badge and the gun and putting it on the line every fucking day?"

"Detective work's mostly detecting, and a boatload of paperwork, legwork. It's not like TV. It's not car chases and shoot-outs."

"You're going to tell me you've never been in either one."

"Some car chases. More foot chases—and why do they run?—but some car chases. They're crazy, I'll give you that."

"Shoot-outs?"

"It's not like the O.K. Corral, Chaz."

Chaz just looked at him, those quiet eyes behind the thick lenses.

"I've been involved a couple of times when we had shots fired."

"Were you scared?"

"Bet your hairy white ass."

"But you did it anyway, and you keep doing it. See, that's the thing about you, Reed. You face up and do it anyway, and you always have. New York's not facing down some asshole with a gun, but it's sort of my 'do it anyway.'"

Chaz paused, smiled. "With a promotion and a big, fat raise."

"Lucky bastard. I bet you've got the rest of a six-pack in a cooler in that rental car."

"Eagle Scout. We're always prepared. But I'm driving, so one's it."

"So let's take it back to my place, polish it off. Tomorrow—well, today now. Sunday, and I'm not on the roll. You can sleep on the couch."

"I could do that. Why are you still living in that dump?"

"It's not so bad, and there's talk about some gentrification in the neighborhood. I could be sitting sweet before you know it. Anyway, I might not be there much longer. I'm looking at a house tomorrow afternoon. It feels like the one from the outside, and the video tour. Nice yard, new kitchen."

"You don't cook."

"Doesn't matter. Excellent master suite, and so on. I like the neighborhood. I can walk to pubs and restaurants. Mow my own grass. Best, if I can whittle the price down just a couple clicks, I can afford it without selling my blood or taking bribes."

"You could sell your sperm," Chaz suggested. "Remember that guy— Fruenski—who did that in college?"

"I think I'll try my hand at negotiation first. Anyway," he said as they rose, "you ought to come with me tomorrow, check the place out."

"I gotta go see my grandparents. Already on the books. Then Monday, I'm heading to New York to check out my own digs."

"Then let's go make the best of what's left of the six-pack."

Reed slept till noon, then threw together some coffee and scrambled eggs, since he had company. He saw Chaz off with the promise of a wild New York weekend once his old friend settled in.

When he showered, in lukewarm water as apparently the building's hot water heater was dying again, he thought how good it had been to spend time with Chaz. And talk about things he realized Chaz had avoided talking about.

He dressed studying his bedroom wall, the one he used as a makeshift case board. He had tacked up photos of every DownEast Mall survivor who'd died, with the death designation above each group: Accidental, Natural Causes, Homicide, Suicide.

He had maps with each of the deceased's location when they died pinned with the name, date, time.

And he crossed-checked each along with their reported locations and any injuries incurred on the night of July 22, 2005.

Too many, he thought again. Just too many.

He couldn't argue with Essie's debate point on the variety of weapons and methods in the homicides, but he knew there was a pattern in there. One that just hadn't come clear for him yet.

He had autopsy reports, witness statements, copies of interviews with next of kin. He'd compiled articles and recordings from a dozen years back right up to the McMullen special.

It had surprised him to see Hobart's sister on there. Patricia Hobart, pale, hollow-eyed, looked older than twenty-six. Then, he guessed, having your brother murder a bunch of people, your mother blow up her house under the influence of drugs and alcohol—as the ME report stated—having your asshole father drink himself drunk and kill a woman and her kid, along with himself, rated premature aging.

She hadn't cried, Reed recalled as he studied her picture on the wall. Plenty of nervous tics though. Hunched shoulders, fingers twisting together or pulling at her clothes.

Dumpy suit, he remembered, ugly shoes. Lived with her grandparents, stood as main caregiver for her grandmother, who'd used a walker since recovering after a broken hip, and her grandfather, who'd suffered two small strokes.

Paternal grandparents—really well-off—who'd disinherited the asshole father and uncle who'd had their shitload of guns available for a trio of fucked-up teenagers to take, to use, to kill what came to be ninety-three people in the space of minutes.

What a fucking family, he thought, strapping on his off-duty weapon, shoving his wallet, ID, and phone in his pockets.

On the way out, he pulled out his phone, called Essie. An actual call because she might ignore a text.

He jogged down the steps as she answered.

"I'm heading to the house I told you about, meeting Realtor Renee. Come on and see it with me. Bring the gang."

"It's a hot, lazy afternoon, Reed."

"That's why it's perfect. We'll go to the park after, the dog and kid can run around. And I'll take you all for pizza to celebrate me making an offer. I really think this is the one."

"You said that with that weird Victorian three months ago."

"I liked the weird Victorian, but it had a bad vibe when we walked through it."

"Yeah, yeah, vibe, bad. You're a house-shopping addict, Reed."

Since it might be true, he evaded. "It'll be fun. This one's only a few blocks from your place."

"It's over half a mile."

"A nice Sunday stroll, right? Then the park, pizza. I'll spring for a bottle of wine."

"That's so unfair."

He laughed. "Come on. I need somebody to talk me out of it if it's wrong, or into it if it's right. The damn water heater's on the death watch here again. I really do have to get out of this place."

He knew by the long, windy sigh, he had her.

"What time's your appointment?"

"Two. I'm heading there now."

"Puck and Dylan could use the walk and the run-around time. Hank and I could use the wine. I've got to get it together first. Don't make a damn offer until we get there."

"You got it. Thanks. See you."

He glanced back at the building. Someone who couldn't spell had added some fresh graffiti advising somebody else to FUK A DUKE.

He assumed they meant *duck*, but maybe they knew somebody named Duke. Maybe they wanted to fuck an aristocrat or something.

In any case, it was just another sign his time there had to end.

Still, a decent coffee shop had opened up a couple blocks away, and somebody had bought one of the neighboring buildings with big talk of rehab and spiffy condos.

Gentrification could happen.

Another reason to get out. He'd appreciate seeing the neighborhood cleaned up, spruced up, but he didn't want to live out his life in a condo.

As he drove, he imagined setting up a grill on his new back deck. He knew how to grill—sort of. Maybe he'd even learn how to cook something besides scrambled eggs and grilled cheese and bacon sandwiches. Maybe.

He'd have parties with the grill smoking—or in the great room in the winter with the gas fireplace going. Keep one of the three bedrooms as a guest room, turn the other into what would be his first ever actual home office.

Buy a big, and he did mean big-ass flat screen for the wall and sign up for every fucking sports channel on cable.

That's what I'm talking about, he decided as he cruised into what he had determined would be his new neighborhood.

Older homes, sure, but he didn't mind older. Most had been remodeled with the ever-popular open concept, the snazzy bathrooms and kitchens.

Lots of families, and he didn't mind that, either. Maybe he'd come across some sexy single mom. He liked kids, kids were no problem.

He pulled up into the drive of the sturdy two-story brick, thought how much he'd liked the unabashed weirdness of the Victorian over this more traditional. But sturdy was good, sturdy was fine. And the owners had definitely put some effort into curb appeal with the plants, shrubs, the new doors on the garage.

He could use a garage.

As he got out, he glanced at the car already parked there. Not Renee's, his extremely patient Realtor. Curious, he noted the license plate—pure habit— as he crossed what he told himself would be his brick walkway.

The woman opened the door before he pressed the (his) doorbell.

"Hi! Reed, right?" The attractive blonde in the tailored red shirt and white pants held out her hand. "I'm Maxie, Maxie Walters."

"Okay. I'm supposed to meet Renee."

"Yes, she called me. She had a family emergency. Her mother had a little fender bender—nothing serious," she said quickly. "But you know moms. Renee's going to try to get here, but she didn't want you to have to delay or postpone—especially when we got the inside scoop the sellers are cutting the price five thousand tomorrow."

"That doesn't hurt a thing." He stepped inside, scanned the high-ceilinged foyer he'd admired on the video tour.

"I've just been familiarizing myself with the property. It does have some lovely features. Original hardwood floors, and I think they did a terrific job refinishing them. And don't you love the open feel of the entrance?" she continued as she gestured him ahead, closed the door.

"Yeah, the house has a good feel." He wandered the living room—staged well, he thought as he'd seen every level of staging—and imagined that big-ass screen on the wall.

He liked the sight line, straight back to the kitchen with the wide breakfast counter, and the dining area, to the wide sliders that opened onto the back deck he wanted for his own.

"So you work with Renee?" He didn't know why he asked. He knew everyone who worked with Renee.

He turned toward her. Blond and blue, mid-twenties, about five-four, and a hundred fifteen. Good muscle tone.

"We're friends," she said as she led the way toward the kitchen. "Actually, she's been my mentor. I only got my license three months ago. Granite countertops," she added. "The appliances are new. Not stainless, but I think the clean white suits the space."

Her voice, he thought. Something about her voice. He stopped on his way to that beckoning deck, turned with the breakfast bar between them.

"Do you cook, Reed?"

"Not really." He thought the flirty smile she sent him just didn't fit the space between her nose and chin.

She stepped up to the counter. "You're a police detective. That must be exciting. Not married though?"

"No."

"It's a great house for a family, when you start one."

She shifted. He couldn't see her hands, but her body language . . . Every instinct went on alert. The eyes, the hair, even the shape of the mouth with that slight overbite were all different. But the voice.

It clicked, just an instant too late. She'd already brought up the gun. He dived for cover, but she caught him twice, in the side, in the shoulder.

He hit the refinished hardwood behind the granite breakfast counter hard, with stupefying pain exploding through his body.

"Some cop." With a laugh, she strolled around the counter to finish him off with one to the head. "You did a better job protecting some idiot kid way back when than protecting yourself now. Say goodbye, hero."

He saw her face change from eager to shocked. Now he had his gun out. He fired three times, forced to use his left hand as his right couldn't hold his weapon.

He heard her scream, thought he hit her, thought at least one shot hit before she used the counter to block. Before he heard her running for the front door.

"You motherfucker!" She screamed it as she ran.

He had to drag himself across the floor, brace the weapon as he cleared the counter. She'd left the door open. He heard the sound of a car starting, tires squealing.

She could come back, he thought. If she came back . . . Teeth gritted, he pushed himself to sit, back to the counter, gasping against the pain as he fought for his phone.

He passed out, felt himself fade. He didn't know how long. Struggling to breathe against the pain, he pulled out his phone.

He started to hit nine-one-one, then thought of Essie and her family.

She answered on the second ring. "We're coming! Five minutes."

"No, no. Don't. Stay back. I'm shot. I'm shot."

"What? Reed!"

"Need ambulance. Need backup. Fuck me, passing out again. Need BOLO . . ."

"Reed! Reed! Hank, stay here, stay with Dylan."

"Essie, what—"

But she was running, the phone in her hand, and her weapon in the other. "Officer down, officer down!" she shouted into the phone.

Hank picked up his son, gripped Puck's leash. And prayed.

She made the last quarter mile in under two minutes, running full out while people working in their yards stopped to gape.

"Police officer! Go inside. Go inside."

She didn't stop running until she hit the porch of the brick house. Weapon out, she cleared the doorway, swept her weapon toward the stairs leading up, then over.

And saw Reed.

"Please, please, please." She checked his pulse first, then leaped up to grab cloth napkins artfully folded on the set-for-company dining room table.

When she padded them, put pressure on the wound in his side, the fresh pain shot him to the surface.

"Shot."

And in shock, she thought. "Yeah, you're going to be all right. Be still. An ambulance is coming. Backup's coming."

"She could come back. Need my weapon."

"Who? Who is she? No, no, no, stay with me. You stay with me. Who did this?"

"Hobart, the sister. Oh fuck, fuck, fuck. Patricia Hobart. Driving—"

"You stay awake. Look at me! You stay with me, goddamn it."

"Driving a late model Honda Civic. White. Maine plates. Shit, shit, I can't—"

"You can. Hear that? Hear the sirens? Help's coming."

And her hands were wet with his blood. She couldn't stop the blood.

"Plates, the stupid lobster." He gasped it out, fighting to stay with her. To stay alive. "Four-Seven-Five-Charlie-Bravo-Romeo."

"Good, good, that's real good. In here! In here! Hurry, goddamn it. He's bleeding. I can't stop the bleeding."

The EMTs pushed her aside, laid Reed flat, got to work.

Cops, weapons drawn, rushed in behind them.

She held up her left hand, felt Reed's blood slide down her wrist. "I'm a cop. We're cops."

"Detective McVee. It's Bull. Jesus Christ, that's Reed. Who the fuck did this?"

"The assailant is Hobart, Patricia, mid-twenties, brown hair, brown eyes. She's driving, or was, a late-model white Honda Civic, Maine lobster plates. Four-Seven-Five-Charlie-Bravo-Romeo. Get it out. I don't know her address—lives with grandparents. Get it out. Get that bitch."

"Detective," one of the officers said. "There's some blood, leading out. She could be hit."

She looked back at Reed and dearly hoped so. "Alert hospitals and clinics. Two of you clear the house. And let's move, let's move!"

Patricia moved. And fast. The son of a bitch shot her. She couldn't believe it! She hoped he died screaming. She couldn't stop to check, but the bullet had gone in just under her left armpit. And she thought, hoped, right out again. A through-and-through they called it, she remembered as she blinked away tears of pain and fury.

If he lived long enough, the bastard would identify her. Plus she knew she'd bled on the way out, and that meant DNA.

She pounded a fist on the steering wheel of the stolen car as she pulled into the sweep of her grandparents' driveway.

She needed her cash, her fake IDs, some weapons, her go bag. She'd have to leave the stolen car behind, just take her own until she could ditch it.

She'd planned for this, she thought. She'd planned for it. She just hadn't expected to hit the road with a bullet wound.

She raced into the house, up the stairs.

It should have gone perfectly, she told herself. She'd cultivated the asshole cop's Realtor, going through some of the same houses he had. Had drinks— girlfriends!—with the clueless bitch. And she'd been right there, sipping hard lemonade, when the should-be-dead guy contacted dumbass Renee about the house.

Simple after that. Go over Sunday morning, get the code for the lock box, and then kill stupid Renee, take her files on the house, and so on. Then just wait.

But he'd made her. How the hell had he done that?

She let out a weeping whine as she doused the hole under her armpit with peroxide, padded it.

She'd *felt* it, just in the set of his body, the way he'd studied her face.

He was probably dead, probably dead, she assured herself as she pulled on a fresh shirt, pulled out her go bag, dumped more cash, more IDs into it.

She'd have made sure of it. She knew he'd be carrying—off-duty weapon, she wasn't a moron. But she'd hit him twice—right side, right shoulder.

How the hell could she be expected to know he'd manage to get his gun out and shoot with his left hand?

How the hell could she know that!

She took two more handguns, her combat knives, a handmade garrote, plenty of ammo, even took the time to grab another wig, some more facial appliances, some contacts, more bandages, and some of the pain pills she'd culled from her grandparents' supply.

It seriously pissed her off she wouldn't cash in on the sale of the house, the life insurance policies when her grandparents finally croaked. But she had more than enough to keep her going for years.

Wincing at the pain, she shouldered the bag and started downstairs.

"Patti? Patti? Is that you? Grandpa's done something to the TV again. Can you fix it?"

"Sure. Sure, I can fix it," she said when her grandmother thumped out with her walker.

She pulled out a nine millimeter, shot her grandmother, center of the forehead. She went down with a soft *whoosh* of air.

"All fixed!" she said brightly, then walked into their bedroom, where the overheated air smelled of old people. Her grandfather sat in his recliner, smacking a hand on the remote while the TV screen buzzed with static.

"Something's wrong with this thing. Did you hear that noise, Patti?"

"I did. Bye-bye."

He looked up, squinted behind his bifocals.

She shot him in the head, too, let out a happy little laugh. "Finally!"

She was in and out of the house inside ten minutes—she'd practiced, after all—leaving two bodies behind her.

Keeping to the speed limit, she drove to the airport, left her car in long-term parking, jacked a nondescript sedan, and was on her way.

CHAPTER TWELVE

He saw lights speeding over his head and wondered if he was dead. Maybe there'd be some sexy angels to guide him through those lights to whatever.

He heard voices, a lot of rapid-fire voices talking doctor talk. He didn't think dead sexy angels worried about GSWs or dropping BPs.

Plus dead couldn't possibly hurt so goddamn much.

Through the pain, the cold—why was he so cold?—the confusion, and the oddly detached wondering about his own death, he heard Essie's voice.

"You're going to be fine. Reed. Reed. You hang on. You're going to be fine."

Well, he thought, okay then.

The next thing he knew was more pain. His body, his mind, his everything seemed to float through it, around it, inside it. Pain was the name of the freaking game.

Since he didn't want to play, he let go.

That pain refused to sit on the bench when he surfaced again, and it pissed him off. Something, someone poked at him, and *that* pissed him off.

He said, "Fuck off."

Even to his dim ears it sounded like *fukov*, but he meant it.

"Almost done, Detective."

He opened his eyes. Everything was too white, too bright, so he nearly closed them again. Then he saw the pretty face, big brown eyes, golden-brown skin.

"Sexy angel." *Sessy ajel.*

Those full, soft lips curved. And he went away again.

He went up and down, up and down, not like a roller coaster, but like a raft on a gently undulating river.

The River Styx. That would be bad.

He heard his mother's voice.

What the hell kind of a name is Yossarian? It's Yossarian's name, sir.

Catch-22. Huh.

He drifted away again, had a long dream conversation about death and sexy angels with the bombardier who had a secret.

When the pain slapped him back again, he decided—once and for all—this dead business sucked.

"It sure would, but you're not."

He blinked his heavy eyes clear, stared at Essie. "Not?"

"Definitely not. Are you going to stick around awhile this time? I just talked your parents into going down for some food. I can get them back."

"What the hell?"

As she lowered the bed guard to sit on the side of the bed, taking his hand, he took stock. Machines and monitors, the annoying discomfort of the IV needle in the back of his hand, the raging headache, the sour, metallic taste in his throat, and a score of other irritations under the full-body pain.

"She shot me. Patricia Hobart—driving a white Honda Civic, Maine—"

"You gave us all of it already."

His brain wanted to shut down again, but he pushed through it. "You get her? You get her?"

"We will. Are you up to telling me what happened?"

"Cloudy. How long?"

"This is day three, heading to four."

"Shit. Shit. How bad?"

She shifted. They'd had pieces of this conversation before, but he seemed more lucid this time. Or maybe she just wanted him to be.

"Good news first. You're not going to die."

"Really good news."

"You took two hits. The one in the shoulder tore some things up, but the docs say you'll regain full mobility and range of motion with PT. You can't screw around with the PT, no matter how much it hurts, or how boring. Got it?"

"Yeah, yeah."

"The second, torso, right side, fractured a couple ribs, nicked your liver on the way down. You had internal injuries, and you lost a lot of blood, but they patched you up. You're going to feel like shit for a while, but if you're not an asshole about it, you'll make a full recovery."

"She didn't hit the, you know, fun factory, did she? Because it doesn't feel right down there."

"That's the catheter. It'll come out when you can move around."

"So I've been mostly dead for going on four days, but not dead yet."

"Leave it to you to do a mash-up of two movie classics. How'd she get the drop on you?"

He shut his eyes, made himself bring it back. "Blond wig, blue contacts, an appliance—sexy little overbite. Said Renee had . . . Renee." His eyes opened, and he saw it. He saw it before Essie told him.

"I'm sorry, Reed. We found her in her house. Two shots to the head. TOD's estimated at roughly two hours before she shot you. From what we've pieced together, Hobart—as a redhead going by the name of Faith Appleby—connected with Renee a few months ago. She claimed she was house hunting, and it looks like she followed your footsteps on properties. She got friendly with Renee, so she must have known about the appointment, saw that as her opportunity to take you out."

"She said Renee was delayed, and asked her to show me through the house. I didn't make her straight off, but her voice . . . I watched some interviews, and I recognized her voice. Took too long to put it together."

"Partner, if you hadn't put it together, you'd be really most sincerely dead."

"And yet another movie classic. She got the drop on me, Essie, and let me just add: Getting shot hurts like a motherfucker. She came around the bar, the kitchen island deal, to finish me off. I couldn't use my right arm, but I got my weapon out with the left. I think I got three rounds off. I know I hit her. I fucking know I hit her."

"You did. Blood trail led out the front door."

"Good."

"We just missed her, Reed. She had to have an escape plan worked out. She killed her grandparents before she walked out the door."

"Come on."

"The bitch dropped her grandmother off her walker, took her grandfather out in his goddamn Barcalounger. We froze their accounts—they all had her name on them—but she'd been systematically clearing them out for what looks like years, and must have millions."

She rubbed his hand between hers. "I owe you a big, giant apology."

"She's the one. She's been killing people her brother and his buddies missed."

"We found her war room, her kill lists, photos, data she's accumulated. Weapons she left behind, more wigs and disguises, maps. No computer. We have to figure she worked on a laptop and took it with her. The car she drove to the house was stolen that morning, and she left it at her grandparents'. We've got an APB out on the car registered to her, and since she's now the prime suspect on unsolved cases across state lines, that's national."

"The feds pushed in."

"I'll take them. She's smart, Reed. She's canny and she's crazy. It's our case, but we'll take the help. You have to get back on your feet, partner. That means rest and meds and PT, and whatever the docs say it means, and no bullshit from you."

"In my apartment, bedroom. I've got a case board going, comp files. Don't let the feds confiscate it. I'll share, but don't let them confiscate the work. Go get it."

"You got it. Look, I'm going to go get a nurse, since you're staying awake longer than you have. And your mom and dad, who've been here pretty much round-the-clock, even with your sibs taking rotation."

Needing to touch, she rubbed her hand over the four-day scruff on his face. "You look rough, Reed, but you're pulling it out. That button there? It's your personal-decision morphine drip."

"Yeah. I'll think about that. There's one nurse—I think nurse—unless I was hallucinating. Really pretty, brown eyes, great smile, skin the color of the caramel my mom used to melt to coat apples on Halloween."

"Trust you. That's Tinette. I'll see if she's on." Then she leaned over, laid her lips lightly on his. "Scared the shit out of me, Reed. Try not to do that again."

He went in and out for another twenty-four, but as much in as out. They wanted him up, taking short walks—and the lovely (unfortunately for him, married) Tinette cracked a velvet whip. She added, if he wanted the catheter removed—oh yes, please—he had to be mobile.

He shuffled, pulling his IV along, usually with one of his family or another cop beside him.

It touched him that Bull Stockwell didn't miss a day, even if Bull harangued him about getting his skinny, malingering ass moving.

In the ten days since steel met flesh, he had lost eight pounds and could all but feel his muscle tone dissolving.

His mother brought him meatloaf, his father snuck him pizza. His sister baked him cookies. His brother slipped him a beer.

His first PT session left him covered in cold sweat and exhausted.

His hospital room, full of flowers, plants, books, and a ridiculous teddy bear outfitted with a detective's shield and a nine mil, began to feel like prison.

The only plus there was that getting in was as hard as breaking out. The one time Seleena McMullen slipped through, Tinette—now Reed's hero— kicked her right out again.

She managed to get a shot of him with her cell phone. When he saw it posted on the Internet, he decided maybe everyone lied to him, and he had died.

He sure as hell looked like a zombie.

Bull lived up to his name and bullied him into getting up and moving after the second round of PT when all Reed wanted to do was sleep off the misery.

"Quit your bellyaching."

"It's not my belly that aches."

"Bitch, moan, whine. You want to be a cop again?"

"I never stopped being a cop." Reed gritted his teeth as they walked. At least they allowed him cotton pants and a T-shirt now, instead of the humiliating hospital gown.

"They'll put you on a desk, and keep you there if you can't draw and fire your weapon like a man."

"Essie'd kick your ass for the 'like a man.'"

"She ain't here."

He walked Reed out to a small garden area where at least the air smelled like air.

"She ain't giving it to you straight, either. Doesn't want to put stress on your poor little feelings."

"What're you talking about?"

"The feds. They're pushing us back, taking over."

"I knew it." Disgusted, Reed punched out at the air. His vision went gray when his shoulder exploded.

"Okay, okay, take it easy, killer." Bull gripped Reed's good arm, pushed him down on a bench. "She fought the good fight, you oughta know. You've been ahead of the pack on this for years, and nobody got on board. That includes yours truly. Thing is, it's not just a hot case, it's hot press. They can put on their stern fed faces and claim the press doesn't have dick to do with it, but that's a crock of shit. But, the other thing is, you were part of the Down East Mall, and now you've been a target of the sister of one of the shooters."

"She had a part in that. I'm telling you she knew what her brother was up to."

"Not saying otherwise. I'm saying the feds see that as two strikes against you staying on the investigation, and the brass on our blue line agrees."

"*That's* a crock of shit."

"It's a big, stinking crock of shit, but that's what they're serving. They're going to lock you to a desk when you come back, and give you grunt work until you pass the physical. And even then, they're going to block you out of the Hobart case."

"Son of a bitch."

"Get your sad, skinny ass back in tune, kid. There are plenty of us who'll work this on the side, but you need to shake off getting shot. And don't tell me it doesn't give you some cold sweats in the dark."

"I see that gun coming up. Slow motion. Like I've got all the time in the world to take cover, return fire. But I'm in slower motion, and the damn gun's as big as a cannon."

"Shake it off. Get back to work."

"Your compassion and sympathy are so heartfelt."

Bull snorted, as bulls do. "You get enough of the soft stuff and forehead kisses. You need a kick in the ass."

"It's appreciated."

"And for shit's sake, eat something. You look like a zombie scarecrow. Now get up and walk."

Reed waited to speak to Essie about it because, at long last, they opened his cage door.

He was going home.

Not home to the shitcan, as he couldn't yet handle three flights of stairs, but home to his old bedroom, his mother's cooking, his father's wonderfully bad jokes.

He'd asked, specifically, that Essie pick him up, deliver him, so he had waited to talk to her.

"Why do I have to get in a wheelchair to leave when all I've heard for two and a half freaking weeks is get up and walk?"

Tinette of the beautiful smile patted the chair. "Rules are rules, my darling. Now put that sweet butt in the chair."

"How about after I'm a hundred percent, we have a hot, torrid affair. It'd be good for my emotional and mental health."

"My man would crush you like a bug, skinny boy. It's too bad my sister's only eighteen."

"Eighteen's legal."

"You go near my baby sis, I'll put you back in this hospital." But she rubbed his shoulder. "I'm glad to see you go, Reed, and sorry at the same time."

"I'll be coming in for the torture."

"And I'll go down and see you don't cry too hard. Here, hold your teddy bear."

He took it, and took a last look at the room. Essie had already hauled down the books, his tablet, and other accumulated stuff.

"I won't miss this place," he said as she wheeled him out, "but I'll miss you. You're the only woman I love, besides my mother, who's seen me naked without me having the same privilege."

"You're going to put some meat back on those bones." She steered him into the elevator. "And you take some advice."

"From you I will."

"Don't go back into it too fast, darling. Give yourself some time. Walk in the sun, pet some puppies, eat ice cream cones, fly a kite. I know enough about you now to know you're a good cop and a good man. Take some time to remember why you're both."

He reached back—left hand—for hers. "I'm really going to miss you."

Essie greeted them with a smile. "You're sprung, partner. Tinette, you're a treasure."

"Oh, I am every bit of that. Come on now, darling, let's get you in the car." She settled him and strapped him in herself. "You take care of my favorite patient."

"One hour in a cheap motel. It'll change your life."

With a laugh, she kissed him on the mouth. "I like my life. Go live yours now."

"What if she'd said yes?" Essie wondered aloud as they drove away.

"Never happen. She's crazy about her husband. You know, she was twenty when the DownEast Mall happened and doing community service as part of her college credits. Nurse's aide, so she ended up being on the front lines at the hospital that night. Small, small world."

He waited a beat. "Bull told me the feds have taken over, pushed us back. Pushed me out."

She let out a hiss of breath. "I was going to talk to you about it once you got out, got home, got settled in. I'm sorry, Reed, they brought down the hammer in the house. You're too close, so I'm too close. I went to the wall on it, and the wall won."

"It's not going to stop me."

She blew out a breath, fluttering the bangs she'd recently tried out. "Look, I didn't support your theory, and that theory's now proven as fact. The feds are scooping that right up from under you. They'll give you a handshake and a brush back. On our end, the same decision goes right to the top."

"It's not going to stop me," he repeated.

"They'll make it an order. Believe me. Whatever you do, you'll have to do it in the dark, on the side. If they find out, they'll write you up and slap you down. It's not right, but that's the line."

"What's your line?"

"I'm with you. We'll do what we can on our off time. I'm going to add, Hank's with us on it."

"Good man."

"He is. He's not going back to full-time teaching. He's going to finish the book he's been writing. Literary cop fiction, he calls it. It's damn good so far—what he's let me read. But part of why he's not going back is to give me more time to work this. With you, when I can."

"I need to think it through, take some time. I need to get back in shape. Apparently getting shot's turned me into a zombie scarecrow."

"You've looked better. But Jesus, Reed, trust me, you looked worse."

He knew it, just like he knew he had a ways to go. "I need to take her down, Essie. I need to be a part of it. But I'm going to think it through. No word on her since they found her car?"

"She's in the wind."

"The wind's going to change," he murmured.

He spent a month with his parents, white-knuckled his way through the PT, managed to put back on a couple of the pounds he'd lost during his hospital incarceration.

He'd dropped twelve before he'd leveled off.

He went back to work—desk duty. And when he got the word from his captain on the Hobart investigation, he didn't argue. No point.

Still, desk duty had its advantages, and gave him plenty of time to access files. He might not have the brass behind him, but he had the blue line.

Traces of Hobart's blood had been found on the driver's seat of the car she'd dumped at the airport. The car reported stolen by a family of four after they returned from a three-week vacation in Hawaii had yet to be recovered.

Reed placed his bets on Hobart dumping it in a lake, torching it in the woods, or otherwise erasing it. She had cash, most likely fake IDs and credit cards. No way she'd stick with a stolen car.

She'd buy one under a fake name, with cash. A solid, nondescript, used car, he calculated. She'd change her hair, her appearance, so she looked little to nothing like the photos on the newscasts and the Internet.

She would watch those newscasts, the blogs, the newspapers, and lie low, at a distance. Until she hit again.

If she had a bullet in her, she'd found a way to get medical treatment.

He tried a check for break-ins, clinics, veterinary hospitals, pharmacies, but found nothing to fit.

He tried a search for deaths, medical profession. Doctors, nurses, aides, vets, ran down a couple, but again, none fit.

He thought about what he'd do, where he'd go in her place. His mind wandered north. Canada. Fake ID—fake passport. Cross the border, settle in, take a breather.

That's just what he'd have done.

No need to risk air travel, no need to learn a new language. Rent a freaking cabin in the woods, keep a low profile.

But she wouldn't be able to cut her losses, he knew. She'd need to finish what she started. Sooner or later, he'd get an alert that someone else who'd shared that nightmare with him had died.

So he shuffled papers, did the PT, ate his mother's cooking.

And one day he woke up realizing he didn't feel like a good cop anymore. He barely felt like a cop at all.

He could rotate his shoulder without agony, and could lift a ten-pound weight for a handful of reps, but he didn't feel like much of a man, either.

He was, well, the zombie scarecrow with a vulture on his shoulder just waiting for somebody to die.

Time to pull it out, he decided, and take Tinette's advice. He needed to walk in the sun, and remember what he'd been and why.

CHAPTER THIRTEEN

For the second day while she enjoyed her morning coffee on her patio, CiCi watched the man on the narrow strip of sand below.

He'd jog a little, walk, jog, back and forth for about a half hour before he'd climb—slowly—onto the rocks to sit and watch the water.

Then, like a man who'd been fit and strong and was recovering from a long illness, he'd do it all again before walking back along the beach to the bike path toward the village.

After day one, she'd gotten his name from the rental agent who'd booked him into a bungalow. A three-week booking in October, heading into November, wasn't without precedent for the island, but it was unusual.

Plus, before she had his name, she'd used her binoculars to get a good look at his face.

Good-looking, but thin and too pale, with a lot of scruff.

Personally, she liked a man with some scruff.

She'd recognized him—she kept up with current events—but she'd wanted to be sure.

So she knew who he was, what had happened, and wondered what went through his mind as he jogged, walked, sat.

Since she wanted to find out, on day three of the morning routine, she did her makeup, fluffed up the hair she'd recently dyed a deep plum, put on some leggings—she still had good legs—a long-sleeve tee, and a denim jacket.

And after filling two lidded cups with mocha lattes, CiCi walked down while he sat on the rocks.

He glanced over as she started to climb up to join him, earned points for immediately getting up to take her hand.

With his left, she noted, and not without a flicker of pain on his face.

"Good morning," she said, offering him one of the cups.

"Thanks."

"It's a perfect morning to sit on the rocks and have a latte. I'm CiCi Lennon."

"Reed Quartermaine. I've admired your work."

"Then you're a man of taste as well as looking tasty. Full disclosure? I recognized you. I know who you are and what happened to you. But we don't have to talk about it."

"I appreciate it."

Gorgeous eyes, CiCi thought. A quiet green with the intensity behind them adding a little magic.

"So what brings you to our island, Reed?"

"Some R and R."

"A good place for just that, especially in the quiet season."

"I've been here a few times in the summer. With my family as a kid, with some pals when I got old enough to drive. But I haven't been in, jeez, I guess about ten years."

"It hasn't changed very much."

"No, and that's nice." Slowly, carefully, he angled around to look back. "I remember your house, and thinking how cool it would be to live there, all those windows—see the water all the time, be able to walk right down to this little beach."

"It is cool. The only place for me, as it turns out. Where's yours?"

"Still looking. Actually got shot looking in the wrong place." He smiled, quick and easy. "That'll teach me. There was another house here I remembered, and it's still there. I walked over from the village to see if it was. Two story, with a widow's walk. What you'd call rambling, like yours. I guess I like rambling. Not as much glass, but enough. Sealed cedar shakes that have weathered. Big double porches on the front. Decks on the back. It's sort of straddling some woods and the water. A little sand beach—not as much as here—then the rocks."

"That's Barbara Ellen Dorchet's place. Just this side of the village, and tucked back some. A riot of lupines in the yard in the summer. Was there a red pickup out front?"

"Yeah, and a Mercedes G-Wagen."

"That's her son's. He's here to help her do some sprucing up before she puts it on the market."

"On the . . . Seriously?"

CiCi, a little bit psychic, smiled and sipped her latte. "Not such good timing for her, as there won't be many looking for a place like that on the island late fall or winter when she's ready to list it. But she lost her husband last year, and doesn't have it in her to stay. She's moving south. Her boy moved to Atlanta about twelve years ago for work. She's got three grandchildren there, so there's where she wants to be."

"She's going to sell the house." He let out a half laugh. "I've been looking for the right house for years now, and I realized after I got here, saw your place, and the other, they're why nothing I looked at rang the bell."

"Looking in the wrong place." She added, "You should make her an offer. I can find out her ballpark easy enough."

"I wasn't figuring on . . ." He trailed off, sipped some of the really excellent latte. "This is downright weird."

"I'm a fan of the downright weird. Well, come on, Detective Delicious. I'm going to cook you breakfast."

"You don't have to—" He broke off to study her, the fabulous hair, the amazing eyes. "Do you invite strange men for breakfast often?"

"Only ones who interest me. Normally, you'd be doing the cooking, but since I didn't spend the night rocking your world, I'll make the cranberry pancakes."

That got a laugh and a grin out of him, earned him more points. "I'd be stupid to turn down a beautiful woman and cranberry pancakes at the same time. I'm not stupid."

"I could tell."

"Let me help you down."

He climbed down, favoring his right side, wincing just a little before he reached his left hand up for hers.

"Still hurting?"

"I get twinges, and I'm still working on range of motion and building back up. Doing physical therapy—exercises—and I'm ferrying back and forth twice a week for the real torture sessions."

"You need to do some yoga. I'm a big believer, and of holistics. But we'll start with pancakes. How do you feel about Bloody Marys?"

"Don't spare the Tabasco."

"Oh, my man." She took his left hand, swung arms with him. "To borrow a phrase, 'This is the beginning of a beautiful friendship.' "

The inside of the house turned out to be as fascinating as the exterior. The color, the light. Jesus, the views.

"It looks like you."

"My, my, aren't you clever."

"No, I mean it." He wandered, looking everywhere. "It's bold and beautiful and creative. And . . ." He stopped beside the bust, stared in wonder at *Emergence*. "Wow. This is . . . Wow."

"My granddaughter Simone's work. It is wow."

"You can feel the triumph, the joy of it. Is that the right word?"

"It's an excellent word. She was in the mall that night, too. My Simone."

"I know." He couldn't take his eyes off the statue, the face. "Simone Knox."

"Have you met her?"

"Huh? What? Sorry. No. I just, I kept track. Even before I became a cop. I needed to keep track of the people, when I could, the people who were there."

"She was there, too." CiCi touched a gentle hand to the bust before she went into the kitchen to mix the drinks. "That's the face of the friend Simone lost that night, as Simone imagines her. So yes, triumph."

"She was the first nine-one-one caller, your granddaughter."

"You do keep up."

"The cop who took out Hobart—the first on scene? She became my partner when I made detective. She's part of the reason I became a cop."

"Isn't the world a fascinating place, Reed? How it intersects, crosses, separates, pulls back? That boy destroyed that sweet girl, and she was a sweet girl. He destroyed all her potential. Simone brought her back, triumphantly, with her talent and the love she had for our Tish. This police officer responds because fate put her right there, and stops that sick boy from taking even more lives than he had, and helped Simone through the start of the awful aftermath."

She stepped over, gave him a Bloody Mary. "That same police officer connects with you, and you become a police officer. I'm a little bit psychic," she said, "and I sense you're a very good police officer. Then that sick boy's sick sister kills, and tries to kill you. And here you are, in my house that you admired as a boy. I believe you were meant to be."

She touched her glass to his. "I'm a decent enough cook, but my pancakes are exceptional. So prepare to be astonished."

"I have been since you sat down on the rocks with me."

"I definitely like you. That's now an absolute, irreversible fact. Sit down while I mix up the batter, and tell me all about your sex life."

"It's flat at the moment."

"That'll change. Exercise, good diet, yoga, meditation, a reasonable imbibing of adult beverages. Some time on the island, and absolutely time with me. You'll get your mojo back."

"Today's a hell of a start."

She smiled. "You rented Whistler's Bungalow."

The Bloody Mary had the kick of an angry mule—just the way he liked it. "You don't miss much."

"Or anything at all. It's not a bad location, but this is better. After breakfast you need to go back, pack up. You can stay here."

"I . . ."

"Don't worry. I won't Mrs. Robinson you. It's tempting, but you need to ease back into that area, not start off with the crescendo.

"There's a guest suite over my studio," she continued. "I only let particular people stay there. You'll have the view, beach access, and my amazing company. Do you cook?"

He couldn't stop staring at her. She had a tattoo on her wrist like a bracelet, a purple crystal shaped like a spear around her neck.

"Not really . . . at all."

"Oh well, you have other qualities. You'd be doing me a favor, too."

"How's that?"

"Simone lives here, works here most of the time. Since she has, I've gotten used to having someone else stir the air around here. Someone simpatico and interesting. You fit. Simone just left the other day for Boston, then New York. Do a lonely woman a favor. I promise not to seduce you."

"I might want you to."

"That's sweet." She sent him a blazing smile as she mixed batter. "But believe me, Delicious, you couldn't handle it."

She was a force of nature, Reed decided. How else did a woman he'd just met feed him cranberry pancakes (awesome) and convince him to move into her guest room?

A force of nature, obviously, as he'd never believed in love at first sight. And now he was a victim of it.

He unpacked. It didn't take long, as he hadn't brought a hell of a lot with him. Still half-dazzled, he looked around the room she'd offered him as cheerfully as someone else might have offered him directions to the local bar.

Like the rest of the house, like all of her, it burst with color and style. No safe neutrals for CiCi Lennon, he thought. She went deep, rich purple on the walls, then covered them with art. Not the beachy scenes you might expect, he noted, but stylized nudes or mostly nude, male and female.

He was especially struck by one of a woman who seemed to be waking, reaching up toward the sky with one hand, a sly, knowing look on her face, and the bloom of just unfurling wings on her back.

The bed, a massive four-poster, gleamed bold bronze with tendrils of vines carved into the posts. The spread had a garden of purple flowers sweeping over bright white. Massed with pillows because, in his experience, women had a strange love affair with pillows. The bases of the lamps formed the sort of trees he'd expect to see in some magic woods.

It offered a sitting area with a small sofa covered in a green you might get if you plugged the color into an electric socket, a table supported by a curled dragon—maybe the mate to the one that stood on a stone pedestal and looked ready to breathe fire—and a dresser with curved feet and fairy faces painted on the drawers.

A magic room, he thought as he took a closer look at the dragon, admiring the detail of the scales, the expression of barely banked power in the eyes.

But for all its wonders, the room didn't hold a candle—whatever that meant—to the view. The bay and out to the ocean, the boats, the rocks, the sky, all as much a part of the room as the magical mix of art and color.

He hadn't come to the island for adventure, but for the time apart, the time to think, the time to recharge. But in one morning, he'd found the conduit to all of that.

He cleaned up first—she hadn't stinted on the bathroom, either, but he bypassed the body jets in the shower. His ribs still troubled him.

She'd told him to come down to her studio once he'd settled in, so he walked down on steps painted hot pepper red and around to the matching side door flanked by grinning gargoyles.

She called out, "Come on in," to his knock. And he entered another wonderland.

It smelled of paint and turpentine and incense—with a hint of weed. Not surprising, since she held a paintbrush in one hand, a joint in the other. She wore a butcher's apron splattered with paint, and that amazing hair—about the same color as the guest-room walls—was piled up with what looked like jeweled chopsticks.

Art supplies and tools were jumbled together on tall red shelves. A long worktable, as splattered as her apron, held more.

Canvases stood, leaned, hung everywhere.

He really didn't know much about art, but he knew spectacular when it was slammed in his face.

"Whoa. It's like . . . nothing else ever."

"Just the way I like it. How's the room?"

"It's magic."

She sent him a beam of approval. "That's just exactly right."

"Thanks doesn't cut it. I feel like I—I was going to say walked into the pages of a really cool book, but . . . What it is? Like I walked into one of these paintings."

"We're going to have a really good time here." She held out the joint, had him half smiling, shaking his head.

"CiCi, I'm a cop."

"Reed, I'm an old hippie."

"Not a damn thing old about you." He wandered over, let his jaw drop. "This is . . ."

"The Stones, circa 1971. That's just a print. Mick bought the original. It's not easy saying no to Mick."

"I bet. I'm now one degree from the freaking Stones."

"You're a fan?"

"Definitely. I know some of these album covers," he added as he wandered. "And posters. I *had* this poster of Janis Joplin."

Intrigued, she drew on her joint. "A little before your time, I'd have thought."

"She's timeless."

"We're made for each other," CiCi decided, watching as he admired her work, and rubbed the heel of his hand at his right side.

"Is that where you were shot?" she asked him.

He dropped his hand. "One of them. Ribs are healing up, but they're still a bitch."

"Got drugs?"

"I'm giving them a pass for now."

She wiggled the joint. "Organic."

"Maybe so, but the couple times I tried it in college, after the high and the insane munchies came the ice-pick headache."

"That's a shame. Me, I loved drugs and did them all. I do mean all. You don't know until you try, right?"

"I know if I jump off the cliff into the ocean I'm going to die."

She smiled behind a thin haze of smoke. "What if there was a mermaid who pulled you out, nursed you back to health?"

He laughed. "Got me there."

"In case you're worried about the cop part, my drugs of choice for the last decade or so have been weed—I've got a prescription for it—and alcohol. No illegal substances stashed around."

"Good to know. I should let you get back to work."

"Before you do, tell me what you think." She gestured to the canvas on the easel in front of her.

He stepped over and his heart gave three hard thuds.

The woman stood in some sort of glade full of flowers and butterflies and sunlight. She looked at him over her left shoulder, a half smile on her lips, in her golden eyes.

A sinuous vine grew up the center of her back, spread its arms over her shoulder blades.

Light and color saturated her, but it was that look in her eyes that made him wish he could step into the canvas and go with her.

Anywhere.

"She's . . . *beautiful*'s not strong enough. Compelling?"

"It's a fine word."

"You wonder who she's waiting for, who she's looking at, and what the hell's taking them so long. Because who in their right mind wouldn't want to walk down that path with her?"

"No matter where it leads?"

"No matter. Who is she?"

"In this portrait? Temptation. In reality, my granddaughter. Simone."

"I have a photo of her in my files, but . . ." It hadn't struck him, not like this. "She looks like you. She has your eyes."

"That's a fine compliment, to both of us. That's Natalie, my younger granddaughter." She gestured to another canvas.

Softer colors here, he noted, edging toward pastels to complement a different sort of beauty, a different sort of mood. Fairy princess, he decided, with the jeweled tiara over the gold halo of hair. Eyes of quiet blue in a lovely face that radiated happiness rather than power, and the slim frame draped in a long white gown thin enough to hint at the body beneath.

"She's lovely, and looking at someone who makes her happy."

"Very good. That would be Handsome Harry, her fiancé. I'm going to give this to him for Christmas. She'd never let him hang it if I'd done a nude, so I compromised."

"You love them a lot. It shows."

"My greatest treasures. I'm going to want you to pose for me."

"Ah, well, hmm."

"I'll ease you into it. It's hard to say no to Mick. Just as hard to say no to CiCi."

"I bet," he said, stepping back. "I'll get out of your way."

"What do you say to cocktails at five?"

"I say I'm there."

She didn't bring up the posing business over the next couple of days—a relief. When he came back, worn out, from physical therapy, she had her acupuncturist waiting. He balked—needles, for God's sake—but she'd spoken truth.

It was hard to say no to CiCi.

He concluded he'd fallen asleep during the acupuncturing because the PT wore him out and not because of weird-ass needles and aromatherapy candles.

She roped him into sunset yoga on the beach with a group of others. He felt stupid, awkward, stiff—and nearly drifted off during *shavasana*.

He couldn't deny he felt stronger and clearer of mind after his first week, but that's what he'd come to the island for. He didn't argue about the next acupuncture session, especially after neither his physical therapist nor his beloved Tinette dismissed it as hooey, which he'd counted on.

When CiCi talked him into a bike ride, his ribs and shoulder cursed him, but not as loudly as they had.

Fall had long since peaked, but he liked the Halloween look of the denuded trees, the way they rattled in the wind. He spotted pumpkins in gardens, and others already carved on porches. The air carried that spicy scent the earth sent out before it went to sleep for the winter.

CiCi stopped her bike in front of the other house he'd admired as a child.

All those rooflines, he mused, and the fussy trim, the spreads of glass leading out to odd little decks, and those double porches. All topped by the ridiculous charm of a widow's walk.

"The silvery gray works," CiCi declared. "And when the lupines and the rest of the garden blooms, it's the perfect backdrop for them. Me? I'd paint those porches orchid."

"Orchid?"

"But that's just me. Cody painted them and the trim that dark gray because it's safer for selling. Can't blame them. Anyway, they're expecting us."

"They are?"

"I called Barbara Ellen yesterday."

He studied the house, yearned. Shook his head. "CiCi, I can't buy a house on the island. Cops have to live where they work."

"But you want to see it, don't you?"

"Yeah, I really do. I just don't want to put them out."

"Cody's had his mother nipping at his heels for weeks now. They could both use the distraction." Once they parked their bikes, she took his hand, tugged him along a flagstone walk.

She crossed the porch that should be painted orchid, knocked on the door—then just opened it and walked in.

"Barbara Ellen, Cody! It's CiCi and friend." She called out over the sound of hammering from up the staircase tucked to the right of the living room.

The living room boasted a wood-burning fireplace and wide-planked floors he guessed were original, freshly sanded and sealed. It opened straight back to the kitchen, where he expected they'd put a lot of effort into modernizing. The peninsula, the prep island, the counters—sticking with gray in granite—and definitely new cabinets in a clean, simple white.

He didn't know why anyone who wasn't a cooking maniac needed a six-burner stove or double ovens, but they looked impressive.

"Go ahead and wander," CiCi told him. "I'll call them again."

He couldn't stop himself and walked back toward the kitchen, noted the double barn-style doors, slid one open. He definitely couldn't buy the house, he reminded himself. Not only for obvious reasons, but because he wasn't worthy of a kitchen with a pantry big enough to hold enough supplies to withstand an alien invasion.

Why had they put those cool Edison lights over the peninsula? He really had a weak spot for those lights.

He turned as he heard someone coming down the stairs, chattering all the way.

"CiCi! I barely heard you with all the noise. Cody's redoing one of the bedroom closets. I don't know what I'd do without that boy."

She was a tiny woman, and made Reed think of a busy bird as she gave CiCi a hug, still chattering.

"He's staying a whole month this time. And he's going to come back this winter to finish up, if need be, so we can get the house on the market come spring. Spring's the best time, everybody says, though I had my heart set on listing it before the first of the year. I'm going home with him when he leaves, to start looking for a little place, maybe a condo. I don't know, but I know I just don't want to spend another winter here alone."

"We'll miss you, Barbara Ellen. Come meet my Reed."

"Oh my goodness, of course! How do you do? CiCi's told me all about you." She put her little hand in Reed's, smiled up at him with dark brown eyes through dusty glasses. "You're a policeman. My uncle Albert was a policeman in Brooklyn, New York. CiCi said you remember my house from when you came to the island as a boy."

"Yes, ma'am."

"Well, it's some different now in here. Cody's been working like a mule."

"It looks great."

"I hardly recognize the place. It's just not mine anymore. But I will say the kitchen's a treat. Let me get you some tea and cookies."

"Now don't worry about that." CiCi patted her hand. "Cody tucked a pretty little powder room under the stairs here, didn't he?"

"He did. That boy's so handy. I don't know what I'd do without him."

Singing Cody's praises, Barbara Ellen—nudged by CiCi—showed off the first floor. Reed had to steel himself against the views of the woods, the water. With CiCi leading, they headed upstairs.

Four fricking bedrooms including a newly remodeled master suite. Gas fireplace, killer views, attached bath nearly as big as the bedroom in his old shitcan.

Everything about the house pulled at him, and pushed against his reality. He met the handy Cody, talked a little construction before CiCi waved him off.

"Go on up to the widow's walk."

"Oh yes, you should!" Barbara Ellen agreed. "It's the crown of the house. I don't go up anymore. Just don't trust myself on the narrow stairs, but you should take it in."

Narrow, yes, but sturdy—Cody at work again, Reed thought.

Then he stepped out onto the circling deck, and couldn't think at all.

He could see everything. The water, the woods, the village, CiCi's amazing house to the west, then the fanciful lighthouse to the east. The world in all its color and beauty spread out for him like one of CiCi's paintings.

It could be his.

Not once, he thought, in all the houses he'd walked through, studied, considered, had he ever felt not that it could be his, should be his, but already was.

"Fuck, fuck, fuck." When he, without thinking, dragged a hand through his hair, his shoulder snarled.

"It's crazy. I'm crazy." He rubbed absently at his shoulder. "Maybe not. Shit. Investment property. What about that? Rent it out during the season, use it for long weekends, for vacation time off-season. What's wrong with that?

"Can't do it. Can't," he muttered as he took one more stroll around the railed deck. "Can't."

As he went back down, he heard CiCi asking Cody what he planned to ask.

"Well, once we get the last bathroom up here gutted and redone, and the last bedroom remodeled, a little more trim here and there, and some this and that. Give everything a nice, fresh coat of paint, and some more landscaping . . ."

He named a price that made Reed wince. Not because it was out of his range, but because it wasn't that much out of his range.

"Of course," Barbara Ellen put in, with a twinkle of a smile toward Reed, "if somebody wanted it before we put it on the market, saved us that trouble, those fees, we'd adjust that price. Wouldn't we, Cody?"

"Some, sure. But we've still got the work left."

"What if you didn't?" Reed heard himself ask, knew he'd just tied a rock to his leg. "I mean, if you didn't gut the bathroom, add more landscaping, the paint, the bedroom. If, say, you finished what you're doing in here with the closet, and that was that?"

"Well now." Cody sniffed, rubbing his chin. "That'd make a difference, wouldn't it?"

Enough of one, when Cody ballparked another figure, to tie on the next rock.

He didn't commit—wouldn't let himself. He needed to run some numbers, give some hard thought to what it would mean to his life. He'd never afford a house in Portland if he did this. But . . . he didn't want a house in Portland.

"You want it," CiCi said as they rode home.

"I want a lot of things I can't have. Like you."

"What if you could?"

"Have you? Pedal faster."

She laughed her glorious laugh. "I'm mad for you, Delicious. You said, and I agree, a cop lives where he works."

"Yeah, that's a sticking point."

"What if you could do that? Live and work on the island. Chief Wickett's retiring. He isn't saying so officially as yet, but he told me. He's giving it until February, maybe March, so he's telling the island council next month. To give them time to find his replacement."

CHAPTER FOURTEEN

Chief of police? That was just more craziness.

CiCi let it drop on him, then blithely went into her studio.

So he took a solo walk on the beach, hoping the air would blow his brain back to sanity.

He sat on the rocks and brooded. He walked some more.

When he finally went back, CiCi sat on the patio, a cozy throw over her legs and a bottle of wine, two glasses, on the table.

"You need a nice glass of wine."

"I can't be a police chief."

"Why not? It's just a title." She poured the wine.

"It's not just a title. It's being in charge of a department. It's administrative."

She patted a hand at the chair next to hers. "You're smart, and the current chief would work with you until you got your rhythm. You've told me enough over these past days and entertaining evenings for me to know you're not happy in Portland. You're not happy with the box your own chief or captain or whatever put you in. Get out of the box, Reed.

"You have a purpose," she continued. "Your aura absolutely pulses with it."

"My aura pulses with purpose?"

"It does. And you'd fulfill that here. You'd also fulfill your just-as-essential purpose of working on the investigation of that Hobart psycho. The off-season here isn't without work for a police chief, but you'd have that time and space."

She looked at him. "Tell me you're happy where you are, and I'll stop."

He wanted to, but shook his head. "No. I've thought about transferring, but there's Essie. And some others. My family."

"You're less than an hour from your friends and family here. You want that house. I don't have to be psychic to know that because it was all over you. But since I am a little bit psychic I know you'll be happy here, happy in that house—because it's your place. Clear as day. You'll have your purpose, your home. You're going to find the love of your life."

"I already did," he interrupted.

She reached over and took his hand. "You're going to find the one who'll share that home with you. You're going to raise a family there."

"I can barely afford the house. Who knows if I'm qualified for chief of police, or if the island council would offer me the position?"

She smiled over the rim of her glass. Silver hoops with bloodred drops glinted at her ears. "I have some not inconsiderable influence. We need good, young, bright blood in the job. And here you are."

"You're biased because you love me, too."

"I do, but if I didn't think this was right for you, for the island—not even just right for you, but the answer—I wouldn't have spoken with Hildy yesterday."

"Hildy?"

"Mayor Hildy Intz. She'd love to talk with you."

"Jesus, CiCi."

Laughing, she poked him in the arm. "Shit's getting real, am I right? It makes me think of Simone. I told you how she tried to fit in the box, and finally realized she couldn't. When she took that leap, she found the answer.

Or one of them. Don't let them keep you in their box, Reed. Damn, that's my phone. I left it inside."

"I'll get it."

He hurried in, brought it back to her.

"Huh. Barbara Ellen." With a wiggle of her eyebrows, she answered. "Hi, Barbara Ellen. Yes. Hmm."

She listened, nodded, sipped wine.

"I see. Oh, I absolutely will. It was wonderful to see you, too. And Cody. Yes, he's done beautiful work. It's no wonder you're proud of him. Uh-huh." She gave Reed an eye roll. "I know you will. Let me get back to you? Bye now."

She ended the call, set the phone down, took another sip of wine.

"Barbara Ellen's anxious to pack up and move, just go back with Cody and be done. Factoring that, she's nagged Cody into lowering the price—for you, if you take it as discussed—another seventy-five hundred."

"Oh, shit."

"She knows you'll love the house she loved, the house where she raised her children. Obviously, she's right about that."

"I shouldn't have gone up on the widow's walk." More rocks, he thought, sinking fast. He rubbed a hand over his face. "It was bad enough before that. It was bad enough just *feeling* that place, but going up there did it. I can't talk myself out of it."

"I've never understood why people are always trying to talk themselves out of things they want. You just got another signpost, my man. You ought to follow it."

"Yeah."

"Why don't I call Hildy, invite her over for a drink?"

He looked at her, nodded. "Why don't you do that?"

As soon as he returned to Portland, Reed contacted Essie, asked her to meet him at the park. He sat on the same bench where they'd sat more than a decade before. He'd taken a new direction right there, with her help.

Now he prepared to do just that again.

In the brisk November breeze, he watched the water, the people, thought back to that hot summer day. Angie's funeral—a girl who'd never had the chance to change directions.

Maybe that was part of the whole—part of his whole anyway. He'd been given the chance—twice—and believed he had to make the best of it.

After DownEast, he'd wondered and worried if there was a bullet on pause, waiting for somebody to hit the play button. Patricia Hobart had hit that button, and two, not one, bullets found him.

And he'd survived.

No wasting time or opportunities, he thought. No looking back later and thinking: Why didn't I?

So he sat while the wind kicked through his hair, while winter began to poke its chilly fingers through the balm of autumn and thought of yesterdays and tomorrows. Because, hell, the right now was already here.

He watched her come, his partner, his mentor, his friend. Quick strides in sturdy boots, dark jacket zipped against the wind, dark ski cap over the short, careless do she called mom/cop hair.

Without her, he'd have bled to death on a refinished hardwood floor. As much as he loved his family, Essie was the person he most wanted never, never to disappoint.

"Okay, let me take a look." She did just that, eyes narrowed and critical on his face. Then she nodded. "Yeah, you look good. A couple weeks on Tranquility worked for you."

She sat, looked him in the eye. "How do you feel?"

"Better. A lot. Walked every day, jogged a little. Kept up the PT. Fell in love with a sexy, fascinating woman."

"That didn't take long."

"Boom." He snapped his fingers. "Have you heard of CiCi Lennon?"

"Ah . . . Artist, right? Local. Isn't she . . . like, your grandmother's age?"

"Maybe. It occurs to me, women have had a profound influence and effect on my life. My mom, sure, and my sister, too. And in a strange, awful way, Angie. You and I sat here the day of her funeral."

"I remember."

"You. You've had a profound influence and effect."

"You made your own way, Reed."

"I like to think so, but you helped me find it. I love being a cop. I hated seeing that worry on my parents' faces in the hospital, and I hate knowing that's going to be inside them from now on. But I know they'll deal. I need to be a cop."

"I never doubted it."

He studied the water. "The thing is, neither did I. Even lying on the floor, wondering if that was it. Game over. The decision I made right here—or at least started to make—was the right one. A big part of that decision was Angie, and that night. I can't stop pursuing that, Essie. I can't stop trying to take Patricia Hobart down."

Essie angled toward him. "The bitch shot my partner. Look, I'm pissed we got locked out, and I can still hope the feds run her to ground. But either way, we'll work it, Reed. We'll work it off the books, on our own time."

"They'll keep me on the desk for a while. Three to six months, I figure. The department doesn't have our backs on it. You've got a family, Essie. We could carve out some time to work it, sure, but by the time they let me come back to full duty, they're going to have you with another partner."

"I'm pushing back on that," she began.

"We've got to work the actives. That's priority. They're never going to let either of us work the Hobart investigation, even peripherally—and I can't get too pissed about it. But Hobart's the key to the rest, and I'm not letting it go. By the time I'm cleared, they'll put me with someone else. We can both push back, but that's a big, gaping maybe. And we'll both have cases that have to come first."

"You're circling around something, and I'm not feeling good about it. Are you thinking of requesting a transfer?"

"Not exactly. I found the house. I found it on the island. It's everything I want and need, and it's the reason I never found that here."

"Well, Jesus, Reed, I get how much you want to find a place, but—"

"*The* place, Essie, that's the thing. I stayed in CiCi's house most of the time I was on the island. Not like that," he said with a quick laugh. "Though if she'd give me a shot . . . Anyway, I found a lot of things. Bloody Marys and pancakes, yoga on the beach—"

Jaw dropping, Essie held up a hand. "Wait. You did yoga on the beach?"

"CiCi's got a way. The thing is, I ended up sitting on the rocks down from her place because her house was one I remembered, especially, from a million years ago when we had a couple of vacations on the island. And she ended up asking me to stay because she recognized me—from the shooting, and from my connection to the mall. Her granddaughter was there."

"Wait, wait, that's it." Now Essie punched her palm at the air. "Nagging at me. She's Simone Knox's grandmother."

"Right. You answered Simone's nine-one-one. I'm looking at all of it, Essie. Angie—I talked to her, made a half-assed date with her minutes before she died. I end up hiding with Brady in her kiosk, with her blood on me. And I end up on this bench with you. I end up on the island because of all of it. I don't want to get all metaphysical or whatever, but it just means something."

"Are you telling me you bought CiCi Lennon's house?"

"No. There were two that hit me back then, back when I was, like, ten years old, and I told her about it because, Jesus, you can talk to CiCi. Or I sure can. And it means something, Essie, that the owner and her son are fixing up the house I remembered—to get it on the market. It matters that when I started going through it, it was—here's another stupid word, but it was visceral. It was mine. I tried to talk myself out of it. But it was all there.

"I said okay, fine, I could think of it as an investment, rent it out, take some vacation time there. Because a cop has to live where he works, and I need to be a cop. But the thing is, I don't want to rent it out."

"Reed, please tell me you're not going for an island deputy job. You're an investigator. You're—"

"No, not a deputy."

"Then what the hell?"

"Chief of police."

"You—" She stopped, let out a *whoosh* of air. "Seriously?"

"I don't have it yet. The island council has to vote and all that. But I did an interview—a couple of them. And I wrote up a résumé. They're going to call you, Bull, the lieutenant pretty soon. If I don't get it . . . I'm young, not from the island—those are strikes against me. I'm a police detective with a few years under my belt, a good closed-case history, who's already got a contract on a house there. Those are pluses for me. And the big guns? CiCi. So I rate my chances at about seventy-thirty."

She sat awhile, saying nothing, working through it. "You want it."

"Downside? Farther away from the family than they're going to like. And not working with you. Not being able to drop by, see you and Hank and Dylan, and mooch a meal. I'm hoping to offset that by having you guys come and hang out. Because, yeah, I want it. I want it because I found things I needed there. And because I think I could do good work. I want it because I'll have the time and space, especially in the fall and winter, to work Hobart. I can't be a cop, look at myself in the mirror, and not work Hobart."

"I hate this." She pushed herself off the bench, walked toward the bay and back. "I just hate it."

"Essie—"

She threw up a hand to stop him as he rose. "I hate it because it feels right for you. It just feels like the right thing. And I'm going to miss you dropping by to mooch a meal. I'll miss working cases with you."

"It feels right?"

"Yeah, it does. When would you leave?"

"I don't have the job yet."

"You're going to get it." It felt too right for otherwise. "When would you leave?"

"Not until after the first of the year. The current chief's leaving in March—see, he told CiCi, hadn't even told the council yet. It all just slid into place."

"Chief Quartermaine." She shook her head. "Isn't that a kick in the ass?"

He felt that kick ten days later when he formally accepted the job as chief of police of Tranquility Island.

In the spirit of fence mending, Simone agreed to a fancy girls' lunch at her mother's country club. She'd have preferred spending the blustery November afternoon in her studio, but her relationship with Natalie had improved.

Natalie wanted the lunch, and pushed. So here they were, eating elaborate salads, drinking Kir Royales, and making chitchat about a wedding that was still nearly a year off.

She'd already gotten her mother's eye for the short, shaggy do in a color her adventurous hairdresser dubbed Burning Embers. But the fact that Tulip held her tongue, for once, helped keep the interlude civilized.

Besides, she couldn't deny she'd chosen the over-the-knee boots, suede pants, and a bold green leather jacket to push her mother's buttons.

In any case, she liked seeing Natalie so happy, even if a lot of it stemmed from debates on wedding dress designs and wedding colors.

When she felt her mind melting over the perfect signature drink for a fall wedding, she steered the conversation toward the house Natalie and Harry had just purchased.

"So the new house. That's exciting. When will you be ready to move in?"

"There's certainly no rush," Tulip began. "Especially with all the holiday festivities coming up. Simone, you really must attend the Snowflake Ball next month. My friend Mindy's son Triston's coming in from Boston for Christmas, and I'm sure he'd be happy to escort you."

"Yes." Glowing, happy, Natalie all but bounced in her seat. "You could double-date with Harry and me!"

Under the table, Simone gave Natalie's leg a quick, firm squeeze.

"My calendar's already full, Mom, but thanks for the thought. About the house—"

"For once I'd like to have my whole family present at an event that's important to me."

Simone picked up her glass, took a careful sip of a drink that struck her as too sweet and silly. "I know the Snowflake Ball's important to you. So's the Winter Gala, the Spring Ball, the Summer Jubilee in July, and so forth. I've come to several of them over the last few years."

"You haven't once come to the Jubilee, and we raise money for the arts with the proceeds."

"It's a bad time of year for me, Mom."

Tulip started to speak, then looked away. "It helps to do something positive."

"I know, and I do. For me. I really want to hear about the house."

"Haven't you hidden yourself away on the island long enough? If you're not there, you're off somewhere else. You're never going to create a social network or meet someone as wonderful as Harry on that island."

Here we go again, Simone thought. "I have the social network I want, and I'm not looking for someone like Harry. And he is wonderful," Simone added with a smile for Natalie. "Mom," she said before Tulip could speak again. "Let's talk about things we can agree on. Like how happy Natalie is, what a wonderful wedding she'll have. How fabulous her new house is."

"About the wedding—again," Natalie said, so obviously trying to right the ship, Simone gave her knee another squeeze, a grateful one. "Will you be my maid of honor?"

It surprised her, touched her, and both showed on her face. "Nat, I'm so honored. Really. It means so much to me you'd ask, and if it's what you truly want, of course I will. But . . ."

Now she took Natalie's hand on the white tablecloth. "Cerise has been your best friend for a decade. The two of you are so close, and she knows exactly what you want for your wedding. She'll know how to make it happen for you. She should be your maid of honor."

"People will expect—"

Simone looked at her mother, so fast, so fierce, the rest of the words died. "What matters is what Natalie wants. Ask Cerise, and let me do something special for you instead."

"I don't want you to feel slighted. You're my sister."

"I won't. I don't. I'd like you to have Cerise stand for you. I'd like to make the topper for your cake. I'd like to do a sculpture of you and Harry. Something you'd keep to remember the biggest day of your lives. Something that shows not only how happy you were on that day, but how happy I am for you."

"We've already started looking at cake designs and toppers," Tulip pointed out.

"Mom." Natalie reached for her mother's hand, effectively joining the three women together. "I would love it. Honestly, I'd just love it. Could you do something fun for the groom's cake? Like Harry putting on a golf green, or swinging on the tee?"

"Absolutely. You get me the cake designs once you have them. And when you have your dress, I'll do some sketches and photos—same with Harry when he's got his groom clothes. We can brainstorm ideas for the groom's cake if you want, but the wedding topper's going to be a surprise."

She looked back at her mother. "I won't disappoint or embarrass you. I want to give something to Natalie, something that's a part of me. How about the two of you pick a couple of desserts to share and order me some black coffee? I'll be right back."

She wound her way through the dining room, escaping to the restroom and vowing no matter how many fences needed mending, she would never agree to another ladies' lunch at the club.

To counterbalance, she decided she'd pick up some of her grandmother's favorite veggie pizza on the way home, and they'd gorge while drinking some good wine.

She had to push herself mentally to go into the bathroom stall—she always did. But the little flutter came and went, as it always did.

When she came out, she barely glanced at the blonde carefully touching up her lipstick in the mirror over the long silver counter with its line of deep vessel sinks.

She needed to figure out how to put a cheerful smile on her face, get through dessert and coffee. And escape.

"Simone Knox."

She looked over at the blonde. She heard the sneer in the voice, saw it on the deep rose lips. Before she realized the physical sneer was caused by the pull of carefully masked scarring.

The left eye—boldly blue—drooped just a fraction. A casual observer might not have noticed, but an artist who'd studied facial structure and anatomy couldn't miss it.

She kept her own face as neutral as her voice.

"That's right."

"You don't recognize me?"

She hadn't, in those first few seconds. But it all flooded over her. All.

"Tiffany. Sorry. It's been a long time."

"Hasn't it just?"

"How are you?"

"How do I look? Oh don't be shy," she continued, waving her hands on either side of her face. "Eight surgeries over seven years. Add years of speech therapy, some brain bleeds. Totally reconstucted left ear," she added, tapping on it. "Of course, the hearing's pretty well shot in it, but you can't have everything."

"I'm sorry—"

"Sorry? The fucking bastard shot me in the face! They had to put it back together. You walked away without a scratch, didn't you?"

None that showed.

"But all these years later, they're still talking about the brave, quick-thinking Simone Knox who hid and called for help. While I lay there under my dead boyfriend with my face in pieces."

She didn't want to see it, didn't want to see the flashes of gunfire through the door wedged open by a dead body. She didn't want to hear the screams.

"I'm sorry for all you've been through."

"You don't know *anything* about what I've been through." The drooping eye twitched as Tiffany's voice rose up another register. "I was beautiful. I was important. And you were nothing. A castoff. You got lucky, and they call you a hero. Why do you think people buy that crap you make?"

"You're sorry? You should be dead. I've waited twelve years to tell you exactly that."

"Now you have."

"It's still not enough. It'll never be enough."

As Tiffany stormed out, Simone thought: Her left shoulder's just a fraction lower than her right. Then went into the stall and threw up the fancy salad and Kir Royale.

When she got back to the table, her mother and sister had their heads together, laughing.

"I'm sorry. I need to go."

"Oh, Simone, we just ordered dessert." Natalie reached up for her hand.

"I'm sorry." How many times would she say that today? she wondered.

"Just because we disagree doesn't—" Tulip's quiet tirade stopped in mid-stream. "Simone, you're white as a sheet."

"I'm not feeling well. I—"

Tulip got up quickly, rounded the table. "You sit. Sit a minute. I'll get you some fresh water."

"This is fine." Water, she thought. Yes, some water. But her hand trembled a little. "Honestly, I need to go. A little air."

"Yes. Some air. Natalie, stay here. I'm going to walk your sister outside." She slid her arm around Simone's waist. "We'll get our coats. I have the check."

Smooth, efficient Tulip retrieved their coats, helped Simone into hers. "Take my beret. You should have worn a hat." She steered Simone out to a patio festively decorated for the holidays.

"Now tell me what happened."

"It's nothing. Just a headache."

"Don't lie to me. Give me some credit for knowing my own child. Give me some respect."

"I'm sorry." There it was again. "You're right. I need to walk. I need to breathe."

"We'll walk. You'll breathe. And you'll tell me what happened."

"In the restroom. Tiffany Bryce."

"Do we know her?"

"I went to school with her. She was in the theater that night."

"Of course. I know her stepmother a little. She—they—have had a very difficult time."

"Yes. She told me."

"I know it's hard for you to be reminded, but—"

"She blames me."

"What?" Absently, Tulip brushed at her hair as the wind disturbed it. "Of course she doesn't."

"She does, and she made that clear. She got shot in the face. I didn't. Nothing happened to me."

"It happened to all of us, whether or not we were physically injured. All of us." Now she gripped Simone's hand. "What did she say to you, sweetie?"

"She gave me a recount of her injuries, harangued me for not having any. And told me I should've died. That she wished I had."

"I don't care what happened to her, she had no right to say that. It's very likely she would have died without what you did that night."

"Don't say that. Please, don't say that. I don't want to be thought of that way."

"You were brave and you were smart, and don't you ever, ever forget it." She took Simone by the shoulders. "That girl's bitter and angry, and I can forgive that. But what she said to you is wrong and hateful. You said in there you wouldn't disappoint or embarrass me. Don't disappoint me now and take one single thing she said to heart."

"I hated her. That night, before, when she came in with Trent, so smug and dismissive of me. I hated her. And now . . ."

"Now you've grown up, and she, obviously, hasn't changed a bit. Not everyone changes, Simone. Not everyone can move through and beyond a tragedy."

Simone let her head drop to her mother's shoulder. "Sometimes I'm still stuck there. In that bathroom stall."

"Then—God, I'm going to sound like my mother—open the door. You have, and you'll keep opening it. Even if I don't like where it takes you. I love you, Simone. Maybe that's why you constantly exasperate me. I mean, honestly, why do you do that to your hair?"

Simone managed a watery laugh. "You're bringing up my hair to take my mind off the rest."

"That may be, but I still can't understand why you'd chop it off and dye it hellfire red."

"I must've been in a hellfire mood when I did." She drew back, then kissed her mother's cheek. "Thank you. I'm better, but I don't want to go back in. I couldn't face dessert anyway."

"Are you well enough to drive?"

"Yeah. Don't worry."

"I will, so you'll text me when you're at your grandmother's."

"Okay. Tell Nat—"

"I intend to tell Natalie exactly what happened so we can gossip about that stupid, ugly woman over dessert and coffee."

This time the laugh came easier. "I love you, Mom. That must be why you constantly exasperate me."

"I'll give you one *touché*. Your color's better. Text me—and have CiCi make you one of her crazy teas."

"I will."

Rather than go through the club, she walked around the building to her car. She hadn't wanted to come, she thought, and couldn't claim she'd had a good time of it.

But she could be glad she'd come. However strange and awful, the fences got mended, and they felt stronger for it now.

Maybe they could keep them that way awhile.

CHAPTER FIFTEEN

Simone couldn't forget Tiffany's face—the before, and the now.

She couldn't forget the smugness on it then, the anger on it now. They pushed and prodded at her, both sides of the coin: the smugness of the young girl who prized her own beauty, and the anger of the woman who believed she'd lost it.

While she worked, those faces revolved in her head.

She'd never gone back to the DownEast Mall or any other. She'd never sat in a movie theater again. She'd done everything to push that night and all that surrounded it out of her mind. Away from her life.

Now, with that single encounter, those two faces playing through her head, that night and all that surrounded it pushed into her.

Unable to block it out, she made it a project. She sketched Tiffany's face at sixteen from memory: the well-balanced features, the confident, blossoming beauty, the perfect sweep of hair.

Then she sketched the now, the woman who'd confronted her at the club: the scarring, the slight drooping of the left eye, the drawn-up lip, the reconstructed left ear.

Flawed, she thought, studying the two faces, visibly flawed. But hardly monstrous. In fact, as an artist, she found the second face more interesting.

But . . . Did the anger come from being reminded, every time she looked in the mirror? Did the horror flood back? Instead of being able to shut it away, move on, the results of that single night lived in the face in the mirror.

Wouldn't it take a particular kind of strength and resolve to face that and move on?

How could she criticize? How could she dismiss that anger and resentment when she'd refused to face her own? She'd just locked hers away.

Rising, she walked to the window. Outside, snow fell soft out of moody gray skies and piled in soft mounds on the rocks. The water blurred with the sky, and winter closed off everything but that water, that sky.

The quiet and peace, the solitude of winter on the island spread before her. The chaos and ugliness of that long ago summer night waited behind.

She heard Tiffany's voice in her head.

You walked away without a scratch.

"No. No, I didn't. So . . ."

On a deep breath, she turned.

She chose her tools, her clay.

Half-scale, she thought as she spread out some canvas and began to roll clay into a rectangle. She could stop anytime, she assured herself. Or just change directions. But if she wanted the faces out of her head, maybe she needed to make them real.

She trimmed the slab of clay before rolling it, bending it into a cylinder. Once she'd flipped it vertically, she used her hands to smooth the walls. She cut the angles, scored, overlapped, joined, compressing the seams, created the void.

The practical, the technical, came first, laid the foundation.

She sketched the outline of the face with a rounded tip, checked proportions.

With her hands, she began to shape it. Eye sockets, forehead, nose, adding clay, pushing from the inside of the cylinder for cheeks, cheekbones, chin.

She could see it just as her hands could feel it. A female face—still any female face.

Depressions, indentions, mounds.

Thinking of the then, the now, the smug, the bitter, she turned the clay to do the same on the opposing side.

The two sides, she thought, of a life.

Now the dome of the head, coiling seams, compressing, adding a slit, until she left an opening only wide enough for her hand.

She studied the work—yes, simple, basic, rough—letting the clay stiffen a bit before cutting another dart, the shape of a football, on the sides. Her transition from neck to skull.

She darted the front, taking her time to create the chin and neck. Repeated on the back with the subtle changes from damage, and the years.

Rising again, she walked around the worktable, studying the roughed-in faces, the sketches.

She sat, made her commitment by using her thumb to draw down the depression of the left eye socket.

"Here we go," she mumbled, and began to roll a small ball of clay. "I don't know what I'm trying to prove, but here we go."

The eyeballs, the corners of the eyes, the lids—she structured with fingers and tools.

As was her habit, she jumped from feature to feature, roughing in the eyes, moving on to the nose, the chin, the ears, and back again. Shifting, as her mind and hands demanded, from face to face.

The mouth, so perfect on the then, and with that hint of smug. On the now, that drawn-up corner—not a smile, she thought, adding clay, scoring with a square-edge, pushing with her thumb, her fingers. Flawed, yes, flawed, but it was bitterness hardening those lips.

As the snow fell, she worked in silence. No music today, no background. Just the clay, giving under her hands, building, forming.

She felt it, real as life even before she went back to the eyes. The anatomy, of course, with the folds, the tear bags, the creases; but it was always the life in them, the expressions that opened the windows. The thoughts and feelings of a single moment, or a lifetime, could come through the eyes.

And here, in the face of a lovely teenage girl, the eyes shined with confidence—borderline arrogance. In the woman, the eyes reflected not just the horror and fear of one night, but the results in the face and the mind and the heart of a woman who'd lived through it.

While Simone worked, so did Patricia Hobart.

Snow fell outside her window as well, as she studied someone else who'd lived through it.

She'd about had it with Toronto, wanted a change of scene, a change of place. Bob Kofax offered just that.

He'd been a mall security guard on the big night, had survived two gunshot wounds. His story, his survival, had garnered him more media exposure than Patricia deemed appropriate. Added to it, he continued to—in her opinion— feed off her own brother's misfortune by continuing to work at the mall.

A slap in the face!

Bob, it seemed, considered his survival a message from a higher power to make the most of the gift of life, to help those in need, and to start and end each day with gratitude.

She knew this, as it said so on his Facebook page.

Part of making the most would be celebrating his fiftieth birthday with his wife and his two children—one of whom was gay and "married" to another gay, which just offended every fiber of Patricia's being. As if that wasn't bad enough, they'd adopted some Asian kid. At least his other son married an actual woman and had a couple of real kids.

The whole damn fam planned to hold the big bash with a week of fun and sun in Bermuda.

Their various Facebook pages held all the details she needed, including— for *God's* sake—a countdown clock.

Bob turned fifty on January nineteenth.

After some thought, Patricia chose her identity, her look, booked her flight and a luxury room at the same resort.

Then she got down to the fun part, planning the best ways to kill Bob before he reached the big five-oh.

Two days before Christmas, CiCi's house illuminated the season. She lit her house brightly enough that, on a clear night, its glow reached the mainland. From her tree hung armies of Santas, mythological creatures, gods, goddesses, and hand-painted balls.

The fire snapped cheerfully. At dusk she'd light the dozens of candles inside, the glass lanterns outside, while the caterers set up the spread for her annual holiday open house.

Christmas Eve was for her and Simone, and Christmas Day was for the family. But tonight was for the island and was one of her favorite nights of the year.

It got a boost when she opened the door to Mi.

"Merry, happy everything." She gripped Mi in a hard hug before grabbing bags.

"CiCi, the place looks amazing. Just like you."

"I'm so happy to see you. Let's get your coat, your bags. Let's get you a drink."

"It's only two in the afternoon."

"It's Christmas! We'll make it mimosas. You can take one up to Simone—and lure her down here, so I can have my girls for a while. I think she's hiding in her studio so I won't bug her about what she's wearing tonight. How's your family?"

"They're really good." Mi pulled her cap off her razor-straight bob. "CiCi, Nari's engaged—well, will be tomorrow night. Everybody knows but Nari. He—James—asked my father for her hand, and earned serious points for that. He's asking her on Christmas Eve."

The boy from Boston had staying power, CiCi thought, pausing with a bottle of champagne in her hand. "She loves him?"

"She loves him."

"Well then." CiCi released the cork with a cheerful *pop*. "We'll drink to her happiness. How about you? Anybody caught your eye?"

"Mmm. Some catch the eye, but . . ." She shrugged. "No one's caught the heart and mind along with it."

"You hold out for that. Sex is easy. Love's complicated. Now, you take this up to Simone, have a little BFF time, then make her come down here. The three of us are going to have another drink, some gossip, then we're going to make ourselves gorgeous."

Mi bounced up two flights of steps, a glass in each hand.

When she turned into the studio, into the music that masked the sound of her boots on the stairs, she saw her friend painting some sort of red wash over a statue.

The nude bent back fluidly, nearly forming a circle from the feet to the crown of her head. She held a bow, with an arrow notched, pointing straight up.

Power and grace, Mi thought. And beauty. She could and would say the same about her friend. Simone wore her hair—a deep brown with bold red highlights—in a short braid, had jeans splattered with clay and paint with holes in both knees, a similarly splattered sweatshirt with ragged half sleeves, and bare feet with toes painted midnight blue.

She felt a rush of love, a click of all's right with the world, and a little tug of envy for Simone's effortless artistic style.

Simone stepped back, angling her head to study the work, and spotted Mi.

She squealed (a sound CiCi heard two floors below, causing her to grin), splattering red wash as she tossed down her brush.

"You're here!"

"With mimosas."

"You're better than a dozen mimosas. I can't hug you. I've got paint all over me."

"Oh, screw that." Mi set the glasses aside, grabbed Simone, danced in a circle. "I missed you."

"Goes double." She took a long breath. "Now it can be Christmas."

"Let's drink to that. Or I can drink to that while you finish what you're doing."

"It's finished."

"Who is she?"

"*The Archer*. She's a shopkeeper I saw in Sedona. She had this . . . bold serenity."

"You captured just that."

"You think? Well." Simone picked up the glasses.

"I love this room," Mi said, taking one of the glasses. "It's so you. So different from my lab—which is so me. But here we are." She gave Simone's hand a squeeze before she started to wander. "These are inspired by your trip out west?"

"Most, yeah. I've sent a couple pieces to my agent so she can see where I'm heading. Anyway—"

"She looks familiar," Mi began, then lowered her glass, turned. "Is this Tiffany? I haven't thought about her in years, but . . ."

"Yeah."

Curious, Mi stepped closer, angled her head. "There's a face on the other side?"

"You can pick it up. It's done."

Mi lifted it, turned it carefully. "Oh. I see."

"One from before, and one from now. I should've put it away," she realized. "We don't want all that spoiling things."

"No, wait. Why? Why Tiffany?"

"I ran into her a few weeks ago." Simone shrugged. "It's so strange. We've got a reversal. Once, I believed, absolutely, that this girl . . ." She trailed a finger over the unlined brow, the smooth cheek. "This girl ruined my life. She stole the boy I loved, the boy I just knew I'd marry and live happily ever after with. I blamed her for my misery. God, Mi. Sixteen."

"Sixteen." Mi slipped an arm around Simone's waist. "But this girl was still a mean, conniving slut."

"She really was."

"To have a reversal means she believes you ruined her life? Blames you? How?"

"I walked out whole." Simone traced fingers over the second face. "She didn't."

"JJ Hobart's to blame for that. What did she say to you, Sim?"

"Do you see this face? Not just the flaws."

"You mean the anger and bitterness? Of course I do. You have a genius for showing what's inside." Mi took a casual sip of her drink, matched her tone to the gesture. "So, she's still a mean, conniving slut?"

And on a laugh, Simone felt the sticky, strangling vines of stress drop away. "Yes. God, yes, she is."

"Tragedy doesn't necessarily change us. More often, I think, it just brings out more of who we are—or were—all along." Deliberately, Mi turned the bitter face out, set the bust back on the shelf. "Tiffany was always this inside."

In a careless toast, Mi lifted her glass. "Maybe she isn't as perfectly beautiful as she would have been—on the outside. But she's alive, and plenty aren't. She may very well be alive because of you. I am. Don't shake your head at Dr. Jung. My blood loss? Another ten minutes—fifteen on the outside? I wouldn't have made it."

"Let's not talk about all that."

"No, let's. Just for a minute because I have something to say. This? What you did with Tiffany—what the hell is her last name?"

"Bryce."

"You remember. I don't. That says something, too. What you did with your art? That's healthy."

"Is it?"

"You're damn right it is. It's not just who she is, Sim, but who you are. We all survived, and we all became who we are right now. Whatever's inside you that created her out of clay? It was always there. The sixteen-year-old girl who thought her world crashed because of some horny jerk who wasn't worth her time—and yeah, maybe I'll go to hell for speaking ill of the dead, but he *was* a horny jerk—could have decided to wallow in misery, to throw away her gifts in bitterness."

Mi turned back to the bust. "But what I see in this face is someone who's throwing away the gift of her life in blame and bitterness.

"We lost a friend, Sim, and it still hurts. It's always going to hurt. But you've brought our friend back to life, you've celebrated the life she had, even the life she might have had, in that amazing sculpture downstairs, and in others."

"I don't know . . ." Simone drew a shaky breath. "I don't know what I'd do without you in my life."

"You're never going to find out. Me? I've channeled my skill, my art, I guess, into working to find ways to alleviate pain, suffering, to improve quality of life. It doesn't make us special, but it makes us who we are.

"We're better than Tiffany fucking Bryce, Sim. We always were."

Simone drew in another breath, let it out on a long exhale. And managed a "Wow."

"I mean every word, including the jerks dead or alive. And now, every time you look at those two faces, you should remember it. Screw the bitch, Simone."

Frowning, Simone took a last study of the bust. "I can be sorry for what happened to her—nobody deserves it—but I can still hate her?"

"Yes!"

"I don't know why I didn't think of that. Even when I formed those faces with my hands, I didn't think of that."

"That's what friends are for."

"Well, best friend ever, you just answered the question I couldn't quite grab on to. Yes. Screw the bitch. Now, let's go down and get a lot more champagne. I'm going to need it to socialize until freaking dawn."

"I love CiCi's parties." As they started out, Mi turned with a cheerful smile. "I bought a new dress just for tonight. It's a killer."

"Damn you. Now she'll be all over me, even more. Well, screw that, too," Simone decided. "I'm throwing caution to the freaking winds. She can pick out my outfit."

Delighted, Mi gave Simone a shoulder bump. "This is going to be so much fun!"

CiCi had already picked the outfit, since she'd bought it and hung it in her own closet with the intention of cajoling Simone into wearing it.

After considerable champagne and gossip, she dragged her girls to her master bath for a makeup and hair session. She decreed sleek and sexy for Mi, then wielded the curling iron to give her uncharacteristically cooperative granddaughter a headful of tousled curls.

She approved Mi's choice of off-the-shoulder red with its flirty skirt and tiny waist, and waited until Simone tugged and shimmied her way into the midnight blue.

The long sleeves and to-the-knees length might have hinted at modesty, but the deep vee front and back, the slit up the right leg hinted at the opposite—especially as it fit like a second skin.

"This is why you handed me the blue nail polish yesterday."

"Good match," CiCi agreed, then pulled out her next weapon. "Especially with these."

The shoes, a series of metallic-blue straps from toe to ankle, boasted high, thin silver heels.

"Sexy bohemian," CiCi declared.

"They're gorgeous." Simone sat, strapped them on, stood. "I may limp for weeks, but it'll be worth it."

"Happy Yule." CiCi grabbed her camera. "Strike a pose, girls."

As they hammed for the camera, CiCi thought she'd paint them as young sirens.

"Crap, that's the caterer. Jewelry! Mi, delicate. Simone, arty and a little over-the-top. Go!"

In a flurry of swirling skirts, lace-up booties, and a flying mane of wild red, she rushed out.

"How does she do it?" Mi asked.

"I don't know, but I'm determined to look just that good, move just that fast, live just that big when I'm her age. Let's play with earrings and get down there, give her a hand."

With the wind kicking, the temperatures dropping, CiCi's house filled with people. The island came out for CiCi, as did off-islanders. People from the art world and the music world mingled with locals over mini lobster rolls, shrimp kabobs, and champagne.

Some spilled out on the patio with its portable heaters. Music blared from the speakers, or when those with talent and the whim picked up a guitar or played a keyboard and jammed.

CiCi mingled, enjoying every moment, even as she kept her eye out for one particular person. When she spotted him, she wound her way over to Simone.

"Sweetie, would you mind running upstairs? I think I might have left my Yule candle burning in my bedroom. Don't want to burn the house down."

"Sure. Great party, CiCi."

"I never throw any other kind."

As her gorgeous girl went on her fake mission, CiCi headed straight for Reed. He broke into a grin when he saw her.

"You said it'd be a party to end all parties. You weren't lying. Merry Christmas." He handed her a gift bag.

"Aren't you sweet? I'm going to put this under my tree." She kissed him first, brushed a hand down the sleeve of his dark gray jacket. "And handsome."

"Gotta dude it up for the party to end all parties. You look amazing. Say, after the party why don't we run away to . . ."

CiCi smiled as his words trailed off, as his face went from flirty to stunned. She didn't have to look to know Simone had come back down the stairs, just as she'd planned.

He knew her—of course he knew her face. He'd studied it as he had so many others in his files. He knew her, too, from photographs artfully scattered throughout CiCi's house, from the painting that had lit a low burn of lust and the fire of wonder inside him.

But that was art, those were photos, witness statements, a couple of TV interviews.

This was the woman, in the flesh, and she shut down his brain for a solid ten seconds where the only thing that got through the buzz was a stunned: uh-oh.

As she walked straight toward him, the buzz got louder.

"All clear," the goddess said.

"Thanks, baby. This is Reed, the island's soon-to-be chief of police, and one of my favorite people in this life and all the others. Reed, my most valued treasure, my Simone."

"Reed, of course." Those lips—those gorgeous lips—curved into a gorgeous smile. The voice was like soft mist over a magic pool. "I'm so happy to meet you, finally."

He took the hand she offered—did she feel that? Did she feel that rush? "Same here," he managed.

"Simone, why don't you take Reed over to one of the bars, get him a drink. You want a beer, right, Delicious?"

"Ah, sure. Beer. Fine. Good." Jesus.

"Let's fix you up."

Simone gestured and led the way while he tried to pull himself together. It helped a little that a few people called out a greeting, or gave him a slap on the back, an easy punch on the arm.

She signaled to the bartender, turned to Reed to make party conversation while they waited on his beer. "So, you bought the Dorchet place?"

"Yeah. I'm, ah, moving in all the way after the first of the year."

"It's a great house."

"You been in it? Sure you have," he said immediately. "I fell pretty hard."

"I can't blame you. The—"

"Widow's walk," they said together.

She laughed CiCi's laugh, said, "Exactly," and he felt some of his balance restore.

He took the beer, took a chance. "You've probably got stuff to do, but can I have a minute?"

"Sure."

He eased her away from the crowd around the bar to a breathing space on the far side of the great room. "I wanted to say, I know a little more about art since hanging around CiCi."

"She's really fond of you."

"I'm in love with her."

Simone smiled. "Join the crowd."

"She opened a door for me I couldn't quite get through. Anyway, I still don't know a hell of a lot about art, but that piece over there?"

He gestured toward *Emergence*.

"If I could ever afford real art, and it didn't already belong to CiCi, that would be mine."

She said nothing for a moment, but reached out to take a flute from the tray of a passing server. "Why?"

"Well, it's beautiful, but mostly when I look at it I see proof of life. That's a weird term for it."

"No. No, it's perfect actually."

"I was there that night."

She nodded slowly, kept her eyes on the sculpture.

"I don't want to get into all that. It's a party. I'm saying it because I'm not sure if it hits me deeper, somewhere deeper, because I was there. I've seen more of your work—CiCi took me up to your studio, and I've seen other pieces here and there. It's all, like, magical. But this one, well, kind of grabs me by the throat and punches straight to the heart."

He took a sip of beer. "Anyway."

"You were shot." She looked at him then, directly into his eyes. "Not that night, last summer. But it's connected."

"Yeah."

"How are you?"

"I'm standing here with a beautiful woman, drinking a beer. I'd say I'm pretty damn good."

"Would you wait here a minute?"

"Okay."

"Just wait here. I'll be right back."

He watched her walk away, and took an internal scan. His heart appeared to be beating normally again, and his brain seemed to be back at full function.

Just some weird reaction, he concluded. Just some strange jolt to the system, and all better now.

Then he saw her coming back, felt that same damn jolt, and had his second *uh-oh* of the night.

She had a pretty woman in a red dress in hand. He recognized her face as well.

"Mi, this is Reed."

"Hi, Reed."

"Mi-Hi Jung. Dr. Jung," Simone added.

"Mi." Smiling easily, Mi held out a hand. "It's nice to meet you."

"Reed bought the Dorchet house—the one with the widow's walk, with its back to the woods."

"Oh, that's a great house."

"He's going to be the new chief of police on the island. He was a police detective—is, I guess—in Portland."

"Was," he said after he shook Mi's hand.

"He was there that night." Simone didn't have to say what night. They all knew. "The three of us were all there. It's odd, isn't it? We were all there. Now we're all here. Reed became a cop. Mi's a doctor, a scientist, a biomedical engineer. And I . . ." She looked toward the sculpture. "Did you become a cop because of that night?"

"It pointed me in that direction. It and Essie. Essie McVee."

Simone's gaze held his, intensely now. "Officer McVee. She's the one who found me. She's the one who responded first. You know her."

"Yeah. She's a good friend. She was my partner the last few years."

"I remember now," Mi said. "You grabbed the little boy, got him to a safe place. You weren't a cop then."

"No. College kid. I was working at Mangia, the restaurant."

"You weren't hurt that night," Simone remembered out loud. "But later. Mi was hurt. A cop and a scientist. Tragedy, you said, Mi, brings out more of who we are. Excuse me."

"I upset her," Reed began as Simone walked away.

"No." Mi laid a hand on his arm, watched her friend. "No, you really didn't. Upset, she'd have been frigid or molten. She's thinking, and she's looking at something she's refused to look at for a long time."

Mi turned back to him, positively beamed. "I don't know what you said or did, but I'm even happier to meet you."

CHAPTER SIXTEEN

Reed's on-the-job training began in January, in earnest. He knew how to be a cop, how to be an investigator, how to interview a suspect, a witness, a victim. How to a build case. He knew the demands and reasons for procedure, for paperwork. He understood the value of community relations and connections.

He wasn't as confident in his skills as an administrator, a boss, or with politics, and in particular, island politics. And he understood, clearly, he came into the job as an outsider.

He did what he could to counteract the outsider status. He walked or biked into the village every morning, had coffee and tried out the menu of breakfast items at the Sunrise Café—open all year from six a.m. to ten p.m. He chatted up waitresses, shopkeepers, bought his first snow shovel from the local hardware, and when January dumped a couple feet of the white stuff on the island, went back and invested in a snowplow.

At CiCi's suggestion, he hired Jasper Mink to deal with a handful of the take-it-as-is items in the house that actually needed addressing.

He hit it off just fine with the Willie Nelson look-alike contractor with the Def Leppard tee under his flannel shirt.

He shopped at the local market, warmed a stool at Drink Up—the only bar open winters—and generally made himself visible and accessible.

He learned the rhythm of the island in winter. Slow, weather-obsessed, self-contained, and proud of it. He made a point of talking to the volunteer firefighters, the local doctors—and got scooped up for an exam.

Same damn thing happened at the dentist.

Because politics had to play a part, Reed sat in on his first town hall meeting, listened to complaints about the power outage on the south side of the island during the last storm, concerns about erosion on the north end. He noted the bitter exchange about mandatory recycling and those—called out by name—who ignored the ordinance routinely.

He hadn't expected to do any more than listen and take note, and felt his stomach sink when the mayor called out his name.

"Stand up there, Reed, so people can see you. Most of you know, or should, that Reed's taking over as chief of police when Sam Wickett retires in a couple months. Come up here, Reed, introduce yourself. Tell people a little about yourself and why you're here."

Crap, he thought, crap, crap, crap. He caught the gleam in Hildy's eye. She was a savvy mayor, knew her people, her politics, and didn't suffer fools.

He'd better not make a fool out of himself at the town hall.

He walked to the front of the room, scanned the few dozen faces of those who'd bothered to show up.

"I'm Reed Quartermaine, formerly a detective with the Portland police department."

"Why 'formerly'?" somebody called out. "You get fired?"

"No, ma'am. I don't think Mayor Intz or the town council would've offered me the job if I had. I guess the best way to say it is, like a lot of people I know in Portland, I spent some time in the summer on the island. I liked it here."

"Summer's one thing," someone else shouted. "Winter's another."

"I found that out." He added a smile with it. "I bought a snowplow from

Cyrus at Island Hardware and Paints, and I learned how to use it. I bought a house on the island last fall, when I was here for a couple weeks, because I remembered the house from when I was a kid, and because when I saw it again, when I went inside it, I knew it was the one. I'd been looking for a home for a while, and I found it on the island, in that house."

"The Dorchet place is a lot of house for a single man." A woman with steel-gray hair wound in a braid eyed him more than a little dubiously while she continued to knit something out of bright green yarn.

"Yes, ma'am. I'm working on finding enough furniture so it doesn't echo. A lot of you don't know me, but I'm around. Chief Wickett's showing me the ropes, and when he leaves, I'm going to continue his open-door policy. I'm going to do my best for you. This is my home now. You're my neighbors. As chief of police, I'm sworn to serve and protect you and this island. That's what I'm going to do."

He started to go back to his seat, stopped when a pudgy guy with a gray-speckled beard stood up in the front row.

"You're cozied up with CiCi Lennon, aren't you?"

"If you mean that in a romantic sense, I can only say: I wish."

The answer brought some laughter, and gave Reed enough time to flip through his mental files and identify the questioner. John Pryor, he recalled—year-rounder, plumber, owned a couple of summer rentals with his brother.

"It seems to me you wouldn't have this job if CiCi hadn't pushed you for it."

"Now just one minute," Hildy began, but Reed held up a hand.

"It's okay, Mayor. It's a fair enough question. It's true I wouldn't have known about the job or the house coming up for sale if CiCi hadn't told me. I'm grateful she did, so I had a shot at both."

"You *got* shot back in Portland. Maybe you figure being chief of police here's going to give you a safe, easy ride."

Mutters rose up, disapproving ones, and Pryor's face only hardened.

"It's not about me getting a safe, easy ride, John. It's about doing my duty, about ensuring a safe ride for the people who live here, for the people who come here during the season to fill the hotels and B&Bs. You and your brother—that's Mark, isn't it?—own one of those B&Bs. You've got a nice place," Reed added. "If you have any trouble after March, you give me a call. Meanwhile, if you've got any more questions for me, we can head over to Drink Up after the meeting. I'll buy you a beer."

Pryor didn't take him up on the beer, but others did throughout January, including his four year-round deputies, his dispatcher, and two of the three part-time deputies who came on from June through September. The third spent six weeks every winter on Saint Lucia.

His only sticky beer came with the sole female deputy. Matty Stevenson had served four years in the Army, put in three years with Boston PD before moving back to the island where she'd been born. She'd taken another eighteen months to work as full-time caregiver to her mother, a widow, when her mother contracted breast cancer, before becoming the first female full-time deputy on the island force. She'd served as deputy for nine years.

Her mother, nine years a cancer survivor, owned and operated a seasonal island gift shop.

Matty sat across from him at a two-top, her hair short, straight, ashy blond, her eyes blue and hard. She wore a flannel shirt, brown wool trousers, and Wolverine boots.

He'd done his research, which was as much a matter of talking to people as reading her file. So he knew, after an angry marriage and divorce, she'd "taken up with" or "started seeing" longtime bachelor John Pryor.

He didn't have to do any research to glean she wasn't particularly pleased with her new, incoming boss.

He decided to play it straight and to the point.

"You're pissed they're bringing me in as chief."

"They snuck you in from the outside. I've got close to ten years on the island force. Nobody so much as asked if I wanted the job."

"I'm asking you."

"Doesn't make a damn bit of difference now."

"I'm asking you," he repeated. "I'm not chief yet."

"You've got the contract."

"Yeah. I'm still asking you. You've got four years military, a dozen years with the police, and a long time on the island. You're probably more qualified than me."

She sat back from her beer, folded her arms over her chest. "I am more qualified."

"Why do you figure they didn't offer you the job?"

"You're male. You took a couple bullets. You're one of the heroes of the DownEast."

He shrugged. "All that's fact—except *hero*'s a stupid word for what happened that night. You served in Iraq. You've got a Purple Heart. *Hero*'s not a stupid word for that. I'm male," he repeated. "Are you telling me you think they passed you over because you're not?"

She opened her mouth. Shut it. Picked up her beer and drank. "I want to say yes. I want to because they never gave us a heads-up. The chief never let us know he planned to retire until it was a done deal. I went at Hildy about it, too, went right at her. I dated her brother when we were in high school, goddamn it."

She drank again. "But I can't say yes because I'm not a liar."

"Then why?"

"You already know why."

"I don't know what you think."

"I've got a temper. I got written up a few times—in the Army, in Boston, and here, too. Not in the last couple years. Not since I got rid of the asshole I was stupid enough to marry. I freaking meditate every morning now."

He stopped himself from smiling, only nodded. "Does it work?"

Now she shrugged. "Most of the time."

"Good to hear. I don't care how you button your shirt."

She smirked at him. "This is a man's shirt."

"Don't care. Other than the chief, who's leaving, you've got more time as a cop than any of the other deputies. I'm going to need to depend on you, and I'm going to need you to give me a chance before you write me off as a dumbass off-islander."

"What if that's my conclusion after I give you a chance?"

"Then I won't last long as chief."

She considered. "That's fair."

"Okay. One more thing? If I need a plumber and call John Pryor, is he going to fuck with me?"

Now she snorted. "He shouldn't have given you grief at the meeting."

"It wasn't that much grief."

"He shouldn't have anyway. Makes us both look like assholes. And bringing CiCi into it made him look like an even bigger asshole. The answer's no. He takes too much pride in his work."

"Also good to know."

Thinking of CiCi, he drove over to her house on his next day off. When she didn't answer, he walked around, as he often did, to her studio.

He could see the art through the glass, but not the artist.

He felt a little tug of worry, told himself it was just the cop always looking for worst-case, but he walked around to the patio. He'd try the door, he thought, just step in and call out.

Then he spotted the woman sitting on the rocks on the snowy beach.

He made his way down, enjoying the slap of the wind, the sound of the water, and the look of it. As hard a winter blue as the sky overhead.

She heard him, turned her head. That face, he thought. That instant sucker punch in the chest.

He climbed up, sat beside Simone.

"Hell of a view," he said.

"A favorite."

"Yeah, mine, too."

She'd wound a scarf with a half dozen bold colors around her neck, pulled a cap of bright blue over her hair.

She looked vivid, Reed thought, and just downright amazing.

"CiCi's not here," she told him. "She's taking a couple days at a spa with a friend. Spur of the moment."

"I wondered when she didn't answer. Her car's out front. Yours, too."

"I drove her to the ferry this morning. He picked her up on the other end."

" 'He,' huh?" Reed slapped his chest. "Heartbreak."

"They've been friends for decades. And he's gay."

"And hope springs yet again." He waited a beat, enjoyed her smile. "Am I in the way here?"

"No. I heard about the meeting the other night. Apparently you handled yourself well."

"People need time to get used to me, judge whether I suck at the job or not."

"I don't think you'll suck."

"I won't, but they need a chance to decide."

"Most islanders like you. I hear."

"I'm a likeable guy." He shot her a smile to prove it. "I can even slide into affable. How about you?"

She looked back out, over the water. "I don't think I do affable very well."

"No, me. Let's talk about me. Am I likeable?"

She turned her head again, gave him a long look with those tiger eyes. "Probably. I don't really know you."

"I could take you to dinner. It's meatloaf night at the Sunrise, or there's Mama's Pizza."

She shook her head. "I'm taking a break, but I plan to work tonight." She took a deep breath of that slapping wind. "The cold's getting through."

When she shifted, he climbed down, offered her a hand.

"It's the meatloaf, right?" he said, making her laugh.

"It factors, but I really do intend to work. I needed some air first. Some . . . mind airing."

"As long as it's not me asking you out that's the problem."

She tipped her head this time, sort of slid her gaze up. "I don't know if it is or not, because I don't really know you. And because I've opted not to go out with your gender the last few months."

"Hey, me, too—with yours. I bet we're due."

"Why?"

"Because," he said as they walked through the lumpy path in the snow they'd both formed in the drifts, "you've got to break the fast sometime."

"No, why are you on a fast?"

"Oh." He concluded a woman wasn't brushing a guy off—altogether—if she kept talking to him. "Well, got shot, had to brood and bitch over that awhile, came here, met the breathtaking CiCi, changed my life. Not a lot of time for meatloaf with a woman in there. You?"

"I'm not really sure. Lack of interest. There may have been some SBZ in there."

"SBZ?"

"Simone Brood Zone. I sometimes reside there. But primarily, I'd say a lack of interest."

"I can be interesting as well as affable." He started up the beach steps with her. "I could clear these off for you."

"That's the affability. It's appreciated, but we're getting another few inches tonight anyway."

"Have you got everything you need in case there's more? Food, drink— Sorry," he said when his phone signaled. "I need to go by the . . ." He trailed off, studied the text. "Ah, I need to go by the market anyway, so—"

"What is it? I know faces," she said as they reached the patio. "You've got a good poker face, or maybe that's cop face, but it slipped for a second. Is your family all right?"

"Yeah. It's nothing like that."

"I know faces," she repeated. "You should come in, have coffee."

She crossed the patio, opened the door. "CiCi would insist, and would be disappointed in me if I didn't."

"Coffee's good." He stomped off his boots, stepped into the house, the warmth.

She turned on the fire first, then stripping off the coat, hat, scarves, gloves, walked to the coffee machine. "Straight or fancy?"

"Just black."

"Manly man." She kept her voice light. "I usually go for lattes myself. I worked in this crappy coffee shop when I first got to New York. But we made excellent lattes."

"I upset you the night of the party. Your friend said I didn't, but—"

"Mi's right, as usual. You didn't. I was thinking about something, and you made me think harder. I was abrupt, but that's because I was inside my own head."

"The SBZ?"

Her lips curved as she shrugged. "Maybe just inside the border."

As she frothed milk for her latte, she glanced over her shoulder. He hadn't taken off his coat. "The phone. It has something to do with that. With the DownEast?"

"Are you a little bit psychic like CiCi?"

"No. It's a logical assumption. You should tell me." She turned back to finish the coffees. "Not all that long ago I'd have made sure you didn't. You couldn't. Now I'd like you to tell me."

He took off his coat, but didn't say anything when she brought him the coffee.

"Let's sit down." She gestured toward the sofa facing the fire. "You're the first person I've asked into the house, and made coffee for in . . . I can't think if ever. I wonder why that is. I don't think it's your famous affability."

"I don't want it to be because of shared trauma."

"But part of it has to be, doesn't it? Nobody who hasn't experienced what we did can ever really know. For years, I shut it out. You can't see if you don't look, can't hear if you don't listen. Do you want to know why I started looking and listening again?"

"Yeah, I do."

Simone shifted to sit cross-legged on the sofa. "I ran into my archenemy from high school. She was golden and beautiful and had breasts. I was brown and gawky and ordinary."

"You were never ordinary."

"That's what I saw in the mirror that night in the bathroom. I thought, Why can't I be beautiful like Tiffany? She'd come into the theater with the boy who'd just dumped me for her because I wasn't ready to put out. Heartbreak, humiliation, with the intensity you can only feel at that age. World over.

"Then it happened. The boy who'd dumped me was dead. Tiffany was shot in that young, beautiful face. Now, years later, she confronts me—another bathroom, in the universe of irony. She said ugly things, and for whatever reason that few minutes of ugliness made me start looking and listening. Not for her. For me."

"I couldn't stop looking and listening," Reed told her. "I don't think it's an obsession, but I'll cop to mission. I followed every story, put together files. It never seemed right, or complete. They barely had a brain among them, and the only one with a brain? Why didn't he go after the girl he blamed for ruining his life? There had to be more, and I wanted to know what it was."

"And you were right," Simone added. "The 'more' turned out to be Patricia Hobart."

"Yeah. That made sense, in a sick, twisted way, once we—they," he corrected, "went through the things she had to leave behind in her rush to rabbit. She was, like, fifteen at the time of the DownEast. Already a psychopath, and a smart one," he added. "Really smart even at fifteen. Smart enough to hide her nature. But before she shot me, before it made that sick, twisted sense, I followed everything. Essie did, too. One of the ways she did—and I did? We get alerts whenever anyone who was there that night dies. Any reason."

So she understood the look on his face, just for that second. "Who died?"

"He was mall security. Took a couple of bullets that night. Went back to work when he recovered. A seriously good guy."

"Did . . . Did she kill him?"

"I'm going to say yes. No proof, not yet. And she's good," he added as he pushed up to pace. "She's damn good. She's been in the wind since she shot me. Not a damn trace. Now Robert Kofax is dead because she laced his drink on a beach in Bermuda."

"Bermuda?"

"I don't know why he was there—I'll find out. I just got the alert: his name, COD. Cause of death," he explained.

"She found a way," he continued, "because that's her mission."

"She's killing survivors? That doesn't make sense."

"Finishing what she started—because she left enough behind to prove she started it. She planned it—hadn't quite finished the plans. Her brother got impatient. My theory, anyway."

She lost some of the color the cold had pumped into her cheeks. "Mi's a survivor. My mother, my sister. Me. You."

"Mi got some press, but she didn't give any interviews. The same with you. Your family didn't get a lot of attention. I think she's after ones who did. But you and me? We got through to nine-one-one. First and second callers. You should be careful, and you can believe I'll be watching for her."

Anxiety churned in her stomach. "The island's mobbed in the summer. Day-trippers, vacationers, summer workers."

"I'm going to be chief of police. Every cop and first responder's going to have her photo. I'm going to have it posted in every fricking shop and restaurant and hotel. On the ferry. I'm not saying she won't try to get here, but I think, for now, she's after easier targets. And if she tries to come here, it'll be to finish me first. I shot the bitch."

He didn't sound affable now, Simone thought. He sounded hard, tough, and very, very capable.

"I think I want something stronger than coffee." She rose. "How about you?"

"I wouldn't say no."

She opted for wine, a full-bodied red, and poured two generous glasses.

"Now I haven't just upset you. I've scared you."

"I don't think so. I don't know how I feel, exactly. Unnerved, you bet. I'm not brave. I wasn't brave that night."

"You're wrong about that. You didn't run screaming, and there wouldn't have been any shame if you had. But you did the smart thing. You hid and called for help. I've heard the nine-one-one call. You held it together. That's bravery."

"I didn't feel brave, and I haven't since. But . . . Come up to my studio. I want to show you something."

"Like etchings?"

She smiled, didn't feel quite as unnerved. "Not in the least."

"I keep striking out with the beautiful artists in this house. I have to try another tactic."

But he went with her. "I can arrange for a cop—a girl cop—to stay with you tonight if you're worried."

"No, but thanks. I've always felt safe in this house. She won't make me a victim again. I know her victims."

In the studio he saw dozens and dozens of sketches pinned to boards.

He knew them, too.

He knew the faces, the few she'd created with clay.

"I started with her. Tiffany." Simone picked up the small bust. "I did her before." She turned the bust. "And after. It, I thought, would be a kind of purge for me. But it didn't turn out that way. You're one of the reasons."

Fascinated, he watched her. "I am?"

"The night of the party, I talked to Mi up here, showed her these two faces. I talked to you. More, I listened to you. And since . . .

"She survived," Simone said, and set the bust down again. "But she's not grateful. I hadn't been, either, not really. That's what struck me. I lived, and instead of being grateful, I wanted to pretend it never happened. What does that say about the ones who died? Was I saying they never happened?"

She took a long drink. "'Proof of life,' you said that night, about *Emergence*. About Tish. It struck me, it rang the damn bell. So, I'm—in my way, I guess—giving them all proof of life."

He looked at her now, at that face, not just because it made his heart thump, not just because she made his blood swim. But because he felt a kind of awe and respect.

"This is bravery."

She closed her eyes a moment. "God. I hope so."

He stepped to the shelf, carefully lifted one of the busts. "I knew her. Angie—Angela Patterson. She was so damn pretty. I had a real thing for her."

"Oh. You were in love with her."

"No, but I liked her a lot." He thought of the kiosk, the blood, the body. And looked at the face, young, lovely, just on the edge of flirty. "I talk to her mother a couple times a year. This? This will mean the world to Angie's mother."

"I want to create a memorial, all their faces. People shouldn't forget who they were, what happened to them. You could help me."

"How?"

"I want to include the people who've died since, because of that night, or because of Patricia Hobart. You could help me."

"I could." He set the bust down. "I will. What will you do with it when you finish?"

"That'll be months—longer. I'll need to take a break from it or I won't see or hear clearly. But I'm hoping my father can help there. He's a lawyer, and has a lot of connections. And, of course, there's CiCi. I'd like to do molds, cast it in bronze, place it in a park."

"I could maybe help there, too."

"How?"

"I talk to the next of kin, survivors off and on. Like Angie's mom. So with that, we might be able to help get that going when you're ready for it."

She nodded, slowly. "An appeal from survivors and loved ones? Hard to refuse. Some might not want this."

"They'd be wrong. So."

He set aside his glass, stepped to her. He took her face in his hands, watched those gorgeous eyes calculate. He kissed her, soft, slow. No demand, no pressure. And felt—hoped he felt—her give just a little before he eased away again.

"Change of tactic," he said.

"It was interesting."

"Told ya. I'm going to head out, for my lonely meatloaf. I'll see you around."

"I don't get around very much," she said as he started out.

"That's okay. I do." He stopped at the doorway, turned for just a moment. "I've gotta say this one more thing. You're the most beautiful woman I've seen in my goddamn life."

She laughed, sincerely amused. "I'm not even close."

"You're wrong again. I ought to know what I've seen in my own life. CiCi's got my number around here somewhere. You need anything, call."

She frowned as he walked out, as she listened to his boots on the stairs. She sipped more wine, then poured what he'd left in his glass into her own, drank a little more.

He *was* interesting, she thought. And could put the affable on and off like a pair of socks. She had a sense he could be dangerous, and that just made him more interesting.

Plus he knew how to kiss in a way that nudged open the door, just a crack.

She'd have to think about that one.

Most of all, he'd looked at her work and seen what she needed to give it, what she'd needed from it.

And he'd understood.

CHAPTER SEVENTEEN

Standing on the widow's walk, Essie McVee marveled. The day shuddered with dead gray February, cold as the lash of a frozen whip, and still the view spread like wonder.

The sea and sky, both that broody, bored gray, couldn't erase the breadth of it or the power of the rocky coastline with the incessant flick of icy water.

She smelled pine and snow, breathed air so cold and damp it felt like she swallowed chipped ice. Far to the right, the buildings of painted clapboard formed the village and a path of trampled snow wound through trees with white-coated branches.

Far off, the lighthouse stood, a beacon of color and joy against the stubborn winter gloom.

Below the house, a rickety pier, with some worrisome gaps, cut on an angle through a break in the rocks.

"You've got a dock."

"Yeah, such as it is. I've got a boat shed, too. No boat. Mrs. Dorchet sold it after her husband died. I might get one. A boat. Maybe."

"A boat."

"Maybe. I've already got the shed and the pier. It seems like I should have the reason for them."

She looked up at him, remembered the sorrowful boy on the bench at the park, the young cop learning his way, the partner she'd gone through doors with. The friend she'd found bleeding.

Now this. A man looking out at what was his.

"It's not a shithole, Reed."

He grinned. "Needs some work here and there, but nope, not a shithole."

"How's it feel to be chief?"

"I'll let you know next month. I'm making some progress, finding my feet. For the most part, people seem to be reserving judgment on whether or not the off-islander can make the grade."

"You'll make it."

"Yeah, I will. It'll be quiet for the next couple of months, so more time to find my feet, get to know who's who and what's what. And take control at the station house."

"Any issues there?"

He made a noncommittal grunt. "The current chief's got my back, and that helps. The deputies, the dispatcher, they know what's what, and things are in a kind of lull during the transition. Got some quirks, like anywhere, but they're solid enough. The best of the bunch is the lone female."

"Do tell?"

"Smart and tough. A little bit of a hothead, but I can work with that."

"Beware the office romance."

"What? Oh no." Laughing, he shook back his disordered mop of hair. "Hell no. Not my type, and I'd be her boss on top of that. Boss—ha ha. Anyway, she's about forty, divorced, and hooked up with an island plumber. Then there's Leon Wendall. Former navy—petty officer. Seven years on the force here. Likes to fish. His wife of thirty years is a teacher. Three kids, one grand-daughter."

"Seven years? And they brought you in over him?"

"He's not a boss," Reed said with a shake of his head. "Doesn't want to be. He'll keep his eye on me though. Guaranteed. We've got Nick Masterson, thirty-three, newlywed. He's competent. His family owns the Sunrise Café. His mom keeps the books. And we finish the full-timers with Cecil Barr. Twenty-four, easygoing, but not stupid. His father's a fisherman, mother's a nurse, older sister studying to be a doctor, younger brother still in high school.

"We wind up with Donna Miggins, dispatcher. Sixty-four, sharp. I've been warned by the lady herself that I can fetch my own coffee, do my own errands, and she won't take any sass. I like her. I'm a little afraid of her, but I like her."

"You're happy."

"I am that."

"And you've put back most of the weight you lost."

"I've been patronizing the Sunrise Café. Most islanders wander through sometime during a given week. And I'm a crap cook anyway."

"You ought to learn to deserve that kitchen."

"If I don't cook," he pointed out, "it stays clean."

"That makes a stupid kind of sense," she conceded.

"Let's head down, get some coffee. I just bought that fancy machine."

"I don't know why," she said as they went in, down the stairs. "When you drink it, it's black."

"The girl of my dreams likes lattes."

"The artist?"

He flapped a hand on his heart. "Thump, thump."

She paused, as she hadn't on the way up, outside the master suite and, with the privilege of an old friend, wandered in.

"Really nice space, great views again. You still don't have a bed."

He pointed to the mattress and box springs. "That's a bed."

"A bed has a frame, a headboard, possibly a footboard. Some style. You're never going to get the girl of your dreams on that."

"You underestimate my charm and sex appeal."

"No, I don't." She looked around, noting the teddy bear cop sitting on what he mistakenly called a dresser. "You need an actual dresser instead of that ugly block of wood you've had since college. Maybe a nice chair. Some tables, nice lamps. A rug. And . . ." She trailed off as she peeked into the en suite. "Jesus, the bathroom's fabulous."

"Previous owner's son, like the kitchen. No more piss-trickle showers for me, baby!"

"Spring for some new towels, find some local art for the walls in here—and a good mirror for the bedroom."

"You're a tough sell, Essie."

"I know what I know."

She walked out, and into an empty bedroom. "What're you going to do with this? Home office?"

"No, I set that up already, down the hall. I figure a guest room—I'll end up having two of them. You and your family could come stay sometime. I'm going to buy a big-ass grill. I'll start paying you back for all the meals and the nights I ended up flopping at your place."

"We'd love it."

"First decent grill-on-the-deck weekend we're both off."

"Deal. Queen bed—you've got the room—simple duvet and curtains, a little desk and chair, nice lamps and end tables—nothing matchy—an old dresser—not a crap one, but an old one."

"What are you, my decorator? Yeah, yeah," he said, before she could. "You know what you know."

She continued her exploration, came across the unrehabbed bath. Sea-green tiles bordered in black. Sea-green john and shower/tub combo. Sea-green sink in a white vanity.

"I like it."

"You do?"

"It's retro and kitschy, and it has possibilities. You need a new vanity, and some paint, and some fun towels, shower curtain. It'll be adorable."

She wandered on—rattling off ideas to the point he figured he should be taking notes. Then opened the door to his office.

"Ah," she said.

He'd put his desk—a big, clunky holdover from college—in the middle of the room. That way, he could see the views, the door, and the pair of rolling boards he'd set up against a wall.

On the first whiteboard, he had tacked Patricia Hobart's photo dead center. Along with photos and crime scene shots of her victims, he'd written in time lines, added copies of reports.

Lines, solid or dotted, fanned out, intersected.

On the second board he'd pinned the three shooters from the DownEast Mall, time lines again, weaponry, and photos, names, ages of the dead. Separated by a red line, he'd displayed photos, names, ages, locations, employment of survivors.

The room held three gunmetal-gray filing cabinets, a couple of folding chairs leaning against a wall—drywalled, mudded, sanded, but not painted—his old mini-fridge—also from his college years—and a kitchen-size trash can half-full of empty cans of Coke and Mountain Dew, water bottles, and take-out coffee cups.

The open closet held office supplies—paper for the printer, the scanner, file folders, a tub of markers, a stack of legal pads.

On the floor of the closet sat a case of water, a case of Cokes, another of the Dew—all opened and pillaged.

Essie moved to the boards, studied them.

"Good, thorough work, Reed."

"It's quiet here now, and I'm not chief yet. I've had the time. Still, she got to another, and she's back in the wind. There's no telling who she'll target next, when or where. Might as well toss the names in a hat and pick one."

"The twisted bitch is more logical than that. To her mind, every target so far got some sort of splash out of that night. A little fame, a little fortune—and a routine she could document or exploit. We can go right down the line on that, ending with Bob Kofax."

"All over his Facebook page," Reed agreed. "Where he was going, when, why. More when he got there. She took herself a working vacation."

"Yeah, she did. The feds tracked her to a room at the same resort."

Reed whipped around. "You're sure?"

"I know how to keep my head down and my ears open. You can add this name to your board: Sylvia Guthrie. She won't use that name again, but she used it to book and pay for the room and her expenses—American Express. And to book her flight, round-trip, first class, direct from New York. JetBlue out of JFK."

"Chaz is in New York. He got a promotion and moved to New York."

"They don't think she had her hole there. They're of the same mind as we've been. Canada."

"She won't stay there now."

"Unlikely. I've got copies of her Guthrie passport and driver's license photos down in my bag. It listed a New York address, but it's bogus. You can have them for your board, too. My information is she flew into Bermuda the day before the target, got herself a fucking massage, charged a hundred dollar bottle of wine and a damn fine meal to her room. Charges also include a couple of virgin daiquiris from the drink service on the beach, on the third day—the target and his family racked up some bar bills there, same time frame, before the target became short of breath, keeled over, and died, thanks to the cyanide in his mai tai."

"The second time she's used poison. Dr. Wu." Reed gestured to the board. "Crowded beach instead of a crowded bar for Kofax, cyanide in his drink instead of jabbing him with a toxin like Wu, but it rings the same. I think she likes to shoot," he added. "I think she likes the impact, the blood, but sometimes poison's easier."

"Same page," Essie told him. "The Kofax family was in and out of the water," she continued as she wandered the room. "Boogie boards, horsing around, using the shaded lounge chairs the resort provides. Target ordered his mai tai—his second of the afternoon—a drink for his wife, a lemonade for one of the grandkids, then dragged his wife up to hit the water with the kids again. He came back, plopped down, started on his drink. And died at forty-nine, a day before his fiftieth birthday."

"All she had to do was stretch out somewhere, mark where he sat, what he drank. Dump the poison in while he's in the water, walk the fuck away."

"Which she did, before she strolled back to the resort spa and enjoyed a facial. Prebooked. It was always going to be poison for this one, I'd say. If not on the beach, then at the pool bar, or the open-air bar, one of the restaurants. She saw her chance, and she took it."

"Did they question her?"

"Busy season at the resort, but the locals spoke with her briefly. She stated she'd been on the beach about that time, had even noticed the big, happy family. She'd left for her spa appointment, and hadn't noticed anyone near the family group. But she'd been engrossed in her book. By the time the feds got wind, she'd poofed."

"That's luck as well as smarts and planning." Studying the board, Reed slipped his hands into his back pockets. "That's a lot of luck."

"She's got plenty of it. The only time we know of she ran low was with you."

"Yeah." Absently, he rubbed a hand on his side.

"How's the side, the shoulder?"

"I'm good. I'm still doing fricking yoga."

"That, I'd like to see."

"No, you really wouldn't. Let me get you that coffee."

"I'll let you practice making the girl of your dreams a latte, but let's have it up here." She looked back at the board. "Bounce things around, see if anything shakes."

"I was hoping you'd say that."

She gave him two hours before she had to drive back to the ferry. Reed couldn't say anything had shaken, but they both speculated Hobart might settle down in warmer climes for a while.

Why not?

Taking that angle, they'd both study survivors who'd relocated south.

"I'm really glad you finally made it out. Next time," he told her, "steaks on the grill for the whole family."

"Do you have actual dishes?"

"Ah . . . sort of."

"Buy dishes, and a bed. Feather your nest, partner. It's a really great nest."

"Okay, okay. Jeez, my mother said the same thing, and even threatened to make my dad haul stuff from the attic out here."

"Buy your own." She jabbed him in the chest. "You're a big boy now." She started to kiss his cheek, then glanced over at the knock on the door.

"Company."

He went to the door, grinned when he opened it to CiCi. "Hello, gorgeous. You're just in time to meet one of my favorite people." Taking her hand, he tugged her in. "CiCi Lennon, Essie McVee."

"We've met." CiCi, a bright green tam over flowing red hair, strode over in her ancient UGGS, took Essie's hand. "You might not remember."

"I do. I met you, briefly, outside of Mi-Hi Jung's hospital room."

"I didn't realize," Reed said.

"You wanted to check on her and Simone," CiCi said. "My impression at the time was of a dedicated and caring woman. I'm never wrong. You're here to spend some time with Reed."

"I've spent it. What a terrific house. Better when it's got some actual furniture."

"Okay, Mom."

"I've got to run, make the ferry. I'm glad I got a chance to see you again, Ms. Lennon."

"CiCi. Reed, next time, you bring Essie over to see us. I hope you bring your husband and little boy."

"I'm planning on it. Reed." Essie hugged him, kissed his cheek. "I'm proud of you, Chief."

"Go on and walk Essie out to her car," CiCi ordered. "There's a package for you in mine. You can bring it in." She unwound a bright green scarf as she spoke. "I'm going to help myself to a glass of wine, if you have some, Reed."

"Got the white and the red you like."

"My man. Come back soon, Essie."

CiCi tossed her coat, scarf, and hat on a truly deplorable sofa. Essie was right about furniture, CiCi thought, deciding on the white Reed had chilling in the refrigerator, as she liked it.

She poured two glasses. He'd rather have a beer, she thought, but she hoped her housewarming gift rated the wine.

He came back, loaded down with the package. "You had to drive with the window down to fit it in there. It's cold, CiCi."

"We islanders are sturdy stock."

"It's a painting." A big one, and he could feel the frame under the thick brown paper she'd wrapped it in. "You did a painting for me."

"I did, and I hope you'll like it."

"I don't even have to see it to know I'll love it."

"It'd be more fun if you did see it. Come on, come on, get the paper off. I have a strong opinion where it needs to go. We'll see what you think."

He had to lay it on the kitchen island to peel off the tape, pull the protective cardboard from the corners of the frame. He flipped it over, took a sheet of cardboard from the front.

And stared, stunned, grateful, overwhelmed.

"Holy shit, CiCi."

"I take that as approval."

"I don't even know what to say. It's amazing."

The beach, the rocks, the strip of sand, all the colors so vivid and strong. Birds winged over the water; a white boat glided toward the horizon. The bluest of blue skies spread, and one of the filmy white clouds formed a dragon like the one guarding her guest room.

A few shells, exquisitely detailed, dotted the sand like scattered treasures.

And two figures sat on the rocks, angled toward each other, looking out.

"It's us," he murmured. "It's you and me."

"It won't be the last time I paint you, but it's a good start."

"I don't know what to say." He looked at her. "I honestly don't know how to thank you. It's magic. Just like you."

"That's a perfect thing to say. We look right, don't we? Kindred souls reunited."

"I really love you, CiCi."

"I really love you right back. Where do you think you want to hang it?"

"It has to go there, over the fireplace. It has to be where you can see it from everywhere."

"You're exactly right. No time like the now. I've got hangers." She reached in her pocket for them. "And a drill in the car, if you don't have one."

"Yeah, I got one."

"And a tape measure. Let's get it done, and done right."

She proved fussy about the accuracy of measuring, and beat him to hell and back on the math part of it. But with her fussing, calculating, and assistance, he hung his first piece of art in his new home.

"I have an original CiCi Lennon. Hell, I'm *in* an original CiCi Lennon. And it's awesome."

She handed him his glass, tapped hers to it. "To you and your happy home."

He drank with her, then drew her in. "Where would I be now if you hadn't walked down that morning?"

"You were meant to be here, so here you are."

"Sure feels like it." He kissed the top of her head. "I guess I'm going to have to get serious about furniture. Nothing down here's worthy of the painting."

"You're right. Start by getting rid of that ugly couch."

He felt a little pang for the memories made on that ugly couch. The naps taken, the sports watched, the girls he'd gotten naked.

Then he looked up at the painting, and thought of memories yet to come.

The island didn't have an actual furniture store, but it did offer a kind of flea market antiquey sort of place. He found some things there, and at the single year-round gift shop he liked, used the Internet for more.

He tried not to think too much about the seeping wounds on his credit card.

Still, the island shopping served the dual purpose of public relations. And trading a six-pack for help hauling, assembling, placing the furniture with Cecil gave him the opportunity to get to know the deputy better.

For instance, he learned Cecil had a more experienced hand with tools. The man wasn't fast, but he was tireless.

Together, they stood back and studied the bed—Reed's first purchase, because he definitely wanted the girl of his dreams in it. He'd even gone for a new mattress set.

"That's a nice bed, Chief."

"You think? Yeah, it works."

Simple, he thought, but not so basic it looked like he didn't give a damn. He liked the vertical slats, the low footboard that wouldn't get in his way, the faded charcoal color.

"You wanna put the sheets and stuff on it?"

"I'll deal with that later. Let's get the rest loaded in. I appreciate it, Cecil."

"Hell, I don't mind. I like putting things together. And it's a cool house."

By the time he passed Cecil the beer, he had a furnished bedroom, a new couch, a second bed—queen-size, as ordered—set up in the guest room along with nightstands and lamps. Not too matchy, he hoped.

Exhausted, he flopped down on his new bed, sans sheets. Considered, bounced a little.

How the hell had he slept on that old piece of shit mattress all this time? He thought about reaching for the beer on his new nightstand—on a coaster, he wasn't a fool. Thought about it again.

And drifted right off.

He dreamed of drills and hammers, screws and screwdrivers. Not so surprisingly, that slid into a rather stupendous sex dream starring Simone.

In the dream, his new headboard banged against the wall as Simone locked her legs around his waist.

He woke hard as iron, a little breathless. And realized the banging didn't stop.

"Shit, fuck, damn." He shoved up, did his best to adjust himself. "Down, boy," he muttered and started downstairs.

The burly deliveryman had been there before.

"Sorry, I was upstairs."

"You got another one." The driver held out his tablet for Reed to sign.

"You know, if I don't answer or I'm not here, you can just leave stuff."

"You gotta say so, in writing."

"Okay. I'll do that."

The driver hulked back to his truck, leaving Reed with a big, ridiculously heavy box on his doorstep.

He hauled it in, pulled out his pocketknife to cut the seal.

"Dishes. Oh yeah, I bought dishes."

White, he remembered, because once he'd started looking, all the colors and patterns made his head hurt. White was easy.

Except now he had to unload them, and he probably had to wash them, which meant loading the dishwasher, then unloading it again, then putting them away.

The idea made him long for another nap.

Plus he still had to put sheets on the bed, and he hadn't unpacked the new towels. Did he have to wash those, too?

How the hell was he supposed to know?

No point calling to ask his mother because she'd just say yes right straight off. He just knew it.

"It can wait," he decided, going back up for his beer. Not altogether warm, he told himself, taking it into the shower.

But the dishes, and towels, the every damn thing nagged at him until he gave up.

He dressed, loaded dishes in the dishwasher, towels in the washing machine. He reminded himself he had a flat-screen coming. Two, in fact, as he'd ordered one for the master. The one downstairs wouldn't go above the fireplace as he'd imagined because he had the magic painting. But he had other walls.

And he had a full week before he took over as chief.

He'd get it done.

He went up to put sheets on the bed—also new (had he lost his mind?). His mother would, undoubtedly, claim they needed washing first, but to hell with it. He couldn't do everything.

He'd gotten a duvet in a color called indigo—mainly because that's what they'd shown on the bed in the picture, and it seemed good enough. It came with shams, which seemed like a lot of fuss and bother, but he finished it up.

He didn't have it in him to go out for food, so went with the reliable frozen pizza.

He switched beer for Coke, carted his dinner up to his office.

He sat, eating pizza, studying his boards.

"Where are you, Patricia, you murdering bitch? I bet it's warm where you are."

He shifted his gaze to his targets board, to the group he'd separated out. One in Savannah, another in Atlanta, one in Fort Lauderdale, another in Coral Gables.

Add the kid who'd joined the navy and was currently stationed in San Diego, and the woman who'd moved to Phoenix with her husband and daughter.

"Which one? Where are you hiding now?"

Patricia, currently Ellyn Bostwick, had a pretty little vacation bungalow in Coral Gables.

Every day she went out with a camera, a wide-brimmed hat, and a backpack. She put on her disguise, had friendly conversations with the neighbors. She was, she told them, a freelance photographer taking three months to do her own photography book of the area.

She cheerfully took shots of the brats next door for their idiot mother. She printed them out, even framed them.

Recently divorced, she told her neighbors, she'd wanted to take some time on her own, and time away from the cold and crowds of Chicago.

Emily Devlon (née Frank) had been eighteen on the night of the DownEast Mall massacre. She'd been coming back from her break from her summer job at Orange Julius when the war broke out.

She knew gunfire when she heard it—her father was a cop—and started to sprint away from the sound. But then it came from both directions.

She knew what to do, even as panic spun through her. You find a hole, and you hide. She aimed for the closest store, ramming through the rush of people. A woman fell in front of her; she nearly tripped over her. Moving fast, Emily had grabbed the woman under the arms—old, frail, moaning—and dragged her into the store.

Glass exploded; they both suffered cuts, but Emily managed to pull the woman behind an entry display of summer tops and sweaters.

A clerk ran by her, eyes wheeling. In her head Emily screamed: Don't, don't.

She closed her eyes at the sound of the scream, the thud of a body.

She held on to the old woman, who'd live another eight years before she died of natural causes. She left Emily a hundred thousand dollars in her will.

Emily, now a wife and mother, used part of her inheritance to buy a house in a pretty community far away from Maine winters and bad memories.

She would live longer than the woman she'd saved, but her clock was ticking down.

CHAPTER EIGHTEEN

Reed dressed for his first day as chief. He had a uniform—khaki shirt and pants, even a billed hat—but chose jeans and a light blue shirt. He'd pull out the uniform for special occasions, but—snagging one of his grandmother's sayings—he'd begin as he meant to go on.

He pulled on boots—not new, not too beat-up—and, since March blew brisk, a leather jacket he'd had for about a decade.

He clipped his service weapon to his belt.

He opted to walk the three-quarters of a mile to the village. Reduce the carbon footprint, he thought, and as chief he had a car available at the station.

The walk gave him time to take some stock. He wasn't nervous. He'd lived on the island for nearly three months now, had felt its pulse. Plenty of the 1,863 islanders—ages from seven months to eighty-eight—hadn't figured he'd last the winter.

But he had.

Some of them calculated he wouldn't finish out the summer as chief.

But he would.

He didn't just like his life here, it was his life.

He had a separate mission, and he'd work the Hobart case until the crazy bitch heard the door slam on her cell; but his priority now, from today on, had to be the island.

He spotted a couple of deer in what he thought of as his woods, took that as a positive sign. Snowmelt made the ground soft under his feet, and the white stuff lay in pools and patches. They weren't done with it, at least according to the old guys who hung out at the Sunrise, drinking coffee, playing cards, and bullshitting in the afternoons.

Their consensus called for one more good nor'easter to blow winter out into spring.

He wouldn't bet against them.

He passed some of the vacation homes that would be closed up until summer came along. Vandalism, even the kid shit, was rare. Everybody knew every damn body, and everybody who knew every damn body also knew that the island economy largely depended on the summer people.

A few more houses—islanders. He'd made a point to find a way to make at least a passing acquaintance with all the year-rounders.

Artists, photographers, shopkeepers, cooks, gardeners, retirees, bloggers, teachers, lobstermen, craftspeople. A couple of lawyers, a scatter of medical types, mechanics, handymen (and women), and so on.

All of them kept the island humming.

Now he did, too.

He watched the ferry glide toward the mainland. Some had business there, or took jobs off-season. A few sent their kids to private school. The forty-minute commute wasn't bad, to his mind. No traffic, after all.

He passed the ferry dock, where he knew, from his own memories, cars would line up by the dozens for the trip home after a summer day on Tranquility Island.

He wound his way into the village. Like the rentals, most shops and restaurants stood closed until the season. Some would get a fresh coat of paint once spring bloomed, so faded clapboard would become bright, drawing in visitors and disposable income.

From there the marina and beach offered everything the summer people could want: sun, sand, water, and water sports.

He wound his way to the Sunrise, stepped into the smell of bacon and coffee.

Val, the counter waitress with bright blond hair and a pink apron, offered him a cheerful smile. "Morning, Chief."

"Morning, Val."

"Got the first-day jitters, do ya?"

"Not so much. I'm going to need six large coffees to go. Two black, one with cream only, one cream and one sugar, one cream double sugar, and one with that vanilla cream you've got and triple sugar."

She gave him a nod as she went for the pot. "Treating the station?"

"It seems like the thing to do on day one."

"Good thinking. I'll mark them with what's what for you. Maybe you want some coffee cake to go along with it."

"I've got an order for a dozen doughnuts from the bakery. Cops, doughnuts. It's what we do."

While Val put the order together, Reed greeted some of the breakfast regulars: the two grizzled men with New England accents so thick he had to retune the frequency of his ears to understand them; the manager of the seasonal Beach Buddies; a birder blogger with his camera, field glasses, notebook; the bank manager; the island librarian.

"Thanks, Val."

"Good luck today, Chief."

He carried the take-out tray down to the bakery, picked up his dozen doughnuts, and chatted briefly with the woman who ran Island Rentals while she waited for an order of sticky buns for what she called a brainstorming meeting.

He continued down, took the right at the corner, and walked to the faded white single-story building with its narrow covered porch. The sign on the strip of grass between sidewalk and porch read: TRANQUILITY ISLAND POLICE DEPARTMENT.

Juggling the coffee and doughnuts, he fished out the keys his predecessor had given him the night before over a transitional beer. Reed unlocked the door and, taking one good breath, walked into what was now his house at seven-twenty sharp.

CiCi, who claimed to be a solitary witch as well as a little bit psychic, had insisted on doing some sort of ritual. Cleansing or opening or whatever. He hadn't seen the harm in letting her light a couple of candles, wave around a sage stick, and chant.

He looked around now at what the city cop in him thought of as a bull-pen. The desks where his deputies worked—four in facing pairs, with the other two shared by the summer deputies. The dispatch station ran along the right wall. Visitor chairs were lined up on the left. A map of the island on the wall, a really sad-looking plant of some sort in a pot in the corner.

The steel door led back to three cells. Another to the small armory. One bathroom, unisex, a tiny break room with a hot plate for coffee, a small re-frigerator, and a microwave. A table with a chipped linoleum top that he hoped to replace if he could find the means in his budget.

He had a budget. Wasn't that a kick in the ass?

He moved through the bullpen to the narrow hall that led one way to the break room, the other to the john, and straight ahead to his office.

He went into his office, set down the coffee and doughnuts, took off his jacket, hung it on the tree by the door. His desk faced the office door, and he'd keep it that way. He had a decent chair, a computer, a whiteboard for schedul-ing, a corkboard, filing cabinets, a single window that brought in some sun.

He had his own hot plate—and eventually he'd replace that with an actual coffee maker.

"Okay then," he said aloud.

He went behind the desk, sat, booted up the computer, entered his pass-word. He'd created the document the night before during CiCi's magic ritual, and now opened it, gave it another look, sent it.

When he heard the station door open, he rose, got the coffee and dough-nuts, and went out to the bullpen.

It didn't surprise him Matty Stevenson was the first to arrive.

"Chief," she said—a little cool, a little clipped.

"Thanks for coming in early. Coffee, black." He pulled her cup out of the tray. She frowned at it. "Thanks."

"Doughnuts." He flipped the lid on the box. "You're first, so first choice." When she continued to frown, he set the box on the closest desk. "When I call everybody in a half hour early, the least I can do is bring coffee and doughnuts."

While she mulled them over, Leon and Nick came in.

"Chief Quartermaine," Leon said, friendly but formal.

"Coffee," Reed said, passing out the cups. "Doughnuts." He waved a thumb at the box.

Cecil strolled in. "Hey. Am I late?"

"Right on time," Reed told him, passing him his coffee.

"Wow, thanks, Chief. Hey, just how I like it."

"Grab a doughnut, take a seat."

"That damn dog!" Donna rushed in. "I don't know why I let Len talk me into that damn dog. What's all this?" she demanded as she took off a puffy jacket, pulled off a boa constrictor of a scarf. "Is this a party or a police station?"

"It's a meeting." Reed handed her the last coffee. "Have a doughnut."

"Doughnuts. We'll end up with a bunch of fat cops." But she took one.

"I appreciate you all coming in early. I had a beer with Chief Wickett last night, and he wanted me to tell you all again thanks for the work you've done under him. I won't be changing much around here."

" 'Much'?" Donna sniffed as she bit into a jelly-filled.

"That's right. I'm going to play with the budget some, see if I can find a way to get us a new table in the break room. I will be keeping Chief Wickett's open-door policy. If my door's closed, there's a reason for it. Otherwise, it's open. If Donna hasn't already given everybody my cell number, get it. And I need yours. I need you to keep your cell charged and with you at all times. On or off duty. I know Chief Wickett used the whiteboard for scheduling. I'm using the computer. I've worked out next month's shift schedule. It'll be on your computers. If anybody needs to switch up, needs time off, you can work that out among yourselves. I just need to know. If we can't work it out, we'll find a way."

"Is your schedule on there?" Matty wanted to know.

"It is. While we're out here, somebody tell me, what the hell is that thing?"

They all looked at the sickly plant.

"It's an eyesore," Donna said. "The chief's wife gave it to him for some damn reason. We ought to put it out of its misery."

"Ah now, Donna," Cecil began.

"The chief had a black thumb—no offense, Cecil."

Cecil, the only black person in the room, just grinned. "I got two of those. But we can't just toss it out. That ain't right."

"Anybody here got a green thumb?" Reed asked. "I don't know what color mine is. I've never tried growing anything."

As one, the group turned to Leon.

"Okay, Leon, you're in charge of the thing over there. If it dies, we'll give it a decent burial. And before the growing season hits, maybe you can tell me something about lupines and whatever else I'm going to have coming up at my place. I don't know a damn thing."

"I can help you out there."

"Great. One more personal thing. I think I'm going to need somebody to give my place a going over, like, once or twice a month. I'm not looking at you." He had to laugh, as the faces ranged from stony to appalled. "I'm asking for suggestions."

"Kaylee Michael and Hester Darby handle turnover for Island Rentals," Donna told him. "They bring in extra hands for that during the season, but Kaylee and Hester are islanders."

"I met Hester."

"Seeing as you're one messy man in that big place, you'd be smarter to hire both of them. In and out quicker, and they're a good team."

"Thanks. I'll talk to them. If anyone's got any questions, comments, snide remarks, now's the time. If they're more personal questions, comments, snide remarks, you can see me in my office."

"Do we get written up for snide remarks?"

He gave Matty a level stare. "I guess we'll have to find out. I'm not much of a hard-ass, but I'm not a pushover. You'll have to figure out the sweet spot. Check your schedules. I'll be in my office."

He grabbed a doughnut on the way out.

It took less than ten minutes for the first to tap on his doorjamb. "Come on in, Nick."

"You've got me scheduled for next Saturday night. It's my six-month anniversary, and I promised to take Tara, my wife, over to Portland for a fancy night out. Cecil said he'd switch with me."

"I'll fix it. How'd you meet Tara?"

"She took a summer job with a friend of hers on the island a couple years ago. A lifeguard. She pulled this guy out—he had a heart attack it turns out, damn near drowned. She pulled him out, gave him CPR, brought him back. I was on beach patrol, so I talked to her, got her statement and all. And that was that."

He smiled, stars in his eyes. "Anyway, thanks, Chief."

Minutes later, Matty came in, sat, folded her arms.

"Is this going to be a snide remark?"

"That depends. It's starting as comment and question. The snide remark depends on your answer."

He sat back. "Fire away."

"Chief Wickett was a good cop, a good boss, and a good chief, but he had one blind spot. We've got one bathroom."

"We do, and I don't see how I can stretch the budget to add a second."

"I don't care about that. I care that the chief's blind spot meant he expected me and Donna to rotate cleaning the bathroom. Because we've got the ovaries, to his way of thinking."

"I don't share that way of thinking. Unless I can, once again, stretch the budget to have somebody come in once a week—"

"Men are smelly and sloppy. Once a week doesn't cut it."

"Okay then, twice a week, if I can stretch it for somebody to come in and deal. Otherwise, daily, full rotation. Including those without ovaries. I'll send out a staff memo on it."

"Are you on that rotation?"

He smiled at her. "I'm the chief of police. That means I don't scrub the toilet. But I'll do my best not to be smelly and sloppy."

"Toilet paper goes on the holder, not on the damn side of the damn sink."

"I'll add that in."

"Toilet seat goes down."

"Jesus." He scratched the back of his neck. "How about this, the lid and all goes down after each use. Seat alone? I'm playing favorites."

"That's fair." But she hesitated.

"More?"

"It ought to be just the deputies on john-cleaning duty."

"Why not Donna? She doesn't use the toilet?"

"You have to get down to scrub the floor. She's fit and she's agile, but I know it hurts her knees."

"Okay, just deputies. Thanks for telling me."

She nodded, rose. "How come you have me patrolling with either Nick or Cecil instead of Leon?"

"Because they both need more seasoning, and you and Leon don't."

"The way it was before—"

"This isn't before. Take your toilet victory, Deputy." He heard the phone ring in the bullpen. "If that's a call, you and Nick are up first. Let's keep it safe out there."

By the end of his first day, he made more adjustments—gave some, held the line more. He took a couple calls himself, just to keep his hand in.

At the end of his first week, he locked up the station feeling satisfied and steady. He left his cruiser at the station, opted to walk. If he got an after-hours call, he'd take his personal vehicle. He picked a couple things up at the market, made his way home in air that tasted of storms.

His weather forecaster at the Sunrise said that nor'easter was barreling in. Since the official weather station agreed, he intended to batten down his own hatches, to be ready if he got a call involving storm damage, accidents, or downed trees.

His trees swayed in that whooshing wind, but they'd come through storms before. He angled to go in the back, the kitchen.

He spotted Simone's car parked beside his, and thought: Oh yeah. Finally!

He didn't see her, so he walked around to the water side of the house. And there she was, standing in the wind, hair blowing. Hair now the color of his grandmother's treasured mahogany sideboard.

Thump, thump, thump went his heart. He wondered if it always would.

"Hey there," he called out. "Nice breeze, huh?"

She turned, eyes alive, face glowing. "Nothing like a storm gathering itself up." She walked over to him. "How'd week one go for you?"

"Not bad. You want to come in?"

"Yeah."

She walked around with him, watched him slide the glass door open to the kitchen. "You don't lock up?"

"If anybody wanted in, they'd just break the glass." He set the market bag on the counter. "You want a drink?"

"What are you offering?"

"I've got CiCi's wine." He got a bottle of each, held them up.

"I'll take the Cab."

She wandered through. "Nice couch. You need some throw pillows."

"Women need throw pillows. I'm a guy."

"A guy who probably wants women on this couch."

"You have a point. Throw pillows it is. I don't know anything about buying throw pillows." He opened the Cab.

"You'll figure it out." She walked to the painting. "Now, this is just wonderful."

"Best gift ever." He got a beer for himself, brought her the wine. "Do you want a tour?"

"Yes, in a minute. You've made a good start down here. You need more art, a couple of chairs, another table or two, including one for over there so you have an actual table when you have someone to dinner."

"I can't cook. Well, scrambled eggs, a GCB."

"GCB?"

"Grilled cheese and bacon. House specialty along with frozen pizza. Are you hungry?"

"More curious." Perching on the arm of the sofa, she sipped wine. "The last time I saw you, and that's been more than two weeks, you kissed me and told me I was the most beautiful woman you'd ever seen."

"I did. You are."

"You never followed up."

He gestured with the beer, drank. "You're here, aren't you?"

Her eyebrows lifted, one disappearing under a sweep of mahogany. "That might make you smart, strategic, or lucky. I wonder which?"

"I'll take some of all three. I figured pushing equaled mistake."

"You'd be right. And you figured waiting would bring me around?"

"I hoped it would. I should also tell you I only had another couple days of waiting in me before I headed your way. I was working on how to be subtle about it."

"Okay then." She rose. "I have something for you in the car. I wasn't sure I'd give it to you. For one thing, I wasn't sure it would suit. I think it will."

She handed him her glass. "Why don't you top this off for me while I get it?"

"Sure."

He topped off the wine, wondered what to make of her. She wasn't really flirting, more conversing. He thought he might drown himself in his strange green tub if she'd decided they'd just be friends.

She came back, traded him a box for the glass.

He broke the seal with his pocketknife, pawed through the packing. Lifted out the sculpture of a woman, no bigger than his hand. Exquisite, she perched on some sort of budded stalk like a flower herself with her hair flowing over her shoulders and down her back between a pair of wings.

She held a hand to her hair as if brushing it back from a face with the lips curved and long-lidded eyes full of fun.

"Your house fairy," Simone told him. "For good luck."

"Jesus, first an original Lennon, now an original Simone Knox."

"Some men might think a fairy too girlie."

"I think she's beautiful." He set her on the mantel at the corner of the painting closest to where he sat with CiCi. "Does she work there?"

"Yes, she does. You need candlesticks on the other end. Something interesting and not—"

He moved in, kissed her with a little more punch than the first time. "Thank you."

"You're welcome." This time she stepped back. "How about that tour?"

"Good timing on that. I hired a bimonthly cleaning crew. They came in today."

"Kaylee and Hester. I heard."

He took her around the main level. She, like Essie, like CiCi, made comments, suggestions.

She paused in front of a closed door.

"Office," he said, placing a hand over the knob to keep it closed. He sure as hell didn't want her to see his boards. "I take care of that myself, so it's pretty messy right now. I've got a guest room over here."

"It's really pretty, welcoming."

"My partner had definite ideas, so I tried to follow them. Mostly. I'm hoping she and her husband will use it this summer. They've got a kid, but I've got a second guest room—or will eventually. And my parents. My sister and her family. My brother and his."

"It's nice, an en suite. Was it the master?"

"No, that's down the other end."

On the way, she stopped at what he thought of as Retro Green.

"This is . . . this is just charming. Anybody else would have gutted this, but you went with it, and it's adorable."

"And now I have to confess gutting was my first thought. Essie, my partner, had different ideas. And she sent me the seahorse shower curtain, and the towels, even the mirror over the sink with the seashell frame. The only thing I did was buy the vanity. Oh, and I had John Pryor replace the faucets. They were pretty awful."

"But you stuck with the old style. Midcentury. You need a mermaid," she decided. "Find yourself a good print of a sexy mermaid, frame it in shabby-chic white like the vanity, and hang it on that wall."

"A mermaid."

"A sexy one."

She walked out, followed him down to the master.

"Well now." She stepped in, circled. "Is this your partner, too?"

"Some. She insisted I get a bed."

"If you didn't have one, what did you sleep on?"

"It was a bed. The kind of bed that's a mattress on top of box springs on top of the floor. I lived in a craphole apartment in Portland. Moved in right out of college, and I stuck with it because I wanted to buy a place. You have to save up for the place, then find the place. It wasn't the sort of apartment where you thought about furniture."

"You thought about this. The colors are good—strong, but relaxing. I like that you didn't go with a new dresser. Did you paint it the navy blue?"

"I found it at the flea market—picked up a few things there. The drawers needed some work, but it was already painted. I saw it, and thought, Deal."

"No curtains at the doors to the porch. I'd never put curtains on that view. If you want to sleep late, pull the sheet over your head."

She turned back to him. "Do you step out there in the morning, look around, and think: all mine?"

He looked around now, nodded. "Pretty much every day."

She opened the door, let the wind roll. "God, doesn't it just rush right through you? All that power and beauty. The *energy*."

Her hair flew back in wild streams. Her skin seemed to glow against the angry, roiling sky. In the distance he saw the first flash of lightning.

"Yes."

She eased the door closed, turned back with that crazy sexy hair, the glow. She walked to the nightstand, set down her glass. "A coaster."

"If I set a glass or bottle down without one, I hear my mother's voice saying—and she's got that exasperated Mom tone down cold—'Reed Douglas Quartermaine, I taught you better.' So . . . coasters, because sometimes you want to stretch out with a beer."

"Sometimes you want." She moved to him and, with her eyes on his, began to unbutton his shirt.

He saw himself grabbing her up like a madman, taking what he so desperately wanted for his.

To his surprise as much as hers, he closed his free hand over her busy ones. "I'm going to slow this down a little," he said.

Her eyebrows shot up again. "Oh?"

He had to take a breath, step back. Since he only had the one coaster handy, he set his beer on the dish he used for loose change every night.

"Did I read this wrong?" she asked him.

"No. A-plus in reading comprehension. I wanted you from the first second I saw you, walking down the stairs at CiCi's party. No, I lie," he corrected. "I wanted you when I saw you in that painting, the one CiCi calls *Temptation*."

"Hence the name," she said, watching him.

"Yeah, good title. But the night of the party, I saw you. I saw you walking down the stairs, and everything turned. Everything stopped, then started again. It was a goddamn moment, Simone."

"You've had moments before."

When she started to turn and reach for her wine again, he put a hand on her arm. "Not like this. Let's get that clear straight off. This is another goddamn moment. I just want to slow it down."

"You don't want to have sex with me tonight?"

"I said I wanted to slow it down a little. I didn't say I'd lost my mind. I want you tonight. I'm going to have you tonight, unless you walk out the door. I just want to slow it down."

He drew her in, took her mouth.

Long and slow, in contrast to the storm breaking outside the glass. Soft and smooth and dreamy.

"Don't walk out the door," he whispered.

In answer, she wrapped her arms around his neck, took the kiss deeper.

"How slow?" she asked.

"Pretty slow, to start anyway." He slipped the jacket off her shoulders. "I've had some pretty intense dreams about you in that bed. We may get there."

He went back to her mouth as the wind kicked. Lightning flashed, thunder rumbled in its wake.

She'd underestimated him, she knew that now. She'd been so sure they'd just jump in, and she'd rid herself of this damn itch he'd left her with.

But he lured her into wanting more, into giving more, feeling more.

When he plucked her off her feet, she felt her heart skip, heard her breath catch. Then he took her mouth again. God, he was good at it. As he laid her on the bed, she drew him down with her, absorbing his weight, the shape of him, before she rolled to reverse positions.

"I can do slow." She dipped her lips to his, a soft brush, a tease. "But I want, too."

Watching him again, she finished unbuttoning his shirt, toed and kicked off her boots. Stretched over him, she nipped at his jaw. "I like your face. Lean, angular, the eyes deep set in that quiet green that's really not quiet at all. I've done sketches of your face."

"You have?"

"Trying to decide what to do with you." She tossed her hair back, smiled down at him. "I decided this part of it." She ran her hands down his sides, then stopped with a jerk. "You're wearing a gun."

"Sorry. Sorry." He rolled her back, sat up. "I didn't think of it." He unclipped it, shoved it in the drawer of the nightstand.

"You forget you're wearing it because it's part of who you are."

"Of what I do."

"And who you are."

He shifted around, saw her kneeling on the bed behind him. "It's all right," she told him. "Just gave me a jolt for a minute. But who knows the good guys from the bad guys better than you and me? I really wish you'd undress me now."

"I can do that."

"But you should take off your boots first, so I can do the same with you."

"Good idea." He bent over to drag at the laces.

"How long since you've done this?"

"Since—" Before he'd been shot, he nearly said. "Since last fall, for one reason or another."

"A long time. It's been a long time for me, too. For one reason or another. Maybe we could speed it up. Just a little."

"Also a good idea." He turned back, knelt with her to pull the sweater over her head. She wore a black bra, cut low. "Man. Sorry, but I'm going to have to take another moment."

When he put his hands on her, she let her head fall back. "You can take a moment. Or two. You have good hands, Reed. Strong, confident."

"I've wanted them on you. Just like this."

"You never pushed."

"Worth waiting."

She lifted her head, opened her eyes. "Wait's over."

She yanked at his shirt, pressed against him, gave herself over to the next kiss. Hungrier now. Harder. She dragged at his belt as the need swamped her.

Around them, the room exploded with lightning, and thunder answered in a roar. Rain lashed, driven by the howling wind.

He pushed her back, dragging at her jeans as she dragged at his.

"We'll slow down after," she managed.

"Best idea yet. Let me . . ."

His mouth rushed over her. So much to taste, so much to feel. When his hands found her, hot, wet, ready, she arched against him with a ragged moan.

"Don't wait, don't wait."

"Can't." He stripped her down, plunged in.

The world shattered, and at last, at long last, he let himself take. He gripped her hands as if to hold them both tethered to the bed. Her legs locked around him as her hips flashed, as she demanded more, more.

She tightened around him, an urgent fist, but he held on, barely held on, so there could be more even when she cried out.

She gathered again, groaning with the build, rising and falling with him.

This time when she broke, she said his name. And buried in her, he let go.

CHAPTER NINETEEN

The two of them stayed tangled, sweaty, breathless while the wind slapped the rain into ice, and the ice hit the windows with the sound of hot grease sizzling. If he'd had his way, Reed would have stayed just as he was, smug and satisfied with the girl of his dreams, until spring.

Seriously smug, he thought as Simone's hands trailed up and down his back. Then her fingers traced the scar from the exit wound in his shoulder.

He shifted, braced on his elbows to look down at her. "You have the most amazing eyes."

"They're brown."

"Some artist you are if 'brown' is the best you've got. They're like a tiger's eyes. Like dark amber. We okay here?"

"Some police chief you are if, with all the evidence, 'okay' is the best you've got."

"I was being modest. You really need to stay. It's bad out there," he continued before she could agree or refuse. "Really bad. I'll admit if this was a balmy night in June I'd want you to stay for, oh, forever. Unless CiCi gives in, then I'd have to kick you out."

"You're talking about making it with my grandmother when I'm naked in your bed."

"Fact is fact. But seriously, you need to stay. I've got wine, frozen pizza, and more sex in store."

She sent him a wicked look with a hint of a smile. "What kind of frozen pizza?"

"Sausage and pepperoni." Rolling over, he grabbed her wineglass for her. "And I've got Dove bars."

"Dove bars seal the deal." She sat up, took the wine. "But I will insist on more sex."

"Before or after pizza?"

"After. I worked up an appetite. I need to text CiCi. She knew where I was going, and she'll figure things out, but it is bad out there, so I want her to know I'm safe inside."

Rising, he walked to the doors. "It really is bad. Tell her to text you back. Let's make sure she's okay."

"CiCi's weathered more storms than both of us put together. And she's got a generator. Which is why she's having her usual nor'easter gathering. A few friends, a lot of food and alcohol. Everyone will bunk there until this blows out. You were invited," she told him. "But I had other ideas."

He switched on the fire, adding the flickering light of flame. "You have good ideas."

"I'm glad you think so. Because another of my ideas? I'm going to have to sculpt you. Guardian. Protector," she mused. "Not with a gun—I don't like them. I think a sword. Maybe in mid-swing. Maybe . . ."

He glanced back. "Like I'm wearing armor?"

She laughed, hitched herself back to prop up on the pillows as she drank. "No, Reed. You'll be wearing the sword."

"I don't really think—"

"You've got a good form, an appealing body. Rangy, but not gaunt. You were on the edge of gaunt at CiCi's party, but you're back in shape."

"Still a couple pounds light." And though he'd never been the modest type, he found himself reaching for his discarded boxers. "I can't seem to get it back."

"You look good. I know the human anatomy, the male body. You look fit and strong along with the rangy." She got up now, walked to him, traced her fingers over the scar on his shoulder, his side. "And these."

"You'd want to leave them out."

"No. They're part of you, part of the protector. You were wounded, but you still pick up the sword. That's admirable."

"It's a job."

"It's you. The boy who stopped to grab a terrified child in the middle of a nightmare, who protected him. I admire that. I might be here if I didn't—it was a long fast for me. But I wouldn't stay." She rose on her toes, brushed his lips with hers. "I need to sculpt you. I could do it from memory now, but I'd rather do some sketches of you."

"You're trying to sex me into it."

"Oh." With a slow, slow smile, she trailed a hand down his chest, his belly. "I will."

"I'm going to have to make you prove that."

He started to pull her in, wanted to ravage that smile.

And his phone rang.

"Crap. Crap, crap. Shit! Sorry." He crouched down for his jeans, dug the phone out of the pocket. "Quartermaine. Okay, slow it down. Where? All right, I'm on my way. Stay calm.

"I've gotta go," he told Simone as he dragged on his jeans. "I'm taking the calls tonight."

"What is it?"

"Car accident, downed tree, a lot of hysteria."

"I could go with you."

"Absolutely no." He pulled on his shirt. "Stay. Toss the pizza in the oven. Eat. I'll text you." He took his gun out of the drawer, clipped it on.

"You need a slicker."

"I've got rain gear downstairs." Sitting, he laced on his boots. "Flashlight in the drawer there, and candles, a lantern downstairs if the power goes."

"Be careful, Chief. It really is bad out there."

"If I only had my sword." He stood, grabbed her, kissed her. "Pizza and ice cream in the freezer. I'll be back as soon as I can."

So, she thought as she stood in the empty room, this is what happens when you start sleeping with a cop.

He hadn't hesitated, hadn't really bitched. He'd just thrown on his clothes and walked out into the storm.

She went to his closet, found herself amused he used about a quarter—if that—of the available space. She checked the bathroom. Apparently the scarred, rangy cop didn't own a robe. She went back to his closet, borrowed one of his shirts.

She texted CiCi, simply tapping in she'd ride out the storm at Reed's.

Two minutes later, CiCi replied with: Woo-hoo!

She considered pizza, but decided she'd wait awhile first. Maybe he'd be quick. She thought about TV, decided against. Books. He had some stacked in the bedroom, and she'd seen some downstairs.

Catch-22, some thrillers. Bradbury's *Something Wicked This Way Comes*. She enjoyed that particular book, but decided it wouldn't be the best choice on a dark and stormy night alone in a still unfamiliar house.

If only she'd brought her sketch pad . . .

On the chance he had a notebook or pad, she opened the nightstand drawers. The flashlight, as advertised, and an iPad that she discovered could operate the TV, a music system, the fireplace.

So the chief liked technology. Something new to add in the getting-to-know-him file.

Home office, she remembered. Bound to have a pad and a pencil in a home office. She wandered out, stopped to smile at the retro bathroom. Maybe she'd paint him a sexy mermaid. She was no CiCi Lennon with brush and paint, but she could manage a fun, sexy mermaid.

She'd while away the time until he got back sketching mermaids—and a few of *The Protector*.

A study from the side—the right side because she wanted the scars—mostly back and butt, his head turned toward the right, sword lifted with both hands, caught in the downswing.

She had to ask him not to get a haircut for a bit. She wanted it a little long and shaggy.

Lightning flashed again as she opened the office door, and she thought of him out in it because someone needed help. She'd come for the sex, she admitted—primarily for the sex. But she stayed, she waited, because of who she'd begun to discover he was.

She switched on the lights, thought he hadn't lied about the mess. Piles of files on a boxy old desk—and a teddy bear with a gun and badge. Folding chairs against the wall, an open trash can loaded with bottles and cans. Maps pinned right to the unfinished walls.

But, hello, a stack of legal pads—they'd do in a pinch—in the closet that had no door.

She walked in, took one, turned to the desk to hunt down pencils.

And saw the boards, saw what was crowded on the two big boards.

"God. Oh God." She had to grip the back of his desk chair, breathe in, breathe out.

She knew the faces, so many of the faces. She'd formed some of them already with her hands.

There, the boy she'd thought she loved. There, her best friend. There, Reed's Angie.

He had photos—not just the faces, but of bodies, blood, broken glass, guns. One of those guns, she realized, had killed Tish, had shot Mi.

She looked at the faces of the killers—boys, just boys. Hobart, Whitehall, Paulson.

And on the second board, Patricia Hobart—her photo and a sketch. She looked different in the sketch, but Simone saw her.

And that face, she realized, had been the one Reed had seen when she'd tried to kill him.

Other faces, other names, other bodies. Times and dates, cities and towns.

He looked at this every day, she realized. He looked, studied, and tried to find the answers.

"My face," she murmured, touching the photos of the girl she'd been, the woman she'd become. "My face on his board. His face and mine. He doesn't look away. He never has."

So she sat at his desk and didn't look away.

When Reed got home, soaked, at just before two a.m., he found Simone wearing one of his shirts, sitting by the fire, drinking a Coke, and reading Bradbury.

"Hey. You didn't have to wait up."

"Couldn't sleep." She rose. "You're soaked."

"Yeah. I think it's starting to ease off some, but it'll probably blow another couple hours." He dragged off a black slicker with POLICE in reflective letters across the back and front. "Laundry room," he said with a gesture, disappearing inside.

When he came out, feet bare, she stood at his fridge, pulling out a carton of eggs.

"It's too late for pizza."

"It's never too late for pizza," he countered. "Didn't you eat?"

"Not yet. I can scramble eggs, too. What happened? How bad was it?"

"Do you know the Wagmans?"

"Priscilla—goes by Prissy—and Rick. They live out by the school."

"They had a fight. Apparently they've been having some marital troubles."

"He had—and likely still is having—an affair with a woman who worked at Benson's Lobster Shack last summer. From Westbrook. Double divorcée."

"So, you know the background. Want a latte?"

"It's too late for lattes."

"You're drinking a Coke."

"Makes no sense, does it? I'll have a latte. Off topic for one moment," she said as she put a pad of butter in a skillet to melt, began breaking eggs in a bowl. "You could use some herbs and spices that aren't salt and pepper and red pepper flakes."

"Write them down, and I'll get them."

"What happened with Prissy and Rick?"

"Big fight, apparently, because, yeah, he's still seeing the woman from

Westbrook. Prissy chose tonight, during the storm, to tell Rick—a drunk Rick—she was getting a lawyer and filing for divorce."

"You can't blame her."

"No, you can't," he agreed. "She found a receipt from some lingerie shop in Westbrook in his pocket—which proves he's a cheater and a dumbass. This when they've been having some money issues, and he swore he'd ended things with the recipient of the sexy lingerie. Prissy started dragging his clothes out of the closet, threatened to light them on fire, busted his MVP trophy from high school softball. He claims she threw it at him. She says she threw it against the wall. I'm going with her because I don't think she'd have missed, and he was too drunk to duck.

"Anyway." He set her latte on the breakfast bar while she scrambled the eggs. "He stormed out in the storm, drunk and pissed. Lost control, hit a tree. Most of the tree fell on Curt Seabold's truck. Seabold runs out, a little bit drunk himself, and he and Wagman get into it, bust each other up, with Seabold having the advantage of only being a little drunk and not already bloodied up from running into a damn tree. Seabold's wife, Alice, runs out, sees Wagman on the ground and her husband staggering around with blood pouring out of his nose, and calls nine-one-one."

"At least somebody acted sensibly."

"Yeah, well. I had to arrest them both, haul their sorry asses to the emergency clinic. Seabold's back home—I figured house arrest until we sort through it all. Wagman's in the clinic with a cracked rib—and I know that's no fun—a mild concussion, busted lip, banged-up knee, and so on. Prissy, who has no sympathy, suggested I tell him to call his slut, which I declined to do."

"Wise." She toasted some of the bread he'd picked up at the market, and set a plate down for him, then one for herself. "This will keep the island entertained for weeks. I hope she doesn't take him back."

"She seems pretty hardened there."

"She took him back at least once before that I know of—another summer worker. They've only been married three or four years. He's never going to be faithful to her, or the slut. He hit on me just last week."

"Did he?"

"In an idiot sort of way." She sampled the latte. "Good latte."

"I've been practicing. The eggs are great."

"They'd be better with some thyme."

"Thyme's on the list." He tapped his temple. "So how did you spend your evening?"

She set down the latte, looked into his eyes. "I have a confession to make."

"At least you could let me interrogate you first. I can already see you've stolen one of my shirts. There'll be consequences."

She laid a hand over his. "I'm going to apologize first. I was rude and intrusive."

"Did you find my stash of porn?"

"You have a stash of porn?"

He stared back, face deliberately blank. "Of what?"

She let out a half laugh. "God, you really are so damn appealing. I was restless after you left. I'm going to say something else because it hit me. With anyone else, I'd have gone home. I'd have said to myself, Well, that was fun, left you a chirpy note, and gone home. Party at CiCi's. But I didn't, and I'm really going to have to think about that. I never even considered leaving."

"I asked you not to."

"It wouldn't have mattered," she insisted. "With anyone else, it wouldn't have mattered. I majored in one-night stands in college."

"Long time ago, Simone."

"Yes, but I have to think about why, when I was restless and alone in a house that's not mine, I didn't even consider leaving. But being restless, I thought I could sketch. Some of you, and maybe a mermaid for your bathroom wall. Only I didn't have a sketch pad with me. So I went into your office to look for a pad."

"Oh." The shutters came down over those interesting green eyes. "Okay."

"You closed the door."

"I didn't lock it," he pointed out. "I didn't say: Don't go in there if you know what's good for you."

"God. You're so steady, so solid." Not feeling as steady, she pushed her hands through her hair. "I saw the legal pads in the closet—no door there."

"I'd just have to open and close it. What's the point?"

"Then I saw your work. Those big rolling boards. I realize some of what's on them is official. What? Crime scene photos and reports."

"Yeah. Since you're not a suspect, we can let that slide. But I'm sorry you saw some of that."

"It's what you see. The dead and destroyed, the bodies, the people who kill. You look right at it, because somebody has to. Isn't that right? Don't say it's part of the job, Reed." She squeezed his hand. "Don't say that."

"It is part of the job, the job I choose to do. It's part of my life. It's a kind of . . . mission, if that doesn't sound too lame."

"Not in the least."

"I won't stop until I take her down. If the feds beat me to it, that's fine. Either way, it closes out. When it does?" He reached over, brushed her hair back from her face. "I take down the boards. I file it all away."

"Can you?"

He sat back with his coffee. "What happened that night's part of us, and always will be. But it doesn't, and it can't, define us. Not you or me, or who you and I are going to be together. We need—however hackneyed the word—closure. And some fucking justice."

"Yes." She let out a breath. "We, none of us, ever had either."

"I'm going to work to get both. Then I'll think about Patricia Hobart sitting in a cell for the rest of her life, and I'll be good with it. Better than."

"You're made that way. That's how it is for you. The good guys go after the bad guys."

"That's how it should be. What are you doing, Simone? You're creating a memorial. You're working on the heart and the soul, honoring the dead, comforting those they left behind. That's a job, too, but it's not just a job. That's your mission."

"I'm pretty late in getting to it."

"So what?"

"You're awfully good for me," she stated. "That scares the crap out of me."

"I'm going to get even better for you, so you'll either get used to it or live scared." He picked up their plates, took them to the sink.

"Will you talk to me about your work? Like, how you believe Patricia Hobart's going to try to kill one of the survivors who's moved south. The two in Florida are top of your list."

"It's what I think, and mostly a hunch. The problem is hundreds of people survived. She's got a lot to choose from. I will talk to you about it, and you'll talk to me about your work. But not tonight.

"Did you check in with CiCi?"

"I did. You got a *woo* and a *hoo*."

"She'll probably never make hot, sweet love with me now." He turned around. "I guess I have to settle for you."

She cocked her head. "There's a gorgeous Italian cellist in Florence named Dante with whom I made hot, sweet love many times. And could again. But since I'm not in Florence, I guess I have to settle for you."

"That's a solid snap back. I did promise you more sex."

"You did."

"I'm a man of my word."

He held out a hand. She took it.

Reed managed a couple hours of sleep before a bright, blustery dawn. He told Simone to sleep and stay as long as she wanted before he headed out with a to-go cup of coffee and an I-had-a-lot-of-sex spring to his step.

He walked, despite the icy patches and slick mud, because he wanted to survey storm damage. He saw plenty of downed branches and hefty limbs—but no trees as unlucky as Curt's.

Needed some cleanup, he decided. He'd have to buy a chain saw, and be careful not to kill himself or others with it. The water might have been bright blue, but it rolled with some violence, white horses galloping.

He spotted a crew of three surveying damage on some of the rentals, stopped to check.

Shingles blown off here and there, plenty of storm debris, and as one of the crew told him, a muddy, bitching hell of a mess, since rain poured in again after the ice.

He found a crumbled bike on the road, but no blood or sign of the passenger. He hauled it up to take with him. Somebody's flag—pink with a flying white horse—lay tattered and soaked in a puddle. That he left behind.

Some, already out clearing their yards, paused to call out to him, asked how he'd fared in his first nor'easter on the island.

He didn't say he'd spent most of it in bed with a beautiful woman.

But he thought it.

He left the crumpled bike outside the Sunrise when he went in to get a refill for his coffee, and caught up with the news there.

Branches and limbs, a collapsed dock, some low-lying flooding. But the big news centered on the Wagman/Seabold incident. Though pressed for details, Reed demurred.

Gossiping about arrests in a café set a bad tone.

He carted the bike to the station, found Donna and Leon already doing some gossiping of their own.

"Where'd you find young Quentin Hobbs's bike?" Donna demanded.

"About a mile out of the village. How do you know it's Quentin Hobbs's bike?"

"I've got eyes. And his mother, who's as ditzy as a drunk cancan dancer, just called in saying how somebody stole her boy's bike during the storm."

"A drunk cancan dancer?"

"Have you ever seen one?"

"Not drunk or sober."

"Take my word. And I said back to her, Did your boy secure that bike in the shed, did he chain it, which he did not, as he takes after his mother and never does either. That bike took flight, that's what happened."

"I'm with Donna," Leon said. "Nobody's going to steal the kid's bike. And nobody's going out in the teeth of a storm to steal it for certain."

"It's trash now. You can tell her we recovered it."

"She'll probably demand you dust it for fingerprints and launch an investigation."

"She'll be disappointed. Leon, I'd appreciate it if you'd go over to the clinic, where I have Rick Wagman handcuffed to a bed, check on his condition. If he's cleared, you can bring him back, lock him up. He's already been charged and read his rights."

"I heard some about that. Did he slap Prissy around?"

"No, he did not, or he'd be charged with that, too. He's charged with OWI, reckless driving, assault—on Curt Seabold—destruction of private property, and resisting, as he tried to take me on when I got there."

"He swing at you?" Donna said, eyes narrowed.

"Half-assed. He was drunk, concussed, and stupid. I charged Curt with assault, as the two of them tried beating the hell out of each other. I let him stay home, and don't see any cause to lock him up."

Frowning, Leon rubbed at his chin. "It seems to me Curt was defending himself."

"He took the first swing, Leon, and said so himself. He'd had a few drinks, but he wasn't driving—and he won't be driving his truck ever again from the looks of it. I expect we'll end up dropping the charge against him, but it has to stand for now. How would he take it if I asked Cecil to go over there with a chain saw and help him cut up the tree on his truck?"

"I'd say he'd take that as good."

"Then that's what we'll do. Nick and Matty are on second shift, but I'll pull them in if we need them. I want Wagman in a cell as soon as he's medically cleared, Leon. I filed the paperwork on him last night. He can get a lawyer, try for bail, but he's in a cell or cuffed to his bed at the clinic. Nobody's going to drive while intoxicated on the island under my watch and shrug it off."

"Yes, sir, Chief."

"You look pretty perky and bright-eyed for somebody who was up half the night dealing with drunks."

Reed smiled at Donna. "Do I? It must just be my sunny disposition. I'm in my office. Send Cecil in when he gets here. And if he isn't here in ten, Donna, you call him and tell him to get moving."

He went in, sat down, booted up his computer. Then contacted the prosecutor who served the island when they needed one.

CHAPTER TWENTY

Rick Wagman got sixty days, a revoked driver's license (not his first drinking and driving rodeo), and mandatory rehab. Since adultery wasn't a crime, Reed decided it was a suitable punishment for being a drunk asshole.

April arrived with a two-day snow. Plows plowed, shovels shoveled while the dawn of spring took the island back to midwinter. Then the sun burst out, popping the temperature toward fifty degrees. The rapid snowmelt gurgled its way into forming streams, chewing potholes into asphalt, swamping the beaches.

Reed spent the lion's share of his first three weeks on the job dealing with weather-related incidents. Off-hours he made himself visible in the village, walking or biking around the island, often with CiCi, Simone, or both. He spent as many nights as he could manage with Simone in his bed.

And dedicated at least an hour every evening to Patricia Hobart.

On his day off in mid-April, he ferried to Portland. He hadn't persuaded Simone to join him. Probably shouldn't have mentioned meeting his parents, he realized.

He drove off the ferry, stopped to buy flowers, ended up choosing a madly blue hydrangea bush instead. Rethought, bought three.

His parents weren't his only visit on this spring Sunday.

He had brunch with his family, played with the kids, bullshitted with his brother, teased his sister, more or less helped his father plant the well-received hydrangea.

And took away an enormous care package of leftovers.

At his next stop he found Leticia Johnson sitting on her front porch potting up pansies. She brushed off her garden gloves when he pulled up.

He thought it amazing she looked exactly the same as she had the night he'd met her.

He glanced across the street, thought the same couldn't be said.

The landlord had indeed sold the lot. The new owners had razed what was left of the house, built a nice little place—currently a soft blue with white trim. They'd added a porch, a concrete walkway, a short, blacktop driveway, some foundation plants.

Next door, Rob's and Chloe's fixer-upper had long since been fixed up into a pretty two-story in a sage green with the addition of a garage on the far side and a bonus room topping it.

He knew they'd added another kid, too.

He pulled the hydrangea out of the car, walked toward Leticia's welcoming smile.

"Aren't you a fine sight on a sunny day."

"Not as fine as you." He bent down to kiss her cheek. "I hope you like hydrangeas."

"I surely do."

"Then pick your spot, and tell me where I can find a shovel."

She wanted it right in front, where she could see it when she sat on her porch. While he dug, she went in the house, came back out with a plastic container.

"Coffee grounds, some orange peels I haven't taken out to the compost yet. You bury these with the roots, boy. They'll help keep the blooms blue."

"You'd like my father. I just delivered one there, and he said just the same. What do you know about lupines?"

They talked gardening, though most of it was like a foreign language to him.

After, he sat on the porch with her, drinking iced tea, eating cookies.

"You look healthy and happy. Island life agrees with you."

He hadn't forgotten she'd come to see him at the hospital—twice. "It really does. I hope you'll come over sometime, let me show you around. We can sit on my porch."

"What you need is a pretty young woman sitting there with you."

"I'm working on it."

"Well, praise be."

"How are the neighbors doing?"

She looked across the street as he did. "Chloe and Rob and their two girls are doing fine. Sweet family. We've got new ones right across now, in that poor woman's place."

"Oh?"

"The family who built the house there—and it's a nice house, too—they just outgrew it. Young couple in there now, expecting their first next fall. Nice as nice can be. I took them over an apple pie to say welcome, and didn't they ask me right in, show me around? And the night before trash day every week, he and Rob, they take turns coming over here to take my bins down to the curb."

"I'm glad to hear that."

"You're still thinking about what was."

"She's still out there."

With a shake of her head, Leticia rubbed the cross she wore around her neck. "A person who'd kill her own mama, kill her grandparents, that's not a person at all. It's something else that doesn't even have a name."

"I have a lot of names for her. I know you didn't talk to her much, but you saw her, Ms. Leticia. Coming and going. I'm looking for patterns, and breaks in them."

"Like we've talked about, she'd drive up with groceries, stay awhile.

Mother's Day, Christmas, she'd bring something. Never looked happy about it."

"Did she ever change her look—like her hair, her style?"

"Not to speak of. But now, I did see her once in one of those outfits the girls exercise in. Like for the gym or running around. Wasn't her usual morning, and she looked downright annoyed. I have to say she had a better figure than I'd have guessed."

"She ran most mornings. We've verified that. Interesting."

"Now that I think on it, I'm putting that at a time her mama took sick."

"Could be Marcia Hobart called Patricia, nagged her into coming by before, and Patricia didn't bother to change from her morning run."

"Now you're putting me in mind of something else." Leticia tapped a finger on her knee. "She didn't look any different that day, or act it all that much, but maybe it's a break in the pattern, like you say."

She rocked, eyes closed, trying to bring it back.

"Wintertime—I can't say just when. But the young ones were building me a snowman right out here, and thinking of the ages, I'm guessing five or six years ago this was. My grandson—the police, you know—was shoveling off my steps, my walk, and he was wearing the scarf I made him and gave him for Christmas, so it was after that. I was out here supervising—brought the young ones a carrot for the snowman's nose—and she drove up."

She opened her eyes again, nodding as she looked at Reed. "I could tell she was annoyed right off when she got out because the walk over there hadn't been done. I called out to her, asked if she wanted one of my kids to do some shoveling, as the girl who did for her was down sick with the flu."

Leticia rocked awhile, nodding again. "I'm remembering now. I walked over while I talked, seems to me, and she ducked her head as she usually did. I just took the bull by the balls, told my grandson to go on over there, shovel off that walk for the lady, told the oldest of the young ones to go get those groceries."

"How'd she handle it?"

"She was kind of stuck, wasn't she? She needed the help, and help was already moving in. I said how it looked like she'd gotten some sun—as it did,

I recall. She said she'd taken a little vacation. My boy's shoveling her walk, the young one's carting the two bags of groceries up to the little porch, so she's stuck, and plainly irritated. She said she hated coming back to winter, wished she could spend all her winters in Florida."

"She said 'Florida' specifically?"

"She did. They had sun and palm trees and swimming pools in Florida, and here we had snow and ice and cold. I suppose that's the most she said to me in our whole acquaintance, so I said it was nice she got a holiday, and where in Florida did she go? She just mumbled about having to get inside to her mother, and went off. Now, she did stop and offer to pay my grandson, still shoveling, but he wouldn't take any money. He's raised better."

"She killed a woman in Tampa, February of 2011."

"Well, my sweet Lord. Her vacation tan hadn't yet faded, so this couldn't have been long after. She'd gotten a tan while taking a life and stood over there bitching about the snow. Do you think she went to Florida again after she shot you?"

"No, I think she went up to Canada. I shot her—she left a blood trail. And she had to move fast."

"She had time to kill her own grandparents." Her fingers reached for her cross again. "Rest their souls."

"She hated them, like she hated her mother. And she had to be hurting. Why not take it out on them? But she *was* hurting, and I don't see her trying to drive all the way to Florida with a gunshot wound. Canada's closer. Fresh ID, over the border, dig a hole, and hide. She had plenty of cash, we figure, and credit cards under fake IDs. But I think she's in Florida now. She had a good time there."

He glanced back at Letitia. "And I think two of her targets are living there now."

"You've got to warn them, Reed. Don't say how the FBI's in charge. Those people should have a chance to take precautions, protect themselves."

After he kissed her goodbye, Leticia watched him drive off. She worried about that boy. The person who wasn't a person but something so bad she didn't have a name for it in her vocabulary had tried to kill him once. Surely he knew she'd try again. She had to pray, and she would, that he was smart enough, and good police enough to catch her before she did.

Essie looked dumbfounded when Reed offered her a hydrangea. "You should plant it with coffee grounds for reasons that make no sense to me. I'll trade you the plant for a beer."

"It's a nice plant. Hank!" she called out. "Reed brought us a plant."

Dylan and Puck came first, on the run.

"My man." Reed slapped high fives with the boy, bent down to rub the wagging dog.

"Are we going to the island? Can we go right now?"

"Gotta hold off on that."

"Aw! Me and Puck wanna go!"

Reed hauled him up. "Not much longer. When you come, I'm making you and Puck the Pug deputies for the day."

"With badges?"

"Can't be a deputy without one. Hey, Hank."

"Reed. That's a nice hydrangea. Nikko Blue. Needs acidic soil to keep it that way."

"Then I'm passing it to the guy who knows."

He had a beer with Hank, admired Dylan's Power Rangers action figures and dinosaurs. Hank caught the subtle signal between his wife and her former partner.

"Hey, Dylan, let's go dig a hole. I've got just the spot."

"Another beer?" Essie asked after her men went outside to dig.

"No, thanks. I've got to catch the ferry back and don't have much time. I stopped by to talk to Leticia Johnson," he began and relayed the new information.

"We always knew she went to Florida, Reed."

"That's right. But I think something about it caught her. She talked about it, and she usually made a point of saying next to nothing. She mentioned it—and the woman at the bakery where she used to stop in the mornings? She said Hobart told her she was taking a few days at a health spa in the mountains."

"She's a liar, which we already know, too. But you've got a point. She slipped. She was pissed off," Essie decided. "Just back from sun and palm trees, and now she's got snow and cold, and nobody's shoveled the damn walk."

"Ms. Leticia had her sort of cornered for a minute, so she let go a little, bitched a little."

"Why would it matter really, what she said to some nosy old woman in her mother's neighborhood? She's irritated with the snow, irritated the kid hadn't shoveled it, fresh off a kill. Yeah." Essie nodded. "She slipped."

"She's in Florida, Essie. I know it."

"Reed, we've got no trail leading there."

"Two targets, and it's been a cold winter." He pushed up, paced. "What did you think when you saw this house, when you bought it?"

"Here's home."

"Yeah, and I felt the same about mine. She lived with her grandparents, and hated them—with her mother before, same thing. She killed them all. Those places were never home for her. I'm betting she thinks Florida is. She comes out of Canada—and even the feds believe she holed up there—and hits Bermuda. You know what I think?"

Nodding, Essie puffed out her cheeks. "It reminded her she loves sun and palm trees."

"Exactly. We figured south already, and I've been leaning toward Florida. Now I'm damn sure of it. I know it's gut, Essie, but it fits."

"I can trickle this to the special agent in charge."

"Not if it brings heat on you."

"Are they getting there? No, they're not. And she's added to the body count. I'll go through channels. Look, Sloop knows you keep in touch with his grandmother, and he can verify. You went by to check in on her—"

"Took her a hydrangea, planted it."

"So much the better. And she hands you this new conversation. You passed it to me. I pass it up the chain. Simple as that."

"Okay. As the person who gathered the information, and as a chief of police sworn to protect and serve, I'm contacting the two likely targets."

"Reed—"

"It'll take time for the feds to process what you pass up, and even then we can't know what action they might take. I'm contacting them, Essie. What can they do to me?"

"Maybe not a lot, if anything."

"They can't slap at you if I make the contacts."

"The contact might have more weight coming from me, a detective on the Portland PD."

"Detective, chief." He grinned at her. "Come on."

"Smart-ass."

"I'm telling you because we've never bullshitted each other, and I don't want you hearing it after the fact. I've gotta go."

He moved to the window first, looked out. "Man, boy, and dog. It's a nice picture."

"My favorite. I'm pregnant."

"Huh?" He spun around. "Seriously? Why didn't you say so right off? It's good, right?"

"It's a lot more than good. I'm only about seven and a half weeks, and you're not really supposed to say before you hit twelve. But . . ."

She looked out the window with troubled eyes. "I'm going to have two kids. Hank found an agent who's going to shop his book around, and by God, he's already started another. He's happy writing, staying home. I'm happy. Dylan's just full of happy. I want the bitch caught, Reed. Sooner or later she'll come after me, too. I'm the one who killed her brother."

"We're going to get her, Essie."

"She doesn't target families. They don't interest her. But now, I've got family inside me."

"Get the word out. Don't wait for the twelve weeks. Look, I think you're high on her list—no bullshitting between us—so it's too soon for her to come after you. But knowing you're pregnant might hold her back if she's bumped you up."

"That's not a bad thought." Because it had tensed up, she rubbed the back of her neck under her short ponytail. "I can let it get out. She came after you, and you were the second nine-one-one caller."

"The second doesn't matter. I didn't bring the cops. Simone did. Simone," he added, "who I'm crazy in love with."

"You—" Essie managed to get her jaw off the floor. "Now it's my turn. Seriously?"

"As serious as it gets. It's either you or Simone on the top of her list. No way she's getting to either of you."

"Is she in love with you?"

"I'm working on it. I've gotta go."

"But it's just getting interesting. How are you working on it?"

"Come to the island, see for yourself," he said as she followed him to the door. "I can't miss the ferry. I'm the chief of police."

On the ferry, Reed made the calls. He spoke to Max Lowen in Fort Lauderdale, identified himself, and said that during a tangential investigation he'd gathered information that caused him to believe Patricia Hobart might be in Florida.

After scaring the crap out of Lowen, Reed spoke of basic precautions, asked relevant questions, gave Lowen his cell number, and suggested he pass that to local law enforcement and contact the SAC at the FBI. He'd be happy to speak with them and verify.

With Emily Devlon, he got an answering machine, left his name, number, and asked her to contact him as soon as possible about information on Patricia Hobart.

Then he got out of his car, watched the island slide into view.

Home, he thought. Where the heart is.

He pulled out his phone again, texted Simone.

On the ferry, about five minutes out. I'm thinking about picking up a pizza and spending some time watching the sunset on the patio with a couple of beautiful women.

She answered back.

CiCi's making what she calls Vegetable Soup For The Ages. And she roped me into kneading bread dough, so no need for pizza. It's too chilly for sunset on the patio. We'll sit by the fire instead.

Deal. Nearly home.

He slid his phone back in his pocket. He'd try Emily Devlon again in the morning if she didn't give him a call back. But for now he put it away.

Emily heard the phone ring as she closed the kitchen door behind her. She hesitated a moment, nearly went back to answer, then kept going. With her husband and kids already off for a little beach time and pizza, she wouldn't worry about it. If Kent needed her, he'd have called her cell.

They had the landline because Kent wanted one for clients and messages. So it had to be a client or another annoying political call or solicitation.

Besides, this was her night. Her girls' night out disguised as a book club, the first and third Sundays of the month—she ran one and just participated in the second. And tonight, she wasn't in charge.

She stepped into the garage—one her husband never used, as he had it so packed with sports equipment, tools, and lawn crap, it barely had room for her car.

She heard a sound, felt a burning flood of pain.

Then heard and felt nothing.

Patricia opened Emily's purse, flipped through her contacts to one of the names on the committee. Texted:

Something came up, explain later. Can't make it. Boo!

In the event a neighbor looked out, Patricia adjusted her wig—same style and color as Emily's. She took Emily's keys, slid into the minivan, hit the garage control.

She drove through the neighborhood, out again, took a direct route to the open-air shopping center a convenient mile and a half away, and parked.

She ditched the wig in her oversize purse with the gun, fluffed up her hair—screw DNA, she *wanted* them to know she'd won again.

She strolled through the mall, basking in the balmy spring evening. Man, she loved Florida! She window-shopped, picked up a couple of things, and walked back to her own car, parked there before she'd taken the mile and a half hike to kill Emily.

Her bags were already in the cargo area.

She let out a sigh. She hated leaving Florida, wished she could stay and just bask awhile. But she had places to go, people to kill.

"Road trip!" she said with a laugh. She opened the bag of jalapeño chips, the Diet Pepsi she'd picked up for the drive. Turned the satellite radio up.

As she drove away, she decided Emily Devlon had been her easiest kill yet.

Her luck was in.

Her luck held. Emily's husband didn't check the garage when he got home. He had no reason to. The kids—hyped up from pizza, and the ice cream he'd been weak enough to indulge them in after—kept him busy and distracted. He didn't expect his wife home until at least ten in any case.

He let the kids go crazy in the tub because they made him laugh even if it did mean some serious mopping up before Mom got home.

He read them a story, tucked them in, mopped up, got what he considered a very well-earned vodka tonic. He didn't check the machine, never thought of it, and fell asleep in the sixth inning of the baseball game on the bedroom TV.

He woke just after midnight, disoriented, then more puzzled than annoyed when he found himself alone in bed.

He shut off the TV, went into the bathroom to pee. Yawning, he checked on the kids and peeked into the guest room where Emily sometimes slept when he snored.

He went downstairs, called for her.

Annoyance flipped over puzzlement. House rule, he thought, for both of them: If you're going to be late, you call.

He reached for his phone, remembered he'd stuck it in the charger beside the bed. He went into his office, off the living area, to use the landline, saw the blinking message light.

He tapped for it, frowned. Why the hell was some police chief from an island off of Portland . . . He heard Hobart's name, and felt his blood run cold.

He called her cell, felt sick when he heard her cheery voice-mail message. "Call me. Call me, Emily. Right now."

He paced, back and forth, telling himself she was fine. Just had too many glasses of Pinot, that's all. She was fine.

But he went out, checked the pool, the hot tub.

Took a shaky breath of relief.

He didn't even think of the garage, or her car, for nearly ten minutes. He wobbled between relieved and shaky when he didn't see her car.

Then he found her.

Reed didn't get the call—from a Homicide cop—until three in the morning. He grabbed the phone, rolled up to sit on what he remembered was Simone's bed instead of his.

"Quartermaine."

"Chief Quartermaine, Tranquility Island, Maine?"

"Yeah. Who's this?"

"Detective Sylvio, Coral Gables PD. I got your name and contact number off a message machine—"

"Emily Devlon." He held on to hope for ten seconds. "Did she contact you?"

"No, Chief Quartermaine."

"Are you Homicide?"

"That would be affirmative."

"Goddamn it, goddamn it. When? How?"

"We're working on that. I've got some questions."

"Ask them." He shoved open the door, walked out on the long terrace overlooking the water. He needed air.

Simone turned on the lights. She felt that air, a strong, chilly flow of it, rush into the room. She got up, put on a robe, walked to the open door to see Reed standing naked in some fitful moonlight, snapping answers into his phone.

He didn't feel the cold, she realized. Not with all that rage burning off him. She'd never seen him angry—hadn't been sure he ever got there. At least not raging.

He didn't rage now, but the rage was in there.

She listened because after he snapped out answers, he snapped out questions. Obviously the answers didn't satisfy him.

"Give me a break, Detective. Give me a fucking break. She might be alive if I'd made that call sooner, if I'd connected with her. Because it's Hobart, goddamn it. She'll have stalked in person, through social media. She'll have a place—or had one—within an easy walk or drive. She'll know Emily Devlon's routine. Where she shops, banks, drinks, eats. She'll have documented every last detail. Did Devlon routinely go out on Sunday nights?"

Reed shoved at his hair, paced.

"For fuck's sake, call the FBI. The SAC is Andrew Xavier. But right now you're standing over a dead mother of two. I was there with her in the DownEast Mall. I didn't know her, but I was in there, too. And I . . . Jesus fucking Christ, are you trying to be a dick? Then give me TOD, and I'll tell you where the fuck I was.

"I was at the home of my former partner and her family. That's Detective Essie McVee." He rattled off her phone number and address. "She'll verify. I left her place, drove to the ferry back to Tranquility. I contacted Emily Devlon, left the message while on the ferry. Prior, I contacted Max Lowen in Fort Lauderdale, as I believed Hobart to be in Florida. The message has a time stamp, goddamn it, you know damn well I called her right before or right after TOD."

He listened and, oh yes, Simone could see that rage in every line and muscle of his body.

"You do that. Fucking do that. You know where to reach me."

He spun around, and the wild fury on his face had Simone taking a step back. He caught himself.

"I need a minute."

But when he reached for the door, to close it between them, she stepped forward.

"Don't do that. Don't shut me out. I heard enough to understand she killed someone else. Someone you tried to warn. Come in, Reed, put some clothes on. You don't know it yet, but you're freezing."

"A lot of fucking good it did. She didn't answer the phone. Maybe already dead. Too fucking late." He tossed his phone on the bed, grabbed his pants. "And this Homicide asshole's grilling me about why I left the message, why I left the Portland PD, how I know so much, where I was during the time in question. Fucking cocksucker."

He caught himself again. "Sorry. I have to go."

"To do what? Put your fist through a wall somewhere else? Once the fucking cocksucker does a minimum of checking, he's going to know he's a fucking cocksucker."

"That won't make Emily Devlon any less dead. She had two little kids. I was too late."

She moved to him, wrapped around him.

"Damn it, Simone. I was too late. She got by me."

"You?" She squeezed hard, eased back. "Why you, and you alone?"

"I'm the only one she's tried to kill who's looked her in the eyes and lived."

"So you're not going to stop. Right now you don't think that counts for much, but it does. I predict the cop in Florida will call you back, apologize, and ask for your help."

"I don't want his fucking apology."

"You're probably going to get it anyway. But now, we're going to take a walk on the beach."

"It's cold, it's the middle of the damn night. I need to go," he insisted. "You should go back to bed."

Odd, she thought, he usually held on to his calm. Now that his had slipped, she had a good grip on her own.

"You're going to wait until I get dressed, then we're going to walk. It's something that helps me, at least sometimes, when I'm really pissed off. Let's see if it helps you."

She went to her dresser for a sweatshirt, sweatpants. "Seeing you in full-blown rage? I realize just how lucky the island is to have you."

"Yeah, nothing like a pissed-off chief of police."

"You have a right to be pissed, and still, already, you're banking it down. And part of the pissed, the part that's still showing, is sad. I knew you were smart and clever as a cop. I knew you respected the job you do, and want to do it well. And I knew you cared about people, but tonight I saw just how much you care."

She got a scarf, wound it around her neck. "We're lucky to have you, Chief. I've got a warm jacket downstairs. We'll get it, and yours, on the way out."

"I'm in love with you. Dear Christ, don't let that scare you off."

It stole her breath for a minute, and she had to take a firmer grip on her calm. "It scares me. It's not scaring me off, but I need a little more gathering myself together before I'm sure what we're going to do about it. I've never felt about anyone the way I feel about you. I just need to figure that out."

"That works for me. And I'm less pissed off now."

"Let's take that walk anyway. You're the first man who's said that to me I've believed. I think we both need a walk on the beach."

It helped, and though he didn't go back in, back to her bed, she knew he'd steadied himself. He kissed her, drove away after he waited for her to go inside.

She didn't go back to her bed, either. Instead, she made a large cup of coffee, went to her studio.

There she found the sketch of Emily Devlon she'd made from the photo on Reed's board. And gathering her tools, began to do what she could to honor the dead.

PART THREE

Proof of Life

Life is real! Life is earnest!
And the grave is not its goal;
Dust thou art, to dust returnest,
Was not spoken of the soul.

—Henry Wadsworth Longfellow

CHAPTER TWENTY-ONE

He did get an apology—stiff and obviously on orders—from the Florida detective. And a follow-up call from the detective's lieutenant, who didn't appear to have his head up his ass.

They exchanged information and promises for updates as they came.

Donna rapped on his doorjamb. "We got a call from Ida Booker over on Tidal Lane, and she's fit to be tied."

"About what?"

"Some dog got into her compost bin, and dug up her flower bed where her daffodils were just coming up, and chased her cat up a tree."

"Whose dog is it?"

"It's nobody's dog, that's the other problem. She's saying it's the second time in two days it's treed her cat, and she asked around having never seen the dog before. The thinking is somebody dumped it. Came over with it on the ferry, went back without it."

"Do we have a stray dog problem on the island I don't know about?"

"We didn't, but it appears we've got one now. Ida says if she sees that dog again, she's going to shoot it in the head. She loves that cat."

"We're not going to have anybody shooting a dog."

"Then you'd better find it before she does. Her blood's up."

"I'll handle it." He could use the distraction.

He drove to Tidal Lane, a pretty neighborhood of eight permanent homes where the residents took pride in their gardens and had formed a kind of informal commune of craftspeople.

Ida, a sturdy woman of fifty, wove textiles, had raised two sons, and loved her cat.

"He scared Bianca, and God knows what he might've done if she hadn't made it up the tree. And look what he did! Dug up my bulbs, spread my composting all over hell and back. And when I came out, he ran off like a coward."

Reed thought he'd rather deal with a cowardly dog than an aggressive one. "Did he have a collar?"

"I didn't see one. For all I know he's rabid."

"Well, we don't know that. Give me a description."

"Some brown mongrel dog, and dirty. Fast. First time he came around and chased Bianca, I was right over there, prepping that bed for planting. I stood up, yelled, and he ran off. Same thing today. I heard the barking and carrying on. Bianca likes to nap on the porch. I came out, and he lit out."

"Which way?"

She pointed. "Tail between his legs. He's lucky I didn't have the shotgun."

"Mrs. Booker, I'm going to advise you against getting that gun and firing it."

"My cat, my property."

"Yes, ma'am, but deploying a firearm in a residential area's against the law."

"Self-defense," she said stubbornly.

"Let's see if I can round up the dog. You say he ran off, so he didn't come at you?"

"He went after Bianca."

"I get that, but he wasn't aggressive toward you?"

"Ran the minute he saw me. Coward."

Not aggressive with people then. Probably. "Okay. I'll look for him. If I don't find him, I'll send a couple of deputies to look around. We'll round him up. Sorry about the daffodils."

He checked the neighborhood, found those who'd spotted the dog—usually after he'd knocked over a trash can and run off.

He cruised awhile, wondering where he'd go if he were a dog who liked to chase cats and dig up daffodils. It calmed him, he realized, the simple task of searching for a stray dog, crisscrossing that area of the island in his cruiser and on foot.

Still, he'd nearly given up and decided to send Cecil out on the hunt, when he heard the barking.

He spotted the dog on a stretch of beach, chasing birds and the lap of the surf. He got the loop leash and the hamburger he'd stopped for earlier, walked down slow and easy as he considered his quarry.

Not rabid to his eye, the way he splashed and ran, and not much more than a puppy. Skinny—ribs showing—so maybe the food would do the trick.

He sat, unwrapped the burger and set half of it beside him.

The dog's nose went up, sniffing, then his head turned. The minute he spotted Reed, he froze.

Reed sat, waited, let the breeze carry that seductive scent of meat. The dog hunched down, crept closer. Long legs, Reed noted, floppy ears, and, yes, tail tucked.

The closer the dog got, the lower he got, until he bellied over like a combat trooper. Eyes on Reed, he nipped the burger, ran back to the surf. Devoured it.

Reed set down the second half, got the loop leash ready.

The dog bellied over again, but this time Reed slipped the loop around his neck when he lunged for the meat.

The dog tried to pull back, eyes wide and wild.

"Uh-uh, none of that. You're under arrest. And no biting."

At the voice, the dog froze, then began to tremble.

"I'd say somebody gave you a bad time." Reed picked up the burger, and his movement had the dog hunching and cringing. "A very bad time." Keeping his movements slow, he offered the rest of the burger.

Hunger overcame fear. The tucked tail gave a hesitant wag.

"Gotta take you in. Attempted assault on a feline, destruction of personal property. The law's the law."

Slow, slow, Reed laid a hand on the dog's head, skimmed it back and over, felt the bumps of scars at the neck. "I've got some of those myself."

He stroked for a few minutes, was rewarded with a tentative lick on the back of his hand.

The dog cringed again when Reed stood up, then shifted his gaze up when the expected blow didn't come. He learned quickly the dog didn't like the leash. He pulled, twisted, froze each time Reed stopped and looked down at him. With that process, they made it to the car.

The tail wagged with more enthusiasm. "Like riding in cars, huh? Well, this is your lucky day." He started to put him in the back, but the dog looked at him with such soulful eyes, the beginning of hope.

"Don't barf up the burger in my official vehicle."

The instant he opened the door, the dog leaped in, sat in the passenger's seat—and banged his snout on the window.

Reed decided a dog could look surprised. He rolled the window down, and his prisoner's floppy ears waved out in the air all the way back to the station.

"Gotta write you up, and see if I can get the vet to come in and take a look at you. Then we'll figure out the rest."

He noted the black SUV in the lot, and knew he had a federal visitor.

In the bullpen Donna took another call, Cecil and Matty sat at their desks, and Special Agent Xavier sat in a visitor's chair with a cup of coffee while he scrolled something on his phone.

The sight and smell and sound of so many humans in one place had the dog shaking, tail tucked, head down.

"Aw, you found the puppy." Cecil started to get up. Reed held up a hand to stop him.

"He's scared of people."

"Doesn't seem to be scared of you," Matty pointed out.

"A little yet, but we came to terms over the burger I fed him. Donna, call the vet."

"Vet's only open Wednesdays and Saturdays, except for emergencies."

"I know that. Call him at home, tell him the situation. I need him to look over the dog, make sure he's not sick. Cecil, why don't you take him back to the . . ."

As he held out the leash to his deputy, the dog whined, pressed against Reed's leg, and trembled. "Never mind. Hang on a minute." Leading the dog, he went to the break room, hunted up a bowl, a bottle of water. "Special Agent Xavier," he said as he came back, "why don't we go into my office?"

"You're bringing the dog?"

"He's in my custody."

In the office, Reed gestured to a chair, then sat behind his desk. Immediately the dog crawled under the desk. Reed poured water into the bowl, set it down.

"So, what can I do for you?" Reed began, over the sound of wet, rapid lapping.

"I felt a face-to-face might make it crystal clear that neither I, nor the Bureau, appreciate your interference with an active investigation."

"Well, you didn't need to take a ferry ride for that, but maybe you needed one to define my interference."

"Detective, you contacted two people—that we're aware of—related information to one of them—that we know of—and stated your personal belief that Patricia Hobart intended to kill them."

"First off, that's Chief. And clearly my personal belief became fact when Hobart killed Emily Devlon."

Xavier pressed his palms together, folded down all but his index fingers. "We have no evidence, at this time, that Hobart is responsible for the death of Emily Devlon."

Reed just nodded. "Would you mind shutting that door? If I get up to do it, this dog's just going to follow me over and back again, and it looks like he's finally settling down."

Reed waited while Xavier obliged.

"I asked you to shut the door because I'd rather my bullpen doesn't hear me calling an FBI agent an asshole."

"You're going to want to be careful. *Chief.*"

"Oh, I don't think so. I think what I have to be here is straight. You may not have any physical evidence, to date, or a handy eyewitness, but you've got everything else. Devlon fits Hobart's pattern down the line. She survived DownEast, and while she was at it, she saved a life. She got kudos— No, my office," he said as Xavier started to interrupt. "She got some kudos at the time, write-ups and so on. More, she benefited financially when the life she saved died of natural causes years later and left Devlon a hundred thousand in her will. Every one of Hobart's victims so far got press and benefited in some way."

"You were ordered, specifically, to stay out of this investigation."

"I don't work for Portland PD now. I'm not interfering in dick-all, and I hope like hell the FBI brings her down, and fast. Until you do, I'll do what I do."

"By tampering with potential targets—"

"Tampering, my ass. I contacted Lowen, laid it out for him because I had information that led me to believe Hobart shifted her gears to Florida."

"And didn't share that so-called information with officials?"

"I put together the information Sunday afternoon, and fully intended to pass it to you Monday morning. I did, in fact, advise Lowen to contact you. Gave him your name and number. I would have done the same with Devlon had I reached her. And had I reached her, maybe she'd be alive. So don't come into my house, Agent Xavier, and try to bullshit me. You're in charge of the Hobart investigation, but I've got skin in this—literal skin."

"Which is exactly why you were taken off the investigation."

"Again, I don't work for Portland PD. I work for the people of, and the visitors to, this island. And, as far as I know, there's no law or regulation saying as such—or as a private citizen—I can't gather information or contact individuals I believe might be in jeopardy."

Xavier just looked down his blade of a nose. "Let me make this clear. The FBI doesn't need the dubious assistance of some obsessed LEO who's playing big shot on some bumfuck island and spends his time out catching stray dogs."

Reed glanced down at the dog now snoring at his feet. "It didn't take that much time. I'll say this, then we should both get back to work: I'm not looking to get in your way, and we both know I haven't been in your way. You're pissed because it's now in the files that some obsessed LEO on some bumfuck island contacted Hobart's next victim—or tried to. And you, Special Agent, with all the punch of the FBI behind you, didn't.

"I'd be pissed, too, in your shoes. But Emily Devlon is still dead, and there are people I care about who fit Hobart's victim pattern. So you're wasting your time trying to scare or intimidate me."

"What I'm doing is warning you. The Bureau has control of this investigation."

"Warning me isn't going to do dick-all, either. I hope you get her. I hope to Christ you take her down before she kills the next on her list. When you do? I'll send you a case of the beverage of your choice. Until then, I'd say we both know where we stand on this."

"You'll cross a line." Xavier got to his feet. "When you do, I'll see to it you lose this cushy job you've got here, and any chance at a badge anywhere."

"I'll keep that in mind. You know, you haven't asked how I determined Hobart was in Florida and would go for one of the two people I contacted. You don't ask," Reed continued, "because you're pissed. I'm going to send you that information, and hope you'll look into it when you're not as pissed. It's relevant because if you haven't confirmed that Hobart's responsible for Devlon as yet, you will. She'll have left something because she wants credit for it."

"Just keep out of my way."

"We're still off-season," Reed said as Xavier went to the door. "So you've got a couple hours before the next ferry back to Portland. The coffee and pie are damn good at the Sunrise Café."

Xavier strode out, leaving the door swinging open behind him.

Reed looked down at the snoring dog again. "That, my friend, was a man who managed to be a dick and a tight-ass simultaneously."

He looked up again when Donna came to the door. "Your visitor didn't look too happy when he left. Rude, too, slamming the door. We figured you were in trouble with the feds for something, but you don't look worried."

"I'm not, because I'm an obsessed LEO playing big shot on a bumfuck island. And that works out pretty well for me."

"Big shot." She snorted.

"Hey, I'm chief of police. That's pretty big for any shot."

"Did he really call the island 'bumfuck'?"

"He did, but we're not worried about that because we know better."

"Did you cut that asshole down to size?"

"He didn't leave happy, did he?"

She gave a sharp nod of approval. "Doc Dorsey said you can bring the dog in."

Reed wondered if he should let sleeping dogs lie. But when he rolled back a couple of inches in his chair, the dog's head shot up. His eyes stared into Reed's with fear and longing.

"I guess I'll do that then."

He opted to walk, hoping the dog would stop shaking every time he saw someone who wasn't his arresting officer. But every time he did, the dog leaned on Reed's leg and trembled.

The vet had his office attached to his house, less than a quarter mile out of the village proper. He lived in the bright yellow house with his wife and their youngest son, now a high school senior.

Doc Dorsey—even his wife called him Doc—kept regular hours two days a week, with a third morning reserved for surgeries. He'd open otherwise for emergencies, even if he was out fishing or working with his three hives of bees.

When Reed walked in, the vet's wife sat at the desk in the waiting area. A kind of animal parlor, Reed observed, with a scatter of mismatched chairs and tables on a floor of pale blue vinyl.

"Mrs. Dorsey, I appreciate you opening up for me."

"Oh, that's no problem." She waved that away, a woman with a long brown ponytail pulled back from a pretty, fully made-up face. "So this is our stray. Poor lost baby."

She hopped up. The dog cringed back and hunched behind Reed's legs.

"People spook him."

"You don't."

"Well, I gave him a hamburger and a ride in the cruiser."

"He's bonded with you." She flicked a finger at Reed, then crouched down to dog level. "I bet he was hungry. He's definitely underweight. That's a sweet face he has. He needs a good wash. I think there's some red under that brown, but he's one dirty dog. Did you bring a stool sample?"

"Ah . . . We haven't gotten to that end of things."

"Well, we'll need one. You take him around the back. Plenty of dogs have pooped and peed there. The scent could get him going. How long ago did he have that hamburger?"

"A good hour I guess."

"Then you should have some luck. Take this."

She pulled a doctor's glove and a widemouthed plastic bottle out of a drawer. "I'll let Doc know you're here."

Resigned, Reed went out, but before he could lead the dog around to the back, said dog squatted and did what dogs do right on the concrete walkway.

"Well, shit. Literally."

Reed put on the glove, did what he had to do.

"That was quick," Mrs. Dorsey said when he came back in.

"He went on the walkway before I realized . . . Sorry." He handed her the sample, which he swore moved. "I got most of it."

"Don't worry, it's not the first time. Take him on back. Straight back through the doorway, first left." She handed the sample back. "You're going to give this to Doc, but I can tell you that poor baby's got intestinal worms."

"Fun."

He went back to the exam room with its counters, long, raised padded table, scales.

The dog trembled again when he saw Doc. The vet had a long brown pony-tail like his wife, but gray streaked through his. He wore John Lennon glasses, a beatific smile, a Grateful Dead T-shirt, cargo jeans, and Doc Martens boots.

"Now, who've we got here?"

"He won't give me his name, but I've got this." Reed, happily, handed over the sample.

Doc said, "Um-hmm," and, like his wife, crouched down. "Hasn't been getting regular meals for a while by the looks of it. Scared of people, is he?"

"Shakes a lot. I felt scars on the back of his neck."

That beautiful smile vanished, and the eyes behind the glasses went hard. "We'll have a look. He's not full grown, I'd say. See if you can get him to stand on the scale."

It took a little convincing, but if Reed knelt down beside him, the dog stood still and trembled.

Doc noted the weight, told Reed to lift him up on the table.

"You stand in front of him, so he can see you. And you talk to him. Just keep your voice calm."

"Nobody's going to hurt you, but we've got to have a look." He kept looking at the dog, talking in that same quiet voice, while Doc gently ran hands over him.

"People reported a stray just yesterday. He chased Ida Booker's cat up a tree, yesterday and again this morning. Dug in her garden, ran off when he saw her. I found him chasing birds on the beach down that way. Lured him in with a burger. I had to sit for a while first."

As he spoke in the calm, easy voice he'd use for an assault victim, he kept his eyes on the dog's eyes. "He liked riding in the car. Kept his head out the whole time. He seems okay with me, but he spooks around anybody else. So far. If you move too fast or raise up your arm, he jerks down."

"Classic signs of abuse."

"I know it. It's pretty much the same in people."

"These scars? They're probably from a choke collar. Yanking and yanking on it until the metal cut him."

"Motherfucker. Sorry."

"No sorry. It takes a motherfucker to do that to an animal. I need a look at his teeth, his ears, and so on."

Reed kept talking. The dog shook harder, but with Reed holding him, Doc examined his teeth, eyes, ears.

"He's got infections in both ears. Teeth are good. I'm going to estimate he's between eight and nine months old, which means you double the 'motherfucker.'"

Doc pulled a couple of dog treats out of his pocket. He put the first on the table, waited for the dog to track his gaze from treat to Reed to treat, then gobble it.

The next he held out. The dog looked at Reed again.

"Tell him it's okay."

"Don't be an idiot," Reed told the dog. "Somebody offers you a cookie, you take it."

The dog did, eyed Doc.

"I can do a test to see if he's had his shots. I'm betting against. He's still got his balls, too, and that needs to change. I'm going to take a look at the sample. So just keep him on the table."

Doc went into a little alcove.

"We can keep him," Doc said, "treat him here, but you're his person. If you can handle it, he'd do better with you until he's healthy. Whoever owned this dog can't have him back. If you find who did, they need to be charged with abuse and neglect."

"Since I'm not home all day, shouldn't . . ."

The dog licked the back of Reed's hand, looked up at him with that same combination of longing and fear.

"We'll take it a day at a time."

"He's got worms. I'm going to give you medicine for that—and we'll need a follow-up stool sample. I'll give you an ointment for the ears, and an antibiotic. We'll write up instructions. I'd recommend you feed him a good puppy brand. Three times a day until he hits his normal weight."

"I need to draw some blood from him, so keep him distracted."

Reed kept them both distracted. He'd rather face a fist than a needle.

"What do you think he is? I mean, what kind of dog?"

"I think there's some coonhound in there." Doc pinched some skin on the dog's flank, slid the needle in. "Might be some Lab, and a lot more of this and that. He's not full grown. I'm going to give you some shampoo. He's got some fleas, and that'll take care of them. You need a bath, boy."

Doc came around, stroking the dog. The dog didn't shake as much, but he watched Doc, as if waiting for the gentle hand to turn mean.

"Somebody did a number on him," Doc said. "In time, with patience and good care, he may get over it. Some do, some don't. I'm going to put the medicine together for you, and Suzanna'll print out instructions for all of it. Should we bill the island PD?"

Reed thought of the budget. "No, go ahead and bill me."

Back came the smile. "In that case, I'm going to charge you cost for the medicine, and we're going to consider the exam a public service."

"I appreciate that. A lot."

Doc offered the dog another treat. The dog just looked at Reed, judged it allowed, and took it.

"If you can't keep him, we'll find a home for him. Right now, he trusts you, and he's had enough trauma in his short life."

Suzanna, as they had progressed to first names, added a list of items he needed for basic puppy care, and walked him through the first application of ointment, gave him a little bag of treats and what she called pill pockets—in a variety of flavors.

He walked back to the station with the dog and the bag from the vet.

"Cecil and Matty just headed to the high school. A little dustup—just off school grounds. A couple of boys punching each other. Probably over a girl."

"Donna."

Her eyes narrowed at his tone. "Chief."

"I know the rule about no personal errands, but I can't take this dog into the market, and right now he's stuck to me like Velcro. Suzanna Dorsey gave me a list of what I need to get for him."

"You expect me to leave my post, go down to the market, and buy stuff for a stray dog?"

"He's got scars on the back of his neck from somebody yanking him on a choke chain so hard and so often it cut him. He's got infections in both ears, and is stuck to me because everybody else in his life so far has hurt him. Doc says he's only about eight months old."

Her chin pushed up so high her bottom lip almost disappeared. "Doc said that about the choke chain?"

"Yeah."

"Give me the damn list."

"Thanks. Sincerely."

"I'm not running a personal errand for you. I'm running one for that dog. Now give me your credit card as you don't know how much this is going to cost."

He handed it over, decided he'd think of his own budget later.

When he finally locked the station for the night, he decided to give himself and the dog a break and drove home in the cruiser.

"You're on parole," Reed told him as he led the dog into the house. "Crapping and pissing in the house, chewing on anything but what I give you violates the terms of your parole. Take that seriously."

The dog sniffed around a little in the bedroom, always with one eye cocked at Reed as Reed changed into his most ragged sweatpants, an old sweatshirt, and a pair of sneakers he hadn't gotten around to tossing out.

Because, of the two of them, Reed knew that what came next would be messy.

He led the dog back outside, got the hose, the shampoo. And spent the first ten minutes of the project wrestling a wet dog who whined and shook and tried to escape the nightmare of soap and water.

The dog finally submitted, just staring at Reed with eyes that spoke of the pain of betrayal.

They were both soaked and not particularly happy with each other when Simone drove up.

"Better keep back. We're a mess."

"Suzanna Dorsey told Hildy who told CiCi you'd taken in a stray dog. I see the grapevine rings true yet again."

"He's on parole." Reed ruthlessly ran the hose over the dog to wash off the shampoo and dead fleas. "And right now skirting close to the edge."

"He has a sweet face."

"Yeah, everybody says so. He's also flea-bitten and has worms."

"Abused, Suzanna said."

"Yeah. That, too."

Simone walked over to sit on the steps because the dog watched her as if she might throw a rock at his head. "I'm supposed to take a picture of him and text it to CiCi."

"You should wait until he's more presentable."

"He's a pretty color, sort of like a chestnut horse."

"Apparently he's got some coonhound in him, whatever that is."

"Do you like dogs?"

"Sure. We had one when I was a kid. My sister named it Frisky before my brother and I could veto. She was a good dog. We lost her right before I left for college." He glanced over. "How about you?"

"We couldn't have a dog—or cat. My mother's allergic. Or says she is. I never really believed her. But, yes, I like dogs. Are you keeping him?"

"I don't know. I'm not here most of the time. Doc said they'd find him a home. He'd probably be better off, once he gets used to being around people who don't smack him around."

He let go of the dog to grab one of the old towels he hadn't gotten around to tossing out—and the dog used the opportunity to shake off the water. It flew up, out, and all over Reed.

At Simone's laugh, Reed used the towel on his own face. "Now I need a damn shower."

"Looks like you just got one."

"Har." He began rubbing the dog briskly with the towel. "How do ya like that?"

The dog responded by wagging its tail and licking Reed's face.

"Sure, sure, now we're buddies."

Simone watched the man rub the dog and grin while the dog wagged and licked his face.

Though she knew she'd been slipping and sliding, in that moment, with that image, she fell in love.

CHAPTER TWENTY-TWO

When Patricia decided she wanted to document her story, professionally, only one person fit the bill. And really, Seleena McMullen had been right there at the DownEast, had ridden the wave of the videos she'd taken of that idiot Paulson.

Who better?

Besides, Patricia felt Seleena had treated her with some respect when she'd done that anniversary interview. She even liked the way she'd looked and sounded; though, of course, she'd put on that poor, shy, sad-me face.

This would be different. This would be real. And when *this* hit cable and the Internet, people would finally know who had the damn brains, who had some damn *grievances*.

Patricia even wrote up a kind of script and practiced. In so doing, she was so impressed by her own skills she decided that when she settled down to the good life in Florida, she'd write a screenplay on her life and times.

When she had it set, when she had everything in place, when she believed everything was perfect, she made contact.

"This is Seleena."

"Don't hang up," Patricia whispered in a shaky voice. "Don't call the police."

"Who is this?"

"Please, I have to talk to somebody. I'm so scared!"

"If you want to talk to me, I need a name."

"It's—it's Patricia. Patricia Hobart. Please, don't call the police!"

" 'Patricia Hobart'?" Doubt dripped. "Prove it."

"You came into the—you called it the green room—before they took me out for the anniversary report last July. You sat with me and you said if I ever remembered anything about my brother, any little thing I hadn't told the police, I should call this number. I could tell you."

"I'm here for you, Patricia." Now excitement rang clear. "I'm glad you called me."

Patricia heard the rustling, imagined McMullen grabbing a recorder, a notebook. And smiled. "I don't know what to do!"

"Tell me where you are. The FBI's looking for you. And a lot of cops."

"It's not like they say, none of it, none of it. I don't know what's happening. I don't understand. I've been running, but I'm scared all the time. I'm going to turn myself in, but I need to talk to somebody first. I need to talk to somebody who'll listen and tell the truth."

She added broken sobs. "You don't know, you don't know what they did to me."

"Who?"

"My grandparents. Oh God, I need to tell someone. I can't keep running, but nobody will believe me."

"You can tell me. I believe you. What did they do to you?"

"No, no, not like this. In person. I need you to record everything so it's, like, on the record. You can't tell anyone or they'll kill me. I know it. Maybe I should just kill myself and end it."

"You don't want to do that, Patricia. You need to tell your story. I'll help you."

Patricia smiled, let her voice quaver with hope. "You—you'll help me?"

"I will. Why don't you tell me where you are?"

"I— You'll call the police!"

"No, no, I won't. You said you're turning yourself in. But you want to tell your story first. You want me to make sure people hear your story. I won't call the police."

A weak voice, Patricia thought, with just a touch of desperate hope. "You swear?"

"Patricia, I'm a journalist. I only want the truth. I only want your story. I'd never betray you. In fact, when you're ready, I know a lawyer who'll help you. We'll arrange for you to turn yourself in so no one hurts you."

Patricia studied the flask of scotch she'd sipped while McMullen spoke. "You'd do that?"

"Tell me where you are, and I'll come meet you. We'll talk."

"If you tell the police, and they come, I'll kill myself. I—I have pills."

"Don't take any pills. I won't do that. Where are you? I'll come now."

"Right now?"

"Yes, right now."

"I'm at the Traveler's Best Motel, off Route 98, right before the Portland exit. Please help me, Ms. McMullen. There's no one else."

"You sit tight, Patricia. I can be there in forty minutes."

"Someone has to listen." Patricia sobbed again. "You're the only one."

She hung up, toasted herself in the mirror with the scotch she'd developed a taste for.

Seleena raced to change into an on-camera suit. If things went well, she'd have the crazy woman in her studio inside two hours. The biggest exclusive anywhere, and it fell in her lap.

Once she had that in the pipe, she'd call the FBI. First the mother of all exclusives, then she'd rake it in as the intrepid reporter who brought down Patricia Jane Hobart.

She checked the time as she grabbed her laptop—she'd start with digital remote. Nearly midnight. She'd beat that forty minutes if she pushed it.

She packed up her recorder in case Patricia was initially shy, a still camera, her phone, tossed in a makeup bag, checked her Glock with its hot pink frame, and was in her garage in five minutes flat.

Emily Devlon could have warned her about Patricia's skill with garage doors, but dead women don't talk.

Seleena slid behind the wheel.

Her eyes widened in the rearview mirror when Patricia sat up in the back seat. Even as she grabbed for her purse and the gun, the syringe jabbed into her neck.

"Night-night," Patricia said.

When Seleena slumped, Patricia got out, popped the trunk. She hauled Seleena out, fixed plastic restraints on her wrists and ankles, added a gag just in case Seleena came out of the sedative and made a fuss.

With some effort, she dragged her to the trunk, hoisted her up, and rolled her inside. "You just take a nice nap," Patricia told her. "We've got a long drive ahead of us."

She closed the trunk.

Simone didn't tell him; she wasn't ready. And in any case, the moment didn't seem right for declarations of love.

She knew he'd keep the dog. If he wasn't already in love, he was—as she'd been—slipping and sliding in that direction.

Because he'd done a very good deed for the day, she did one of her own and fixed a simple pasta dinner. She didn't mention she'd learned how to make it from a certain Italian cellist.

As Reed explained how easily the dog spooked around people, and why, Simone strategically ignored him.

Reed fed the dog, who ate as if he'd been starved for weeks. Her heart ached as she wondered if he had.

By the time she had their meal together, the dog had stopped hiding behind Reed and was curled up under the table asleep beside his empty food bowl.

"He needs a name."

Reed shook his head as they sat down to eat—at a drop-leaf barnwood table he'd bought from a friend of CiCi's. "If he goes somewhere else, they'll name him something else, and it'll just add more confusion. Man, this is great," he said after a bite of pasta. "You've been holding out on me. You can cook?"

She shook her head. "I can make a couple of things well, a few other things reasonably edible. That's surviving rather than cooking."

"It's cooking on my scale. Thanks. How'd things go for you today?"

"They went well, but I realize I need a break from my . . . mission. A change of pace. I need those sketches of you."

"How about a loincloth? I could wear a loincloth."

"Do you have one?"

"No, but maybe I can rig one up. The naked thing . . ."

"I've seen you naked."

"It's different seeing me naked and studying me naked, drawing me naked. You're on the other side of that."

"I've been on both sides."

"What?" He stopped eating.

"I subsidized my income in New York by modeling."

"Naked?"

"Figure studies." Amused, if unsurprised, by his reaction, she stabbed a noodle. "It's art, Reed, not voyeurism."

"I can guarantee some of the guys—and probably some of the girls—were voyeuring."

She laughed. "I got paid either way. So, tonight's perfect. I brought my sketchbook. You can consider it a trade for the meal—and what I'll give you after the session."

"Bribing me with sexual favors? That will . . . completely work."

"I thought it might. You haven't mentioned the FBI paying you a visit today."

"Grapevine," he said.

"It drips with juice. Did you not mention it because you thought it would upset me?"

"It didn't amount to all that much."

She'd heard differently, but wanted his side of it. "So tell me what it did amount to, and trust me to handle it."

He picked up the wine she had insisted went better with the pasta than beer. He couldn't say she was wrong. "It's not about you handling it. I guess, it was more about bringing work home."

Arching her brows, she angled to look deliberately down at the dog under the table.

"Okay, you got me there."

"Proving your work doesn't come to a hard stop, and neither does mine. So?"

"Special Agent Dickhead didn't like some LEO with a cushy job in bum-fuck stepping on his sensitive toes."

"He called you a lion?"

"A—oh. No." On a laugh, Reed ate more pasta. "LEO as in 'law enforce-ment officer.' L-E-O."

"Oh. And he considers the island bumfuck."

"It kind of is. I'm fine with serving and protecting our bumfuck. I'm not fine with him coming into my office trying to strong-arm me." He gave her the gist, shrugged, and added, "So basically I told him to blow me, and he left."

"Didn't it matter to him that a woman's dead?"

"I have to believe it did, and does, which is one of the reasons he decided to take a swipe at me. Swing and a miss. Look, most FBI I've crossed paths with are dedicated, want to catch the bad guys, and are willing to cooperate with local LEOs—to integrate them into investigations where it makes sense. This guy? He takes the *special* in 'Special Agent' literally. He just thinks he's better than cops."

"I don't like him."

"Hey, me, either. He's a raging dick. That doesn't mean he's not good at his job."

"Then why hasn't he caught Hobart?"

"She's slick. Smart, slick, and fucking canny. She's got skills, focus, and a boatload of money. I wouldn't punch at Special Agent Dickhead for not tak-ing her down yet." He jerked a shoulder. "I did it for him being so self-important and territorial that he flips off information and assistance from outside sources—especially, for whatever reason, me."

"CiCi knows people. I bet she knows people who know the head of the FBI, or people who know people who do."

"Don't go there." He gave her hand an easy pat. "I've got this, and if it turns out I don't?" He polished off his wine. "Then we can revisit the idea of pulling out the awesome power of CiCi."

He rose to clear the pasta bowls. The dog jumped up immediately, smacking his head on a chair leg in his haste.

"Jeez, chill. I've got to give him another pill, do another ear deal. The pill's easy. They've got this little flavored thing you push it into. The ear deal could get ugly."

"I bet he's a very good dog." Simone turned in her chair as the dog followed Reed to the sink. "I bet he's very brave."

Glued to Reed's leg, the dog watched her.

"You're so handsome, and you have such kind eyes." As she spoke, she eased down to sit on the floor. "How could anyone have been mean to you? But it's going to be okay now. You landed in a big bowl of Milk-Bones."

The dog took a cautious step toward her, retreated, but she kept talking.

"And weren't you smart to find Reed? He's going to keep you. He's telling himself he's not, but he will."

Another cautious step, then one more.

Standing still and silent so he didn't distract, Reed watched, thought the dog looked half-hypnotized. He bellied over to where Simone laid a hand on the floor. Sniffed it, tried a lick.

He cringed when she lifted the hand, trembled when she put it on his head.

"There now. No one's going to hit you anymore."

He edged closer, eyes on her face as she stroked.

"I feel the scars," she murmured. "He's got heart and fortitude. He must have a very pure soul to be able to trust any human. They couldn't turn him mean. He doesn't have mean in him."

She bent down, kissed the dog on the nose. "Welcome home, stranger."

Reed took out one of the pills, pushed it into the soft little pocket. And accepted he'd gotten himself a dog.

The downside of that showed itself when he took the dog out to walk him. Eventually, he thought, the dog would learn the territory, just go out on his own. But for now he'd walk him over into the woods.

If bears shit in the woods, so should dogs.

When the dog didn't mimic a bear, Reed assumed he didn't have enough food in him yet to pass it along.

Until they hit the slate walk, then the dog squatted and relieved himself.

"Goddamn it, what's wrong with the woods? Now I need a shovel."

When he got one, the dog cowered and quaked.

"Ah, Jesus, it's not for you."

He found his gut burning in fury at the idea of someone beating some poor dog with a shovel.

Back inside, he got one of the dog biscuits, crouched down, offered it. "That's not a reward for crapping on the walkway because, man, that's just uncivilized. It's just because. Now, I have to go upstairs and get naked, and not for fun and sex. I'm already mortified."

He started upstairs, the dog at his side. Then looked back when he reached the top and heard the whining.

"How'd you do that?" Stumped, Reed walked halfway down to where the dog now had his head through the pickets, and was stuck. "Why did you do that? Hold on. Stop squirming."

He managed to angle the head, shift the body, reangle, and work the head free.

"Don't do that."

This time the dog followed close on his heels to the bedroom.

Simone sat in the chair by the fire doing random sketches in her pad. Of body positions—naked body positions. *His* naked body?

If that wasn't weird enough, he glanced toward the bed. Took a step toward it.

"That's a sword. There's a sword on the bed."

"I told you I wanted you holding a sword."

"You've got a sword."

"I borrowed it from CiCi."

"CiCi has a sword." He picked it up—weighty—studied its long, carved sheath.

It looked old, he realized. Not all jeweled up and fancy, but old and . . . battle-tested.

"This is so cool." He drew it out, wondered at the shine and sleekness. Battle-tested, he thought again, spotting a few nicks. Steel against steel.

"This is just out-and-out cool. Why does CiCi have a sword?"

"It was a gift. From some ambassador. Or maybe it was Steven Tyler. She has a katana that I considered, but you're an all-American boy and a katana's too exotic for this."

"She has a katana and a . . . Is this a broadsword?"

"I couldn't say. Strip it off, Chief."

Holding the sword, giving it a slow swing right, left, because you just had to, he frowned back at her. "A man would have to be crazy to swing a sword around naked."

"The Celts did."

"But they got crazy first."

"Strip it off," she said without mercy. "There's a bottle of wine for courage."

"Maybe you should spell out the sexual favors first."

"Then they wouldn't be a surprise, would they? Don't be shy. I repeat, I've seen you naked."

"The dog hasn't," he countered, but set the sword down to undress and get it over with.

"It was sweet of you to get the little stuffed dog for the dog."

"I didn't. Donna tossed it in. No dog of mine plays with dolls."

"Really? You'd better tell him that."

Shirt off, hands on the button of his jeans, Reed looked over to see the dog, curled up, one paw on the stuffed toy while he lovingly licked its face.

"He's already an embarrassment to me." Heaving out a breath, he stripped down to the skin.

"Stand closer to the fire—it's nice light. With the sword," she added. "Pivot to the left, but angle back toward me from the waist. We're going to try a couple with you holding the sword at the hilt, point down. You can talk."

"I have no words."

"The island's starting to gear up for the season."

Naked small talk. Naked small talk with swords. Jesus. But he gave it a try. "Yeah, a lot of spring-cleaning and painting going on."

She wove casual conversation through directions to turn or to change his stance.

"I want you to raise the sword over your left shoulder, as if you were going to strike down. Just hold it there a minute."

Good lats, she thought, strong biceps, a lean torso. The scar puckering over the right oblique, the latissimus dorsi, the deltoid added that tangible proof of violence.

"Lower it for a minute, shake it off."

She got up, got him some wine. "Relax."

"We done?"

"Not yet. I want you to turn your head, look at the doorway. Imagine your enemy there, coming at you."

"Can it be Darth Vader?"

"Not Kylo Ren? He killed Han Solo, and Vader never could."

"It matters that you know that." He handed her back the wineglass. "But nobody out-dark-Forces Vader."

"Darth Vader it is." She took the glass, set it down, went back to her chair. "I want you to take a couple breaths, then look toward the door. There's Vader. Then keep your eye on him and swing the sword up, and hold that. Hold the look, the pose. I want you tensed, primed for the first blow. Got it?"

"Yeah, yeah."

"Make it real. Believe it, and it'll look real. When you're ready."

He tried to make himself hear that spooky Vader breathing, and when he had it in his head, looked, swung.

"Hold it, just hold that."

Perfect, she thought. The angle, the muscles in his glutes, hamstrings, quads. The ripple along the shoulders and arms. The tension in the jaw, the back.

"I've got it. I've got it," she muttered, bringing him onto the paper. "Just hold the pose."

She grabbed her phone, took three quick photos to back up the sketch.

"That's it. You've defeated the Empire. Relax."

He lowered the sword, rolled his shoulders. "We're done?"

"I've got what I need. You're an excellent model."

"Let's see."

"Uh-uh." She slapped the sketchbook closed.

"Come on."

"I want you to see the finished piece. Besides." She rose, walked to him. "Now that we're done with the session, I'm thinking I have a naked man all to myself."

She took his mouth, gave his lower lip a teasing nip.

"Watch the sword," he told her.

Trailing a hand down his chest, over his belly, she asked, "Which one?"

"Ha."

"Put the metal one away. There's a full moon tonight. By the time I'm done with you, you'll be howling at it."

By the time she was done with him, he had decided that if this was the payment scale, he might make naked modeling a career.

He woke groggy, in desperate need of coffee, and remembered the dog when he tripped over him.

"Sorry. I got it," he said when Simone murmured.

He yanked on clothes, took the dog out through the kitchen, grabbing a Coke on the way because it was faster than coffee.

He needn't have bothered with speed, as the dog used the patio before he could lead him off and toward the woods.

After dealing with that, he went back in, fed the stupid dog, made coffee, drank it while the dog bolted down the food. He went through the medicine routine, headed back up for a shower.

Stopped halfway when he saw the dog had, once again, gotten his head stuck in the pickets.

"What is your deal? Are you just a fucking moron?" He did the angle/re-angle shift, then herded the dog upstairs in time to see Simone getting out of bed. "I named the dog."

"What's his name?"

"Fucking Moron."

"You're not naming that sweet dog Fucking Moron."

"It fits, and a name's gotta fit. He can be FM for short."

"Think again."

"He crapped and peed all over the patio, and he got his head stuck in the railing again. How is that not Fucking Moron?"

As Reed spoke, the dog stared up at him with eyes full of love.

"At least he waited until he was outside," Simone pointed out. "He should have a sweet name. Like Chauncy."

"Chauncy's a—" He stopped himself before he said *pussy name.* "I wouldn't have a dog named Chauncy," he amended. "I need more coffee. I need a shower. Shower. You're coming with me." He grabbed Simone's hand. "You're not," he told the dog.

Sex in the shower put him in a better mood.

Dressed, with her first cup of coffee drained. Simone grabbed her jacket. "Bring Herman over to CiCi's tonight."

"I'm not naming him Herman. But I'll bring him over."

"Good. I'll see you then." She kissed Reed. "And you, too, Raphael." Kissed the dog's nose.

"He's no Raphael, either."

Reed gathered dog supplies—pills, pockets, food, the chewy things, a couple of biscuits.

"We're going to work. It's time you started earning your keep." He led the dog out, stopped when he noted things starting to poke out of the ground. "How about that? Spring's coming. You dig in all that, there'll be no Milk-Bones for you. Get in."

The dog happily obliged, immediately rapped his head against the closed window.

"See, Fucking Moron. You are what you are." Despite the chill, Reed lowered the window. "I guess I'm going to have to deputize you, if I'm hauling your ass to work every day. That makes you Deputy Dog. Get it?"

The dog just stuck his head out the open window.

"Is that it? My amazing detective abilities lead me to conclude you think the damn pickets are a window, and the wind's going to blow your ears back. Some dumbass deputy that makes you."

Shaking his head, Reed backed out of the drive, turned toward the village. Inspiration struck. "Dumbass, yet loveable, deputy. Barney Fife, right? That's it. You're Barney. Deal is done."

Barney seemed fine with it as his tongue lolled and his ears blew.

Reed unlocked the station, went to his office. He filled Barney's water bowl, gave him one of the chew sticks. "Don't make me regret this."

He got a cup of coffee, and heard Donna come in—she almost always arrived first—as he went to his desk to boot up his computer.

"Are you going to bring that dog in every day?"

"Barney's been deputized."

"Barney?" She set her fists on her hips. "Like the purple dinosaur?"

"No. Like Barney Fife. Deputy Barney Fife."

"Isn't that show before your time?"

"It's a classic."

"I can't argue there. You can just stop giving me the spook eye," she said to Barney. "I picked up the mail on the way in."

She walked over, dropped a short stack on his desk.

She and the dog exchanged another look before she went out.

As he started opening the mail, his phone rang. Suzanna Dorsey, doing a follow-up. He ran her through, then listened to her response when he asked about the dog's insistence on using walkways and patios.

"Considering the rest of it? I'm going to say he was kept in a pen most of the time. Concrete floor. He only knows hard surfaces, poor thing. He'll learn, Reed, but it may take a little time."

"I'll keep a shovel handy."

After the call, he looked down at Barney. Barney looked back, bellied a little closer, gave him that look of trusting adoration.

"We'll work on it," Reed told him, giving his head a scratch before he went back to the mail.

The letter addressed to him at the station, postmarked Coral Gables, Florida, stopped him cold.

He pulled out a pair of crime scene gloves, took out his pocketknife to carefully unseal the flap. Drew out the greeting card.

CONGRATULATIONS!!!

The foil letters shined over colorful bursts of fireworks. He opened it with a gloved fingertip, read the printed sentiment inside.

LET'S PARTY!

She'd drawn skulls and crossbones around the words, then added a hand-written message.

> *You lived! Enjoy that while you can. We're not finished,*
> *but you will be when I come for you.*
> *XXOO, Patricia*
> *P.S. Here's a little souvenir from the great state of Florida.*

He picked up the little sealed plastic bag, studied the lock of hair inside. It would be, he had no doubt, Emily Devlon's.

"Okay, bitch, it's on. You let it get personal, and that's a mistake."

"Hey, Chief, you—" Cecil pulled up short at the cold glint in Reed's eyes. "Ah, I can come back."

"What do you need?"

"I thought I should tell you they were painting over at the Beach Shack, and knocked a whole gallon of paint off the ladder. It's splattered over some of Jewels of the Sea, and on Cheryl Riggs as she was out there washing the display window. She's pretty mad, Chief."

"Can you handle it?"

"Yeah, well, I was walking to work when it happened, so I did what I could. Paint's all over the sidewalk, too. But Ms. Riggs wants you to come down there."

"Tell her I'll be down, but I have to take care of something first."

"Sure thing."

"Do it in person, Cecil. Block off the sidewalk so people don't end up walking through wet paint. And have Donna contact village maintenance to see about getting it off the sidewalk."

"Yes, sir, Chief."

"And close the door, Cecil."

Spilled paint, angry shopkeepers had to be dealt with, Reed thought. But they'd just have to wait.

With his phone, he took pictures of both sides of the envelope, of the front, inside, back of the card. Another of the lock of hair.

Then he dug Xavier's card out of his drawer, made the call.

CHAPTER TWENTY-THREE

Seleena surfaced and moaned. A terrible hangover, she thought, groggy and queasy. Her head pounded, her eyes throbbed, her throat felt sand-papered, her stomach roiled.

How many drinks had she . . .

And she remembered.

She shot awake with a jolt, and light ice-picked into her eyes. When she tried to lift her hands to shield them, she felt the bite of restraints.

She let out a wild, crazed scream.

"Boy, you wake up cranky." Sipping coffee from a mug, Patricia walked into view. "You probably feel pretty rough, and screaming's just going to make you feel worse. Nobody's going to hear you, so do yourself a favor."

"Where are we? Why are you doing this? God, don't kill me."

"Where we are is deep in the north woods. I already told you why—I want to tell my story. If I was going to kill you, you'd be dead. Relax."

She offered a glass with a straw. "Just water. I need you awake and ready to go. Sorry about the needle in the neck, but I wasn't sure I could trust you. It's better this way, for both of us."

Her body quaked as she looked into Patricia's eyes. Her bladder threatened to release. "You don't have to do this. I told you I wouldn't call the police."

"Yes, I trusted that part. You want the story, so you wouldn't start off calling the cops. But it's still better this way." With a roll of her eyes, Patricia
used the straw and sucked down some water. "See? Just H-two-O."

Desperate, Seleena accepted, drained the glass.

"Can't make you a macchiato—that's your coffee drink, right? But I bet
you'd like some coffee, get your brain up and running."

"Yes. Please."

"Let me lay out some ground rules."

"First? I'm sorry. I need a bathroom."

"Understandable, but hold your water, Seleena. You'd better hear the rules
first, so we don't have a spat. I'll release you, and you use the facilities." Patricia pointed. "I took the door off. Hey, we're both girls, right? Then you'll
come back, sit. I'm going to put restraints back on your left hand, your ankles, but I'll leave your right hand free so you can drink your coffee, eat a
yogurt bar—keep up your strength. If you try anything, I'll start by breaking your fingers. I won't kill you—we need each other—but I will hurt you."

"I understand."

"Great."

When Patricia pulled out clippers—long, sharp points—Seleena cringed
back.

"For cutting the plastic. I've got plenty more zip ties."

She snipped them off, stepped back, took the gun out of her belt holster.
"Go on and pee."

Seleena's legs wobbled when she pushed to her feet.

"The sedative—you're just a little shaky yet. Take your time. We've got
plenty."

"People will look for me."

"Maybe. I sent your assistant a text from your phone, letting her know
you got a hot tip and you'd be out of town for a day or two. But that may not
fly for long."

"A day or two." Struggling to take in details—a cabin, she realized, with the shades pulled down. Rough, rustic furniture, no sounds of traffic. No sounds.

"It won't take us longer than that. Then you'll have your big story."

"And you'll let me go." Blocking embarrassment, Seleena lifted her skirt, did what she had to do.

"Why wouldn't I? That's the deal. I tell you my story, you get it out there. I want it out there. I want people to listen to me."

"You're going to turn yourself in?"

"Well, I did lie about that." Patricia grinned. "And the business about killing myself. But look."

She gestured.

"I've got the tripod, a professional video camera, the lights, the works. Consider this our on-location studio. We'll sit here. You can ask questions. I'll talk. I'll lay it all out. That's what I want. It's what you want."

Out of the corner of her eye, Seleena spotted her purse. Inside her purse was a gun. "I would have kept all this confidential. You don't have to strap me to the chair."

"Think about this. Some of what I'm going to tell you is, well, we'll say graphic. You might get upset, or scared. You might think: Oh no! She's going to kill me, too, and try to run or pull something. Like, right now you're wondering if you can get to the cute pink Glock you had in your purse. Then? Ouch. Broken fingers."

She reached back, drew the gun out from where she'd tucked it into the back of her belt. Held it up.

"So you'd have all pain with no gain. I'm saving you from that." She smiled, all charm. Then her lips peeled back. "Sit the fuck down, or instead of breaking a finger, I'll shoot you in the foot with your own girlie gun."

"I'm going to cooperate." Keeping her eyes direct, her voice calm, Seleena walked back to the chair. "I want to hear your story."

"You will." Patricia holstered her own gun—an all-business Sig—kept the Glock pointed at Seleena. The pink was growing on her.

She picked up some zip ties, tossed them onto Seleena's lap. "Do your ankles to the legs of the chair. Then your left hand to the left arm.

"We'll have some coffee, a little bite to eat, and talk about how we'll set this up. Your makeup's faded off and smeared, and your hair's a wreck. But don't worry, I'll fix you up. I'm good at hair and makeup, trust me."

While Patricia made coffee, Reed dealt with the incident of the paint, calmed the shopkeepers, worked things out with the clumsy painter—barely out of his teens and terrified he'd lose his job or get arrested.

On the walk back with his canine deputy, Barney started to squat on the sidewalk.

"Don't you do it!" Risking his jeans, Reed grabbed the dog up, quickened his pace. Barney shook, lapped nervously at Reed's chin.

"You just hold that in. Just hold it."

He rushed into the station, startling Donna and the human deputies. "I need an evidence bag. Fast!"

Matty leaped up with one. "What is it?"

"Town Ordinance 38-B."

Matty rolled her eyes as Reed ran back out. "Scoop the poop," she told Cecil.

Reed set Barney down on the grass behind the station.

"Now you can go."

Since the dog looked anxious and bewildered, Reed walked him back and forth on the grass.

"She's pissed. She didn't kill me, and worse yet, I put a hole in her somewhere. And because of that she had to run. Shot her own grandmother right off her walker. Imagine that."

Barney sniffed dubiously at the grass.

"So she didn't inherit that big house. Worth an easy million and change right there. And everything in it? A lot more change. Add frozen bank accounts. She'd already skimmed plenty there, but there was plenty more.

"Yeah, I cost her, and that burns her psycho ass. Psycho," he repeated, looking across to shops, eateries, some with apartments above them that he knew the owners rented out to summer workers.

"That's a big part of it. She always got her way before me. Her brother screwed things up, but he's her brother, and blood's thicker, right? But before me, she hit all her targets. A hundred percent success rate, and she was just getting started."

Rolling it around in his head, he stopped walking. "I didn't just knock down her batting average, right? I cost her a fricking fortune she, in her psycho brain, figured she'd earned. It's like I stole it from her. And I hurt her. I made her bleed. She's been breaking down since, that's what's happening."

He thought back, the look on her face when he'd fired at her—the shock and fear. More, he thought, the sound of her voice as she'd screamed at him, and ran.

Insult and tears as much as fury and fear.

"I always knew she'd be pissed, and want another try at me. But sending the card? She wants to make sure I don't forget her. She wants to make me feel what she felt, that shock, that fear. But that's a mistake. Once you make a mistake, it's easier to make the next."

Barney whined, tugged on the leash.

"It's the grass or nothing. She mailed that before she left Florida. She mailed it fresh off a kill, feeling full of herself. She'll be heading north, that's how I see it. Maybe not all the way back, but coming this way."

He looked down at the dog. "We'll be ready for her."

In answer, and looking apologetic, the dog squatted.

"Now, that's how it's done." When he finished, Reed gave Barney a good rub. "Looks like we both worked things out. That's a good boy. That's what I'm talking about. Too bad I can't teach you to clean up after yourself, but that's what partners are for."

Back inside, bag or no bag, he scrubbed his hands, then went out to the bullpen. "Donna, I need you to call Nick and Leon in."

"What for?"

"Because I need to talk to everybody."

He went into his office for the file he kept there, just in case. He took out Patricia Hobart's photo.

"Cecil, I need you to make copies of this—the full-color ones."

"How many?"

"Start with fifty."

" 'Fifty'?" Cecil blinked. "That'll take awhile."

"Then you'd better get started. Donna, the feds are coming in. I know your stand on it, but I'd appreciate if you'd make a pot of fresh coffee when they do."

"I'll make an exception. Leon and Nick are on their way."

"Good. You take calls as they come in, but anything that isn't urgent waits for a response until after the briefing."

He sat down across from Matty. "Give me your opinion on the summer deputies. On who can handle more trouble than fender benders and spilled paint."

"You've read their files, you've talked to some of them."

"I have, and did, and I've got my opinion. Now I want yours."

She frowned, but she gave it. He nodded, then stood as Leon came in.

"We got a problem, boss?"

"Not yet. Take a seat, Leon." He went to take one of the photos Cecil had run off, and as Nick came in, pinned it to the main board. "Have a seat, Nick. Cecil, that's enough for now. Finish it after the briefing. I want everybody to take a good look at this picture. You'll all have copies, and we're going to distribute some around the village, to the rental agencies, to the ferry personnel. This is Patricia Hobart, age twenty-eight. So far she's killed ten people, that we know of. Add an attempted on me."

Though he figured they knew the history, at least most of the particulars, he ran through it anyway. He wanted it fresh, and he wanted them to hear it from him.

"She sent me this today."

Out of his file, he took an evidence bag containing the card, the envelope, the lock of hair. "I'll be turning this over to the FBI when they get here."

"Bullshit on that," Matty grumbled. "They've been after her for damn near a year, and they've got nothing."

"We don't know what they have, or how close they've come, because they're not telling. That's how it works." He set the file aside, opened another. "This is my file—our file—with a copy of the card, the envelope, and a couple strands of the hair I'm going to have run. I've got contacts. We're going to cooperate fully with the FBI, but that doesn't mean we sit on our hands.

"She'll come here sooner or later," he continued. "Simone Knox was in that mall, too. She's another target, and as the first nine-one-one caller, I believe a prime one. As of today, we're going to start regular patrols by CiCi's house. We're going to sit on the dock, watch who gets off the ferry. I'm going to bring two of the summer deputies on now to help with that."

"She uses disguises," Matty said.

"She does, and she's good at it. So get that photo of her in your head. Don't let yourself be thrown off by hair color, hairstyle, eye color, glasses, or subtle changes to facial structure, body type. She'll be alone. She'll need to rent a place, take some time to study the routines. She'll be armed, and she's damn sure dangerous. I need islanders warned, and for you to make it absolutely clear they are not to approach, not to confront. If she goes into the market for supplies, they ring her up, wish her a good day, then they contact us. She isn't looking to hurt anyone but me and Simone, but that won't stop her if she's cornered.

"It's an island," he added. "When she comes, she's boxed in. It's our island. We know it better than she does. She's patient. She may come next week, or she may wait another two years."

But he didn't think she'd wait long. He didn't think she could.

"None of us can get complacent, because she will come."

He stopped as the door opened, and Xavier walked in—with a female colleague.

"Donna, I'd sure appreciate that coffee."

"Sure thing, Chief." She gave Xavier the evil eye as she went to the break room.

"Agents." Reed gestured to his office.

The female agent wore a black suit, white shirt, practical shoes. Reed judged her as an athletic early forties with dark brown hair cut short—practical like the shoes—and minimal makeup on an attractive face with serious brown eyes.

Reed figured she probably ranked as much of an asshole as Xavier. Until she smiled at the dog.

"Isn't he sweet?"

"He's shy around people," Reed explained as Barney burrowed under his desk. "Somebody dumped him on the island—after abusing him."

"I'm sorry to hear that. My sister rescued a mixed breed under similar circumstances. She's the best dog in the world now."

"We're not here to exchange dog stories."

The woman sent Xavier a short stare, then held out her hand to Reed. "Special Agent Tonya Jacoby, Chief."

"Thanks for coming." Since he liked her a great deal better than Xavier already, he offered her the evidence bag. "It came in this morning's mail."

Jacoby snapped on gloves, unsealed the bag. "Your photos came through clear," she began.

"And this contact, the threat therein, makes it only more imperative that you back off."

Reed barely flicked a glance at Xavier. "Since that's not going to happen, and there's no point in going over the same ground as yesterday, let's try this: I've briefed my deputies."

"The last thing we need is a bunch of armed yahoos shooting at shadows."

Reed got slowly to his feet. Jacoby started to speak, but he beat her to it. "You want to take potshots at me, you go ahead. But you watch what you say about my officers. You've been invited here today. You can be uninvited just as easy."

"This is an FBI investigation."

"Special Agent Xavier, why don't you take a walk?" Jacoby's stare turned longer, harder. "Take a walk."

He strode out—and once again slammed the station door behind him.

"Are you in charge now?" Reed asked her.

"As a matter of fact. I was brought in on this investigation just last week. He's not happy about that, which may account for his behavior yesterday. I caught the drift of it from his report. I'll apologize."

"No need."

Donna came in with coffee—a pot, mugs, the fixings on a tray. He didn't know they had a tray.

"Thanks, Donna."

"Yes, thanks." Jacoby added a dollop of milk to her coffee, sat. "Let's talk."

He spent thirty minutes with her and, when they shook hands again, felt better about things.

After she left, he finished the briefing with his team, took questions, answered.

"Special Agent Jacoby, now the SAC on the Hobart investigation—"

"Did they can that dick?" Leon asked.

"He's still on the investigation, but no longer the Special Agent in Charge."

"At least somebody in the FBI's not a total idiot," Matty decided.

"Since Jacoby didn't strike me as any kind of idiot, I'm going to say there's more than one. She informed me they're following up a lead in Tennessee. Memphis. If that pans out, we may be able to put this to bed. But until we do, I want those patrols, and an eye on the ferry. My partner and I will be in rotation."

" 'Partner'?" Matty asked.

Reed patted the dog's head. "Deputy Barney. He's one of us now."

In the cabin, with her laptop streaming Fox News in case anything broke she needed to know, Patricia redid Seleena's makeup.

"You take care of your skin," she said as she applied foundation. "Me, too. My mother let herself go. I mean hag time, especially after they killed JJ. But even before, she didn't fix herself up. I wouldn't've blamed the old man for screwing around on her or giving her a smack now and then, but he was such an asshole.

"I'm going to use a neutral palette on your eyes. Classy, professional. Close them."

Engage, Seleena ordered herself. Connect. "Did he hit you, too?"

"Barely noticed me, so he couldn't be bothered. I got fat—that's her fault, too. Always bribing me with candy and cookies, and letting me eat bags of chips. He called me 'Tub O Lard,' 'Tubbo' for short."

"That's cruel."

"Didn't I say he was an asshole? I got bullied in school, did you know that?"

She had to draw back before she messed up her work. Seleena's eyes popped open.

"But I'm getting ahead of myself. Close your eyes, keep them closed until I tell you otherwise."

She closed her eyes, kept them closed. Listened. She heard the crazy, oh God, she heard it. And the bitterness, and worse. God, worse, the cold dispassion when she talked about doing her mother a favor by killing her.

"They— The police classified that as an accident."

"Because I'm just that good, girl. Loopy, whiny old bitch made it easy, but you have to be good. Open your eyes."

Seleena opened them, tried to mask the fear.

"Oh yeah, I'm good. Close again. You know, I learned all about makeup and hair, skin care, all of it, on the Internet. YouTube because my mother taught me nothing about nothing. I've got an IQ of a hundred and sixty-four, and I sure didn't get it from her or dear old dad. Open," she said, beginning to brush and blend liner on the bottom of Seleena's eyes. "You're used to having your makeup done."

"Yes."

"I do my own. I do everything myself because I'm smart. JJ wasn't stupid, but he wasn't very smart, either. I used to do some of his homework and assignments for him, even after those asshole parents of ours tore us apart. They shouldn't have done that."

"No, they shouldn't have. That was cruel, too, and selfish."

"You're damn right! JJ's the one who taught me how to shoot because the old man couldn't be bothered with me. Look down while I do your lashes. Not that much!"

"Sorry."

"He was good with guns, but I was better there, too. He didn't mind. JJ was proud of me. He loved me. He was the only one who did. And they killed him."

"You must miss him."

"He's dead, what's the point? He knew I was smart, but he didn't listen to me, went off half-cocked. Get it? Guns, half-cocked."

Trying to read the eyes boring into hers, Seleena let her lips curve, just a little. "That's a good one."

"I can be funny when I want to be. I don't get to talk to people much, and never as myself. I have to talk to fuckheads when I'm stalking a target, but that's not me. I'm on the inside then, and only show the outside they expect. You're lucky, because you get to see inside."

"It's been hard for you, to keep yourself inside."

"I had to do it for *years*, goddamn years in that mausoleum with those dried-up, whiny grandparents. 'Oh, I'll do that, Gram. Don't worry about that, Grandpa, I'll clean it up.' They just wouldn't die and leave me alone. Nobody would've put up with their shit as long as I did. The eyes look good."

She studied her kit, chose a blush, a brush.

"They said terrible things about JJ, especially after he was dead. Terrible things, and I had to hold myself back from just slicing their throats. Maybe he wasn't very smart, maybe he didn't listen to me, but they shouldn't have said those terrible things about him."

"Their own flesh and blood," Seleena said.

"They said he was sick, defective, even evil. Well, they paid for it, didn't they? Not enough, but they paid. He just didn't listen to me, that's what happened."

"You tried to stop him."

Patricia eased back, studied the blush, approved. "We'll polish that off," she said and reached for translucent loose powder.

"I would've stopped him if I'd known he'd upped the time line. I still had some details to work out. And what does he do, he hits in July, when too many people are on vacation or whatever. It was supposed to be December, holiday crush. He'd have taken out twice as many. More, and I'd have worked out the escape route by then."

"You would have?"

Patricia tipped her head from side to side, lifted Seleena's with fingertips under the chin. "You look good. Classy professional, as promised. Want a cold drink?"

"Yes, please. Thank you."

She rose, walked over to the kitchen. "I've got Diet Coke, water, V8 Splash."

"The Diet Coke would be great, thanks. A little caffeine boost before we start recording."

"Good idea." She uncapped the bottle, poured some over ice in plastic cups. "Now, what were we talking about?"

She came back, handed Seleena the cup. "Right. JJ. Haven't I been telling you he wasn't really that smart? You don't think he and those two idiot friends of his came up with all that? DownEast was my idea, my plan, and it would've worked if they'd waited for me to tweak the details."

"You . . . planned the attack?"

"Thought it up, planned it out, stole Grandpa Shit-for-Brains' credit card long enough to order the vests, the helmets." She tapped a finger to her temple. "I let them give JJ credit as the mastermind up till now. We're going to change that, you and I. Anyway."

She lifted her own cup, sipped. "You're set, except for lips. I'll do them right before we start. I'm going to do my makeup now, and change into my on-camera wardrobe. It'll take a little while. I want to look good, then we'll get this party started. You think of some good questions, Seleena. I'm counting on you."

CHAPTER TWENTY-FOUR

Seleena sat for four hours under the lights, her chair angled to Patricia's, the camera recording.

After hour two, Patricia let her use the toilet again, and changed batteries in the camera. She allowed Seleena to drink water through a straw as she touched up her own makeup, then Seleena's.

But then it was right back to it.

As the time passed, as Seleena fell into the rhythm of interviewing, as the subject drew her in, her fear dimmed under her ambition.

She had the biggest story of her life, unfolding right in front of her. Being drugged, abducted, faded off as her own ego spiked.

She'd copped a face-to-face, exclusive interview with the mastermind of DownEast, a female serial killer. And due to her interviewing skills, Seleena's ambition and ego told her, Patricia had given her chapter and verse on all of it. On every kill, every detail, the stalking, documenting, choosing the time and the method.

When the restraints on her ankles, her left hand (Patricia left the right free so Seleena could take notes) bit into her skin, she assured herself (and believed herself) Patricia kept them on as visual evidence to protect Seleena from any charges of aiding or abetting, of obstruction.

They were in this together, just as Patricia claimed.

The excitement of what she had right there, of what she'd produce once she got the video in? Fear couldn't hold a candle to that fire.

Caught up, she began to imagine the benefits.

She knew how to play an interviewee, how to stroke, add understanding, empathy. This woman, this monster, poured out her sickness, her rage, her cold and calculating belief in her right to kill because Seleena skillfully led her down that path.

One day, they'd study this video in journalism courses—and she'd make a mint on speaking fees.

For Patricia, she concluded, the three boys had been her weapons, ones that had misfired on her. Her feelings for her brother came across as a strange mixture of love and disdain. And still she justified her killing, as far as she felt the need to justify it, as payback for his death at seventeen.

By Jesus, it fascinated. And if it fascinated her, just think, just *think* of viewer reaction.

"You're the best interview I've ever had, Patricia. I'm struggling to keep up with you! Could we take another break?"

"I'm not done!"

"No, no, just taking ten?" Seleena flashed a smile. She had a powder keg on her hands, and didn't want to light a match.

Flattery, she reminded herself. Just pour it on.

"I need to get some thoughts organized. I want to set this up for you in segments—some of that we'll do in editing, but I'd like to organize my next questions. I could really use something to eat, another drink to keep the energy up. Plus," she said quickly, "I'd like you to take a breath, too, recharge for a few minutes. We want you to be fresh in each segment."

"Fine." Patricia shoved to her feet.

"It's so powerful, Patricia. I need a little time to absorb."

"Fine," Patricia said, mollified. "I've got some whole wheat crackers and hummus."

"That would be great. Give us a little pickup for the next segment. And do you think I could stretch my legs a little? You're a runner," she said, "I'm active, too. If I could just walk around the cabin a little." She flashed a smile again. "I've gotta tell you, my ass is numb."

"Think about your fingers, Seleena."

Seleena laughed that off because she no longer believed it. "I'm in the middle of the mother of all exclusives. We're talking Pulitzer, Emmys. You can believe I'm not going to do anything to mess it up."

"You'll be a real big fucking deal after this." Patricia cut the restraints.

"We both will. Everyone's going to know your story."

And mine, Seleena thought as she walked the aches and tingles out of her legs. Just wait, just wait until she did a special report on her experience. Kidnapped, held by Patricia Hobart. And the intrepid reporter conducts a brilliant, hard-hitting on-camera interview, drawing all the details out. Motives, victims, method, movements. All of it.

"'Pulitzer, Emmys,'" Patricia repeated. "The sky won't be the limit for you." She opened the box of crackers. "You got a big boost by being in the mall that night, recording what you did. That put you on the map."

"I kept my head," Seleena agreed. "That's what you have to do to get ahead. Especially when you're a woman. A smart woman, a tough woman. They say you're pushy, bitchy, arrogant, when what you are? Is strong, ambitious."

"You do a program about DownEast every year in July, because that's your main claim to fame."

"Up until now. Oh, that's better. I can almost feel my ass again." She rubbed her butt with both hands as she walked back and forth.

"This interview, that's serious fame and fortune for you. You wrote that book about DownEast, but others did, too. And you're not that good a writer."

"I'm not bad, but you're right, book form isn't my strength. I'll hire a ghost this time. The ratings for this, Pat? We're going to have enough for a five-part series, and the ratings are just going to build and build. Fuck the Super Bowl, we're going to blow it and everything else out of the water."

"Because millions of people will watch."

"They will, they will. They'll be glued to their screens and devices. The fifteen-year-old girl planning a massacre because she hated her life, her parents, and could manipulate her brother. How she handled it when he pushed her aside to do it on his own. The years of holding her true nature inside, hiding it."

Seleena shook her head, let out a breath. "It's so powerful, so compelling. Your first kill? God, you were so young! Then your own mother. The calculation that went into you eroding her will, the years of gaslighting her, up to luring her into being complicit in her own murder. It's brilliant. Just brilliant."

"Sit down, have some food."

"Thanks. I'm starving." She took the paper plate, scooped up hummus with crackers. "The irony, Pat, do you see it? Of just missing with the cop—the one who saved the kid in the mall. Just missing that kill, getting shot yourself, but getting away, holding on to get back to your grandparents'. God, that's a segment on its own. Has to be."

"You think the cop deserves a segment," Patricia said slowly.

"Absolutely. That moment when you realized you hadn't finished him, and that he'd shot you—I want to talk about that a bit more. And about what you thought, felt, while rushing back to get money, weapons, IDs—and *still* taking the opportunity to kill your grandparents before you ran."

"I didn't run. I regrouped."

"Mmm." She scooped up more hummus. "We'll touch on your time in Canada, but that's not a highlight. It's more of a bridge, so *regrouping*'s a good term. But the turning point came when you realized you'd failed to kill Quartermaine, and that he managed to wound you—and then you have the serendipity of the cop who killed your brother helping to save the man you tried to kill."

"'Serendipity.'"

"It's great TV, just great TV. I want to focus more on that turning point next, how the mistake with Quartermaine changed your direction, forced you to regroup. Thanks," she added when Patricia handed her another cup of Diet Coke.

"You see that as a mistake. With that fucking cop?"

Seriously hungry, and far too caught up, Seleena forgot a good interviewer let the subject do the talking. A good interviewer observed changes in tone and body language.

"A miscalculation anyway, and again a turning point we want to punch. Up to that point, you weren't even on the radar, right?"

She drank some diet soda, went back to the crackers.

"It's just what you said before—you let JJ take the blame."

"Credit."

"Credit. You were the sister of a teenage killer, the devoted granddaughter, living a quiet life. And the next minute you're a fugitive who'd tried to kill a cop in cold blood because he'd survived the DownEast. Who *did* kill her elderly grandparents in cold blood before she ran to hide—and regroup—in Canada.

"You'd killed before, Pat, but that near miss with Quartermaine changed everything."

"He got lucky."

Seleena nodded. "He did, he got really lucky. Recognizing you just an instant before it would have been too late, then wounding you, not to mention the irony of having his police partner already heading to that house—the same woman cop who was, ironically again, just outside the theater. She killed JJ, helped save Quartermaine. Great TV."

"You think so?"

"Believe me, I know so. Okay, I've got the next segment organized."

"Your segments, your ratings, your claim to fucking fame."

"Sorry? What?"

"It's my story. Mine."

"And it's going to blow the roof off. I think we should freshen up the makeup a little before we roll again." She shook out her shoulders, then crossed her legs.

"You don't need it," Patricia said, "because that's a fucking wrap."

Seleena glanced over, managed one choked sound before Patricia shot her, and shot her, and shot her again. *Ironically*, in Patricia's mind, with Seleena's own pink Glock.

She expelled air, and anger. Felt better. "And don't call me 'Pat.'"

She made herself a plate of crackers and hummus, ate while Seleena's body bled out on the cabin floor. She'd take the camera, she decided, leave the tripod and the lights. Too much to take back on her flight south.

Since she'd already stopped to change the plates, and she'd taken some time to beat some dings into it, she considered Seleena's car a safe ride for the distance she had to drive.

Time to grab some cash and another couple IDs out of the bank in New Hampshire, she calculated. Then she'd leave the car at the airport, catch a flight. She'd pick up a rental in Louisville.

They'd find the body in a few days, she imagined. She'd booked the cabin for a week, and had four days left. By then, she'd be . . . somewhere else.

She laughed a little as she washed down crackers with Diet Coke, and smiled over at Seleena's body. "Now who made the mistake?"

After shift, Reed walked home with the dog. He picked up some supplies, and drove his personal car to CiCi's. He'd have to tell them—Simone and CiCi—about the card, the threat, and lay out precautions he needed them to take.

When he arrived, he considered the house. All that glass, all that damn glass. So beautiful, and so vulnerable. Still, breaking in doors and windows wasn't Hobart's usual style.

She liked subterfuge. Breaking windows? That just wasn't elegant.

He heard music—some of the windows were open to the spring air—recognized the steady, sexy beat of "After Midnight." He walked the dog inside, and saw CiCi—tight cropped jeans, black T-shirt, long wild hair flowing while she danced.

She had some moves, he thought as she shoulder swayed and hip bumped her way around the room to Clapton's genius guitar and seductive voice.

He didn't notice Barney plopping down to watch beside him, and thumping his tail.

CiCi made a pivot, spotted him. Still moving, and now with a slow smile, she crooked a finger at Reed. "Let's dance, Delicious."

He stepped to her, put an arm around her waist and swept her into an impressive dip.

"Look at you!"

"Guys who dance get more girls," he told her, sweeping her back up and into a slow spin.

"You've been holding out."

"You never asked me to dance before."

Simone came down the stairs to see her grandmother and the police chief dancing—smoothly—while the dog sat watching them with apparent fascination.

They ended the dance with his arms around CiCi's waist, and hers linked around his neck. And grinning at each other.

"So that's how it is."

"Simone, you are my greatest treasure." With a happy sigh, CiCi rested her head on Reed's shoulder a moment. "But now that I know this man can move sexy to Clapton, I may have to steal him from you."

"I'm yours," Reed told her, and kissed the top of her head.

He caught the scent of her shampoo, a whiff of turpentine, and a faint, fading drift of weed.

It all said CiCi.

She gave him a squeeze, then turned to study the dog. "And here's the four-legged cutie. You're right, Simone, he has a sweet face, and eyes full of heart."

She didn't crouch, just held out a hand. "Come on and say hello, little darling."

"It takes him awhile to . . ."

Reed trailed off as Barney stood, and walked straight to CiCi.

He couldn't say Barney had gotten used to people by spending the day around them. Though he'd warmed up to Cecil, he'd cringed away from every human being they'd come to on the walk home.

And here, with only a hand held out, he'd gone to CiCi, wagging his tail as she bent down to pet him.

"Maybe you are a witch."

"Of course I am, and I have an innate affinity for animals, especially canines as I was a she-wolf in an early life. Plus this sweetie and I recognize each other, don't we, my handsome boy? We've danced, too, in yet another life."

It wouldn't have surprised Reed a bit.

"He's Barney."

"Acceptable," Simone decreed, then picked up the remote to turn the music down a few notches. "Since we've all finished work for the day, I'm ready for some wine. Any takers?"

"Twist my arm," said CiCi.

"Maybe we could sit outside with that. It's warm enough. I've got some things to talk over with both of you."

"Sounds serious."

"It is."

"You get the wine, Simone," CiCi told her. "Let's see how Barney likes the view from the patio."

Deliberately, she led Reed and the dog out. "This is about Patricia Hobart."

"Is that grapevine or psychic?"

"I'm going to say I felt a disturbance this morning."

"In the Force?"

"I know what I know when I know it." She tapped a finger to his chest. "Then Hildy called me this afternoon, after you met with her. Hildy's no blabbermouth, but we go back. She wanted to talk this through with me. I haven't said anything to Simone. She's been working, and I didn't want to distract her. And I thought you'd want to tell her yourself. I can take Barney for a walk on the beach, if you want privacy."

"No, but thanks. I'd like to talk to both of you."

"I believe strongly in the threefold rule. What you send out into the universe, good or bad, comes back at you threefold. But I'd risk whatever came at me to send out something that would drop that bitch like a stone down a bottomless well for trying to hurt you or my baby."

"I won't let her hurt Simone, or you."

CiCi framed his face with her hands. "Add yourself to that."

"I've . . . danced with her before. I know her moves."

"And they're at it again." With an exaggerated eye roll, Simone brought out a bottle of wine and three glasses. After setting the wine and glasses on the table, she pulled a long, fat chew stick out of her back pocket. "Now everyone has a treat."

She poured the wine as Barney settled down with his treat. "God, I had a really good day, and now it's a gorgeous evening."

"I'm sorry to have to put a hitch in that."

Simone glanced at Reed. "Seriously serious then."

"Let's sit down." He'd tried out several approaches in his head, hadn't settled on any. So in the end, he went with straight ahead.

"I got a card in the morning mail. From Patricia Hobart."

As she sat beside CiCi, Simone reached for her grandmother's hand.

"What kind of card?"

"The kind that cost her three-ninety-nine, plus applicable tax and postage." He described the card, then relayed the message.

"She's threatening you. Has she ever done that sort of thing before?"

"No, not to me, and I confirmed with the FBI today, there's no evidence she contacted or threatened anyone else. She's pissed off she missed with me, and I shot her. I cost her the big house and a lot of money. Being pissed, she had to take another shot—metaphorically. And that break in pattern tells me she's going to make more mistakes. That's the good part."

"There's a 'good part' to getting a death threat?" Simone demanded.

"More than one. It tells me I shook her enough to get inside that twisted brain of hers. It tells me that fresh off killing Emily Devlon, she thought of me, sent the card. It had a lock of hair inside it. It's going to be Emily Devlon's hair."

"Jesus, she's a horrible, sick, vicious creature," CiCi said. "Karma will make her its bitch, but until then . . ."

"The justice system will make her its bitch first," Reed told her. "She mailed the card from Florida, and the FBI will track exactly where."

"But she won't be there," Simone pointed out.

"No, but it tells us where she was. It tells us when she was there. Where is that in relation to the Devlons? They work on triangulating that and they'll find where she lived while she stalked Emily. They'll talk to people who talked to her, who saw her. Every piece of information counts. On top of it, she warned me. She did it to scare me, but she missed again. Warned, I take steps."

"What steps?"

"I bring in the FBI for one of those steps."

"The dickhead?" Simone reminded him.

"He's no longer SAC—Special Agent in Charge. The new SAC is Special Agent Tonya Jacoby."

"A woman." CiCi gave a satisfied nod. "Now we're getting somewhere."

"After meeting her today, I can agree. She's also not a dickhead. At this point, and very likely due to Hobart's misstep, we'll be sharing information. I'll know more, and they'll—including Xavier, who takes orders from her—listen more."

"It takes a woman." CiCi raised her glass.

"A lot of times it does. I've briefed my deputies and Donna. We've got Hobart's photo front and center on the bullpen board. And we're going to distribute her photo. I talked to the mayor about that, and about bringing on a couple of the summer deputies early. She's good with it."

"We're an island," Simone said. "She needs the ferry, a charter, or a private boat to get on or off. It's harder to run."

"You're exactly right."

"She could wait until you're in Portland for something."

"How would she know?" he countered, as much in truth as to soothe Simone. "I don't do the social media thing, and that's her main source. It'll be here, and that's an advantage for us."

"You're right." Nodding, Simone sipped her wine. "You're exactly right, too, but—"

"There are a lot of buts, and we'll get to them. Another advantage for us is she's trying to take on a cop, again. And a forewarned police force. I've studied her, and I'm going to bet I've studied her closer and longer than she's studied me. Or you, Simone."

Now CiCi reached for Simone's hand. "We have to face that, don't we? The fact that by coming here, she could try a two for one."

"She has to get here first, and stay here long enough to observe routines and make a plan. That's to our advantage, too—even in the summer, which is when she'll come. Summer's smarter. We're crowded, lots of people, a lot going on, busy shops and restaurants. We'll start watching for her now, but she'll wait for summer. This year, maybe next. Now, to the buts."

He leaned forward. "She's smart and she's cagey and she's patient— though I think the patience is ripping under the anger and the crazy. She knows how to look like someone she's not, and to act like someone she's not. She knows how to go unnoticed, how to blend, and how to bullshit. On the other side of that? The two of you know faces. You're going to study hers until you know every inch of it. I believe you'll recognize her if you see her, no matter how she looks. You'll know."

"She won't get by us." CiCi gave Simone's hand a squeeze. "Will she, baby?"

"No."

"Here's a list of rules," Reed began.

"I hate rules. Too many stem from the patriarchal system designed to oppress the female."

Reed aimed a long look at CiCi. "I'd like to see the patriarch or system that could oppress either one of you."

CiCi smiled into her wine. "Many have tried and had their balls bruised in the attempt."

"At the risk of my balls, these aren't suggestions or guidelines. These are rules, like them or not. If you see her, you don't approach or confront. You contact me or the nearest officer. If you see a strange car, bike, hiker going by the house more than once, you contact me. If you start getting hang ups or wrong numbers, you contact me. We're going to do regular patrols."

"What about your place?" Simone asked him.

"I'm a cop. It's already patrolled. But if you're there and I'm not, you lock up, and you don't answer the door. Someone comes around, you contact me.

If you're driving into the village, or anywhere, and you see somebody broken down on the side of the road, you keep going."

"And contact you," CiCi figured.

"You get the idea. You take no chances. Those are simple precautions. I need you to vary your routines. Not that you have hard and fast ones anyway. But don't shop on the same day of the week or the same time of day. Don't take walks the same time and day. Whether or not you expect a delivery, if a truck pulls up, they leave the delivery outside. You don't open the door, you don't go out. Anything, anyone gives you an off feeling, you contact me. And no social media about plans."

He sat back again. "You could put in an alarm system."

"That," CiCi said decisively, "isn't going to happen."

"I figured that, but you need to lock up, whether you're here or out. Do that for me, okay?"

"I can do that. I don't like it, but I can do it."

"Good. I'm not going to insinuate the two of you can't take care of yourselves. Especially since I don't want my balls bruised, and I'm hoping for dinner. But I'm going to say I love both of you, and I'm going to look out for you. That's it."

"Don't think we're not going to look after you for the same reason." CiCi rose, topped off her wine. "I'm going to start doing that now by making you a hot meal."

"Don't cook," he said quickly. "I'll go get takeout."

"Cooking's going to rebalance my chi." She leaned over, kissed Reed. "You're a lot smarter than she is, and so's my girl. I'm damn well a lot cagier."

Simone waited until CiCi went inside. "I didn't bring it up, all this is enough, but if Hobart comes here, she'll go back to Portland. My sister, my mother."

"I've talked to Essie, and I talked to Jacoby. They'll have eyes on your family."

She got up, wandered over to look out at the water. The dog, finished with the treat, now lay stretched over Reed's feet. "I should've known you'd think of them."

"I talked to Boston PD, so they're on alert. You'll want to talk to Mi about it. I also talked to a friend of mine who I think she has on her list. He's in New York now. I'm sorry to bring all this here."

"You didn't. She did. She started it all. It was her plan, and as horrible as it was, it didn't work out the way she wanted. Neither will this. It's funny. I love the island, always have. But I didn't realize how much I do, how much it's mine, until I realized she might come here and try to hurt someone who matters so much to me. Hurt someone else who matters so much. Who could try to stain this place the way she did the mall, and Portland? I never felt completely safe in Portland after that night."

She turned back. "I went to New York as soon as I could. I went to Italy, I went wherever I could that wasn't there. Most of the time, though, I came here. I sheltered in place, but I kept looking for somewhere or something else. I'm not sure I knew, until you, that it was more than that for me, more than sheltering in place. It was *my* place, my home. Nothing she can do will change that."

She came back, slid over the arm of the chair into his lap. "There's more than one kind of shelter. You're another for me. I'm going to be the same for you."

"I looked a long time for my place, and for you. It's damn good luck I found them both."

"You know what I thought when I came down the stairs earlier?"

"How easy you could be replaced?"

Laughing, she nuzzled in. "Besides that. I thought, I want to sculpt them—Reed and CiCi—just like that. Holding each other in a dance and smiling."

"Naked? Listen—"

"There's art, Chief, and there's weird and inappropriate. No, not naked."

"Okay then. You looked happy when you came down."

"I'd had an excellent day working on a fascinating new project."

He nuzzled back. "You're not going to let me have a look at it?"

"When it's done. Stay tonight. Stay with me."

"I was hoping you'd ask. I've got our gear, mine and my new deputy's, out in the car."

In the kitchen, CiCi watched them out the window. This, she thought, just this—the blush in the sky as the day wore down; the strong, good man; even the sweet-faced dog—filled all her hope pockets for her girl.

No bitch from hell would rip holes in those pockets.

Two days later Reed got a call from Essie.

"We've got a Missing Person's out on Seleena McMullen."

"How long has she been missing?"

"Over forty-eight hours now. Her assistant got a text that she was going to be out of town on a hot tip, but she's missed appointments, and doesn't answer her cell."

"She fits the profile, Essie, but this would be the first abduction. Even killing her and dumping the body doesn't fit Hobart's MO."

"There's no sign of a break-in or a struggle at McMullen's house or office. She got a call on her landline just before midnight on the day she went missing. Untraceable. A burner."

"Lured her somewhere." Reed frowned. "That's not Hobart's usual method, either."

But.

"The fact is, Hobart might not be the only one who'd want to cause her harm. She's got an ex who isn't fond of her, and plenty of people she's burned along her way. But I'm having officers check for McMullen's car at the airport. That is Hobart's MO. Right now, with no direct link to Hobart, it's with Major Crimes—because I snagged it. If we find that link, it goes to the feds."

"Jacoby's all right."

"I agree. But, Reed, if we find that link, it means she's back in the area. Watch yourself, partner."

"I will. You, too."

He hung up, thought it over. McMullen, yeah, that could fit. But coming after Essie now—way far up from the opportunistic blogger—didn't fit. And coming after him right after sending the card? No, that didn't fit, either. She had more to say first.

So, if Hobart grabbed or killed McMullen, came back to Portland for that? Why?

He had to think about it.

Two days later, the turnover crew for the cabin found McMullen's body. Essie sent him a report on the rest.

A camera tripod, two theatrical lights on stands, food and drink enough for several days, traces of makeup on the floor, on two chairs, a number of cut zip ties.

And Hobart's prints all over the cabin.

Why did someone kidnap a reporter/blogger with her own local show and hard-core Internet following?

It seemed to Reed that somebody had a story to tell.

Between the kidnapping/murder and the card, he decided Patricia Hobart wanted some attention.

He'd be happy to give it to her.

With Jacoby and Essie coordinating on the McMullen case, Reed concentrated on his own. He found a deputy badge charm on the Internet and, amused, ordered two. One for Barney, one for Puck when Essie and the gang came out.

He bought the dog a bed, and had to start out with it right next to his own or Barney ignored it and slept on the floor. Strategizing, Reed moved it away an inch or so every morning.

When he tried throwing the red ball he'd picked up, Barney looked at him without a clue.

They'd work on it.

April edged toward May, and flowers began to bloom. In a peace offering, he bought a pot of daffodils and took it, and Barney, to Ida Booker.

She came out, kept the cat inside.

"He'd like to apologize for the trouble he caused you."

Ida folded her arms. "That dog's a menace."

"He's being rehabilitated. Ms. Booker, when I took him to Doc, he had infections and all kinds of physical issues. He's scarred from where somebody choked him with one of those chain collars."

Her fierce frown deepened. "Somebody choked that dog?"

"Yes, ma'am, Doc and Suzanna said that's what happened. He was so scared of people because somebody'd caged him up and hurt him. Doc said he maybe chased your cat because he wanted to play. Now, I can't promise that, and I won't bring him around your cat—or your gardens—off the leash. He was half-starved, Ms. Booker."

"He looks better now." She cursed under her breath. "I'm not much on dogs, but anybody who'd treat an animal that way isn't worth spit on a skillet. I heard you were keeping him."

"He's Barney now, and he's coming along. We've just come from Doc's, and he's on his way to a clean bill of health. He's put on a few pounds, too. There's not a mean bone in him, but he could be a habitual cat chaser. He runs at birds on the beach, too."

"I guess that's just the nature of things. I appreciate the flowers." She huffed out a breath, took the pot. "I was on the side of those who thought it was a mistake to bring in someone from off-island to be chief. I may have been wrong about that. Time will tell."

Reed drove back to the village, stopped off to watch the ferry come in. He had the two part-timers on that duty, but a look for himself didn't hurt a thing.

Some families with kids young enough not to be in school, a couple of islanders coming back, delivery trucks, a couple of hikers who walked off.

Satisfied, he drove back to the station.

"What did Doc say?" Donna demanded.

"Barney's back in tune. He's cleared for active duty."

She snorted. "You keep him from nosing in the trash or I'll give him some active duty."

"He was just looking for clues." His desk phone rang, so he went back with Barney at his heel. "Chief Quartermaine."

"Special Agent Jacoby. I'm in Louisville, Kentucky, following up a lead. We've got a witness—former cop—who's followed the case. He swears he spotted her."

"'Kentucky'? She backtracked? How reliable's the witness?"

"I'm buying what he's selling."

"Okay, where did he spot her?"

"In a mall here. He says he got a good look at her, and when the face clicked tried to follow her out of the mall. He lost her. The place was crowded. A popular shopping center anyway, and on top of it, Derby's coming up. But he got lucky again, when he spotted her driving out of the parking lot. I've got the make and model, the color, the plate. You ready for it?"

"Yeah, I am."

He noted everything down.

"She bought a pair of sunglasses, a couple of shirts, jeans. She's a size six. Some workout clothes. We're checking store by store, but our wit made a couple of the bags she had before he lost her. She charged everything to a Visa in the name of Marsha Crowder, bogus San Diego address. She had her hair in a tail—medium brown. We've got an all-points on the car and the plates. No luck yet."

"This is good news. I don't have Louisville, or Kentucky, on my list. No targets there I know of."

"The Memphis lead turned shaky, but with those plates, it may have been more solid than we thought. She's likely headed north. You watch for that car, those plates, Chief."

"Believe it."

"We're on her. I've gotta move on this."

"Thanks for the heads-up. Good hunting. Donna!" he shouted it the minute he disconnected.

"You want me," she said, eyes firing up as she walked up. "You come out."

"Get this information to the deputies, on and off duty. A white Toyota Sienna, maybe a 2016, Tennessee plates. Six-Eight-Three-Charlie-Kilo-Oscar. Hobart was spotted driving that car in Louisville."

"I've got it."

Reed opened the file, never far from hand, studied Hobart's face. "Maybe we've got you."

* * *

She switched the plates in a Walmart parking lot off I-64. She had an itchy feeling. She was damn, dead sure some old guy had trailed her for a while back in Louisville.

Better safe than screwed, she decided, and destroyed her current ID and cards, ditched them.

She went in the Walmart, to the hair products section. She bought auburn hair dye, paid cash. She took the back roads, winding around until she spotted a junker outside a double-wide with a FOR SALE sign on the windshield.

She bargained with the yahoo and told him she'd be back with the cash. Plenty of woods around to ditch the car.

She walked back, bought the junker, drove it rattling back to the Toyota. Once she transferred her luggage, she beat the crap out of the Toyota, released some tension.

She expected some other yahoo—or maybe the same one—would stumble on it eventually, and pick it clean for parts.

In the junker, she drove to a cheap motel, paid cash.

She dyed her hair, trimmed it, put in green contacts, and switched her ID before walking out. Though the junker coughed and shimmied, she managed to get to a decent-size town fifty miles away. She parked the junker, walked the half a mile to the car dealership she'd spotted.

She paid cash, did the paperwork, and got back on 64 inside an hour. With her things once again transferred, she drove off in a freshly washed secondhand Chevy Tahoe with fifty-three thousand and change on the odometer.

Carrie Lynn Greenspan, with auburn hair and green eyes, drove north.

She had a stop to make in Wild, Wonderful West Virginia.

CHAPTER TWENTY-FIVE

Essie brought her family to the island for a pre–Memorial Day cookout. The Memorial Day weekend didn't rate as the island's biggest day, but it started them off. Reed would have his full team on the entire weekend, including himself.

He gave himself the weekend before to mark his second entertaining venture in his new home.

His first, earlier in the month with his family, had gone just fine.

His second looked to follow suit.

After an intense sniffing introduction, Barney fell in love with Puck. He romped with the other dog, romped with Dylan, and accepted the boy's hugs and squeezes with eyes filled with bliss.

He accepted Essie; she probably carried scents of the kid and the dog—and maybe something of the baby inside her.

With Hank, he trembled and cringed.

"I think it's the beard," Reed told him. "My brother's got one, and Barney wouldn't come near him. I'd say whoever abused him has a beard."

"Kids and dogs flock to me," Hank claimed. "I'm a kid and dog magnet. I'm going to win him over before we get back on that ferry."

Hank walked to the rail of the back deck where Reed had the grill heating up, looked out into the woods. "This is a hell of a nice spot. A hell of a nice house, Reed. I like your lady, too. Or should I say your ladies?"

"I plan to keep all of them."

"I'd love to see CiCi Lennon's studio. And more of Simone's work."

"You've got the weekend for it."

Dylan, his deputy badge pinned to his T-shirt, raced over, leaped into Hank's arms. Barney stopped dead, bellied down.

"Watch me win him." Hank sat down on the top step of the deck. He found his son's tickle spot, sent the boy into happy giggles.

Puck trotted over, shoved his pug face under Hank's arm.

"Daddy!"

"That's my name." Hank kissed and cuddled—boy and dog—listened with apparent fascination to Dylan's rapid-fire talk about dogs and fish and going to the beach.

"Why don't you call Barney over?"

"Hey, Barney. Hey, Barney."

The dog whined, bellied an inch back.

"Try this." Reed pulled a biscuit out of his pocket, gave it to Dylan.

"Cookie! Get the cookie, Barney!"

Puck took that as an invitation, rushed right in for it.

"Try another." Reed pulled out a second.

"Your turn, Barney!"

Obviously conflicted, Barney edged a little closer. He wanted the biscuit; he wanted the boy; he feared the beard.

"It's a good cookie. Yum, yum, yum!" After feigning taking a bite, Dylan belly laughed at his own joke.

The laugh did it. Barney ran forward, snatched the cookie, ran back. Eyed the man as he ate it.

"Just the first step," Hank claimed. He set Dylan down, watched him run off. "Are you thinking of having any of those? Kids?"

"I've got to talk her into moving in with me. Just the first step."

Hank got up, retrieved the beer he'd set aside. "My money's on you."

"Your boy's a charmer," CiCi said as she walked with Essie into the kitchen.

"One of the nurses in the maternity wing swore he winked and smiled at her. It wouldn't surprise me."

"He told me I had pretty hair. He's going to have girls sighing over him. Have a seat while I shake up these vegetables. Are you hoping for a girl or a boy this time?"

Taking a seat at the counter, Essie lifted her eyebrows. "How did you know? I'm not showing . . . much."

"Aura," CiCi said wisely, and shook the chunks of vegetables marinating in a sealed bag.

"'Aura,'" Essie repeated. "Since the cat's out, I'm hoping for healthy, and I'd be satisfied with half as happy as Dylan. He wakes up happy."

"Some of that's his nature, and some of it's a testament to you and your man. You've been a steady compass point for Reed. His parents raised him right. They're good, loving people, but you crossed paths with him at a defining moment, and you helped him look down the right turn."

"I think crossing paths helped both of us. You know, I would never have imagined him here, chief of police, a house like this. But when he talked about it, I could."

"Because you know him, and you love him."

"I do. And seeing him here? I see a really good fit. You must know he's completely in love with Simone."

"Oh, I know it. She's in love with him, but she'll hold that back for a while. My girl's strong and smart, but not as confident in some areas as our Reed is. They're just exactly what the other needs."

"A really good fit," Essie said with a smile.

"Yes, they are. I saw that before Reed and I had finished our first stack of cranberry pancakes."

At home, CiCi went to the refrigerator for a jug. She'd taught Reed the process and the value of sun tea, and refilled Essie's glass with it.

"I'd say these vegetables are ready to grill."

"Reed grilling vegetables." Essie rose. "Something else I never imagined."

"He's a good boy, and ordered the grill basket I told him about. Now we'll see if he makes good use of it."

He made good use of it, and enjoyed seeing everyone dig in to a meal he'd put together. With some help, sure, but he'd actually pulled off his second entertaining experience with adult food.

"You're officially a man," Hank told him.

"I'm relieved to hear it."

"A man is not a man, my friend, until he can grill steaks and grill them right," Hank added.

"I believe Shakespeare said: A man's worth is oft proved by the grilling," CiCi countered.

Hank laughed, toasted CiCi. "The Bard's never wrong. I wonder if I could see your studio while we're here. I've still got the poster of Guitar God I pinned to the wall in my college dorm."

"It's now framed on the wall of his office at home," Essie added.

"Come by tomorrow."

"Really? A thrill of a lifetime. I'm not exaggerating. Simone, any chance I could see your studio while I'm there?"

"Sure. Not you." She pointed at Reed. "I'm working on a sculpture of Reed. He doesn't get to come into my studio until it's finished."

Essie nearly choked on her tea. "You got Reed to pose?"

"She vamped me."

"Whatsa 'vamped'?" Dylan wanted to know.

"It's, like, if Pink Power Ranger got mind-control powers."

"That'd be awesome!"

"It really is," Simone agreed. "The power of the mind's a strong weapon against evil, like the wicked Rita Repulsa."

Reed sat back, stared. "You know Power Rangers?"

"Why wouldn't I? I was Pink Power Ranger for Halloween when I was five or six."

"She vamped me into getting her the costume," CiCi confirmed. "I have pictures."

"I've gotta see. I absolutely have got to see."

"I'm adorable." Simone stabbed the last grilled pepper on her plate.

"I just bet."

"Can we go to the beach now?" Dylan tugged at his father's arm. "I finished all my vegables."

"Ta-bles."

"I finished my ta-bles. Can we?"

"I vote for it." Reed's phone rang in his pocket. He hitched up, took it out. After a glance at the display, Simone saw his gaze cut to Essie. "Sorry, I need to take this. Don't worry about the dishes. Take the kid to the beach. I'll catch up."

He started out of the room. "Chief Quartermaine."

Simone put an easy smile on her face, rose. "Go ahead and head to the beach. CiCi can show you the best way. I'll wait for Reed."

"Yay! The doggies, too. Let's go."

Essie gave Simone a subtle nod. "Dylan's personal paradise, dogs and the beach," she said. "Yes, let's go."

As they left, Dylan and the dogs in the lead, Simone carried dishes inside. She'd keep busy, she thought, try not to think too much, just clear the picnic table, load the dishwasher, and wait.

Because what was coming wasn't good news.

Five minutes passed, then ten, then fifteen before she heard him coming back.

She got out a cold beer, offered it to him when he came in.

"I sent them on. Essie knows there's trouble, and I know you'll want to talk to her about it. But I need you to tell me. It's not island trouble, not from the way you looked at Essie."

"No, not island trouble." He took a chug from the beer. "I didn't want Dylan to hear my end of the conversation."

"I know. Now he's playing on the beach. Was it Agent Jacoby?"

"Yeah." He could work his way up to it. "They found the car Hobart was driving when they spotted her in Louisville. She'd changed the plates, busted it up some. The idiot who found it decided to claim it as his own, did some half-assed bodywork. They found it when the Staties stopped him for speeding—and driving while stoned as it turned out. And hauling a batch of opioids. He did some basic bullshitting. Not my car, man. I just borrowed it."

"I don't know where those drugs came from," Simone finished.

"Yeah, except he had some of said drugs in his pocket. Anyway, before they had all that nailed down, they found Hobart's prints and the rental agreement with the alias she'd used in the mall down there in the glove box. It came out he'd found the car, busted up and abandoned. Which led to them finding another guy who'd sold her a junk Ford for cash and no worries about paperwork."

"Now they have a description of that car."

"She won't still have it. They're trying to run that down."

"That's not all."

"No." He brushed her arm as he wandered to the glass doors. "No, that's not all. I told you they tracked the card she sent me to where she mailed it."

"And they were able to track her to where she'd stayed in Coral Gables. That helped track her to Atlanta and the flight to Portland."

"A little late for McMullen, but yeah. Got the name she used to book the cabin."

"When they had that sighting in Louisville, verified the name she used to charge those purchases at the mall, the car and tag. You said that was good, good work. You said she's making mistakes."

"Yeah." He turned back. "That didn't stop her from killing Tracey Lieberman."

Simone braced a hand on the counter, then sat. "Where, how?"

"Near Elkins, West Virginia. Lieberman worked as a guide. National forest right there. She was in the theater with her mother, her aunt, her cousin. She was fourteen then. She got married last year. Back then she was Tracey Mulder."

"God. I knew her—a little. She was a year behind us, but she and Mi were in gymnastics together. I knew her."

He came over to sit beside her. "Her mother was killed that night. She shielded Tracey with her own body. And still Tracey took hits in both legs. Her aunt and her cousin, minor injuries, but Tracey's were severe. They weren't sure she'd walk again without assistance, or without a profound limp. She'd never be competitive in gymnastics again. She got a lot of press."

"And Hobart targets that."

"Yeah. She got more, even as the story faded off some, because she didn't give up. She had all the surgeries, and didn't give up. She did years of PT, and caught the attention of a couple of medalists from the U.S. gymnastics team. They gave her a gold medal for courage. More press.

"She not only walked again, on her own, but at twenty completed her first 5K marathon, and came in fifth. More press. A couple years later, a 25K, third place, and she dedicated the race to her mom."

"More press."

"She did some motivational speaking, went to work for the Park Service, moved to Elkins for the job. Got married. McMullen, among others, did a splash on her. Pictures of her after a marathon, looking healthy, more of her in her wedding dress, with the gold medal in her bouquet."

"She's everything that Hobart detests. She made strength and heart and endurance out of tragedy and pain."

"And got the gold—a kind of symbol of wealth and fame."

"Social media?" Simone asked.

"She was active on a couple of sites for runners. She had two of her own, a public page, about the national forest, the trails, photos, anecdotes. And a private one with her personal stuff."

"But it's never really private, is it?"

Reed turned the bottle, shook his head. "All it takes is basic hacking or finding a way to have the page owner let you in. Either way, Hobart knew enough to track her on her early morning runs. She ran every day, not always the same route, but she ran every morning. Hobart's known to be a runner."

"She could run one of the routes a couple of times, let Tracey see her, get used to seeing her. Even strike up a conversation."

"Easy enough," he agreed. "She was killed this morning between six-thirty and eight-thirty. A bullet in each leg, one in the head."

"The legs." It burned in Simone's heart. "Hobart wanted to destroy her before she killed her."

"Take out her legs again," Reed agreed. "Bring back that pain and terror. The feds will track back to where she lived in that area, how long, what she drove."

"But she'll be gone, and driving something else."

"That's her pattern, but every piece of information counts. It adds up. It should add up," he muttered.

"Was Tracey on your, I guess I'd call it a watch list?"

"I had her, but . . . She didn't really benefit financially, she didn't get media hero status out of the incident itself. She didn't affect the outcome. I had her, but we weren't focused there."

He shoved up to pace. "Damn it, she drove out of Florida after Devlon, flew out of Atlanta, back to Portland to snatch McMullen, held her in a cabin in the White Mountains, miles east of here, for hours."

The admirable calm's slipping, she noted. So she'd be calm for him. "She'd never abducted and held anyone before."

"She wanted more than a straight kill with McMullen. She wanted attention. The tripod, the lights, makeup traces, and a reporter? She did a video, had to."

"God, she taped killing McMullen?"

"That might've been bonus footage. She wanted the interview, it's what makes sense. She booked the cabin, had supplies for a full week, but killed McMullen within twenty-four of the snatch. She couldn't hold on to it, couldn't maintain for longer."

To keep her hands busy, Simone dealt with more dishes. "What does that tell you?"

"She's breaking down. She's sure as hell breaking down. It tells me she needed to talk, to tell somebody—on the record—how goddamn smart she is, tell them what she's done and why."

Simone turned back to him. "She's isolated, has been all of her life really. A lot by choice, but isolated and playing roles."

"That's exactly right."

"I haven't been, not really, because I had CiCi and Mi—but I pulled away from my family, and some of that was them pulling away from me. I played a role for a year, to try to please my parents, and ended up making myself sick and miserable before I stopped."

"What role?" He dragged himself out of his frustration over Hobart, looked at Simone. "You never told me about that."

"A long time ago—college time. The business major, corporate suit, date-the-fortunate-son-like-the-parents-want role. It's awful to try to be what you're not. She does that all the time, has done it all the time."

"Except with her brother. She could be herself with him."

"First her parents took him away from her, then we—because it's all of us to her, isn't it? Then we killed him. Now she's alone, playing roles. You're the only one alive who's seen the real Patricia Hobart."

"You're on the money. She needed to make a statement, spend some time being herself. I bet she plays that recording over and over."

Frustrated, disgusted, he dropped onto a stool at the kitchen peninsula. "But she's still covering her tracks, and goddamn well. She leaves McMullen's body in the cabin, calculating it won't be found for a few days—and she's right. Meanwhile, she takes McMullen's car west into New Hampshire, changed the plates along the way, dumps it in the airport lot in Concord— her favorite ploy—and she's in the wind again. They'll backtrack her with the sighting in Louisville, and the murder in West Virginia, but we started looking west. Why come all the way back here, drive McMullen west, take the car west, if she was going to double back south?"

"Kentucky's still west of Maine," Simone pointed out.

"Yeah, we factored that in. Looking for a reason for her crossing into New Hampshire, then with the sighting, looking at the southwest. So I'm looking at this guy who moved to Arkansas a couple of years ago, another in Texas, and didn't give West Virginia or Tracey much of a thought."

"If you take one fraction of one degree of blame over this, I'll be seriously pissed off at you."

"Not blame, but . . . I don't know the word for it. She doubled back again, and none of us saw it coming."

"You'll go over it with Essie later tonight. I'll go home with CiCi." She held up a hand before he objected. "From what I've seen of Hank, he'll keep Dylan occupied. We're all going to get out of the way, and you can go over it with Essie."

He slid off the stool, drew her off hers, rested his forehead to hers. "You're right. Let's go walk on the beach." He kissed her. "With friends and dogs and a wild and crazy kid."

Simone went with him. She didn't know where Elkins might be, but felt certain if she traced a northeast route on the map from Louisville, she'd find it.

Despite the pall of another murder, Reed saw Essie and her family off on the ferry early Monday morning after a good, happy weekend.

They glided away, waving, in a steady rain that had held off until just before dawn. He appreciated the timing—and now that he had lupines and tulips and other unidentified things popping up around his house, he appreciated the rain, too.

He and Essie had spent time in his office, the old partner rhythm still there. They agreed, unless she veered off course, her next area of interest should be the D.C. area.

They had a congressional aide, a victim's advocate lawyer, a political reporter, and a couple who ran a women's shelter—all within a fifty-mile radius.

Reed intended to pass their theories, conclusions, and newest list to Jacoby when he got to the station.

At his side, Barney whined as the ferry drifted away.

"They'll be back. You did okay, pal. You even took a biscuit from the scary bearded man, even if you did run away from him afterward. Progress. Let's go to work."

He got in early, made coffee, sent the report he and Essie put together to Jacoby, settled down with the memos and incident reports on his desk.

A drunk and disorderly—Saturday night, off-islander, cited, sobered up, and fined. Somebody TP'd the Dobson house, also Saturday night. So much action!

As Richard Dobson taught math at the high school, and wasn't known for the warm fuzzies or grading on a curve, the investigating officers—Matty and Cecil—suspected a student, possibly a student in danger of failing his class.

Marking period was nearly over, Reed calculated. He agreed with his officers' conclusions.

A complaint about loud music and noise, also during the island madness of Saturday night. Responding officers—again Matty and Cecil—broke up a party comprised of a group of teenagers taking advantage of parents away for the weekend.

Underage drinking discovered.

Reed noted the party poopers arrived at twenty-two-thirty. And Dobson saw no sign of TP dripping from his trees when he let his dog out for a last tour at twenty-three hundred.

Dobson discovered same when he woke just before two hundred hours, answering his own call of nature, and glanced out the bathroom window.

Reed looked at Barney. "I deduce, my young apprentice, certain party-goers aren't doing so well in algebra or trig—and I sympathize. I suspect some gathered again after the raid, got their supplies, and exacted their revenge."

Normally, he'd let it go. It was just toilet paper, but he noted Dobson called in twice on Sunday demanding pursuit of the vandals. A memo informed him, Dobson had also complained to the mayor and wanted a response personally from the chief of police.

"Okay then."

He noted from the schedule that Matty and Cecil were off, but the clarity of their report meant he didn't need a sit-down.

He got up when he heard Donna come in.

"Morning, Donna."

"Chief. Nice weekend?"

"Yeah. You?"

"The rain held off, so that's good enough."

"I hear you. Donna, how much of a hard-ass is Dobson—the math teacher?"

"Ass as stony as his heart. My grandson's studying his brain out of his ears, and barely making it in geometry. Dobson won't accept extra credit, no re-tests, no nothing. This is about them rolling his yard?"

"It is."

"I'd have bought the TP for them, that's how I feel about it."

"I'll pretend I didn't hear that. I have to go talk to him."

"Good luck with that," Donna said, bitterly. "He won't be satisfied until whoever did it is slapped in stocks."

"We have stocks?"

"He probably has some in his garage. It wouldn't surprise me."

"Was your grandson at the party at the Walkers' Saturday night?"

She pokered up. "Maybe."

"Donna." He gestured to her chair, took one of his own. "Nobody's going to be put in stocks, drawn or quartered, tarred or feathered. Nobody's going to be arrested. I'm damn sure not going to screw around with kids over something like this. But it'd help if I knew who was involved, so I could talk to them. I'll handle Dobson."

"I'm not ratting out my own flesh and blood."

"Do you want me to take an oath he won't get in trouble, and neither will anybody else?"

She yanked open a drawer, pulled out a King James Bible.

"You're serious?"

"Right hand on it, and swear."

"Jesus Christ."

"Don't you take the name of the Lord in vain when I'm holding the Bible."

"Sorry." He put his right hand on it. "I swear I'll keep your grandson and the rest of them out of trouble regarding this matter."

She nodded, put the book away. "He's a good boy. He's getting all A's and B's except for that one class. He's already grounded for the party, and he deserved it."

"He did. There was drinking."

She pointed at him. "Are you going to sit there and tell me when you were coming up on eighteen or already hit it, fixing to graduate high school in a few weeks, you didn't drink a beer or two?"

She yanked the drawer open again.

"Don't bring that out here again. I'm not going to deny it. I bet he listens to you."

"Everybody listens to me if they know what's good for them."

"Then you back me up with this. You have a talk with him later, tell him to avoid the drinking and the . . . mischief, to steer clear of Dobson outside of class, and Dobson's house altogether."

"I'll do that."

"Good. Who's his best pal?"

"Damn it, Reed!"

"I took an oath, on the Bible."

"Cecil's brother, Mathias, and Jamie Walker."

"Jamie Walker of the infamous party?"

"That's right."

"Okay then. Let's go, Barney."

"Don't you let me down, Chief."

"I won't."

As he and Barney walked to the school, Reed thought it good to be back to work.

He caught Dobson as the math teacher—briefcase in hand, sour expression in place—strode toward the main doors of the high school section of the building that also housed the middle and elementary.

At the moment, grouping the three levels, and the one-room kindergarten class, two hundred and twenty-seven students attended the Tranquility Island Education Complex.

"It's about time," Dobson snapped. "My taxes pay your salary."

"That they do. Why don't we talk inside, out of the wet?"

"You can't bring that dog inside the school."

"He's deputized." To solve it, Reed opened the doors, led Barney in.

"I expect better—"

"We can talk in your classroom, or the teacher's lounge, whichever you prefer." Or you can try to haul me into the principal's office, Reed mused.

Dobson strode off. A little guy, Reed thought. Maybe five-seven, on the stocky side, and with a serious stick up his ass.

It might have been small as high schools went, but it smelled like school to Reed—commercial cleaner, tinged with the messy mix of jittery hormones and teenage boredom. Sounded like one as his wet sneakers slapped on the floor. Looked like one with its administrative offices straight to the left, and its facing walls of dull gray lockers.

"It's a nice school," Reed said conversationally. "I had a tour of it, along with the middle and elementary, over the winter."

"Nice isn't relevant. It's a place for education and discipline."

Though he felt like he'd regressed to high school, Reed rolled his eyes behind Dobson's back as the man unlocked a classroom door.

"My time's limited."

"Then I'll be as quick as I can. According to the incident report, you didn't see anyone in your yard or around your house at the time you woke and saw the toilet paper in your trees."

"At the time I saw the vandalism. It had already been done. If you can't identify and apprehend a gang of vandals, you have no business in your office."

"I'm sorry you feel that way. What did you do with the evidence?"

"Evidence?"

"The TP."

"I removed it, of course—at considerable time and trouble—and disposed of it."

"Well, that's a shame. I might have been able to find prints. Can't guarantee that, as the perpetrators might have worn gloves. But at this time, no one, including you, saw anyone, heard anything, and the evidence has been disposed of by your own hands. You could give me a list of names, people who would wish you harm."

Dobson's mouth popped open in shock. "No one wishes me harm! There are several teachers in this school, any number of students, and certainly some parents who have issues with me, but—"

"'Issues'?"

"Many who don't approve of my teaching methods or philosophies."

"'Many,' 'any number,' 'some,' and 'several.' That's a lot in a school this size. Did any of them threaten you or your property?"

"Not in so many words."

"Mr. Dobson, I'm going to keep my eyes and ears open, as will my deputies. But without a witness, without the evidence, without you being able to name individuals who might have had the time, opportunity, and motive for committing this act, we don't have a lot to go on."

"I expect better! I expect justice."

"Mr. Dobson, if I identified the individual or individual responsible, the most justice would offer is a few hours of community service, maybe a negligible fine. And by pursuing that, demanding that, you'd have more people than you do now who have issues with you."

"I'm going to speak to the mayor again."

"Okay. Have a good day."

He led Barney out. A handful of students began to file in, bringing color and chatter and the smell of wet hair.

Reed went outside, waited.

Mathias spotted him at the same time he spotted Mathias with two other boys.

Mathias looked instantly guilty. Reed sauntered over.

"Mathias, how you doing?"

"Fine, sir. Ah, we've got to get to class."

"There's time yet. Jamie Walker?"

The kid wearing the hipster hat with his hair shaved on the sides and floppy front and back shrugged.

"I need to talk to you about the party the other night," he said loudly enough for anyone passing to hear. "Let's walk over here. You, too," he said to the third boy—the one with the hood of his orange hoodie over ginger hair. Adding more of his cool by wearing sunglasses in the rain.

"We already caught it for that, Chief," Mathias began. "I'm grounded for two weeks."

"You do the crime, you do the time. Who else is grounded?"

Both the other boys raised hands. "I'm eighteen," Jamie said with overt disgust, "and I'm grounded for having a party."

"In your parents' house, without their permission. With beer—and weed."

"Nobody found any weed," Jamie insisted.

"Because you were smart and quick enough to get rid of it. My officers smelled it. But that's done, and you're lucky, as they could have hauled you in."

"It was just a party," Jamie grumbled.

"I might agree, but you were stupid enough to make enough noise and get caught. Be smarter next time. Now, where'd you get the TP?"

"I don't know what you're talking about."

Reed turned from Jamie to Mathias. Cecil's brother had his hood up, too. "You know Donna the dispatcher."

"Yes, sir. She's grandmother to a friend of mine, and friends with my mom."

"Here's the deal. She had me take an oath with my hand on the damn Bible—shit, she'd skin me for saying 'the damn Bible'—I'd keep her grandson, who I suspect was in on this, and the rest of you out of trouble."

"She would." Mathias ducked his head, but Reed saw the grin.

"I'm not risking the wrath of Donna to slap you back for TPing a house. I'm asking because if you were stupid enough to buy it, that's going to come out, and I'll have to do something."

Mathias hunched his shoulders, scuffed the ground with his already scuffed Nike KD's. "We each took a couple of rolls from home."

"Not completely stupid. Don't do it again—and pass that to the ones I haven't caught. Yet. Meanwhile, stay away from Dobson outside the classroom, keep your heads down. Don't go around his house, and for Christ's sake, don't go bragging about doing this. You hold to that, all that's going to happen is you're all—plus Donna's grandson, who I have caught but haven't talked to yet—going to do some community service. Two weekends of yard work, or whatever your mother needs around the house. No bitching about it. I'm going to check."

"You're not going to tell Mr. Dobson?" Mathias asked.

"No. You're all going to college or into the world of employment. You're going to run into more Dobsons, trust me. Figure out a better way to deal with them. Get to class."

"Thanks, Chief," the three of them said, almost in unison.

Reed walked off satisfied. Yeah, he thought, it was good to be back to work.

CHAPTER TWENTY-SIX

Mail took its time getting to the island. Reed got the next card five days after his weekend off, and right before the Memorial Day weekend with its village parade, LobsterFest, early bird summer specials, and the first influx of summer people.

As always, Donna picked up the mail on the way in and arrived shortly after him. He'd made his first cup of station coffee from the machine he'd paid for himself. He'd settled the dog down with a chew bone and, though it humiliated, the little stuffed dog Barney loved.

Reed expected Barney to chew the toy to bits, but Barney habitually clamped it gently in jaws or paws and did no real damage.

As he booted up his computer with an eye toward looking over the June calendar again, Donna came to his open door.

"Chief."

"Yeah. So this Arts and Crafts Festival the second weekend in June? I remember my mother being all about that one year. Do we have an estimate on . . ."

He trailed off as he glanced up, saw her face.

"Problem." It wasn't a question.

"You got another card in the mail. It's the same handwriting, I know it. The postmark's from West Virginia. I only touched it by the corner to stick it in my tote."

"Let's have it."

He hadn't expected another card as much as he'd hoped for one.

Another trail. Another break in control.

Donna set it carefully on his desk, sat.

"I've got something to say first, before you open it."

"I need to get to this, Donna."

"I know you need to get to this, but I've got something to say first." She clutched her big summer straw purse in her lap. "I want to say it before you open it, because we both know this is another threat against you."

"Go ahead then," he said as he got out a pair of gloves, his penknife.

"You kept your word. I believe you'd have kept it whether or not you took an oath on the good book. But that's a kind of insurance. You did the right thing and didn't let those boys—including my grandson—off scot-free, but you didn't mess up their lives over a prank. Dobson hammered at you, pushed at the mayor, but you did the right thing."

"It was toilet paper, Donna, probably biodegradable."

"That's not the point. I didn't know what to think about them bringing you in as chief, but I didn't think very well. You're young, you're from the mainland, and you've got a sassy way half the time."

He had to smile, even with the slow burn working inside him over the card waiting on his desk. "I'm sassy?"

"That's not a compliment. But you do a good job, you treat the deputies with respect, and you kept your word. You're good to that idiot dog."

"He's only half an idiot these days."

"I didn't like the idea of you bringing him in here, but I'll tell the truth and say I've got a fondness for him now."

Her fondness, Reed knew, included sneaking the dog tiny bone-shaped treats from a bag she now kept at her station.

"Barney grows on you."

"I think you need a decent haircut and real shoes instead of old beat-up sneakers."

Reed frowned down at his high-tops. They weren't that beat-up. "Noted."

"Otherwise." She sniffed. "You're doing reasonably all right. More or less."

"I'm touched."

"And you're chief, so that's that." She dug into her bag, pulled out a black ball cap with CHIEF over the crown in white. "So this is for you."

"You got me a hat."

"I watch these TV movies all the time and the chief of police has a hat like this one."

Touched, sincerely, Reed took it, settled it on his head. "How's it look?"

"Well, you need a decent haircut, but it'll do."

He took it off, studied the CHIEF, put it back on. "I appreciate it, Donna. I'm proud to wear it."

"At least people will see it and not think you're some beach bum with that ragged hair and those beat-up sneakers." She pushed up from the chair. "I'll call in the off-duty deputies, so you can brief them after you've looked at that card."

"Thanks."

She paused at the door. "You be smart and you be careful."

"I intend to be both."

"See that you do. I paid good money for that hat. I don't want anything to happen to it."

He smiled for a moment as she walked out, then put on the gloves, slit the envelope with his knife.

This one read:

THINKING OF YOU

On a floral background.

Inside, over a rainbow and more flowers, the sentiment read:

YOU MEAN SO MUCH TO ME, I NEED TO LET YOU KNOW.
NO MATTER WHAT I SEE, NO MATTER WHERE I GO.
YOU'RE ALWAYS IN MY THOUGHTS.

She'd signed it *XXOO Patricia*, and on the inside cover had written her
personal message.

> *I can't wait until we're together again. It's been too long!*
> *I hope you think of me as often as I think of you, and with*
> *the same—should we call it passion?*
> *Enclosed is another token of my undying loathing.*
> *Until . . . Patricia.*

He lifted out the lock of hair inside the sealed bag.

It wouldn't be McMullen's, he thought. McMullen, the abduction, the
video, the killing, all that had been not just personal for Hobart, but intimate.

This lock of hair was Tracey Lieberman's.

He took photos, sealed the original and the lock of hair in an evidence
bag.

"Just come, bitch. Just stop screwing around and come. We'll finish
this."

He contacted Jacoby, shot her the photos, did the same with Essie.

Then he swiveled in his chair, gazed out the window at the flowering
bushes. Azaleas—even he knew that much. They made a nice show. He had
a couple of them at his house, in flaming red, and the wild dogwood—CiCi
had identified—had burst out in late March between snowstorms.

The fishing boats would be out, and the lobstermen. Before long they'd be
joined by sailboats, powerboats, boogie boards, sunbathers, and sandcastles.

Whenever she came, however she got there, he'd find a way to stop her
from leaving a scar on the island.

He flicked a finger down the bill of his cap, got up to brief his deputies. The dog, toy in his mouth, followed him.

In her studio, Simone circled the clay. She searched for imperfections, for possibilities of improvements. For the last few days, she'd touched up details, cutting minute bits of clay with hook and rake tools, smoothing out with kidney tools, delicately brushing with solvent to remove those tool marks.

She knew, from experience, an artist could cut and rake and smooth a piece—searching for perfection—and destroy the soul of it.

Her hands itched for her tools, but she walked out, called down the stairs to where she knew CiCi sat with her morning coffee.

"CiCi, could you come up, take another look at Reed?"

"I'm always ready to look at Reed. You haven't let me look for days— covering him up even when you had Hank and Essie up there."

"I know. He wasn't ready. I know he's ready now, but I can't stop looking for reasons to tweak just a little more. Stop me," she said as CiCi reached the landing. "Or tell me to keep going."

CiCi stepped in, flipped her long braid behind her back, then circled as Simone had.

The image stood two feet in height on a base she'd created to resemble a platform of rough stone. She'd caught him, as she'd envisioned, in mid-swing, the sword gripped two-handed over his left shoulder, his body turned at the hip, legs braced, with the right foot planted ahead of the left, and in a pivot.

His hair, tumbled and with that hint of curl, seemed to flow with the motion. For his face, she'd sculpted the barely banked rage and cold purpose.

Behind his left leg, Barney stood, leaning in, head up, eyes full of hope and trust.

"God, he's gorgeous," CiCi stated as she circled.

"In person, or here?"

"Both. Absolutely both. Simone, this is brilliant. It's stunning, and it's absolutely Reed. *The Protector* you said you called it. And that's just perfect.

Leave it alone. Perfect's often the enemy of done, but you've already gotten perfect."

She traced a finger a hairbreadth from the scars. "Perfectly flawed. Real. Male. Human."

"It got more important to me every day. And the more important . . . I want to cast it in bronze."

"Yes. Yes. Oh, I can see that." CiCi shifted, slipped an arm around Simone's waist. "Will you let him see the clay model?"

"Nope."

"Good. Let him wait."

"I've let it dry. Most of me knew it was done. I can start the molding process this morning."

"I'll let you get to it. My talented girl? It's going to be a masterpiece."

"Okay then," she murmured when she was alone.

She got her brush, the latex rubber mixture. Stopped herself, got a bottle of water, turned on music, going with one of CiCi's New Agey playlists. Soothing harps, bells, flutes.

With the brush, she painted the mixture onto the clay. Avoiding air bubbles while coating every millimeter took patience and care, and time.

She knew his body so well now, the length of torso, the line of hip, the exact placement of the scars.

Once done, she stepped back, searching for any tiny area she might have missed. Then she cleaned her brush, put the mix away.

This process took more patience. She'd apply the next coat the following morning, then another. Four coats, she determined, before she made the mother mold of plaster.

When that dried, she'd remove the mother mold, cut the rubber away from the clay. She would have the negative image, and could pour the wax replica.

She decided she'd wait until she reached that stage before booking the foundry she used on the mainland. Pouring the wax replication took several steps, then she'd need to chase that—repair imperfections, remove seams and mold lines.

Painstaking, but she preferred doing her own wax chasing as she'd learned in Florence.

But by then, even with the steps that followed, she'd have a good sense of when she'd be ready to have it poured.

Sipping water, she turned toward her board, and the faces that waited. Time, she thought, to get back to her mission. A walk on the beach to clear her head, then she'd go back to work.

Reed walked Barney home in air soft with spring. Buildings, many freshly painted for the season, stood in soft roses, bright blues, quiet yellows and greens. Sort of like a garden, with touches of more in baskets of pansies or window boxes spilling with—he didn't really know, but it looked nice.

Walking instead of driving reaped benefits. People along his stroll knew him now, stopped to have a word, ask a question. The best way, in his mind, to weave yourself into the fabric of a community was regular visibility—and compliments on flowerpots, paint, a new hairstyle didn't hurt.

Barney still shied, but not as much, and not with everyone. The dog had his favorites on their comings and goings.

Barney's top favorite—and Reed's—got out of her car in his driveway as they approached. Barney let out a happy yip, wagged all over, so Reed unclipped the leash and let him go.

"Perfect timing." Simone bent down to rub and stroke. Her gaze tracked up, amused. "Nice hat, Chief."

"I like it. Donna gave it to me."

"Donna?" Now her brows shot up as she straightened. "Well, well. You are accepted."

"Seems like it."

"Congratulations," she said, moving in, winding around him, and capturing his mouth in a long, deep, steamy kiss.

"Wow. That's an amazing way to end the workday."

"I had a really good workday myself, so." She kissed him again until he fisted a hand on the back of her shirt.

"Why don't we just—"

"Mmm-mm." She gave his bottom lip a quick bite. "Things to do first. You can carry in the supplies."

"We have supplies?"

"We have pasta salad—another draw from my limited culinary repertoire—and some marinated chicken breasts—courtesy of CiCi. She says if you don't know how to grill chicken, Google it."

"I can do that, and supply the wine."

He got out the bag as she took a square package out of the other side. He'd seen enough of them now to recognize a wrapped painting.

"What's that?"

"Your mermaid, as promised. Get me that wine, I'll unveil her."

"Hot damn." He smiled over at her as they started inside—across the porch he'd—with Cecil's and Mathias's help—painted orchid. "You must've had a really good workday."

"I did. How about you?"

"Let's get that wine, then we'll talk about it."

He'd started to develop a taste for wine, so he poured two glasses while she unwrapped the painting.

It was maybe eighteen inches square, and full of light. Blue skies blurred pink and gold at the horizon, blue water streaked with those rich tones.

But the mermaid was the star.

She sat on a stand of rocks at water's edge, her tail a treasure of gleaming blues and greens with touches of iridescent gold. She ran a gold comb through waving masses of red hair, which spilled over bare breasts, back, torso. Her face was turned toward the onlooker.

And that face, he thought, eerily beautiful, exotic, bold green eyes all-knowing, the perfect lips curved in a sensual smile as water sprayed white against the rocks.

"She's . . . wow. One sexy mermaid."

"CiCi framed her—she's better at that than I'll ever be. Let's go put her up."

"In a minute. First, one more wow, and thanks." He set the painting down, drew her in for another kiss. Held her an extra moment.

"I think you didn't have such a good workday."

"That depends on your perspective. I want to get this said and done so we can put it aside, and just be." He eased back. "I got another card this morning."

"Oh God."

"Wait now. What this tells me is: She's still hung up on me, and has lost her main focus. She's letting emotion and personal bitchiness get in the way. She's given us that trail, Simone, communicating rather than concentrating on evading only. That's a plus for us."

"She wants to *kill* you."

"She tried once," he reminded her. "I always knew she'd try again. Now, instead of letting it all lie, then coming at me when I'm unprepared, she's giving me a trail and a time line. Not just me, but the FBI. Jacoby's all over this."

"If you're trying to placate me—"

"I'm not. She's one dangerous, crazy, bloodthirsty psychopath. You're not only on the island, too, you're with me on the island. She wouldn't know that second part yet, but she'll figure it out, and she'll want both of us. I'm not placating you."

"That's clear now." Simone blew out a breath. "Tell me about the card."

"This one was a 'Thinking of You' deal," he began, and ran it through, took out his phone, showed her.

"And the lock of hair again," Simone added. "It's not McMullen's, is it? That's been too long a gap."

"McMullen, for whatever reasons, hit another category for her."

"It's poor Tracey's, isn't it?"

"That's my take. Forensics will confirm."

"I barely knew her, and only through Mi, but . . ." She had to take a moment, steady herself. "That link to me, links her to me. It's harder than the others because of that."

He brushed a hand over her hair. "I love you. This island's my home—I even have a dog to prove it. The people who live here, who come here, they're my responsibility now. I need you to trust me, trust I'll take care of all of it."

She thought of the sculpture, the heart of it. She'd created it because she knew who he was. "I do trust you. You'll make her pay for Tracey and all the others, and that makes it easier. I'm glad you told me first, so we can put it away."

"Good. Let's do that. Put this away, and have a normal evening."

"Normal sounds just right."

"Okay then." He scooped her off her feet, heading for the stairs.

"What's this?"

"This is me, Rhett Butlering you up the stairs and into bed."

"That's a normal evening?"

"That's how I see it."

He made the turn, dumped her on the bed, dropped down to cover her. "You started it. Driveway kiss. So now I have to finish it."

Barney, who'd witnessed this behavior before, padded over to his bed with his toy, settled down to wait it out.

"Big talk. Maybe I like to finish what *I* start."

"You'll get the chance." He lowered his mouth to hers, let the kiss spin and spin and spin out.

Everything she wanted, Simone thought. Too much what she wanted. All these feelings and needs, the weakness and power rising and whirling inside her.

She held on to him and let herself fall.

He undressed her, slowly, piece by piece. No hurry, not when he felt drunk on her already. He glided his hands over bare skin, felt it heat under his touch, trailed his lips over it, felt it quiver.

Time seemed to slow; the air thickened. Every sigh, every murmur, soft as moth wings, floated out and away as they moved together, came together.

He loved everything she was, had been, would be. She loved, he knew, so he could wait for her to look at him, into him, and say the words. Because here and now, she showed him, and no words were needed.

He opened her; she couldn't explain it. He unlocked things in her she hadn't known existed, and he held those secret things so carefully.

She ran her hand down his side, over the scars. The Protector, she thought, but who protected him?

I will. She cupped his face, rose up to him. I will.

He slipped inside her, slow, slow, with his eyes on hers.

I will, she thought again, and surrendered.

When she lay beneath him, feeling his heart trip against hers, the beauty flooded her throat with tears.

"I like your version of normal," she managed.

"I was hoping." He brushed his lips over the curve of her shoulder. "I could spend a couple lifetimes being normal with you."

Not yet, she thought. Not yet. "Does normal include dinner?"

"Right after I Google how to grill chicken." He levered up, looked down at her. "Hey." Brushed a tear from her lashes.

"They're the good kind," she told him. "The very good kind. You make me feel more, Reed. I'm still getting used to it. Let's do this. You figure out how to do the chicken, and I'll hang the mermaid. I suspect we'll both be playing to our strengths."

"Let's see if you feel that way after you eat the chicken. The good kind?"

"The very good kind."

He fed the dog and grilled chicken that was pretty damn okay. He admired the sexy mermaid on the bathroom wall. They took a walk, and he studied the spearing green of his emerging lupines, before they wound through the woods and down to the beach.

They gave each other normal.

He tried tossing the ball for Barney, to no avail. Then Simone picked it up, threw it. Barney trotted after it, snagged it, brought it back.

"Why does he fetch for you?"

"Because he's a gentleman."

"Throw it again."

She obliged with the same results.

"Let me have that thing. Go get it, Barney!" Reed tossed it. Barney stared up at him. "Well, for—"

"Barney." Simone pointed to the ball. "Get that for me."

He wagged his tail, raced down the beach, and brought the ball back to her.

"He's messing with me," Reed decided. "I can get him to sit. We've got about a ninety percent success rate on that. But he gets his head caught in the stair rail a couple times a week. And he's getting bigger, so it's not as easy to get him out again."

They walked on, and he tried a new tactic. Reed tossed the ball back over his shoulder. Barney ran back for it.

"I've got his number now."

With Simone's hand in his, and his dog trotting along with a red ball, he watched the moon come up over the water.

"Can you stay tonight?"

"I have to leave early. It's a timing thing, but I can stay."

He brought her hand to his lips, watched the moon, and thought he couldn't ask for better normal.

CHAPTER TWENTY-SEVEN

Summer came to the island, and so did the summer people. Day-trippers with their sunscreen and beach blankets, weekenders prepared to pack fun and sun into their two days. Others flooded in to spend a week or two, a month, or the season.

The ferry ran every hour on the hour with cars, bikers, hikers lined up at the dock on both sides of the bay.

Every hour on the hour Reed himself or a team of deputies stood watch.

He'd checked on a scatter of bookings by single females, but none panned out.

He worked every day, on the roll or off, he walked the village, the beaches, cruised by rentals.

Sooner or later, he thought.

On a lovely June evening at a well-attended fund-raiser in Potomac, Maryland, Marlene Dubowski—victim's advocate attorney, political activist, DownEast Mall survivor—gave a short speech, raised her glass in a toast.

She sipped, mingled, sipped, schmoozed, sipped. And began gasping for breath. As she collapsed, Patricia, in the guise of a wealthy donor, dropped down beside her, quickly snipped a lock of hair. "Oh my God, call nine-one-one!"

"I'm a doctor," someone shouted. "Let me through!"

In the confusion, Patricia slipped away.

She drove by the fine homes, sweeping driveways, to the post office she'd already earmarked. Humming to herself, she slipped the lock of hair into the bag and the bag inside the card she'd already signed, addressed, and stamped.

She'd chosen:

JUST BECAUSE
YOU'RE YOU!

After sealing the card, she slipped it into the mailbox in front of the post office.

Pleased with herself, she took the Beltway, cruised off the exit ramp to the mid-level hotel she'd prebooked, as she'd considered the crowds of vacationers.

She only needed a night, a good meal.

In her junior suite—the best she could do—she pulled off the ash-blond helmet wig, took out the blue contacts, the device that pushed her jaw out to prominence.

With a grunt, she removed the matronly designer cocktail dress and the body padding beneath. She took the lifts out of her evening shoes.

She ordered room service, took a long shower to start fading the self-tanner she'd used.

In the morning, she'd dump the car she'd rented in long-term parking at Dulles airport, rent another. A change of plates somewhere along the way, and she'd be off again.

She set the photo of Reed on the table beside her bed—she'd bought a frame for it.

"We've got a date, don't we? Just because."

Jacoby sat in Reed's office, frustration in every line of her body. "We had an agent at the damn fund-raiser, and she slipped through. People panicked, crowded in, cut him off. He got a look at her, and gave chase, but . . . He believes she fled in a black Mercedes sedan, but he couldn't get the plate. No plate light."

Reaching in her bag, she took out a sketch. "Artist's rendering."

"She added some years, some weight, changed the jawline. And she went back to cyanide."

"She stayed to see her target collapse, and even got down beside her for a moment when keeping back, leaving would be smarter."

"She's gotten more arrogant, and she didn't know how close you were."

"Not close enough. She's going to send you another card."

"I'm counting on it. Her time between kills is compressing."

"Another sign she's losing the control that kept her under for so long. It goes back to you, Reed, and putting a bullet in her. Initially I thought, and our analysis agreed, she might string you along. Play it out because, for her, it must be torturing you. I don't think that now. She needs to right that wrong."

"Agreed. If she wants to take out another on her way here, and at the rate she's escalated, I think she will, you need to put Mi-Hi Jung and Chaz Bergman under some protection. I think Brady Foster falls in there, too. She won't go after Essie yet. Essie's too high up the chain. She wouldn't go after Simone yet if I didn't live on the island. But she won't be able to resist a doubleheader. But . . ."

He rose, wandered over for a Coke, held out a second.

"Have any Diet?"

"Hold on." He went out, through the bullpen, into the break room, took a Diet Pepsi out of the fridge.

"I owe you one," he said to Matty, and took it to his office, closed the door.

"Thanks. 'But'?"

"She's escalating, and she's devolving, but she's still smart, she's still cagey. We saw just that in how she played us with and after McMullen. She knows, has to know, you're following her route, connecting dots."

"You think she'll veer off, take another detour."

"If she needs another kill before me, she'd be stupid to take a direct route to Maine. She's not stupid."

Jacoby rose, walked to the map he'd pinned to his wall, studied the push-pins that represented Hobart's kills since she'd started the journey.

"Any instincts on where she might detour this time?"

"I have to think about it. Would she stick to driving, book a flight? Will she stick to fame and/or fortune, or go off pattern there, too? I have to think about it."

"So will I, and the rest of the task force. I had a man in the same room with her, and she killed her target, drove away."

Reed picked up the sketch. "Do you see Hobart when you look at this?"

"I probably wouldn't have, and witnesses confirmed a Southern accent—a good one. She mixed with people, Reed, made small talk, and worked up tears when she spun a story about her daughter and what she went through after a rape. She paid the five thousand to be there."

"She lives the role while she's in it. She's good. Crazy good."

"I've got to get back. Contact me when you get the next card."

He had traffic issues, parking issues, beach issues, boating issues, drinking issues, even some petty theft to deal with. Every day was a holiday, and people swarmed the streets, shops, trails, beaches.

Most days he worked until after sundown, and then some. But most evenings he had Simone. If he found an hour or two of quiet and solitude, he settled into his office, studied the map, the faces, tried to put himself in Patricia's mind-set.

He stepped out one morning—Simone tended to leave at the crack of dawn these days— and found CiCi in his yard with canvas, easel, and paints.

"Morning, Chief Delicious."

"Morning, love of my life. You're painting."

"I want the morning light. I've been out here a couple times this week later in the day—which shows how sneaky I am—but I need this light."

He walked around to her—the dog had already hurried over to wag and lean.

"It's the house." And the lupines, he noted. Those rivers of color he still marveled belonged to him.

"They're not at peak yet. Next week they will be. But I need this light, and a good start before they peak. I like the lines of this house, always have. Somebody was smart enough to paint those porches orchid."

"Somebody had someone with an artist's eye tell him to."

"You figured out painting the main doors that plum would add punch all by yourself."

"I have my moments. And HGTV."

"More than a few moments. The lupines, they're a study all on their own."

"Leon helped me out there, and with the other flower stuff. He knows his fertilizer. I had to buy a composter. He wouldn't take no."

CiCi studied him as he spoke. "You haven't been getting enough sleep, my cutie. I can see it."

"Summertime. Busy time."

"And not just that. Why can't they catch her?"

"She's slippery." He leaned in to kiss CiCi's cheek. "But we will." He pulled out his key ring, took off a spare.

"To the house. Help yourself—and go ahead and lock it when you leave. Keep the key. Just don't roll a joint while you're out here. I'm the chief of police. I have a hat."

He clipped on Barney's leash, walked to work, stopping at a rental along the way to wake up the tenants—college kids—and tell them to pick up the beer and wine bottles scattered every damn where. Left with a warning that a deputy would be back within the hour to fine them if it wasn't done.

So, he thought, begins a summer day on the island.

And since he'd estimated the arrival, it didn't surprise him when Donna brought in the third card.

"Don't call everybody in, we're too busy for that. Just contact them, let them know we've gotten a third, and this one from Potomac, Maryland."

"That crazy woman's ruining my damn summer."

"Not making mine a picnic, either," he replied as he got gloves, the penknife, and opened the card.

"Cute," he said as he read the printed greeting.

This time she'd drawn hearts with blood dripping from them and arrows through them.

> *What do you think? I could try some archery. Or maybe we'll just stick with bullets in the heart, and the head. Maybe I'll shoot you in the balls first for shits and giggles. The fancy, bleeding-heart lawyer climbed on my brother's dead body to get on her pedestal. I knocked her off. She didn't know what hit her. Neither will you, asshole.*
>
> *XXOO, Patricia*

She even drew a very distinct middle finger after her name.

Devolving, he thought. Angrier, or less able to control that rage, so a more overt threat.

She'd need that next kill, no question about it. She'd need that rush.

But who? And where?

He looked at the map as he contacted Jacoby.

Simone inspected every inch of the investment casting over the wax mold. She'd done the wax chasing, using delicate tools for minute scraping, hot tools for filling in imperfections. She studied it now, and deemed it ready.

She'd taken hours to design, create, and attach the sprue system, the channel system of wax rods and gates to feed the molten bronze into the mold.

More hours still coating the wax with slurry. First, the very, very fine grain—two coats—to pick up all the minute and delicate details. More layers—nine in all—of various grades and mixtures, letting each dry between coats to create that thick ceramic shell.

All the tedious, technical work had kept her mind occupied for days, and off the anxiety of that third damn card.

She didn't know what hit her. Neither will you.

Don't think about it now, she told herself. Don't let a madwoman dictate your life.

She boxed the shell, carried it downstairs.

"Is that Reed?"

"All ready to go." Simone set the box on the kitchen counter with a little huff from the effort. "I appreciate you giving up a pretty summer day to go with me."

"I love a trip to the foundry. All those sweaty men—and women," CiCi added. "I'll get some sketches out of it." She checked her hair in the mirror—long and loose with a trio of enormous hoops showing through at her ears. "And I really am looking forward to hearing Natalie's wedding chatter. We'll make it a fun day." She shouldered on a straw bag the size of the Hindenburg. "Let's get our pretty boy out to the car. You did tell him we're going to the mainland this morning."

"I'll text him from the ferry."

CiCi narrowed her eyes as they walked out of the house. "Simone."

"It gives him less time to worry."

"And no time to try to talk you out of going off-island."

"Exactly." Simone settled the box in the cargo area, tossed her satchel back with it, popped on sunglasses as CiCi slid on her rainbow-lensed ones. In the driver's seat, she cranked up the radio, shot CiCi a grin.

"Girl trip!"

"Wee-hoo!"

Under usual circumstances, Simone might have booked a hotel room near the foundry, instead of pushing the work there to a single day. It wasn't that she didn't trust the supervisors, or the workers who were, in their way, artists themselves. But she preferred being in on every step and stage.

These weren't usual circumstances, and she didn't want to be away from Reed and the island, so the push was on.

He looked after her, she thought, and she looked right back after him.

Still, she left CiCi to entertain herself on the pouring floor or to wander around the furnaces while she hovered over the worker who placed her piece into the autoclave.

She'd used the lost wax method, her preference, and the heat and pressure from the oven would force the wax out of its shell.

If she'd done good work, she thought, *The Protector* would be perfectly formed inside the empty, hardened shell.

CiCi joined her when the workers transferred the hot shell to the pouring floor.

"And here we go," CiCi said.

Workers in helmets, face masks, protective suits, thick gloves, and boots always put her in mind of rugged astronauts.

They secured her work in sand while others heated solid blocks of bronze into liquid. She imagined muscles tensed and rippling inside those thick suits as they stirred that glorious molten bronze.

Here was art, too, she thought, in the enormous heat, the scent of chemicals and sweat, of liquified metal. And magic in the glowing light as workers lifted the crucible of molten metal out of its furnace.

And the pour—that moment of truth—always enthralled her. Those quick movements of workers moving in unison, the fluid flow of deep, glowing gold like melted sunlight.

Inside the shell, her work, her art, her vision filled with that melted sunlight. The negative became positive, and the symbol and study of the man she'd come to love would be born.

"Not as good as sex," CiCi murmured beside her. "But it's a damn fine rush all the same."

"Oh boy." On a long sigh, Simone released her breath.

Since the shell and the form within required several hours to cool, she drove with CiCi into Portland, had a long lunch—thank God not at the country club—with her mother and sister.

Wedding talk dominated, but Natalie radiated happy, and that glow reflected on their mother. If you can't beat them, Simone thought, join them.

"You saw the pictures I sent of the attendants' dresses." Natalie sipped from her second glass of champagne.

"I did," Simone told her. "They're lovely—sleek and elegant, and I love the color."

"Boysenberry." Tulip indulged in more champagne herself. "I had my doubts, and I admit I tried to talk Natalie into something more traditional. But she was right. It's a striking color, especially with her accent colors."

"The blush and pale silver." CiCi nodded. "You've got an artist's eye when you want one, sweetie."

"I was hoping you and Simone would wear the silver. If you'd look for a dress in that color. The boutique I'm using has some really beautiful choices. And there's still time to customize."

"I look good in silver," CiCi mused.

"You're not in the wedding party." Natalie shifted her gaze to Simone. "But I'd like you to . . . I want you both to be part of it."

"Why don't we go to the boutique after lunch?" Simone suggested. "You can help me pick out a dress."

Natalie blinked. "Really?"

"You're the bride, Nat." Simone tapped her glass to her sister's, and caught the glint of tears in her mother's eye. "Let's all go shopping."

Just a dress to her, she thought, but a symbol that mattered to both her sister and mother. And it would fill in another couple of hours while her bronze cooled.

By the time she and CiCi drove back toward the foundry—with dresses, shoes, bags, wraps for a fall wedding—she felt energized.

"I actually enjoyed that," she marveled.

"It never hurts to get out of our own comfort zones. You made them happy."

"We did."

"Yes, we did." She gave Simone an elbow. "Now they owe us."

"Big-time."

Since she wanted to do the rest of the work herself, and didn't want to spend her days off-island, Simone had the foundry load the encased bronze back into her car.

"I'm texting Reed," CiCi said as they drove onto the ferry. "I want him to know we're on our way back."

"I don't want him coming back to the house until I've done the breaking out and have the bronze back in my studio for the metal chasing."

"I'll hold him off, and I'll call on a couple of strong men to haul it out on the patio." As she texted, she glanced at Simone. "I want to be there for the breaking out."

"I wouldn't have it otherwise."

Two and a half hours later, Simone swiped sweat off her forehead. Bits and chunks of shell lay over the tarp along with a variety of hammers and power tools.

And the bronze stood in the early evening light.

"Gorgeous, Simone. Gorgeous."

"He will be." She'd grind off the sprues, finish the surface with pads from coarse to fine, retexture here and there, and perfect. "Few more steps." She circled it. "The metal chasing, a good sandblasting, then the patina, but I can see it, CiCi. I can see it's exactly what I hoped."

"So's he, whether you know it or not."

"I didn't hope for him, that's the thing. For a while I didn't hope for anything, and that was useless. Then I woke up and I hoped to be able to do something like this. That was enough, it honestly was because I had you, and this place, and could always come back. And then . . . he looked at me."

She crouched down, traced a finger over the bronze face. "He loves me."

"A lot of men, and a few women, have loved me. It's not enough, baby."

"No, it wouldn't be. It wouldn't be even though he's beautiful and kind, he's brave and smart and so many things. That wouldn't be enough."

She pulled off the bandanna she'd tied over her hair. "But he unlocked something inside me, CiCi. And unlocked, I see more, feel more, want more. He made me believe. I love him because of who he is, and who I am with him."

"When are you going to tell him?"

"When this is finished, and I show it to him." She straightened. "Is that silly?"

"I think it's profound. I'm going to help you clean this up and get this beauty upstairs."

While Simone chased metal, Reed rounded up a couple of kids who felt tossing lit firecrackers into trash cans in the public bathrooms was the height of vacation fun.

He might have let it go with simply confiscating the rest of the cherry bombs and ash cans and a lecture, but the father, who'd apparently enjoyed more than his fair share of booze on the beach, got in his face about it.

"What's the big deal? They're just having some fun. Didn't hurt anybody. And I paid good money for those cherry bombs."

"The big deal is they broke the law, endangered public safety and their own, and destroyed property."

"Buncha trash is all."

Still trying for some diplomacy, Reed nodded. "Which they'll clean up."

"My boys aren't janitors."

"They are today."

"Hell with that. Come on, Scotty, Matt, let's go."

"They're not going until they clean up the mess they made."

Drunk Dad puffed out his chest. "What're you going to do about it?"

Diplomacy, Reed concluded, couldn't always work. "Since they're minors, I'm going to fine you for contributing to their delinquency and for bringing illegal explosives onto the island."

"Bullshit."

He smiled an affable smile. "No shit about it."

"I'm not paying a red cent to some rinky-dink play cop trying to hose me down and harass my boys on our vacation. I said, let's *go!*"

He turned. Reed shifted to block him.

Red-faced, riled up, he shoved Reed.

"Well, we'll add assaulting an officer to that list." Only slightly amazed, Reed dodged a wild swing, then settled the matter by spinning the man around and snapping cuffs on his wrists.

"This is not the way to behave," Reed told the boys as the older one gawked and the younger began to cry. "Sir, you're considerably inebriated," Reed continued as the man struggled and swore—with several in the crowd that gathered taking pictures and videos with the ever-present cell phone. "You're resisting, are now a public nuisance, not to mention showing yourself to be a bad influence on your minor children. Is your mother around?" Reed asked the boys.

The younger one blubbered, "It's our week with Dad."

"Okay. Let's settle all this at the station. Sir, I can perp walk you there, or you can come along quietly."

"I'm going to sue your fucking ass."

"Perp walk it is. You need to come with us, Scotty, Matt." He glanced down at the dog, sitting, waiting. "Let's go, Barney."

By the time he got to CiCi's—he had a dinner invitation—it was after nine, and he wanted a drink like he wanted his next breath.

"Rough one?" she asked him.

"Ups and downs, with the deepest down a couple of kids with cherry bombs scaring the crap out of people, and their drunk, argumentative father, who capped it off by puking in my office from a combination of temper and booze. It wasn't pleasant."

"I'm going to get you a beer, then plate you up a spicy barbecue sandwich that's one of my specialties when I'm not a vegetarian."

"I love you, CiCi."

"Go sit out, drink your beer, and look at the water. Some Ujjayi breathing wouldn't hurt."

The beer helped, and so did the water—the look, scent, sound of it. Maybe the breathing didn't hurt. But Simone stepping out—her hair was kind of coppery lately and right now tied up with a blue bandanna—carrying a plate of barbecue and potato salad smoothed out all the rest.

She offered the plate, tugged on the hair under his cap, bent down to kiss him. "Cherry bombs and drunk vomit."

"Yeah." He gestured to the dog already snoring at his feet. "It wore my deputy out. How are things on the mainland?"

"I bought a dress for my sister's wedding—so did CiCi—and we earned major points by letting Natalie and Mom help pick them out. And shoes. I did the sketches—well, several, but settled on the winner—for Natalie and Harry's wedding topper."

"I'd like to see it. It's happy," he said. "Happy's a good way to counteract drunk vomit."

"I'll get it."

He ate, watched the water, listened to his dog snore.

She brought out her pad, sat on the arm of his chair. "This is the one that speaks to me."

He studied the sketch of a woman—cotton-candy pretty—in what he thought of as a princess dress. All billowy in the skirt, sparkly up top, it suited the bride with the tiara on her upswept blond hair.

The groom wore tails in a deep gray, a long silver tie, and that suited his golden god good looks.

The groom spun the bride into a dance—more billowing from the skirt. And they looked at each other with all that happiness, as if they'd each found the answers to all the questions.

"You need to frame this for her."

"It's a little rough."

"It's not, and I bet she'd really love having it. Sign it, date it, frame it."

"You're right. She would love it. I'll have CiCi mat and frame it. I'm going to do the topper in porcelain, and paint it."

"From the look of the dress and the tails, this says big, formal, fancy wedding."

"Two hundred and seventy-eight—so far—on the invite list. Black-tie apparel for guests. That covers the big and the formal. The rest? As fancy as they can make it."

"Is that what you want? An as-fancy-as-you-can-make-it wedding?"

"I never said I wanted a wedding."

"We'll get to that, down the road a bit. And the three kids we'll never hand cherry bombs and a fricking match."

She felt a flutter in her belly, couldn't decide if it was anxiety or pleasure. "That's a lot of projecting, Chief."

"It's just the way I see it. Unless CiCi changes her mind and takes me as her sex slave. Then the deal's off."

"Of course."

"Before all that, I have to talk you into moving in with me. That can wait, too. We need to build on a studio for you first. I'm working on that."

"You're—what?"

"Not working, working. Summer's too busy for that. I just asked Donna's cousin—you know Eli, he's an architect. I just asked him to draw up some ideas for it."

He drank some beer, and thought how cold beer and spicy barbecue smoothed out a thorny day just fine.

"Of course, if CiCi answers my prayers, I'll just move in here, and we'll kick you out. It would be awkward for everybody otherwise."

He closed his eyes as he spoke. Smoothed out, but, Jesus, he was tired.

She stared out to the horizon, at the glimmer of moonlight on the water between them and the end of the world. "In this fantasy of yours, do I have any input into the design of the potential studio?"

"Sure, that's why Eli's drawing up a few ideas. Then you can look them over, play with them. Plenty of time."

She thought of the sculpture in her studio, and the time she needed to finish it, perfect it, show him. Maybe she should show him now, as it became. The way he'd shown her what could be.

"I think we should—"

She broke off when his phone signaled, and shifted so he could pull it out. She saw the readout: Jacoby.

What could be, she thought as she left him to talk of murder, had to wait.

Hobart hit and hit fast in Ohio, in an upscale suburb outside of Columbus. The target, a popular local newscaster, had received the warnings from the FBI, and had taken them seriously.

He'd never forgotten that night at the DownEast Mall. He'd been twenty-eight, working at the Portland TV station, mostly covering fluff and trying to work his way to hard news. He'd been shopping for a video camera when hell had come.

He'd taken cover, and he'd recorded some of the carnage, with his own shaking voice struggling to describe what he saw, heard, felt.

McMullen had gone one way with her reporter's luck, and Jacob Lansin another. He'd turned the recording over to the police with his still-trembling hands, but when he got out of the mall, he'd found the crew from his station. He'd given them a firsthand, real-time report.

He'd moved up the ranks, and snatched the local anchor job in Columbus when it had come his way. He'd married a Columbus native, the daughter of a wealthy businessman.

He'd achieved fame and fortune.

Patricia's luck came when a woman driving and texting a friend that she'd be late for a lunch date struck Lansin's BMW convertible.

He suffered a wrenched shoulder, broken ankle, and whiplash.

Grateful it hadn't been worse, Lansin took some time off to recover and arranged for in-home physical therapy.

It only took Patricia two days to determine the therapist wore a bouncy brown ponytail, favored T-shirts and jeans, and carted a massage table when she arrived every day at two in the afternoon.

Patricia rented a car of the same make and color as the therapist's and, wearing a brown wig, a simple T-shirt, and jeans, arrived ten minutes early. She angled the massage table to obscure her face.

Lansin, in his ankle cast, sling, and neck brace, checked his security monitor, disengaged his alarm, and opened the door.

"Hey, Roni, you're early."

"Right on time," Patricia told him, and shot him in the chest, adding two head shots when he went down.

She shoved the table inside, snipped off a lock of hair, closed the door, jogged back to the car. All done in under a minute. Since she intended to dump the car at the airport, she didn't care if anyone saw her drive off.

After the dump, she took a cab back to Columbus and bought a second-hand luxury SUV, for cash.

Time for an island holiday, she thought as she stopped long enough to mail Reed what she intended to be his last card.

Over Fourth of July week, visitors flooded onto the island. Hotels, B&Bs, and rentals ran at capacity, and strips of beach became a sea of umbrellas, blankets, and beach chairs.

In the little park off High Street, the band shell rang with patriotic music while kids—and more than a few adults—lined up for face painting, snow cones, and funnel cake.

To beat the heat—and there was plenty of it—people bobbed, swam, floated in the water. Boats glided in and out of the marina, white sails rising, motors humming.

The air smelled of sunscreen, peanut oil fries, sugar, and summer.

Reed worked twelve-hour shifts and realized that, without the little problem of a serial killer, he'd have enjoyed every minute of it.

In the winter, the island held the quiet, peaceful beauty of a snowglobe. In the spring, it bloomed and awakened. But in the summer, it burst bright with sound and color and crowds and clashing music.

Like a daily carnival, he thought.

And with summer, two ferries ran, one disgorging cars and pedestrians at the island dock, while the second loaded up departures and sailed them back into reality.

On the Fourth, as he did every day he could manage it, he watched the ferry dock, watched cars, trucks, campers, people spill off.

Beside him, Simone scanned faces as he did.

"You think she'll come today."

"I think today's the biggest influx of people, and it's a good day to slip through. The ferry operation has people at both docks looking for a lone female. And I've got two deputies down there." He lifted his chin toward the cruiser. "They've spotted a few since June, and all of them checked out. The marina's doing the same with private boats and charters."

"But a lot of people."

"Yeah. On the other hand, she's smart enough to know that we'd look and look hard on the holiday weekend and the Fourth. If I'm her, I wait."

"Like you're waiting for the next card."

"No mail service on the Fourth." He watched the last passenger, a minivan loaded with kids, drive down the ramp. "Barney and I have to go to work."

"You could deputize me."

"Can't afford you." He gave her a kiss. "I'd feel better if you stayed out of the crowds today. You said you and CiCi avoid most of it anyway, and watch the fireworks tonight from the patio. Just do what you always do."

"I'd feel better if you did that with us."

He tapped the CHIEF on his cap.

"With the parade, the park, and the beach activities, the general craziness in the village, she could be anywhere, Reed. She could, God, get you in the crosshairs from a window in the Overlook Hotel."

"She won't come at me that way. She won't. It's personal. She needs to see my face, needs to look in my eyes, and have me look in hers. And she needs to get away with it. Trust me."

"I am." She gripped his hands. "I'll wait for you."

"At CiCi's. Stay there tonight. I'll be there after the fireworks. She's not here yet. Maybe some of CiCi's a little bit psychic's rubbing off, but she's not here yet."

It didn't stop him from searching crowds, picking out women, watching for someone watching him. After the long day, he stood with the crew of volunteer firefighters and watched the sky fill with color, listened to air ringing with blasts like gunfire.

Not yet, he thought as people cheered. But soon.

CHAPTER TWENTY-EIGHT

She came three days later, sliding the secondhand SUV into the line waiting at the mainland dock. Like many who waited, she stepped out of her car to wander.

She'd let her own hair grow to her shoulders, colored it a beachy blond. She'd used self-tanner religiously over the past few weeks, and with careful layers of makeup, she'd achieved a healthy glow. Under big, stylish sunglasses, contacts turned her eyes into bluebells.

And under her breezy blue summer dress—one with short sleeves to hide the scar under her armpit—she wore a fake baby belly filled to simulate a woman at about twenty weeks. On the third finger of her left hand, she sported an impressive wedding set—cubic zirconia, but sparkly enough to pass for real.

She'd sprung for a good mani/pedi, French for class, and carried a Prada summer bag to go with her sandals.

She looked like a polished young pregnant woman of some means.

She spotted the pair of hikers—man and woman—sitting on their packs while they waited to board. Young, too, she thought, and the woman looked hot and tired.

She wandered over, a hand on her fake baby as she'd observed pregnant women did. "Hi. I hope you don't mind if I ask if you know any easy—really easy—hiking trails on Tranquility? My husband's a serious hiker, and when he gets here later in the week, he's going to be all about it. I'm just not up for the serious hikes."

She smiled as she said it, rubbing that bump.

"Sure." The woman answered Patricia's smile. "You can get a map at the information center back there."

"You can get them on the island, too," the man told her. "The ones at the info centers are free, but they have better ones at some of the shops. They don't cost much, I guess."

He got a map out of his pack. "We can show you a couple nice, easy beach hikes. The one out to the lighthouse is a little longer and tougher, but it's worth it."

"Great. Mostly I just want to sit on the beach, read, watch the water, but Brett loves to hike. Where are you coming from?"

She chatted them up. She—Susan "Call me Susie" Breen—had driven up from Cambridge. Her husband—Brett—had been called out of town suddenly on business, but she was happy to have a couple of days to get the cottage, one they'd rented for six wonderful weeks, ready, lay in supplies, have that time to sit and read and watch the water.

They—Marcus Tidings and Leesa Hopp—chatted right back.

"Say, why don't I give you a ride over? I have to pay for the car anyway, and they don't charge for passengers. It would save you the pedestrian fee. Plus I can take you into the village, at least as far as the rental office where I have to pick up my keys."

Grateful, they walked to her car before Patricia realized she'd missed changing plates at the rest stop with the Massachusetts plates on a Suburu. Smiling as she cursed herself for the slip, she came up with a cover story—borrowed her brother's car.

But her friendly hikers didn't notice as she chat, chat, chatted.

She told Leesa to sit in the front with her, so she didn't feel like a taxi driver.

They embarked, a group of three, having hung out at the rail on the trip over.

When Patricia drove off at Tranquility dock, the deputies on ferry duty didn't look twice at the SUV with Ohio plates carrying three passengers and a cargo space full of luggage.

As Patricia stopped at the rental office for her keys and welcome package, Simone used a blowtorch to heat the bronze until it turned gold. She brushed ferric nitrate over Reed's hair, over Barney, over areas she wanted hints of red and gold to shimmer with the bronze.

She'd use silver nitrate on the sword, on the collar she'd given Barney to bring out a silvery-gray patina. The work would take hours—but she considered it an improvement on the ancient method of burying the bronze to oxidize it. And this gave her control, allowed her to highlight, add a kind of movement and life.

She'd worked and studied with patineurs in Florence and in New York to learn the art, the science, the techniques. For this, a piece that had become so intimate to her, she called on all she had, asked herself for more.

When she paused in the work, she walked her studio, drinking water, clearing her mind. And she studied the faces on her shelf. More now. Throughout the finishing of the bronze, she'd taken breaks, worked on those faces.

The last one she'd completed looked back at her with wide, smiling eyes. Trent Woolworth, the boy she'd loved—as a young girl loves. He'd never had a chance to become a man. She'd thought he'd broken her heart, but he'd barely pricked it. She knew that now, and felt for him only regret and grief.

She'd join his face with the others, all the others, and cast them in bronze as she had Reed. Cupric nitrate, she thought, for the subtle and beautiful greens and blues, to mirror the water.

She could do this, would do this, not only because she'd finally found it inside her, but because the man she did love helped her open the rest.

She put on her gloves, turned back to the sculpture of Reed.

Hours later, her shoulders stiff from the final steps of sealing—waxing and buffing—she went down to CiCi's studio.

Through the glass she saw her grandmother at her framing station, so she walked in.

"I wondered if you'd surface."

"So did I, but I— Oh, CiCi, I love it. Reed's house, the lupines like a sea of color, the woods, the *light!* Fairies in the woods, just a hint of them in that dappled shade." She murmured, "And Reed standing on the widow's walk with Barney, with me."

"That's how I see it. I'm going to give this to him—and, as I see it, you— for Christmas. You'll be living with him by then unless my granddaughter's an idiot. Which she's not. I think this would work in the master bedroom."

"It's perfect. You're perfect." She took CiCi's hand. "Can you stop for a minute, come outside?"

"If there's an adult beverage involved, I can."

"That can be arranged."

"Give yourself and Reed a break," CiCi said as they walked out and across to the patio. "Go to his place tonight. You've both been working crazy hours. You're both tense waiting for that next shoe to drop since that last ugly card arrived. Go, crack a bottle of wine, and have a lot of sex."

"I'm on that same path because, you see? I finished him."

CiCi's breath caught—the artist and grandmother felt her heart soar. "Oh, oh, Simone." She walked to the counter where it stood in the late afternoon light. "It has life, a pulse, a soul, and more. Oh, the patina, such light and depth and movement. The detailing, the flow."

She let the tears burning her throat free. "Get me that wine, baby, and a tissue. I'm overwhelmed."

She took a breath, moved around the sculpture as Simone opened a bottle. "Years ago, back in Florence, at your first show, your use of Tish, your *Emergence*, grabbed me just this way, brought me to tears this way. You do beautiful work, Simone, some of it stunning. But this, like *Emergence*, has your heart and soul in every line, curve, angle."

She took the glass, the tissue. "He's magnificent. He breathes. You won't have to tell him you love him when you show him this. Unless he's an idiot. Which he's not."

"I'm ready to tell him."

"Then go do it." CiCi drew Simone close. "Go get your man."

In her beach cottage, Patricia used the second bedroom for weapons—guns and ammo, a night-vision scope, poisons, syringes, knives. Her HQ, she thought. She would put up maps of town, document her target's routines, his close associates. She'd learn where he drank his beer, ate his lunch, who he fucked.

She'd keep the door locked, tell the housekeeper her husband was territorial about his office space. No entry allowed.

She set men's toiletries in the master bathroom, put men's clothes in the master bedroom closet, the dresser. Later in the stay, she'd leave men's shoes here and there and other items carelessly tossed around.

She set out a copy of *What to Expect When You're Expecting*, which she'd dog-eared and marked up in advance. Hiking gear that read male, a bottle of top-shelf gin, which she'd pour out into the sink a bit now and then, her unblended scotch—which she'd drink herself—a couple bottles of fancy wines and craft beers, the food supplies she'd bought at a stop at the market.

Satisfied, she went out for her first stroll through the village.

Easy to mix and meld with groups and crowds, simple to wander into a shop and buy a few trinkets—including a pair of bathing trunks and a Light of Tranquility T-shirt she told the shopkeeper her husband would love.

She spotted Reed within a half hour, holding a dog on a leash while he—from the looks of it—gave a bunch of people some directions.

You've come down low, big-shot detective, she thought.

She didn't follow him directly. She strolled, crossed the street, window-shopped. But she kept an eye on him all the way back to his rinky-dink police station. And considered it a good start.

After Simone's text, Reed decided, for once, he could go home before dark. Maybe the day only seemed quiet after the craziness of the holiday, but it was quiet enough.

He walked Barney toward home. The itch between his shoulder blades had him circling a little, scanning a lot, but he saw nothing and no one that drew his attention.

"Can't let the waiting psych us out, Barney. Take it a day at a time."

Seeing Simone's car parked in front of the house lifted him up. Seeing her sitting on the porch, sipping wine, finished the job.

"You're early."

"Pretty quiet today. The chief of police is taking the night off."

"That's handy. So am I. I've missed nights off with you." She pulled a chew bone out of her pocket. "And you, too, Barney."

"Just sit right there. I'm going to get a cold beer, and we'll sit awhile."

"Actually, I have something to show you." She took his hand. "And things to say," she added as she drew him inside.

She'd found a stand for it at the flea market—knowing he'd appreciate that sentiment, too. It stood in the entryway, a statement, to her mind: He'd protect all within.

And there, the bronze caught the early evening light just as she wanted.

He stared, speechless, and she saw on his face what she'd hoped to see. The stunned wonder changed to something else when he looked at her.

No, she thought, he wasn't an idiot. And still, cautious.

"I . . . I need a second. Or an hour. Or a month. It's hard to take in. I never expected—I don't know why I never expected . . . when I've seen your work."

"It's different when it's you."

"That, yeah, but . . ." He just couldn't wrap his brain around it. "It's— You put Barney in it."

"I thought at first I'd use a woman, or a child. And then I watched you with him, him with you, saw how his trust in you has changed his life, his world. Like mine for you has changed mine."

"It's the most amazing thing. You made me look—"

"Exactly as you are," she interrupted. "Every hour I spent on this work showed me more and more of who you are. More of who I am. And we are. I didn't fall in love with you during the work."

She laid a hand on his heart. "You can give Barney some credit for when I did, how I fell when I saw you, the first time with him, washing that poor, skinny, scared dog, laughing when he soaked you and licked at your face. I fell realizing you had that inside you."

He closed his hand over hers. "Say it, okay? I don't care if he gets the credit. I'll buy him caviar Milk-Bones. But I really want you to look at me, Simone, look at me and say the words."

"This is who you are to me." She touched the sculpture. "This is who you are," she repeated, pressing her other hand on his heart. "This is the man I love. You're who I love."

He lifted her to her toes, then an inch higher, capturing her mouth as she hung suspended, holding it as he brought her down. "Don't ever stop."

"I cast your heart, and mine, together in bronze. That's forever." She gripped him tight, pressed her face to his shoulder. "You waited for me. You waited until I could tell you."

"Waiting's over." He took her mouth again, circled her toward the stairs. "Come with me. Be with me. I need—"

His phone went off. "Fuck. Just fuck."

He yanked it out. "Yeah, yeah, it better be—" His eyes went flat, cold. "Where. Anybody hurt? Okay. I'm on my way. Sorry. Damn it."

"I'll come with you."

"No, no, cop business."

"What cop business?"

"Somebody shot through the window of a cabin up on Forest Hill."

"Oh my God."

"Nobody's hurt. Cecil's already there, but . . . I need to go."

"Be careful."

"Probably some asshole trying to shoot a deer, and probably long gone. Let's go, Barney. I'll be back." He caught Simone's face in his hands, kissed her.

When Reed arrived at the cabin, one neatly tucked into the inland woods, Cecil walked out.

"Hey, Chief. I heard the dispatch go out when I was on my way home, so I radioed Donna I'd take it, since I was close."

"What've we got?"

"Family from Augusta renting the cabin for a week—couple and two kids. They're having some ice cream, talking about going for a walk, and hear a shot—a sort of *pop*—and breaking glass. This window here."

He walked Reed over to examine a side window with a hole and radiating cracks from it in the glass.

"Hit a lamp inside, too," Cecil told him. "The wife grabbed the kids up, kept them down and away from the windows. The husband called nine-one-one. He looked around out here some after, but didn't see anything."

Reed examined the damaged window, turned to study the trees and the shadows deepening in them with dusk.

Inside, he spent some time soothing nerves and tempers before hunkering down by the broken lamp. Avoiding the shards from the globe, he pulled out a penlight, shined it under a chair.

And came up with a BB.

While he soothed, reassured, apologized to the frazzled family, Patricia watched the cabin through field glasses. She'd noted Reed's response time, the make, color, tags of his car for future reference. When he stepped out again, she lifted the BB rifle onto her shoulders, softly said, "Bang!" and laughed.

"No island kid's stupid enough to shoot a BB gun like that, Chief. It has to be some dumb-shit summer kid."

"We're going to go by all the cabins and cottages in this area, see if we can find a dumb-shit. I appreciate the overtime, Cecil."

"Aw, that's no problem."

They split up to handle it, but Reed's thoughts kept circling. A small cabin, he thought, four people inside. But the pellet hits in an area no one's near at that time. And bull's-eyes a lamp.

Maybe a dumb-shit. Maybe not so dumb.

For the next week, Reed dealt with a rash of petty vandalism. Spray-painted obscenities on the window of the Sunrise, flowerpots stolen right off the porch of the mayor's house, three cars keyed while their owners enjoyed dinner at the Water's Edge, all four tires of another slashed as it sat in front of a rental overlooking the south inlet.

He sat in the mayor's office as Hildy unloaded.

"You have to put a stop to this, Reed. Every damn day it's something else, and it's not the usual summer problems. I'm spending most of my time on the phone dealing with complaints. If this keeps up, it's going to cost us revenue and damage our reputation. Dobson's making noises about writing up a petition to have you removed as chief. You need to handle this."

"We're doing full-island loop patrols, on foot, in cruisers. I added night patrols. We're on twenty-four hours."

"And still can't catch some nasty kids."

"If we were dealing with nasty kids, we would have. This is too smart for that." He rose, went to the map on her wall, tapped various points. "Every sector's had a hit of some kind. That means whoever's doing it needs to have a car or bike. And the time frames are all over the clock."

"You think this isn't some nasty, bored kid or kids, but a deliberate attempt to undermine the island?"

"Something like that. I'm going to shut it down, Mayor. This is my home, too."

As Reed walked back to the station, he couldn't blame Hildy for the anger. He had plenty of his own. He couldn't blame her for the shaky faith in him, as he believed that was one of the purposes of the vandalism.

Hit every point of the island, he thought, see how he responded, how long it took, where he went, how he got there. Not bored kids, he thought. Hobart, and she was stalking him.

He'd checked the rental offices, the B&Bs, the hotel. No single check-ins. But she'd found a way around that because he knew she was on the island. And watching him.

He ran through the content of the last card—number four. A sympathy card this time, why be subtle?

Enjoying the summer, asshole? Soak up those rays because you're going to spend a lot of time in the cold and dark. I won't come to your funeral, though all those tears would be delicious! But I'll come back, and spit on your fucking grave.

My luck's in. Yours is running out. It's time to die.

XXOO, Patricia

Pretty direct, he thought, but what had interested him more had been the scrawling handwriting, and the pressure of the pen on the card. She'd written this one while riding hard on emotion, and she hadn't been as clever with the rental car she'd used for her last kill. Not when they'd tracked it with GPS within an hour of that kill. He had to leave it to the feds to track down if she'd taken a cab or bus from the airport, rented another car, bought one. Maybe she'd already had one waiting in the lot.

But whatever she'd driven out of Ohio, she'd driven onto the ferry in Portland and onto the island.

Because she was here.

Patricia opened the door to the twice-a-week housekeeper in a robe, her wet hair slicked back. "Oh my! We overslept."

"I can come back."

"No, no, please. It's fine. We wouldn't want to throw you off schedule. My husband's still in the shower, but maybe you can start in the loft? He told me to tell you thanks for offering to at least vacuum in his office, but it's fine." She rolled her eyes. "I swear he thinks about his work like state secrets or whatever. I'm going to go get dressed. You're welcome to make yourself some coffee. I sure miss being allowed that one cup a day."

She patted her belly as she crossed the living area to the master. She opened the door to let the sound of the shower she'd left running spill out before she closed it again.

As she dressed—capris and a pink T-shirt, fancy hiking boots—she held a conversation with no one, added some laughter, opened and closed drawers, the closet door.

She inspected the room—bed tumbled on both sides—a spy thriller and a nearly empty glass of wine on one nightstand, a historical romance and teacup on the other. A man's belt slung over the back of a chair. Damp towels in the bathroom—two toothbrushes—bristles damp. Male and female toiletries.

Satisfied, she opened the door, looked back over her shoulders. "Yes, Brett, I'm coming! Go ahead. We're going for a walk, Kaylee," she called out to the housekeeper. "You can do the bedroom anytime."

"Have fun!"

"Oh, we will. We love it here. I'm just getting my water bottle and pack, honey. Men," she said for the benefit of the housekeeper in the loft above. "So impatient."

She left by the opposite door, and decided she'd take a stroll to the house a little chatter and gossip had revealed belonged to the chief of police.

A long hike for a pregnant woman, she thought with a smirk. But she felt up to it.

For the next few days, the vandalism eased off, making most conclude the troublemakers' vacation had ended, and they'd gone off-island.

Reed didn't buy it.

"She's still here." Reed drank a Coke on CiCi's patio while the sun set like glory at water's edge. "She's smart enough to know screwing around could get her caught with the extra patrols, but she's still getting the rhythm."

He turned to them, these women he loved. "You could do me a big favor, get on the ferry in the morning, take a trip somewhere."

"She won't leave you," CiCi said. "I won't leave either one of you. Ask for something else."

"If you were off somewhere," he persisted, "Florence or New York—"

"Reed," Simone interrupted.

"Damn it, staying just means I have to worry about you. She's gearing up. It's no goddamn coincidence she's here—and she's here—when we're coming up on the thirteenth anniversary of DownEast. She slipped it in the card.

My luck's running out, hers is coming in. Unlucky thirteen. It's less than a week, and I don't need the two of you scattering my focus out of sheer, wrong-headed, *female* stubbornness.

"You're in my way." He didn't shout, and his deliberate tone added edgy barbs to every word. "So get out of it and let me do my goddamn job."

"That's not going to work, either," CiCi said, cool and calm. "Trying to pick a fight, make us mad isn't going to change a thing. But damn good try."

"Look, this isn't—"

"I hid before," Simone interrupted.

"Bullshit!" Now he did shout, and had Barney bellying under a table. "Don't start that bullshit with me."

"I did hide. I'm not saying it wasn't the right thing to do because it was. But it's not the right thing now, and it would strip away what it took me years to build back up again."

"Simone." At wits' end, he pulled off his cap, dragged a hand through his hair. "I swore I'd keep you and CiCi safe."

"You said you want to start a life with me. This is our life. You think she'll try to . . . do this on the twenty-second?"

He'd try calm reason, again. "I think that makes a circle for her, yeah. I think she knows damn well you and I are together, and if she can take me out, she'll come for you. Not you first," he said. "You're still higher on the chain than me. And she'll want to eliminate the biggest threat. I'm the cop with a gun, you're not. If the two of you went off-island until after the twenty-second, I wouldn't have to factor your safety into the mix."

"For me—and CiCi—not to be safe means she'd have eliminated you. You won't let that happen. You won't let that happen," Simone repeated, rising and moving to him, "because you know if she kills you, she'll kill me. Maybe not now, but sooner or later, and you won't let her. I believe that, trust that, absolutely.

"Besides." She framed his frustrated face with her hands. "I have too much to do to go off to Florence or New York or anywhere else. I have work, and it occurs to me the twenty-third's a good time for me to move in with you. I have a lot to pack up."

He dropped his forehead to hers. "That's a damn sneak attack."

"The twenty-third, Reed, because you'll have ended this. I'm moving in. CiCi, you'll come to dinner."

"I'll bring champagne."

"I'll need to keep my studio here until Reed and I finalize the design and plans for my workspace at . . . our house."

"It's always here for you, my clever, clever girl."

"That day, the twenty-third, it's going to be a symbol for us," she told him. "A reminder that whatever terrible things happen, we're together."

"I think this calls for a big pitcher of sangria."

Reed shook his head at CiCi. "I can't. I've got to get back. Stay here," he told Simone. "I'll be back as soon as I can. Come on, Barney, we're not going to get anywhere with these two. Cast in the same damn mold."

"That's why you love us," CiCi called as Reed walked out. "I'm proud of you, Simone."

"I'm terrified."

"Me, too."

As Reed completed another patrol, Patricia sat in her war room, sipping a gin and tonic—heavier on the gin as time passed. It felt like a waste to pour it down the sink.

And the gin made a nice change of pace from scotch.

A couple of drinks—or three—helped her sleep. How was she supposed to sleep without a little help when her mind was so full, so busy?

It wasn't like her father—she didn't get drunk, did she? It wasn't like her mother. She wasn't using the booze to wash down pills.

She just needed a little help to calm her mind. Nothing wrong with that.

So, sipping gin, she studied her maps, her time lines, the photos taken with her phone.

The fact that two of her top targets were lovebirds both infuriated and delighted her. They didn't deserve even an hour of happiness. But then again, she would slit their happiness at the throat and watch it bleed dry. And with a little more time—she still had a little more time—to observe the bitch, maybe she'd kill two birds with one stone.

On the other hand, she thought as she rose to pace, she'd always planned to take out the bitch who'd called the cops last. She still had a half dozen targets on her board, leading up to the cunt cop who'd killed JJ, then finishing it off with the interfering little bitch who'd hidden like a coward.

She'd come this far following the plan, she assured herself, and had the cops and FBI running in circles. She should stick with the plan. If JJ had stuck with the plan . . .

It hadn't been his fault, she thought, rapping a restless fist on her thigh as she paced and sipped, paced and sipped. Simone Knox killed JJ, and she wouldn't forget it.

So, maybe if—and only if—the opportunity fell into her lap, she'd take the bitch out early. Otherwise.

She picked up her gun, aimed it at Reed's picture. "It's just you and me, asshole. And taking you out? Yeah, that's going to break your little whore's heart—and the cunt cop's, too. Delicious tears. That works for me."

CHAPTER TWENTY-NINE

Sometimes the gin and tonic, the pacing, the planning, didn't work. To relax, to calm the increasing busyness of her mind, Patricia indulged in her favorite late-night pastime.

In the beach cottage she'd grown to hate—and planned to burn to the ground before she left the island—with the doors locked, curtains drawn, Patricia switched to scotch on the rocks and watched her video.

It enthralled and entertained her, no matter how often she viewed it.

She looked good! Damn good. Long gone was the fat girl with pimples and bad hair who'd sat in her room watching TV and learning how to hack.

In fact, she looked amazing, trim and fit in the camera-friendly red dress she'd chosen. "Body conscious" they called it, she mused as she started it over from the beginning. Flawless makeup, but *her*. No contacts to change eye color, no appliances, no wig.

All Patricia.

She looked better than that hack reporter, that's for sure. Younger, stronger, and damn it, prettier, too. Maybe she should have taken the time to press out the suit McMullen wore—it looked like she'd—ha ha!—slept in it.

But it didn't matter. Patricia Hobart was the star, just as she was meant to be.

Gone was the girl who'd dreamed of being important, who'd curled up in the dark and imagined killing the boy who'd dubbed her Patty the Porker, the girls who'd stolen her panties and pinned them to the elephant, her mother, her grandparents, the perfect families she saw in the mall.

Dreaming, dreaming of killing all of them, all of them.

All of them.

Crunching on sour cream and onion chips (a well-earned reward, just this *one* time), she listened to herself. How clearly she told her story, told the world how mistreated and abused she'd been. Her parents, her grandparents, teachers, fucking bullying kids. She laughed, as she always did, when she got to the part about the asshole kid taking that header off the bike she'd rigged, busting up his face.

She wished, how she wished, he'd broken his neck.

See how smart she'd been? She'd been born smarter than anyone else. The video proved it.

And look how fascinated McMullen looked. Hear that awe in her voice? She'd known she'd been outclassed. She understood what kind of brains, what kind of *will*, it took to accomplish all Patricia Hobart had accomplished.

Too bad McMullen had started babbling, had shown herself to be what she'd always been. Just another opportunist looking to get rich, to get in front of the cameras and brag.

"Too bad you pissed me off," Patricia muttered, pouring another finger of scotch before she fast-forwarded to the kill.

Her only regret there? She hadn't thought to step out, move into camera range. She'd have enjoyed watching herself raise the gun and fire. But McMullen made up for it, made her laugh again.

"There it is, shocked face, and bang, bang, bang." Howling with laughter, she grabbed more chips. "Talk about a ratings bonanza! But not for you."

No, not for you, she thought as she went back, chose the clip. One where *she* was the star, one where she told the frigging world that before her fifteenth birthday, she'd had the brains, the skills, the freaking vision to begin to plan a mass shooting the size and scope of DownEast.

She studied it again, and once again, nodding, nodding, pleased with her own clarity, approving what she thought of as the stunned admiration on McMullen's face.

There, only a scant mile and a quarter from Reed's home, she hacked into some dumb-shit in Nashville's Facebook account, attached the video to his wall.

Just the start, she thought, and decided she deserved another drink. After the twenty-second, after she—ha ha again—shot the sheriff, she'd send another clip to the FB fucking I.

With satisfaction, she looked up at her wall of targets, pointed a finger.

"Then, Chaz Four-Eyes Bergman, you're up." She lifted the scotch to toast him. "New York, here I come."

She started the video over, watched it all again.

"I'm so glad you came." In her studio, Simone clung to Mi. "I wish you didn't have to go so soon. One day isn't enough."

"I'll see you at Nari's wedding in September. You and CiCi. You'll bring Reed."

"I will. Then you'll come for Nat's wedding in October."

"Absolutely. And I'll be back in December for CiCi's big bash. A one, two, three. But . . . Come with me, Sim—I have to ask again. You and CiCi come back to Boston with me for a few days."

"You know why I can't. Reed shouldn't have asked you to try to persuade me."

"He loves you. I love you."

"I know. It's why he asked, and why you came. I love him, so I can't go. I love you, so you have to."

"That wouldn't make me, but he made me swear I'd be on that ferry back to the mainland with or without you." In frustration, Mi jammed her hands in her pockets. "I shouldn't have given him my word. Tomorrow's the twenty-second. Why wasn't it enough for her, Sim? All that death her brother caused wasn't enough."

"It was always her underneath it all. I think he was just a defective weapon. Reed says she's devolving, making mistakes. Jesus, Mi, she put that video clip on Facebook. She needed attention so much, she risked hacking an account and putting it out there."

"But they haven't traced the hack yet."

"They will. But Reed's going to stop her whether they trace it or not."

"I've never known you to believe in anyone but CiCi the way you do him."

"And you."

"Thirteen years," Mi said with a sigh, turning to the shelves holding the faces of the lost. "What you're doing here matters so much. People forget, then there's another nightmare followed by another. And still, after the grief and outrage, people forget. No one can forget when they look at what you're doing."

"I tried to forget."

"But you never did. And Tiffany?" Carefully, Mi took down the bust. "Still right here."

"To remind me that everyone who survived July twenty-second carries the scars. But we survived, Mi. We can remember those who didn't, and still treasure the life we have. Tiffany didn't intend to give me the gift of that insight, but she did. So I'll keep her face in my studio as a thank-you."

Mi replaced the bust. "You haven't done Tish."

"I want to do her last. She means more to me than anyone else, so I need to finish it with her."

"I still miss her. Will you do me a favor? No, I'm not going to push you to leave," Mi said when Simone tensed. "When you're ready to start Tish's bust, will you let me come? I know you don't like anyone in your space when you're working, but I'd like to be here."

"I can do better. When I'm ready, you'll help me. We'll do it together."

"You always said as an artist I made a good scientist."

"So true." Simone smiled. "But we'll do it together. Now I'm kicking you out so you don't miss the ferry."

"If anything happens to you—"

"Positive thoughts." She took Mi's hand, led her out.

"Maybe she's not here, not on the island. That's a positive negative."

CiCi came in from her studio as they walked down the stairs. "It's nearly sunset. How about drinks to toast day's end?"

"Mi has to go."

"I could stay for a drink."

"And miss the ferry."

"I'll take the next one."

"You're stalling," Simone said. "You gave your word."

"I shouldn't have." Annoyed with herself, Mi picked up her purse. She'd caught the first available plane after Reed's call, hadn't even packed a bag. Now she sighed. "He thought I'd just phone you, and he put the hammer down on me when I said I was coming. He's sneaky and smart. I really like him, Simone. I really like him."

"Me, too. You'll have more time to get to know him when you come back. We'll have time to show you the house—and by then, finalized plans for my studio. More time," she added as she walked Mi to the door.

"I want you to text me tomorrow. Every hour."

"If that's what it takes."

"We're going to look out for each other." CiCi kissed Mi goodbye. "You come back soon."

"I feel like I'm abandoning you," Mi said as Simone walked her to the car she'd rented in Portland.

"You're not. You're trusting me. This island's always given me shelter when I needed it. That's not going to change. Text me when you land in Boston."

"And tomorrow—every hour on the hour, Sim."

"I promise."

Simone watched her drive off, turned back to the house. She caught the movement, stopped, saw the woman walking along the quiet road hesitate.

"Can I help you?" Simone asked.

"Oh no. Well, I'm sorry. I was just admiring the house. It's so beautiful. So unique."

The woman laid a hand on the swell of a baby bump, adjusted her sunglasses.

"I'm being nosy," she said with a sheepish smile. "I heard in the village a famous artist lives here, and I wanted to see it from up here. I've seen it from the beach. Are you a famous artist? CiCi Lennon, the lady in the gallery said."

It happened several times a summer—an off-islander wandering by, often taking photos of the house, and hoping to catch a glimpse of CiCi Lennon.

So Simone smiled. "My grandmother."

Blond hair, Simone noted, with a floppy-brimmed sun hat over it. A backpack, expensive hiking shoes, a pink T-shirt that read: BUN IN THE OVEN, and well-toned, athletic legs in mid-thigh khaki shorts.

"I bet my husband will know her work—Brett's the art buff. I can't wait to tell him. We're here on vacation for a few weeks, from Columbus."

No, Simone thought, because there was too much Maine in the voice for Ohio. Columbus, where another survivor had been shot—and the postmark on the last card.

"I hope you're enjoying your stay." Simone took a step back toward the house. She saw it now, despite the dark glasses, the hat, the mound of belly. She saw it in the jawline, the profile, the shape of the ears.

She knew faces.

"Oh, so much. It's our pre-baby vacation! Do you live here, too?"

"The island's my home." Another step back, another, a reach behind for the doorknob.

She knew faces, she thought again, and saw the change. In the flash of a moment, they recognized each other.

She bolted inside as Patricia dragged at her pack. She locked the door, leaped toward a stunned CiCi.

"Run," she said.

Reed briefed his men again, gave his thanks to the pair of FBI agents Jacoby had sent him. Then he went out to walk the village, the beach. He intended to walk home—keeping visible. Maybe, just maybe, he'd draw Hobart out, he thought.

He saw Bess Trix through the glass door of Island Rentals, decided to give that another shot.

"Chief, Barney." She shook her head. "The answer's the same as always. And look, Kaylee can back that up. She does a lot of the cottages and cabins, and along with Hester, supervises the rest of the housekeeping crew."

"Okay, let's try this. Have you had anyone—eliminate families, people with kids—anyone who strikes you as strange? Or that one of the crew's told you about that strikes them?"

Kaylee rolled her eyes, bent down to pet Barney. "Chief, if I start on the strange with summer people, we'd be here till next Tuesday. There's the four friends out in Windsurf who pay for three times a week, and I know damn well are swapping partners about as often."

"Oh now, Kaylee."

"It's the God's truth, Bess. You can ask Hester, we clean that one together." She wound the tip of her braid around her finger as she got into the gossip. "Then there's the couple easily going on eighty who want daily and go through a bottle of vodka between them every twenty-four. There's the guy who keeps the second bedroom locked up, and the shades pulled on the windows. The wife says it's his office, and I have to wonder what kind of work a man does that has him lock everything up."

"He keeps the door locked to that bedroom?"

"Well now, Chief, you've got an off-limits room in your place."

"I don't lock the door."

"I guess you're more trusting I won't—or Hester, either—go poking in."

"But he locks the door," Reed repeated.

"He does, and works a lot, it seems. That doesn't stop him from going through a goodly amount of scotch and gin—expensive stuff. Wine and beer on top of it."

"Is he on his own?"

"With his wife. And I'm going to say he's got a nice-looking young wife, too, but they haven't cuddled up—if you get me—since they got here. The person who changes your sheets knows."

"Kaylee."

"Well, he's asking about strange, Bess, and that's strange. Makes you wonder how the wife got pregnant in the first place. He tosses clean clothes in the hamper, which is better than the group at the—"

"Let's stick with the couple in— Where's the pregnant woman and the secretive husband?"

"Oh, that's the Serenity. It's tucked back in there. Got nice views from the deck off the loft, but it's a walk to the beaches and the village."

"Some want more quiet and privacy," Bess pointed out.

"Some do. He likes hiking, and doesn't he make that poor woman go with him? And if he's not dragging her off to hike, he's closed up in his office. At least on the days I clean."

"What's he look like?" Reed asked her.

"I . . ." She wound the tip of her braid around her finger again, frowned. "Well, I couldn't say, now that you ask. I haven't laid eyes on him."

Every muscle in Reed's back tensed. "You've never actually seen him?"

"I have to say I haven't, since you ask. I guess that's strange, too. He's been in the shower or the bedroom or that other bedroom whenever I've come by. Then they head out for a hike. I always start that place in the loft. And I'm done before they get back."

"Pull up the booking," he told Bess. "Have you met him?" he asked her.

"I don't think so. He made the booking online. If I remember right, she picked up the keys and package because he'd been delayed a couple days. I've seen her around, but . . . Here it is. Brett and Susan Breen, Cambridge, Mass."

"Well now, that's strange, too," Kaylee said. "Their car, a nice silver SUV, has Ohio plates."

"Make, model, year," Reed demanded.

"How'm I to know?"

"I don't know the year," Bess put in. "But it's a Lincoln. My brother has one. I saw it when she came in. It's silver, like Kaylee said, and it's pretty new, I'd say."

"Describe her," Reed snapped at Kaylee.

"Ah, ah, she's young and pretty in a made-up sort of way. I've never seen her not made-up even with her hair still wet from the shower. Can't be more than around twenty-six or so. Blond hair, and I guess about my height. I think her eyes are blue, but I haven't seen that much of her, either. Like I said, they go out when I'm there. She's pregnant, that's a fact."

Not necessarily, Reed thought.

He yanked out a card. "Call this number, tell Special Agent Jacoby I need a full run on those names."

"The FBI?"

"Now."

He rushed out, yanked out his radio. "Matty, I might have something. I want you and Cecil to meet me at the Serenity beach rental. Don't approach. Just watch. I'm getting my car, and I'm on my way."

He beat them there. No car in the drive, he noted, no lights on in the encroaching dusk. He didn't leash the dog as he circled the house. If trouble came, he wanted Barney to be able to run.

Through the windows he studied the great room, the open living, kitchen, dining areas. A pair of men's hiking boots—from the size of them—stood by the door. Funny, he thought. A man who hiked routinely ought to put more wear on his boots. Those looked straight out of the shoebox.

A single plate, a single glass, sat on the counter by the sink.

He tried the door—locked.

He walked to the bedroom windows. Another solo glass—one side of the bed, and the pillows propped up on only one side. A single towel hanging over the doors of the shower, he noted. The door from the bedroom onto a small deck, also locked.

He walked down to the master bath windows—locked—but through them he saw makeup, a lot of it, scattered on the vanity counter—double sinks—with men's toiletries shoved in a pile on the opposite side.

"You put on a good show, Patricia, but not good enough."

He tried the back door before rounding the house to the second bedroom windows. He considered the drawn blackout shades, gave the windows a try, found them locked.

As he reached in his pocket for his penknife, he heard his deputies pull up. "Get out a BOLO on a Lincoln SUV, silver," he ordered. "Ohio plates. And a blond female, mid-twenties, she'll look pregnant. Go on around front and do that."

Matty eyed him, eyed the shaded windows. "Are you planning to jimmy that window, Chief?"

"Around front, Deputy."

She took out a hefty multi-tool. "This will do the job better and faster than that measly penknife you carry. Is the looks-pregnant Hobart?"

"We're going to find out." Reed took the multi-tool.

"Oh, shit. We're going to break and enter?"

Without glancing back at Cecil, Reed worked on the window. "Get that BOLO in. If I'm wrong about this, we're going to owe a pregnant woman and her paranoid husband an apology. If I'm not, I'm going to be doing a lot of dancing around probable cause."

"Not unless you're sloppy with the jimmying. That window was unlocked when we got here," Matty said easily. "And the shade open just enough to see in. Nothing to see? No harm."

Reed eased the window open a couple inches, pushed up the shade.

"My turn for holy shit," Matty said as she peered in with him.

"Cecil! Suspect as described is Patricia Hobart. She's armed and dangerous. I want the ferry shut down."

"Shut down?"

"It doesn't leave the island again until I clear it. Matty, I want a three-man team sitting on this house—out of sight. Nick, Cecil, and . . . Lorraine's solid. Get that started. The rest of us, with our FBI friends, are going to start a manhunt."

He pulled out his radio to begin coordinating when his phone rang.

"Simone, I need you to—"

"She's here, at CiCi's." The voice breathless with fear turned his blood to ice. "I saw her—she's blond, wearing a fake pregnancy belly. She's—"

He heard wind, the *whoosh* of water, and the breathless fear in her voice. "Where are you?"

"Running. The beach, the rocks. I heard glass break, but she hasn't come out yet. You need to hurry."

"Take cover, stay down, stay quiet. She's at CiCi's," he said as he ran for his car. "I want everybody to move in there. Nick and Lorraine out here, on this house, in case she slips through. Shut down the fucking ferry."

As if he sensed urgency and trouble, Barney leaped through the open passenger window, but for once, didn't stick his head back out.

CiCi nearly stumbled when they reached the beach.

"You're faster. Go, baby. Go."

"Save your breath. We just have to get to the rocks, get behind them." She risked a glance behind. "She'll think we're in the house. She'll have to look through the house first."

Unless she looks out the big windows. Simone gripped the kitchen knife she'd grabbed on the run out. Run, she thought, hide. And when there was no choice, fight.

They reached the rocks, crouched down behind them. Water soaked through shoes, over ankles and calves; spray buffeted and chilled.

"Reed's coming."

"I know, baby." Winded, CiCi struggled to find calming breaths. "You got us out safe, and he's coming. Tide's coming in."

"We're strong swimmers. And we may need to swim. She might see our footprints on the beach."

Calmer now, determined to stay that way, CiCi shook her head. "It's getting dark, that'll make them harder to spot. If she sees them, if she starts down, I want you to swim out, swim toward the village. Now you listen," she said when Simone shook her head. "I've lived my life, and done more than most with it. You do what I tell you."

"We sink or swim together." Simone risked a peek over the rocks, ducked down again. "She's on the patio. Keep close to the rocks. The sun's gone down, and the moon's not up yet. She can't see us."

Knee-deep now, with the tug and pull of the surf dragging at them.

Reed saw the SUV a quarter mile from CiCi's, took a turn at a speed that had his tires screaming nearly as loud as his sirens.

Hear that, Patricia? I'm coming for you.

She heard them, but she'd already started down the steps to the beach. Nine-one-one, bitch, she thought on a quick slice of panic. Full fucking circle. She considered making a run—maybe she could get to her car—but odds were against it.

Maybe she shouldn't have had that drink before she walked down to the old hippie freak of an artist's house, she could admit that. And maybe she shouldn't have stood there watching that bitch and her Asian friend. The way they'd hugged and kissed disgusted her. Lesbians, no question.

She shouldn't have started talking to Simone fucking Knox, shouldn't have moved in that close, but she'd gotten caught up.

So close, so close. Bang, bang, you're dead.

Gone off half-cocked, she thought, just like JJ.

No point worrying about that now. She just had to be smart, as always, and she'd finish this just a little ahead of schedule.

As the light dimmed, she edged back toward the rise. It would conceal her until the cops—let Quartermaine be one of them—got at least halfway down the steps. She'd take them out, every last one of the half-assed island cops.

Take them out, she thought, and unhooked the damp fake belly for more mobility, use the dark for cover, and get to the water. She'd swim to the marina, steal a boat.

Pull in somewhere down the coast, jack a car. She'd need to get into one of her bank boxes for cash and IDs, another weapon, but she'd figure it out.

She always figured it out.

And she would come back one day for the bitch who'd caused this god-damn bullshit. Who'd caused it all.

She considered the rocks, wondered if she could make it before the cops came. Wondered if the bitch and the old hippie freak were hiding there.

She gathered to sprint, heard the sirens cut off.

"I need to look again," Simone whispered. "I need to see."

"She had to hear the sirens. She has to know Reed's coming."

"I need to see."

Simone eased up, strained to see through the encroaching dark. No moon yet, no stars. That in-between slice between night and day.

Then she saw him, stepping onto the patio, gun drawn and sweeping right, left, right again. Her breath came out on a wave of relief, then stopped again when she saw the movement below the house.

"Damn it, what's happening?" CiCi edged up beside her. "Thank the gods and goddesses, there's our hero."

"He can't see her. He's coming down for us, and he can't see her."

"What are you doing? Simone, for God's sake—"

Simone dragged herself onto the rocks, kicked off her shoes as the surf tried to pull her back. She made it to her knees and shouted for him.

It happened fast, though he'd relive it countless times in slow motion. He heard her, over the *whoosh* of the water, saw Simone, the silhouette of her kneeling on the rocks. Even as she waved her arms, pointed, Barney exploded with happy barks, and raced down the beach steps.

At the base, Barney looked right, went into his protective crouch, and quivered.

Patricia stepped out and swung left to take her shot.

Reed took his first. Hers grazed his shoulder, just above the scar. He put three in her, center mass.

He kept his weapon trained on her as he continued down, kicked her gun away from where it had fallen out of her hand.

Conscious, breath coming in pants, she stared at him out of blue eyes glazed with pain and fury.

"Don't you die on me, Patricia. Call for an ambulance!" he shouted as his deputies poured out onto the patio, and more came from the north side of the beach as ordered. "Suspect's down. She's down. I want a couple of you to help get Simone and CiCi in the house so they can get warm, get dry."

"Chief." Matty stopped beside him as he knelt down, applying pressure to Patricia's chest wounds. "You're shot."

"Not really. I know how that feels. She just nicked me. Thanks to my woman and my fucking moron of a dog, she just nicked me. Keep breathing, Patricia. I want to think of you doing a whole bunch of consecutive lifetimes in a cell. Keep breathing."

"Reed."

He glanced up at Simone and CiCi, both pale, their eyes too dark, both shaking.

"I need you to go on up, get on dry clothes. When you can, you're both going to give statements to Matty and Leon. Separately. I'll be there as soon as I can. There's nothing to worry about now."

He wanted to grab them both, hold them both, but not with his hands covered in blood.

"She shot you. She—"

"You're going to make me say it. It's just a flesh wound. I'm okay. CiCi needs to get warm and dry. Take Barney, would you? He's a little shaken up, too."

"The ambulance is here." Cecil rushed down. "They're heading down now."

"Good. Cecil, I want you to unclip my holster, take my weapon until we have all the statements. Matty's in charge until this is cleared."

"No, sir, Chief."

"Cecil, that's how it's done."

"I won't do it. You can fire me, but I won't do it."

"He'll have to fire me, too," Matty put in. "And the rest of us, because none of us are doing that."

"Ah, well." Reed straightened, stepping back as the paramedics took over.

CHAPTER THIRTY

Though Matty corroborated Simone's eyewitness account, as she'd been ten steps behind Reed, he gave his statement to Leon.

"I'm going to ask you to take my weapon."

"Nope."

"Deputy Wendall, I'm going to ask you to take the weapon I fired, so we keep the chain of evidence clean. I'm not asking you to take over, just to take the weapon, bag it, seal it, label it. I've got a backup in an ankle holster, and have had since Memorial Day."

Leon considered, rubbed his chin. "Okay then. You get that arm fixed up, Chief."

Reed gave his statement to the feds while one of the island doctors stitched him up right in CiCi's kitchen.

Shutting down the ferry brought Mi back, so the three women sat together, refusing to budge while the crime scene work went on around them.

Jacoby came in, sat across from him. "Tranquility Island, huh?"

Reed had to smile. "Usually. What's the word on Hobart's condition?"

"They airlifted her to Portland. Your clinic's not equipped for wounds that severe. She's in surgery. I asked your former partner to work with us on that side of the water. She'd like to hear from you when you have a chance, and wanted me to tell you she'll contact your family, let them know you're okay."

"You're okay, for a fed. My deputy Leon Wendall has my weapon—sealed and labeled. Three shots fired from it. Do you want me to run it through for you?"

"No, I've got it. We're working on the rental cottage, and the car. If she makes it to trial, we've got everything we need. Unless she's got another stash, it looks like she was running low on IDs. Only a couple left at that cottage. It's clear her control's deteriorated since you shot her. The first time. We'll talk again, but I want to say . . ." She rose, held out a hand. "It's been a pleasure working with you, Chief."

"A pleasure for me, too, Special Agent."

Since Matty wouldn't take over, Reed coordinated his deputies, talked to the mayor when she raced up in a frilly pink tank and a pair of pajama bottoms with starfish all over them. He dealt with the publisher of the *Tranquility Bulletin*.

He'd need to make an official statement, and do more dealing with the reporters flooding in from the mainland, but that would wait.

Since Essie had reassured his family, he'd follow up with all of them just a little later.

Leaving the rest for now, Reed walked over to sit on the coffee table across from Simone, CiCi, Mi. "How're you doing?"

He put a hand on CiCi's knee first.

"I'll be better when I can have a couple tokes, but I'm waiting on that until the cops clear out so I don't embarrass the chief of police."

"I appreciate it. I'm sorry I wasn't faster. Sorry I didn't find her before she—"

"Shut up. Shut up. Shut up." Simone gripped his face, pressed her lips to his and poured every piece of her heart into the kiss. "You did exactly what you promised. So did I. So shut up."

"I'm going to get you a whiskey," CiCi decided.

"It's going to have to be coffee for a while yet. Chief on duty."

"I'll get it. You sit." Mi rubbed CiCi's arm, got up, then leaned over to put her arms around Reed's neck. Just held on. "They're my family," she told him. "Now so are you." She straightened to go into the kitchen.

"These girls are treating me like an old lady," CiCi complained. "I don't like it, so don't you add to that. When are these cops going to get out of my house—present company excepted."

"It won't take much longer." He looked back at the broken glass door. "We'll board that up for you."

She nodded. "Mi wants to call her family. The news is going to get out about this, and while she didn't tell them she was coming, they'll worry about me and Simone. So will Tulip and Ward and Natalie."

"You can call your families."

"Then I'm going to get a whiskey and do just that." CiCi rose. "Stop hogging the man for a minute." She leaned into Reed. "You're the answer to all my prayers to all the gods and goddesses. You clear these cops out as soon as you can—I need to white sage my house. And you take Simone home."

"We're staying here tonight," Reed told her.

"Because I'm an old lady?"

Deliberately, he brushed Simone aside, whispered in CiCi's ear. "You're the love of my life, but I have to settle for her." When she laughed, Reed kissed her temple. "And because Simone's not moving in until the twenty-third, and you're coming to dinner."

"I'll accept that. Mi, pour me a whiskey, and yourself whatever you're having. Then we'll go upstairs and make these calls. Mine will result in hysterics on the other end, so make that a double. We'll talk in the morning," she told Simone, then smiled at Reed. "Over cranberry pancakes and Bloody Marys."

"She could still change her mind," Reed considered, taking the coffee Mi brought him.

"Can we just go outside for a minute?" Simone asked.

"Sure. I'm still the chief of police. Don't let this spoil this house for you, the beach, any of it."

"It won't," Simone told him as they stepped out on the patio, as she took a deep, clear breath. "It can't."

Lights still shined on the beach below, cops still did their work. She didn't care. He was here.

"When they leave, can we take a walk on the beach?" She leaned her head on his uninjured shoulder. "Our version of a couple of tokes and some white sage."

"Let's do that."

"You need to call your family."

"Essie talked to them, so they know I'm okay."

"You need to call them. They need to hear your voice. Do it now. I'll wait."

"You call yours, I'll call mine."

"CiCi's already talking to Mom and Dad."

"Call your sister."

"You're right." Simone drew a breath. "You're right."

As she spoke to her sister, she heard Reed glossing over some of the details on his end while he soothed the still anxious Barney with long, easy strokes.

She didn't blame him for the glossing over as she did exactly the same. The hard truths could wait a little longer.

She put her phone away, watched the water, waited for Reed.

"They're coming out tomorrow," he told Simone. "I couldn't talk them out of it."

"Good, because Natalie's coming out with Harry, and I'm going to bet my parents will, too."

"I guess we'll have to heat up the grill."

She kissed his bandaged shoulder. "And tomorrow, you can tell me everything. I caught bits and pieces, but you can tell me everything. Not tonight, tomorrow. Except I guess it's already tomorrow, but in the morning, after those pancakes."

"That's a deal. You saved me. She might've gotten the drop on me again."

"I don't think so. I watched it all, and I don't think so. But we can say we saved each other. And he helped," she added, looking at Barney.

"Caviar Milk-Bones for life."

"With champagne chew-bone chasers."

"It's the high life for Barney. Sorry." Reed pulled out his phone. "Jacoby? Yeah." He blew out a breath. "Yeah, thanks for letting me know."

He stared at the phone a moment, then put it away.

"She didn't make it. Hobart. They called it at twelve-thirty-eight."

"July twenty-second," Simone added. "Thirteen years to the day." She gripped his hands. "CiCi would say it's karma, or it's the hand of fate, and she wouldn't be wrong. It's a door closed, Reed, for both of us. And for all the people she meant to hurt just because they lived."

"She heard the sirens, had to, but she didn't even try to run. So, yeah, it's a door closed."

He turned her hands over, kissed them. She'd scraped them up a little on the rocks.

"We're going to take a walk on the beach," he told her, "and start the next part of our lives. And since I've already talked you into step one—the moving in together—I'm going to start talking you into step two. Especially since the door's closed, and I'm wounded."

"What, exactly, is step two?"

"We need to talk about a few things. You never answered the fancy wedding question. Me, I'm more in favor of simple, but I'm flexible."

"Not nearly as much as you pretend. Step one hasn't even happened yet."

"Today's the day. Plus, ouch, I'm wounded. They're clearing out. Let's take that walk on the beach."

She went down with him, down the steps she and the most important woman in her life had run down only hours before.

Now the moon spread light over the water, spilled it silver onto the rocks that had given her and a woman they both loved shelter.

She didn't look at the sand where blood had spilled. Time and wind and rain would wash it away. She would cast the lost in bronze, and they would stay. She would walk with him into tomorrow, and he would stay.

They'd tend a house together, and a good, sweet dog, and remember every day as a precious gift.

She turned to him. "I'm not saying I'm ready for or can be talked into step two—even though you're wounded."

"Blood. Needles. Stitches."

She touched her lips to his shoulder again. "I'm just willing to say, at this time, I like simple."

He smiled, kissed her fingers, then walked the beach with her with the dog trotting at his heels.

— *One Year Later* —

In the park where a nineteen-year-old Reed Quartermaine asked Officer Essie McVee how to become a cop, hundreds gathered. Survivors and loved ones of those lost each held a single white rose with a sprig of rosemary.

The mayor of Rockpoint gave a short speech under a sky blue with summer while white gulls winged over the water. Among the gathered, children fidgeted, a baby fussed.

Simone took her place, looked out at the faces, the tears already shed. She looked at Reed, standing with his family and hers.

"Ah, thank you, Ms. Mayor, and thank you to my father, Ward Knox, and my grandmother, the amazing CiCi Lennon, for making it possible to place this art in Rockpoint Park. Thank you to my mother, Tulip Knox, for helping to arrange this . . . gathering today to unveil it."

She'd tried to prepare a speech, to write one out and practice, but everything she'd attempted came off stiff and stilted and, well, prepared.

So she did what CiCi advised. She said what came to her mind from her heart.

"I was there," she began, "on July twenty-second, fourteen years ago tonight. I lost a friend, a beautiful girl," she continued, looking toward the Olsen family. "A friend I still miss, every day, as so many here lost someone they loved and miss every day.

"For a long time I tried to forget what had happened. Some of you may understand what I mean when I say I tried to pretend it was over, and didn't affect my life. I thought I needed to do just that to survive it. But I was wrong, and everyone here, everyone knows that while we have to go on, we can never, should never, forget.

"You know their faces, the son or daughter, the mother or father, the brother or sister, husband, wife. You know them. I came to know them, and hope by knowing them, by honoring them, no one will ever forget. I hope you'll think of this, not as a memorial, but a remembrance. I'd like to dedicate this work not only to those we loved and lost, but to all of us. They are, as we are, all connected but not just by tragedy. By love."

She reached out for Reed's hand, waited for Essie and Mi to take their place on the other side of the drape.

"Okay." She took a long breath. "Okay."

Together, they lifted the drape.

She'd cast the bronze in a graceful curve. More than a hundred faces formed it, all connected by twining roses and rosemary. All softly washed in a patina of quiet blues and greens. On the curve of the base, she'd listed all the names, every name in bas-relief.

Simone gripped Reed's hand as she heard weeping, and couldn't bring herself to look away from the faces she'd cast to the faces of the weeping.

Then she heard CiCi's voice, the amazing CiCi, begin to sing "The Long and Winding Road."

Others joined in, hesitantly at first, then more fully if they knew the words.

Now she looked, and saw hands clasped as Reed clasped hers. She saw people embracing. She saw tears, she saw comfort.

When her own tears came, she turned into Reed and found her comfort there.

And when the song ended, people came forward. Some reached down to touch a hand to a face. Some came to her to take her hand or to embrace her.

Reed brought a woman to her. "Simone, this is Leah Patterson. Angie's mom."

"I need you to know." Leah gripped both Simone's hands. "I need you to really understand what this means to me. People will know she was here. She lived. Thank you more than I can say."

Then Leah walked over, laid a white rose on the grass at the base as others had.

Tulip waited until the crowd thinned before she went to Simone. "I'm very proud of you."

"We're very proud of you," Ward said and kissed her cheek, smiled. "You'd have made a terrible lawyer."

"Boy, wouldn't I."

"I got two good ones in the family." He glanced back at Harry and Natalie as Natalie ran a hand down the mound of her belly. "And maybe a next-generation one in the works."

"Ward." Tulip patted his arm, narrowed her eyes at Simone. "What color is that hair?"

"Magnificent Maroon with Golden Goddess highlights."

"I'll never understand it, or you." She drew Simone into a hug. "I love you anyway."

"Ditto."

"Reed." When Tulip offered a cheek, Reed bent down to kiss it. "I don't suppose you can talk my daughter into the two of you, and my mother, joining us at the club for dinner tonight."

"We appreciate that, but we have to get back. I'm on duty tonight."

"Well." She straightened his tie to her satisfaction, brushed at his lapels. "I hope we see you both soon."

Reed shook hands with Ward, watched them move off.

"You took the day and evening off," Simone reminded him.

"Grill duty. Let's say goodbye to Essie and her gang, scoop up Mi and CiCi, and go home. I've got to ditch this tie."

"You go ahead. I'll be there in a minute. I want to talk to Nat first."

He made his way to Essie, and the baby in the stroller.

"Hey there, Ariel."

She gurgled, grinned, waved a pudgy fist, then went back to gnawing on a teething ring.

"Where are the men and dogs?" Reed asked her.

"Over on the swings. Or Dylan is while Hank deals with him and the dogs."

"He sure won Barney over. I appreciate him riding herd while we did all that." He looked down toward the bench where they'd once sat together. "Sometimes it seems like a lifetime ago, sometimes like yesterday."

"I wouldn't change a single thing from the moment we sat down on that bench."

"Me, either. Well, maybe getting shot, except one thing leads to another. Did you get to see Ms. Leticia?"

"I did."

"It was good of her to come." He looked back at the gentle curve of bronze. "It was good."

"It's beautiful, and wrenching and important. I look at it and I want to hug my kids so tight, and Hank, and everybody I love."

"Bring it in," Reed offered. "Get the gang, come for the rest of the weekend. I'm grilling tonight. Don't say no. Go pack some stuff and catch a ferry."

"Do you have a clue how much stuff's involved in packing up a baby and a kid?"

"Not yet. One of these days. Come on, Essie, let's cap this day off with some happy, kick some sand over what happened on the island a year ago."

She blew out a breath. "You're on."

"Great. I'll go get my dog, tell Hank."

Simone waved Natalie off, hooked arms with CiCi. "Did you plan the Beatles?"

"No. It just came to me. It seemed the right song, and it seemed we needed a song. My treasure." She sighed, tipped her head to Simone's as they looked back at the bronze with the flowers spread at its base.

"I put Tish in the center. I needed to. She was mine. They all became mine, but she was mine first, and always."

"And that's how it should be. I see our Reed heading this way with Barney. I'll get Mi. It's time to go home, let him smoke up the grill, put some music on. I want to dance in the sand."

"I'll dance with you. I just need one more minute."

"It's about damn time." And CiCi did a little boogie on the spot. "I'm a little bit psychic," she added. "Go on, make him smile." She gave Simone a nudge.

With a half laugh, a quick shake of her head, Simone decided her grandmother just might be a little bit psychic.

She crossed paths with Reed and the faithful Barney in front of the bronze.

"I asked Essie, Hank, and the kids to pack up and head over. I think we need a good party."

"I think that's a great idea. Mi can bunk with CiCi."

"That works. Are you ready?"

"Almost." She took his face—oh, she knew that face—in her hands. "I want simple. Maybe a wild party after, but simple for the main event."

"I was going to do burgers and . . ." The smile came, slow. "When? I've got to clear my schedule."

"Summer's busy for the chief of police. How about the Saturday after Labor Day? The island's pretty quiet again."

"I can do the Saturday after Labor Day."

"At CiCi's. Nobody throws a wild party like CiCi, and she and Mi are going to be my maids of honor. No black tie, no tails."

"Can I begin to tell you how much I love you?"

"You'll get to that. CiCi's going to want one of her Wiccan priestess friends to perform the ceremony. I'd like to let her have that one."

"As long as said priestess is licensed to marry, I'm good. Can I start telling you now?"

"Almost. I want the ceremony part at sunset. I don't want traditional vows, but I do want an exchange of rings. And I want Florence for a honeymoon."

She considered, nodded. "I think that covers the absolutes. After those you can have your input."

"I can agree to all of that. My only provision, at this time, and up to the vows—when it's legal? If CiCi crooks her fingers and says: Come on, Reed, let's catch a slow boat to anywhere, you're out."

"That's fair."

Grinning, he swung her off her feet and in circles while Barney leaped and wagged.

CiCi put an arm around Mi's shoulders as she watched.

"You're spooky, CiCi. Really good spooky."

"Dr. Jung, we're going to throw our girl one hell of a wedding."

She watched through a blur of happy tears as a man she adored whirled her greatest treasure in front of the curve of bronze, the hill of white roses.

UNDER CURRENTS

Available July 2019

CHAPTER ONE

From the outside, the house in Lakeview Terrace looked perfect. The dignified three stories of pale brown brick boasted wide expanses of glass to open it to the view of Reflection Lake and the Blue Ridge Mountains. Two faux turrets capped in copper added a European charm and that quiet whisper of wealth.

Its lawn, a richly green skirt, sloped gently toward a trio of steps and the wide white veranda banked by azaleas that bloomed ruby red in spring.

In the rear a generous covered patio offered outdoor living space with a summer kitchen and those lovely lake views. The carefully maintained rose garden added a sweet, sophisticated scent. In season, a forty-two-foot sailing yacht floated serenely at the private dock.

Climbing roses softened the look of the long, vertical boards of the privacy fence.

The attached garage held a Mercedes SUV and sedan, two mountain bikes, ski equipment, and no clutter.

Inside, the ceilings soared. Both the formal living room and the great room offered fireplaces framed in the same brown brick as the exterior. The decor, tasteful—though some might whisper *studied*—reflected the vision of the couple in charge.

Quiet colors, coordinated fabrics, contemporary without edging over into stark.

Dr. Graham Bigelow purchased the lot in the projected development of Lakeview Terrace when his son was five, his daughter three. He chose the blueprint he felt suited him, and his family; made the necessary changes and additions; selected the finishes, the flooring, the tiles, the pavers; hired a decorator.

His wife, Eliza, happily left most of the choices and decisions to her husband. His taste, in her opinion, couldn't be faulted.

If and when she had an idea or suggestion, he would listen. If most often he pointed out why such an idea or suggestion wouldn't suit, he did—occasionally—include her input.

Like Graham, Eliza wanted the newness, the status offered by the small, exclusive community on the lake in North Carolina's High Country. She'd been born and raised in status—but the old sort, the sort she saw as creaky and boring. Like the house she'd grown up in across the lake.

She'd been happy to sell her share of the old house to her sister and use the money to help furnish—all new!—the house in Lakeview Terrace. She'd handed the cashier's check to Graham—he took care of things—without a second thought.

She'd never regretted it.

They'd lived there happily for nearly nine years, raising two bright, attractive children, hosting dinner parties, cocktail parties, garden parties. Eliza's job, as wife of the chief surgical resident of Mercy Hospital in nearby Asheville, was to look beautiful and stylish, to raise the children well, keep the house, entertain, and head committees.

As she had a housekeeper/cook three times a week, a weekly grounds-keeper, and a sister who was more than happy to take the children if she and Graham needed an evening out or a little getaway, she had plenty of time to focus on her looks and wardrobe.

She never missed a school function, and in fact had served as PTA president for two years. She attended school plays, along with Graham if work didn't keep him away. She embraced fund-raising, both for the school and the hospital. At every ballet recital since Britt turned four, she'd sat front row center.

She sat through most of her son Zane's baseball games as well. And if she missed some, she excused it, as anyone who'd sat through the nightmare of tedium that youth baseball provided would understand.

Though she'd never admit it, Eliza favored her daughter. But Britt was such a beautiful, sweet-natured, obedient young girl. She never had to be prodded to do her homework or tidy her room, was unfailingly polite. In Zane, Eliza saw her sister, Emily. The tendency to argue or sulk, to go off on his own.

Still, he kept his grades up. If the boy wanted to play baseball, he made the honor roll. Obviously, his ambition to play professionally was just a teenage fantasy. He would, of course, study medicine like his father.

But for now, baseball served as the carrot so they all avoided the stick.

If Graham had to pull out that stick and punish the boy from time to time, it was for his own good. It helped build character, teach boundaries, ensure respect.

As Graham liked to say, the child is the father of the man, so the child had to learn to follow the rules.

Two days before Christmas, Eliza drove the plowed streets of Lakeview toward home. She'd had a lovely holiday lunch with friends—maybe just a couple sips more champagne than she should have. She'd burned that off shopping. On Boxing Day, the family would take its annual ski trip. Or Graham and the kids would ski while she made use of the spa. Now she had a pair of gorgeous new boots to pack along with some lingerie that would warm Graham up nicely after his time on the slopes.

She glanced around at the other homes, the holiday decorations. Really lovely, she thought—no tacky inflatable Santas allowed in Lakeview Terrace— by order of the homeowners' association.

But, no point being modest, their home outshined the rest. Graham gave her carte blanche on Christmas decorating, and she used it wisely and well.

The white lights would sparkle when dusk rolled in, she thought. Outlining the perfect lines of the house, twining around the potted firs on the front veranda. Gleaming inside the twin wreaths with their trailing red and silver ribbons on the double doors.

And of course the living room tree—all twelve feet—white lights, silver and red star ornaments. The great room tree, the same color scheme, but with angels. Of course the mantels, the formal dining table, all tasteful and perfect.

And new every year. No need to box and store when you could arrange for the rental company to come sweep it all away afterward.

She'd never understood her parents' and Emily's delight in digging out ancient glass balls or tacky wooden Santas. They could have all that with their visit to the old house and Emily. Eliza would host them all for Christmas dinner, of course. Then, thank God, they'd head back to Savannah and their retirement.

Emily was their favorite, she thought as she hit the remote for the garage door. No question there.

It gave her a jolt to see Graham's car already in the garage, and she checked her watch. Let out a breath of relief. She wasn't late; he was home early.

Delighted, especially since someone else had the car pool, she pulled in beside her husband's car, gathered her shopping bags.

She went through the mudroom, hung her coat, folded her scarf, removed her boots before sliding into the black Prada flats she wore around the house.

When she stepped into the kitchen, Graham, still in his suit and tie, stood at the center island.

"You're home early!" After setting her bags on the wet bar, she moved quickly to him, kissed him lightly.

He smelled, lightly like the kiss, of Eau Sauvage—her favorite.

"Where were you?"

"Oh, I had that holiday lunch with Miranda and Jody, remember?" She gestured vaguely toward the family calendar in the activity nook. "We topped it off with a little shopping."

As she spoke, she walked to the refrigerator for a bottle of Perrier. "I can't believe how many people are still shopping for Christmas. Jody included," she said, adding a scoop of ice from the ice machine, pouring the sparkling water over it. "Honestly, Graham, she just never seems to get organized about—"

"Do you think I give a damn about Jody?"

His voice, calm, smooth, almost pleasant, set off alarm bells.

"Of course not, my darling. I'm just babbling." She kept the smile on her face, but her eyes turned wary. "Why don't you sit down and relax? I'll freshen your drink, and we'll—"

He heaved the glass, smashing the crystal at her feet. A shard dug a shallow slice across her ankle with an added sting as scotch splattered over it.

The Baccarat, she thought with a little frisson of heat.

"Freshen that!" No longer calm and smooth, not nearly pleasant, the words slapped out at her. "I spend my day with my hands inside a human being, saving lives, and come home to an empty house?"

"I'm sorry. I—"

"Sorry?" He grabbed her arm, twisting as he slammed her back against the counter. "You're sorry you couldn't be bothered to be home? Sorry you frittered away the day, and my money, having lunch, shopping, gossiping with those idiot bitches while I spend six hours in the OR?"

Her breath began to hitch, her heart to pound. "I didn't know you'd be home early. If you'd called me, I would've come straight home."

"Now I have to report to you?"

She barely heard the rest of the words that hammered at her. *Ungrateful, respect, duty.* But she knew that look, that avenging angel look. The dark blond hair, perfectly groomed, the smooth, handsome face suffused with angry color. The rage in those bright blue eyes so cold, so cold.

The frisson of heat became electric snaps.

"It was on the calendar!" Her voice rose in pitch. "I told you only this morning."

"Do you think I have time to check your ridiculous calendar? You will be home when I walk in the door. Do you understand me?" He slammed her against the counter again, shooting a jolt of pain up her spine. "I'm responsible for everything you have. This home, the clothes on your back, the food you eat. I pay for someone to cook, to clean so you can be available to me when I say! I say. So you damn well will be home when I walk in the door. You'll damn well spread your legs when I want to fuck you."

To prove it, he rammed his erection against her.

She slapped him. Even knowing what was coming—maybe because of what was coming—she slapped him.

And that rage went from cold to hot. His lips peeled back.

He plowed his fist into her midsection.

He never hit her in the face.

At fourteen, Zane Bigelow's heart and soul centered on baseball. He liked girls—he liked looking at naked girls once his pal Micah showed him how to bypass the parental controls on his computer. But baseball still ranked number one.

Numero uno.

Tall for his age, gangly with it, he longed to get through school, be discovered by a scout for the Baltimore Orioles—he'd settle for any American League team, but that was his number one pick.

Totally numero uno.

He'd play shortstop—the amazing Cal Ripken would have retired by then. Besides, Iron Man Ripken was back at third.

This comprised Zane's ambitions. And actually seeing a naked girl in the—you know—flesh.

Nobody in the world could have been happier than Zane Bigelow as Mrs. Carter—Micah's mom—drove the car pool gang home in her Lexus SUV. Even if she had Cher singing about life after love playing.

He didn't have a passion for cars—yet—just a young male's innate knowledge. And he preferred rap (not that he could play it in the house.)

But even with Cher singing, his sister and the other two girls squealing about Christmas, Micah deep into *Donkey Kong* on his Game Boy (Micah's desperate Christmas wish was the new Game Boy Color), Zane hit the highest note on the happy scale.

No school for ten whole days! Even the prospect of being pushed into skiing—not his favorite sport, especially when his father kept pointing out his little sister skied rings around him—couldn't dampen his mood.

No math, ten days. He hated math like he hated spinach salad, which was a lot.

Mrs. Carter pulled over to let Cecile Marlboro out. There was the usual shuffling, hauling of backpacks, the high-pitched squeal of girls.

They all had to hug, because Christmas vacation.

Sometimes they had to hug because it was, like, Tuesday or whatever. He'd never get it.

Everybody called out Merry Christmas—they'd called out Happy Holidays when dropping Pete Greene off, because he was Jewish.

Almost home, Zane thought, watching the houses go by. He figured to fix himself a snack, then—no homework, no freaking math—close up in his room and settle in with an hour on *Triple Play* on his PlayStation.

He knew Lois—off till like après-ski—planned to make lasagna before she left for her own family holiday stuff. And Lois's lasagna was awesome.

Mom would actually have to turn on the oven to heat it up, but she could handle that much.

Better yet, Grams and Pop got in from Savannah tomorrow. He wished they could stay at his house instead of with his aunt Emily, but he planned to ride his bike over to the old lake house the next afternoon and hang awhile. He could talk Emily into baking cookies—wouldn't even have to talk hard for that.

And they were coming for Christmas dinner. Mom wouldn't even have to turn on the oven for that one. Catered.

After dinner Britt would play piano—he sucked at piano, which equaled another regular dig from his dad—and they'd do a sing-along.

Corny, totally corny, but he sort of liked it. Plus, he sang pretty good, so he didn't get ragged on.

As the car pulled over at his house, Zane exchanged fist bumps with Micah.

"Dude, Merry."

"Dude," Micah said. "Back atcha."

While Britt and Chloe hugged as if they wouldn't see each other for a year, Zane slid out. "Merry Christmas, Chloe. Merry Christmas, Mrs. Carter, and thanks for the ride."

"Merry Christmas, Zane, and you're always welcome." She shot him a smile, made eye contact. She was really pretty for a mom.

"Thank you, Mrs. Carter, and Merry Christmas." Britt practically sang it. "I'll call you, Chloe!"

Zane slung his backpack over one shoulder as Britt climbed out. "What are you calling her for? What could you have left to talk about? Y'all never shut up all the way home."

"We have plenty to talk about."

Britt, more than a full head shorter, shared his coloring. The dark hair—Britt's nearly to her waist and pinned back with reindeer barrettes—the same sharp green eyes. Her face was still sort of round and babyish while his had gone angular. Because, Em said, he was growing up.

Not that he was ready to shave or anything, though he did check carefully every day.

Because she was his sister, he felt honor bound to give her grief. "But y'all don't actually say anything. It's like: *Ooooh, Justin Timberlake.*" He followed up with loud kissy noises, making her blush.

He knew Timberlake was her not-so-secret crush.

"Just shut up."

"You shut up."

"You shut up."

They back-and-forthed that until they reached the veranda—switched to snarling looks, as both knew if they went inside arguing and their mother heard, an endless lecture would follow.

Zane dug out his key, as his father decreed the house stayed locked whether or not anyone was home. The second the door cracked open, he heard it.

The snarl dropped from Britt's face. Her eyes went huge, filled with fear and tears. She slapped her hands over her ears.

"Go upstairs," Zane told her. "Go straight up to your room. Stay there."

"He's hurting her again. He's hurting her."

Instead of running to her room, Britt ran inside, ran back toward the great room, stood, hands still over her ears. "Stop!" She screamed it. "Stop, stop, stop, stop."

Zane saw blood smeared on the floor where his mother tried to crawl away. Her sweater was torn, one of her shoes missing.

"Go to your rooms!" Graham shouted it as he hauled Eliza up by her hair. "This is none of your business."

Britt just kept screaming, screaming, even when Zane tried to pull her back.

He saw his father's hate-filled eyes track over, latch on his sister. And a new fear flashed hot inside him, burned something away.

He didn't think, didn't know what he intended to do. He shoved his sister back, stood between her and his father, a skinny kid who'd yet to grow into his feet. And with that flash of heat, he charged.

"Get away from her, you son of a bitch!"

He rammed straight into Graham. Surprise more than the power of the hit knocked Graham back a step. "Get the hell away."

Zane never saw it coming. He was fourteen, and the only fights he'd ever participated in consisted of a little pushy-shovey and insults. He'd felt his father's fist—a blow to the gut, sometimes the kidneys.

Where it didn't show.

This time the fists struck his face, and something behind his eyes exploded, blurred his vision. He felt two more before he dropped, the wild pain of them rising over the fear, the anger. His world went gray, and through the gray, lights sizzled and flashed.

With the taste of blood in his mouth, his sister's screams banging in his head, he passed out.

The next he knew, he realized his father had slung him over his shoulder, carrying him up the stairs. His ears rang, but he could hear Britt crying, hear his mother telling her to stop.

His father didn't lay him down on the bed, but shrugged him off his shoulder so Zane bounced on the mattress. Every inch of his body cried out in fresh pain.

"Disrespect me again, I'll do more than break your nose, blacken your eye. You're nothing, do you understand me? You're nothing until I say you are. Everything you have, including the breath in your body, is because of me."

He leaned close as he spoke, spoke in that smooth, calm tone. Zane saw two of him, couldn't even manage to nod. The shaking started, the teeth-chattering cold of shock.

"You will not leave this room until I permit it. You will speak to no one. You will tell no one the private business of this family or the punishment you forced me to levy today will seem like a picnic. No one would believe you. You're nothing. I'm everything. I could kill you in your sleep, and no one would notice. Remember that the next time you think about trying to be a big man."

He went out, closed the door.

Zane drifted again. It was easier to drift than to deal with the pain, to deal with the words his father had spoken that had fallen like more fists.

When he surfaced again, the light had changed. Not dark, but getting there.

He couldn't breathe through his nose. It felt clogged like he had a terrible cold. The sort of cold that made his head hammer with pain, had his eyes throbbing.

His gut hurt something terrible.

When he tried to sit up, the room spun, and he feared throwing up.

When he heard the lock click, he started to shake again. He prepared to beg, plead, grovel, anything that kept those fists from pounding on him again.

His mother came in, flipping the light as she did. The light exploded more pain, so he shut his eyes.

"Your father says you're to clean yourself up, then use this ice bag on your face."

Her voice, cool, matter-of-fact, hurt almost as much as his father's.

"Mom—"

"Your father says to keep your head elevated. You may leave your bed only to use your bathroom. As you see, your father has removed your computer, your PlayStation, your television, items he's generously given you. You will see and speak to no one except your father or me. You will not participate in Christmas Eve or Christmas Day."

"But—"

"You have the flu."

He searched her face for some sign of pity, gratitude. Feeling. "I was trying to stop him from hurting you. I thought he might hurt Britt. I thought—"

"I didn't ask for or need your help." Her voice, clipped, cold, made his chest ache. "What's between me and your father is between me and your father. You have the next two days to consider your place in this family, and to earn back any privileges."

She turned toward the door. "Do as you're told."

When she went out, left him alone, he made himself sit up—had to close his eyes against the spinning and just breathe. On shaky legs, he stood, stumbled into the bathroom, vomited, nearly passed out again.

When he managed to gain his feet, he stared at his face in the mirror over the sink.

It didn't look like his face, he thought, oddly detached. The mouth swollen, bottom lip split. God, the nose like a red balloon. Both eyes black, one swollen half-shut. Dried blood everywhere.

He lifted a hand, touched his fingers to his nose, had pain blasting. Because he was afraid to take a shower—still dizzy—he used a washcloth to try to clean off some of the blood. He had to grit his teeth, had to hang on to the sink with one hand to stay upright, but he feared not doing what he'd been told more than the pain.

He cried, and wasn't ashamed. Nobody could see anyway. Nobody would care.

He inched his way back to bed, breathed out when he eased down to take off his shoes, his jeans. Every minute or two he had to stop, catch his breath again, wait for the dizziness to pass.

In his boxers and sweatshirt, he crawled into bed, took the ice bag his mother had left, and laid it as lightly as he could on his nose.

It hurt too much, just too much, so he switched to his eye. And that brought a little relief.

He lay there, full dark now, planning, planning. He'd run away. As soon as he could, he'd stuff his backpack with some clothes. He didn't have much money because his father banked all of it. But he had a little he'd hidden in a pair of socks. His saving-for-video-games money.

He could hitchhike—and that thought brought a thrill. Maybe to New York. He'd get away from this house where everything looked so clean, where ugly, ugly secrets hid like his video game money.

He'd get a job. He could get a job. No more school, he thought as he drifted again. That was something.

He woke again, heard the lock again, and pretended to sleep. But it wasn't his father's steps, or his mother's. He opened his eyes as Britt shined a little pink flashlight in his face.

"Don't."

"Shh," she warned him. "I can't turn the light on in case they wake up and see." She sat on the side of the bed, stroked a hand over his arm. "I brought you a PB&J. I couldn't get lasagna because they'd know if any was missing from the dish. You need to eat."

"Stomach's not so good, Britt."

"Just a little. Try a little."

"You need to go. If they catch you in here—"

"They're asleep. I made sure. I'm staying with you. I'm going to stay with you until you can eat something. I'm so sorry, Zane."

"Don't cry."

"You're crying."

He let the tears roll. He just didn't have the strength to stop them.

Sniffling at her own tears, swiping at them, Britt reached down to stroke his arm. "I brought milk, too. They won't notice if a glass of milk is gone. I cleaned everything up, and when you're done, I'll wash the glass."

They spoke in whispers—they were used to it—but now her voice hitched.

"He hit you so hard, Zane. He hit you and hit you, and when you were on the ground, he kicked you in the stomach. I thought you were dead."

She laid her head on his chest, shoulders shaking. He stroked her hair.

"Did he hurt you?"

"No. He sort of squeezed my arms and shook me, yelled at me to shut up. So I did. I was afraid not to."

"That's good. You did the right thing."

"You did." Her whisper thickened with tears. "You tried to do the right thing. She didn't try to stop him from hurting you. She didn't say anything. And when he stopped, he told her to clean up the blood on the floor. There was glass broken in the kitchen, to clean it up, to clean herself up and have dinner on the table by six."

She sat up, held out half the sandwich she'd neatly cut in two. In that moment he loved her so much it hurt his heart.

He took it, tried a bite, and found it didn't threaten to come up again.

"We have to tell Emily and Grams and Pop you're sick. You got the flu, and you're contagious. You have to rest, and Dad's taking care of you. He won't let them come up to see you. Then we have to tell people at the resort you fell off your bike. He said all this at dinner. I had to eat or he'd get mad again. Then I threw up when I went upstairs."

He took another bite, reached for her hand in the dark. "I know how that feels."

"When we get back, we have to say you had a skiing accident. Fell. Dad took care of you."

"Yeah." The single word rang bitter, bitter. "He took care of me."

"He'll hurt you again if we don't. Maybe worse. I don't want him to hurt you again, Zane. You were trying to stop him from hitting Mom. You were protecting me, too. You thought he was going to hit me. So did I."

He felt her shift, saw in the faint light of the flashlight she'd set on the bed that she'd turned to stare toward the window. "One day I guess he will."

"No, no, he won't." Inside the pain, fury rose. "You won't give him any reason to. And I won't let him."

"He doesn't need a reason. You don't have to be a grown-up to understand that." Though her tone sounded adult, fresh tears leaked. "I think they don't love us. He couldn't love us and hurt us, make us lie. And she couldn't love us and let it keep happening. I think they don't love us."

He knew they didn't—had known for sure when his mother had come in, looked at him with nothing in her eyes. "We've got each other."

While she sat with him, making sure he ate, he understood he couldn't run away, couldn't run and leave Britt. He had to stay. He had to get stronger. He had to get strong enough to fight back.

Not to protect his mother, but his sister.

Nora Roberts is the #1 *New York Times* bestselling author of more than two hundred novels, including *Come Sundown, The Obsession, The Liar,* and many more. She is also the author of the bestselling In Death series written under the pen name J. D. Robb. There are more than five hundred million copies of her books in print.

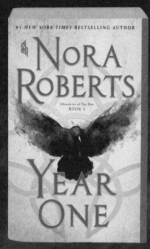

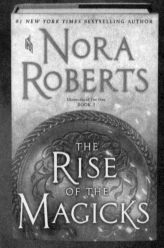